ALSO BY FIONA DAVIS

THE
STOLEN
QUEEN

A NOVEL

Fiona Davis

DUTTON

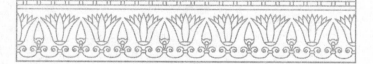

DUTTON

An imprint of Penguin Random House LLC
penguinrandomhouse.com

LIBRARY OF CONGRESS CATALOGING-IN-PUBLICATION DATA

Names: Davis, Fiona, 1966– author.
Title: The stolen queen: a novel / Fiona Davis.
Description: 1. | [New York] : Dutton, 2025.
Identifiers: LCCN 2024019655 (print) | LCCN 2024019656 (ebook) |
ISBN 9780593474273 (hardcover) | ISBN 9780593474297 (ebook)
Subjects: LCGFT: Novels.
Classification: LCC PS3604.A95695 S76 2025 (print) |
LCC PS3604.A95695 (ebook) |
DDC 813/.6—dc23/20240502
LC record available at https://lccn.loc.gov/2024019655
LC ebook record available at https://lccn.loc.gov/2024019656

Printed in the United States of America
1st Printing

Book design by Nancy Resnick
Title-page frame art by Liudmila Klymenko/Shutterstock.com

For Mom

THE
STOLEN
QUEEN

CHAPTER ONE

Charlotte

NEW YORK CITY, 1978

The staff meeting of the Metropolitan Museum's Department of Egyptian Art was supposed to start at ten, which meant associate curator Charlotte Cross arrived at nine to prepare her colleagues for battle.

The department had never been so busy. Two months ago, Charlotte had overseen the opening of the Temple of Dendur, which had been plucked from the banks of the Nile (with the blessing of the Egyptian government) and reconstructed at the Met in a special exhibit hall featuring a slanted wall of glass overlooking Central Park. Next month, the King Tutankhamun exhibition—which had been touring America to great acclaim for the past couple of years—was scheduled to have its final stop at the Met. The prospect of millions of visitors descending upon the museum had put pressure on everyone, including Charlotte's boss, Frederick, who much preferred wooing donors to dealing with departmental logistics.

The Met was closed on Mondays, but only to visitors. For the employees, much of the behind-the-scenes work was accomplished on the first day of the workweek: handlers moved paintings from one gallery to another, the curatorial team might oversee the installation of a new exhibition, technicians performed condition checks of antiquities, while lampers wandered from gallery to gallery, necks craned, searching for blown-out lightbulbs. Monday was Charlotte's favorite day, when the museum felt like a private playground, the staff free to roam about without being accosted for directions to the nearest bathroom.

She started in the gallery that housed the ten-foot-high, four-thousand-year-old Colossal Seated Statue of a Pharaoh. The figure depicted was all muscle and power, with broad shoulders and a narrow waist. Even though his face and one arm were damaged, he looked as if he were about to declare something important: an act of war, or maybe a death sentence.

A group of handlers were already gathered around the statue. Joseph, a budding sculptor who led the team, looked up expectantly as Charlotte approached. "Morning, boss."

Charlotte nodded. "I wanted to give you the heads-up that Frederick is considering moving this piece to the Temple of Dendur gallery."

They all moaned in unison. "This old guy's been in the same spot since the 1930s," said Joseph. "He's way too fragile."

"That was my first impression as well," answered Charlotte. "But I was thinking about it last night, and there might be a way." They talked through the procedure, which would involve a mechanical hoist and several carefully placed padded blankets and straps, until the team's uneasiness abated. Luckily, the Met's staff were the best in the business, as professional as they were serious, and Charlotte knew they'd leave nothing to chance.

In the Old Kingdom gallery, Charlotte pulled aside a technician.

"Denise, I'm still concerned about the humidity in here. Can you talk to Steve in the conservation department today and see if silicone gel will help absorb the moisture?"

"That's a great idea. Will do."

Just before ten, Charlotte finished her circuit and headed to the spacious plaza in front of the Temple of Dendur, where Frederick stood among a group that included the more junior assistant curators, as well as handlers, technicians, and conservators.

"There's so much to cover, I don't even know where to begin." Frederick ran one hand through his thick mane of hair and gave his head a tiny shake, a nervous habit that meant he was about to lose it. "The humidity in the vitrines *must* be better controlled. I don't know how many times I've said it, but if any of these loaned antiquities get damaged on our watch, one of you will be to blame. I will not allow the Met to become the laughingstock of the country. Denise? Do you hear me?"

"I do, sir," answered Denise in a strong alto. "I've already spoken with Steve in the conservation department. He thinks silicone gel will help, and we'll have it taken care of by tomorrow morning."

"Oh. Okay." Frederick sniffed. "What about the updated budget information for the exhibition? I need to see where we stand."

An administrative staffer threw Charlotte a grateful glance before speaking up. "It's on your desk."

"Huh." Frederick paused, the ends of his mouth turned down, as if he found his staff's industriousness slightly disappointing. He scanned the crowd before settling his gaze on Joseph, who immediately snapped to attention. "Joseph. I'm going to tell you something that you will not like. Not at all. Are you ready?"

Joseph nodded.

"The Colossal Seated Statue of a Pharaoh is to be moved into the Temple of Dendur for the duration of the King Tut exhibition."

Joseph replied without missing a beat. "Yes, sir. We can do that."

"Really?" Frederick's voice rose in pitch. "I mean, it hasn't been moved in ages. You really think you can handle it?"

"Sure thing."

"Okay, then. Glad to hear it." Frederick sounded like he was trying to convince himself of the fact.

The mood in the room relaxed noticeably. So far, so good.

"Charlotte, have you proofed the King Tut catalog yet?"

Frederick had insisted on writing the copy himself for the exhibition catalog, which meant Charlotte had spent most of last week editing it so that readers unfamiliar with terms like "cartouche" and "New Kingdom" wouldn't end up befuddled. "It's on your desk, and I've integrated Mr. Lavigne's notes as well."

"You got notes from the director already? Well, then, I suppose all is in order. Oh, wait, I almost forgot." He snapped his fingers. "One of our donors suggested we should sell King Tut scarves as part of the merchandising. Nancy, look into that and get me samples by next week."

Nancy was Frederick's assistant, a tough divorcée from Queens who usually managed her boss with a firm hand. But merchandise was not part of her job description, as Frederick well knew.

"Scarves?" she repeated. "You must be confusing me with someone else. I don't do the souvenirs."

"Not my problem," he snapped before breaking out in a wide smile. "That's all, folks." Frederick clapped his hands twice and trotted away, his mood obviously lighter now that he'd ruined at least one person's day.

Charlotte approached Nancy, who was barely concealing an eye roll. "Reach out to Wendy Metcalf, she's the merchandise planner in the Met Store who handles textiles and women's apparel," said Charlotte. "Tell her I sent you."

"Will do. Frederick's lucky to have you, Charlotte Cross. I was just about to tell him where he could stick his scarves."

Charlotte had been working at the Met Museum her entire career, except for a brief stint in Egypt when she was a young woman. While her colleagues had climbed the ranks and been appointed head curators at other museums, she was still an associate, her career stalled out, and for the past fifteen years, her job had basically consisted of cleaning up after Frederick. He liked to consider himself a "concept guy," which meant all the details fell to her. But it also gave her a chance to reconfigure his concepts so that they appealed to the museum's visitors and could be smoothly executed by the staff. All the responsibility and none of the accolades. Sometimes she felt more like the protector of Frederick's legacy than associate curator, but she adored the people she worked with and loved being surrounded by some of the most precious antiquities in the world.

Still, in recent months, Charlotte had been thinking more and more about her own legacy. A few years ago, without sharing her plans with anyone, she'd begun to investigate a bold theory about an ancient Egyptian ruler who modern historians had largely dismissed. And now, in the wake of hundreds of hours of painstaking research, Charlotte had something up her sleeve that she hoped would change everything. After a decade and a half of living in Frederick's shadow, Charlotte might finally have a chance to shine.

The administrative offices of their department were located through an unmarked door down one of the gallery's long hallways. After the grandeur of the collection, the offices were something of a letdown— Charlotte considered herself lucky that her particular cubicle looked out onto an air shaft. Her duties included answering letters from people asking if the object they'd found in their grandmother's attic was an ancient Egyptian relic or not (she could usually tell from the enclosed snapshot that it was not), handling requests for loans from other museums, spending a couple of hours in the storerooms checking on items that weren't currently exhibited, and working on the infernal Egyptian Art collection catalog that eventually would list every artifact the department owned. It had been started in the 1950s, and Frederick hoped one day to have a third volume published that would include all the pieces from the Twentieth to Thirtieth Dynasties, a massive undertaking.

As soon as she sat down at her desk, Charlotte caught sight of a large envelope from Egypt that lay next to a well-worn accordion folder bursting with notes and research papers.

For the past three years, Charlotte had been studying the complicated life of an ancient Egyptian woman named Hathorkare, who married the pharaoh Saukemet I but was unable to bear him a son, which meant that, upon his death, the infant son of one of the lesser queens was chosen to be the next leader of Egypt. Hathorkare, seething with resentment of this child king, quickly named herself regent and stepped in to rule, ostensibly until Saukemet II came of age. Yet seven years into her regency, she named *herself* pharaoh, maintaining her hold over Egypt for the next twenty years. After her death, Saukemet II finally seized the throne and immediately ordered many of his stepmother's images to be violently hacked out of the stone walls of temples and shrines.

Or at least that was the conventional wisdom among Egyptian scholars—including Frederick, who had published a seminal article on the early struggles and triumphant rise of Saukemet II.

But Charlotte had a different theory about Hathorkare.

After doing some meticulous research, she'd concluded that the vandalization of Hathorkare's likenesses couldn't have occurred right after her death, as historians believed. In fact, according to Charlotte's calculations, the proscription had to have been undertaken twenty years *after* her death—and not long before Saukemet II's own demise—which seemed an awfully long time to hold a grudge. It made no sense that Saukemet II's rage would suddenly erupt in his waning years. Perhaps there was another, less emotional reason for the erasures.

Charlotte also noticed that historians ignored all the good Hathorkare accomplished during her reign: building glorious temples, making savvy trades with neighboring countries, and providing a long stretch of economic and political stability for her countrymen. Instead, she was unilaterally disdained and dismissed. In fact, the Met's own depiction of Hathorkare—written by a male archaeologist in the 1950s for the museum's catalog—described the female pharaoh as a "vain, ambitious, and unscrupulous woman."

If correct, Charlotte's findings would completely transform the way Egyptologists—and the world—viewed Hathorkare. Finally, after three years of hard work and multiple dead ends, this envelope containing photos taken at the Temple of Karnak in Luxor, Egypt, was crucial to proving her theory. She spent an hour studying the photos with a magnifier, making notes, checking her timeline. By the time she was done, she knew for certain that her initial instincts about Hathorkare and the timing of the erasures were right.

Charlotte was about to turn a long-held assumption upside down, revive the name and reputation of Hathorkare, and make a major contribution to the study of ancient Egyptian history.

The ringing of her phone brought her out of her daydream.

"Frederick wants to see you down in the basement storeroom," said Nancy. "There's a new piece that just came in."

That was odd. They weren't expecting anything other than the Tut artifacts. "I'm on my way. Hey, does Frederick have time in his schedule for me today? I have something important I want to show him."

"He's not free until six tonight."

"I'll take it."

"And thanks again for your help earlier," added Nancy. "The King Tut scarves have been ordered."

"Let the merchandising begin."

Out in the galleries, Charlotte paused in front of one of her favorite depictions of Hathorkare in the collection, a fragment of a statue known as the Cerulean Queen. While many of the other figures from Egypt were made of limestone or red granite with a rough finish, the Cerulean Queen was made of finely polished lapis lazuli. The only remnant of the statue was a tantalizing fragment of the lower portion of its head, consisting of the cheeks, the chin, and a large portion of the lips. And what lips they were: beautifully curved and utterly sensuous. The lips of Hathorkare. If the rest of the statue came anywhere close to being as beautiful as the lips, it must have been a sight to behold. Charlotte wondered how it came to be smashed. Was it accidentally dropped while being moved from one location to another? Or did someone take a hammer to it on orders from Saukemet II? The thought was too awful to contemplate.

The fragment was small, only around five inches across. It had been found at the turn of the twentieth century, by a British earl who fancied himself something of an Egyptologist, in a trash heap containing destroyed statues of Hathorkare, just outside her temple. Nearby had lain a broken slab of limestone with a warning that translated to "Anyone who removes an object dear to Hathorkare outside of the boundaries of the kingdom will face the wrath of the gods."

The earl was killed in a hunting accident two weeks after bringing the Cerulean Queen to his estate in Hampshire. His widow quickly sold it off to the Met, and died less than a month later choking on a gumdrop.

As she stood before the artifact now, Charlotte reflexively looked around for a young woman in a red coat before remembering it was a Monday, the Met closed to visitors. "Little Red Riding Hood," the staff called her, because in cold weather she always wore a bright red coat with a large, floppy hood. Judging from how often Charlotte spotted her in front of the statue, Little Red Riding Hood was a big fan of the Cerulean Queen. She was always alone, probably a graduate student or an artist, and had the saddest eyes Charlotte had ever seen.

A voice drifted in from the hallway.

"Charlotte's been around how long?"

"Way longer than Frederick." Charlotte recognized Joseph's voice. He was speaking with one of the younger technicians, a new hire. "Since the 1930s."

Charlotte slid behind the statue, hoping they wouldn't peer into the gallery as they walked by.

"Then why isn't she in charge? It would make our jobs a whole lot easier."

"She's never been back to Egypt, not since she was there in the '30s. There was some kind of accident, a tragedy. No one ever shares the details, but she's never been back."

"An Egyptologist who won't go to Egypt. Huh."

They moved out of hearing range. Charlotte's cheeks flamed with embarrassment as she sidled her way back around to the front of the statue, trying to find her equilibrium again.

The curse of Hathorkare hadn't ended with the death of the earl's widow. Charlotte had fallen under its spell as well.

It was dangerous to think about that time.

She took a couple of deep breaths, studying the curve of the statue's chin, trying to imagine the shape of the nose and eyes. The Cerulean Queen gave her hope. Hope that one could be broken and crushed and still carry on, the gleaming remnant proof that something beautiful once existed in this terrible world.

Downstairs, Frederick and several others from their department stood around a large worktable in the storeroom, one of many bursting with artwork and sculptures in the Met's basement level.

"Ah, Charlotte. I know you'll want to see this," said Frederick, waving her over. Whatever lay on the table was hidden due to the crush of bodies surrounding it. "We've just received a very generous one-year loan from an anonymous donor."

Frederick usually consulted with Charlotte on any loans. Why now, when they had their hands full managing the loans for the King Tut exhibition, would they need one more? Typical Frederick, to have his attention pulled by the latest shiny new thing. She hoped it was worth it as she maneuvered her way closer.

But once she was at the edge of the table and the object came into focus, she gasped, one hand going to her heart. The conservators on either side of her looked at her curiously.

In the middle of the table lay a broad collar, a type of necklace popular in ancient Egypt. But this one was exquisite, made of gold and glass, and Charlotte knew even before she leaned in closer that she would find a gap on the right side of the bottom row where one of the nefer amulets was missing.

The piece was exceptional, distinctive.

She'd first seen it in Egypt, in 1936, when it was lifted from the bowels of a tomb, covered in dust.

And she'd last seen it a year later, right before it was lost at the bottom of the Nile.

"Does it have the cartouche of Hathorkare on the back of the clasp?" she asked, not bothering to hide the panic in her voice.

"It certainly does." Frederick nodded to the technician, who turned over the necklace with gloved hands to show off the hieroglyphics that represented the pharaoh's name, enclosed in an oval. "I'm impressed."

"Where did this come from?" she demanded.

"Charlotte, are you all right?" Frederick regarded her with concern. "You're as white as a sheet."

She had so many questions, the words got stuck in her throat. "Why are we getting it? Who was the donor?"

"The donor asked to remain anonymous. We have the broad collar for one year. I thought you'd be pleased."

She could almost hear the screams from that fateful night echoing in her head. The night that changed everything. And the reason she could never return to Egypt.

Frederick ordered the technicians to take the necklace away and turned to leave. Charlotte followed him out the door.

"You have to tell me who the donor is," she said. "It's important."

Frederick looked at his watch. "I have exactly four minutes until my next meeting at the other side of the building. Why exactly do you need to know this information?"

She couldn't tell him. That would reveal too much, and she was barely hanging on as it was. "I was there when it was found."

"Ah, back in Egypt, in the olden days." He laughed at his joke. Charlotte did not. "What does it matter who owns it now?"

"It doesn't make sense, how it suddenly reappeared like this. It was lost."

"Then lucky for us it was found. I would think you would be pleased."

Charlotte forced herself to back off. It would do her no good to anger Frederick right now, not if she wanted him on her side when she told him about her Hathorkare finding.

Besides, she had other ways to figure out who the donor was. Charlotte took the elevator up to the fifth floor of the building, where the director of the Met, Mr. Lavigne, had his office. The last time they'd interacted, he'd expressed his thanks to Charlotte for providing a reference for a friend's daughter who was applying to a PhD program in art history. Charlotte had insisted on interviewing the woman before she wrote the reference and was relieved to find her smart and ambitious, so it hadn't been a difficult request to honor. But Mr. Lavigne didn't need to know that. As far as he was concerned, he owed her a favor.

Unfortunately, his secretary informed Charlotte that he was away in Europe, back on Thursday. She made an appointment for the afternoon of his return; she wasn't giving up so easily.

She had to know where the broad collar came from, how it got to the Met.

And why it was haunting her from the grave.

CHAPTER TWO

Charlotte

EGYPT, 1936

When Charlotte Cross signed up to study abroad in Egypt for four months, she did not expect her responsibilities to include administering antivenom to counteract cobra bites. As the only undergraduate among an international team of professional archaeologists and PhD candidates, she was there to observe, assist, and pretty much stay out of the way as the others excavated the ruins of a small walled village where ancient Egyptian artisans and craftsmen had once resided.

So far, the majority of the artifacts unearthed from the villagers' brick homes were flakes of limestone covered with writing, called ostraca—the equivalent of ancient Egyptian notebooks. The team, under the leadership of a curator from the Met Museum named Grayson Zimmerman, had amassed bills, wills, wedding announcements, medical diagnoses, and prescriptions, dated as far back as 1500 BC, which all together told a detailed story of the average ancient Egyptian's life. One of Charlotte's duties was translating some of the items into English, a painstaking process that left her right hand sore but which she performed with great zeal. Just that morning, she'd spent two hours transcribing a contract between a scribe named Ankhsheshonq and a master craftsman that involved detailed instructions for altering existing reliefs, as commanded by the reigning pharaoh, before turning to a transcription of a shopping list written by some long-lost servant girl.

That afternoon, though, a group of strangers approached the camp, led by a grim-looking Bedouin with a bloody bite between his finger and thumb. One of his fellow tribesmen carried a limp six-foot-long serpent. The dig team's leaders were off in Luxor, overseeing the transfer of artifacts onto a barge on the Nile, which meant there was no one else present who knew what to do, other than Charlotte.

Not that Charlotte was all that qualified. She'd grown up in New York City's Greenwich Village, where snakes were only read about in books or viewed postmortem in dioramas at the Museum of Natural History. But her father was a doctor and her mother suffered from diabetes, requiring regular injections, which made Charlotte less queasy about grabbing the medical kit from the dispensary, located next to the kitchen tent where she'd been helping the cook prepare lunch (another one of her assigned duties that had nothing to do with digging, but which she gladly performed). Box in hand, she found the Bedouin sitting stiffly in one of the camp's foldable chairs. His hand was already the size of a grapefruit and the color of a plum; Charlotte didn't have much time.

Charlotte knelt beside the Bedouin and opened the emergency kit, withdrawing the prefilled syringe with care.

"I don't see why we should waste our supplies on the natives," murmured a voice a few feet behind her. She recognized it as that of Leon, an archaeology doctoral candidate from England who was never satisfied with his lot, always wanting to have the first go at a promising location and quick to move on if his desultory efforts weren't rewarded.

She ignored him. By now, a large cohort of the team had gathered. One of the other archaeologists, Henry, who'd only recently joined them from England, knelt beside her. "What's going on, can I help?" he asked brightly. But his demeanor changed when he caught sight of what was in Charlotte's hands. He blinked a couple of times, then stared intently into her eyes. For a split second, she thought he was flirting with her. Even though she was the only woman in the group, the work was dirty and backbreaking, and at the end of the day, everyone simply wanted a bath in one of the two galvanized iron tubs, followed by bed. There was no time or energy left for such silliness as flirtation, a fact she appreciated.

But Henry wasn't flirting. He was staring hard at her face because he couldn't bear to look back at what she held in her hand. She stifled a smile. The poor man obviously had a deathly fear of needles.

"That's fine, I can handle it," said Charlotte. Henry, looking relieved, ducked away, and Charlotte turned her attention back to the Bedouin. "Roll up your sleeve, please."

One of the Egyptians on their team translated, and the Bedouin did as he was told.

She cleaned off a spot near the top of his arm and quickly administered the shot. The man didn't flinch. After, she brought him water and waited to see if the swelling went down, as the others headed to the long table where their group of twenty gathered every afternoon for lunch.

She brought a glass of water to Henry as well.

"Oh, thanks." He gulped it down. "I needed that."

"Maybe more than *he* did," said Charlotte, pointing her elbow in the direction of the Bedouin.

"Was it that obvious?" Henry wiped his forehead with a hand-kerchief.

"Just a little."

"I swear, nothing else gets to me. I can stand heights, small spaces, spiders. But needles—" He shuddered.

"I'd recommend you stay far away from cobras, in that case."

"Let's hope I do well here, then, so I don't end up working at the Regent's Park Zoo." Henry had large ears that stuck out either side of his head and brown hair that had been flattened by the wide-brimmed pith helmets they both wore. His was hanging off his neck, and his Adam's apple bobbed just above the strap.

Charlotte laughed. "I guess that means you're from London?"

"Correct, and you?"

"New York City."

"You've come from quite far for the glory of being a notetaker and de facto medic. King Tut, I presume?"

Even though Henry was a little older, probably in his early twen-ties to Charlotte's eighteen, their generation was united in their love for all things Egyptian thanks to the 1922 discovery of King Tut-ankhamun's tomb by the Englishman Howard Carter. The poor man had been digging for years in the Valley of the Kings, the royal burial ground for pharaohs, without finding much of note, and was close to having his funds cut off by his wealthy patron. Since most of the tombs had been plundered and stripped of their riches in ancient times, the chances of finding a tomb intact were slim to none, but Carter held out hope. At the eleventh hour, he came upon a step that eventually led to the burial chambers of a pharaoh named Tutankha-mun, who'd reigned for around ten years and been entombed with a wondrous treasure trove of artifacts. His burial chambers were stacked to the ceiling with gleaming antiquities, including thrones, jewels, three golden coffins, and even a royal chariot. Charlotte had been four years old when the discovery captivated the world, and she decided then and there that finding buried treasure would be her life goal. In her teens, she spent copious amounts of time at the Metropolitan Museum and the New-York Historical Society, reading everything she could on ancient Egypt, including Amelia Edwards's marvelous account of her 1874 travels, *A Thousand Miles up the Nile*. By the time Charlotte enrolled in New York University at seventeen, she was already fairly proficient in translating hieroglyphics, which gave her an edge when she applied to be part of an excavation team funded by the Met for her study-abroad program.

"You're right, it was Carter's discovery that pulled me in," she admitted. "Although, being here now, I understand what a small part of history King Tut actually takes up. That there are thousands of other stories that are just as interesting, if not more so."

"That's certainly true."

The Bedouin was beckoning Charlotte, so she excused herself to attend to him. He was already able to gently flex his thumb—a promising sign—and addressed her in a low, solemn voice. One of the Egyptian workers translated. "Mehedi says that you will always be sacred to his tribe, and you will always be safe."

A lovely sentiment, thought Charlotte. She thanked Mehedi in Arabic and they nodded to each other, and then Charlotte invited him and his tribesmen to join them for tea before they headed back out into the desert. They politely declined, and eventually the robed men disappeared over the sandy ridge to the west.

Charlotte returned to the lunch table and began collecting the team's dirty plates and glasses.

"You seem to have made an admirer out of our visitor," said Leon as Charlotte reached past him to grab an errant spoon. "I wouldn't be surprised if he comes back to make you his concubine." He twisted the gold ring he always wore on his pinky, embedded with an ostentatious yellow jasper stone.

"That's enough, Leon," said Henry sharply.

By the end of the working day, the team leaders had returned from the shores of the Nile, along with provisions carried on the backs of donkeys. Mr. Zimmerman was sorry to have missed the Bedouin and complimented Charlotte for a job well done. "I think you've earned a chance to do some real work, don't you?" He regarded her with his pale blue eyes.

He was one of the best Egyptologists in the world, and Charlotte was lucky to land under his tutelage, even if it mostly consisted of observing. Until now.

"I'd welcome the opportunity," she said.

Later that evening, she climbed the steep ramp to their living quarters, located in an empty tomb that branched off into a series of smaller chambers and offered neither running water nor electricity. At night before bed, she refilled the cups of water that sat under each leg of her cot to prevent scorpions from climbing up, a detail that she made sure to omit in her letters home. She had a small desk and chair, as well as a basin where she could wash her face and hands. The caverns were cool and quiet, and she'd never slept better.

As the sun set, she liked to sit outside and watch the sand drift across the desert's edge and listen to the howl of hyenas. To the east, the Nile River lazed its way north to Cairo and then Alexandria before draining into the Mediterranean Sea. The majority of Egyptians lived along its shores, an area that took up a mere four percent of the entire country. But every spring, the Nile would flood, spreading silt far across the fields, a rich nourishment for the next planting. The ancient village they were currently excavating, as well as the Valley of the Kings, was located only a few miles away from the fertile plains of Luxor, but it might as well have been on the moon. Beyond the flood zones, the landscape changed dramatically into a barren desert, not a palm tree in sight. It was like working in an oven on days when the temperature climbed.

In high school, Charlotte had learned that the deserts to the west and south and the seas to the north and east of Egypt offered the country protection from the threat of invaders. That, together with the rich abundance of food from the fertile Nile valley, meant that most of the ancient Egyptians lived well, with time to study the sky and create an accurate solar calendar, build follies like the pyramids of Giza, form a written language, and make great strides in civil engineering and medicine, all long before Christ was even born.

And now here she was, in a place she'd only dreamed about. The orange sun set in a hazy sky full of dust particles as Henry joined her, bringing along his own wooden chair.

"How was your day?" he said as he planted himself next to her. "Translate anything of interest?"

"A shopping list that was eerily like ours of today. Oh, and a contract between a master craftsman and Ankhsheshonq about altering some images."

"Ankhsheshonq?" repeated Henry. "He was a scribe to Saukemet II, I believe."

"You would be correct."

"Sounds like a camel's sneeze." He covered his nose with his hand. "*Ankhsheshonq!*"

"Gesundheit."

He laughed. "Here's a question for you: Why are we called 'Egyptologists,' yet no other country has a name as a job? 'Greece-ologist'? 'Italiologist'? You can't think of one, can you?"

"Now that you say it, I can't. Although 'Italiologist' is fun to say."

He sat back, looking quite pleased with himself; she liked the way his eyes twinkled in the dimming light.

"It's probably because the ancient Egypt civilization lasted for three thousand years," she said. "Compared with Rome, which eked out one thousand, and Greece with fifteen hundred, I would say the Egyptians deserve their own 'ology.'"

"Good point. And how has your experience as a budding Egyptologist been so far? Between treating snakebites and cleaning dishes, I imagine it has been a bit of seesaw between moments of high adventure and hours of painful monotony."

"I don't mind the dish-washing. I've learned so much from listening to the conversations between the rest of the team. It's enough to write an entire book."

"Is that what you'd like to do?"

"Maybe." She could only imagine the face her mother would make when presented with the idea. Her parents had reluctantly allowed her to go on this trip after meeting with Grayson Zimmerman in person, when he assured them she'd be safe under his wing. They expected her to be back home by Christmas, and, after graduating, to become a history teacher. This trip was a lark, a once-in-a-lifetime experience, in their minds. She was only a girl, after all.

Sometimes, as Charlotte translated the ostraca, she wished she'd been born in ancient Egypt, when women and men had many of the same rights under the law. If a woman divorced or her husband died, she retained a third of the property. Divorce and remarriage weren't frowned upon, nor were children born out of wedlock, nor sexual relations between unmarried people. In fact, life in old Luxor sounded a lot more fun to Charlotte than life in the modern world, where women had limited rights and the idea of a dalliance was considered shocking and immoral.

"I understand Grayson is offering you a chance to get your hands dirty," said Henry, cutting into her thoughts.

"He is. Do you think he'll make good on his promise?"

"He's a good man. I would bet on it. Just don't get your hopes up. Not everyone can be a Howard Carter."

The last of the sun faded into the horizon. Called Ra, the sun was the ultimate god to the ancient Egyptians, the king of the other deities and the father of all creation.

"Maybe so," she answered. "But not everyone can be a Charlotte Cross, either."

Four weeks later, Charlotte was still waiting for her chance to excavate. However, after finishing up their work at the village, the team was given permission to relocate three miles away at the final resting place of the pharaohs of Egypt, including Tutankhamun: the Valley of the Kings. But Mr. Zimmerman had put off Charlotte's entreaty, saying that logging everyone's findings was a more valuable activity for her than taking over a man's spot. It didn't help that this was the final dig site for everyone involved—not only Charlotte—as funding issues connected with the Great Depression meant that the Met Museum would be withdrawing its presence from Egypt.

With only a couple months left on the site, the members of the dig team were feeling peevish at the thought of having to return home. The one bright spot was that they were no longer living in caves, but had taken up residence at the swanky Metropolitan House, the home base for the museum's expeditions in the Valley of the Kings. The long, pale building, tucked into the hillside, boasted several domes and a spacious veranda behind thick arches. Its decor was spare but comfortable, with a library, a dining room with a long oak table, and dozens of bedrooms. The air inside was cool and the furniture modern.

One evening at the Metropolitan House, after a hearty dinner and multiple rounds of drinks, Charlotte and Henry slipped away at the same time.

"Can I ask you a favor, Charlotte?" asked Henry, one hand on the doorknob to his room.

"Of course."

"I need a haircut, badly. Any chance you can lop off the long bits?"

"I have absolutely no experience as a barber. You might regret it."

"I'll take that chance."

In his room, Henry pulled the chair from the small desk and placed a towel around his shoulders as Charlotte stood awkwardly in the entranceway, hands clutched together as if she were in church, unused to being alone in a man's bedroom. Once Henry was seated, he handed her a pair of scissors. Gingerly, she pulled out a curl at the back of his neck and clipped off a couple of inches, the only sound their breaths and the metallic slice of the blades.

As she worked, the silence stretched on. Henry had gone very still and the air felt strangely electric.

"Are you worried I'll take off your ear?" she said, attempting to alleviate whatever weirdness had descended upon them. "I promise to avoid any bloodshed."

He laughed. "No. It's not that. It just reminds me of my mum. When I was a very small child, she'd cut my hair. I'd completely forgotten that until just now. She was lovely. Died when I was seven. From then on, I was at the mercy of the school barber."

"I'm sorry about your mother," said Charlotte.

"Thank you. She always said it was easy to cut my hair because we had the exact same curls."

"My mother and I share the same silver streak." She pointed to her right temple, where a stripe of gray had appeared a year ago, just as it had when her mother was eighteen, and her grandmother before that. Charlotte's mother covered hers with hair dye, but Charlotte refused. "I overheard one of the boys at college say it reminded him of a skunk." She hadn't told anyone that before.

"He should be shot. It lends you an air of gravitas and fierceness, which is required for anyone crazy enough to dig in this infernal Egyptian sandbox."

She turned pink from the compliment and quickly changed the subject. "I overheard Leon saying you attended the same boarding school. Sounded quite fancy."

"It was, but I certainly wasn't. My father was the school's maintenance man, and I attended on a scholarship. The rest of the students were the sons of the aristocracy, like Leon."

That explained a lot. Out in the field, Henry stood out from the other archaeologists, winning the local Egyptian workers' respect by addressing them without condescension, or charming the upper-crust wife of some duke who'd insisted on viewing a dig as part of their around-the-world itinerary. He was a chameleon in many ways, and she found him intriguing, drawn in by his authentic charm as well as his unerring knowledge when it came to the field of ancient Egyptology. Not to mention the fact that he was near fluent in Arabic.

When she was finished with his haircut, Henry examined the results in the mirror. Charlotte had gotten carried away trying to make both sides even, which meant his large ears stuck out even more than they had before.

"Oh, God, I'm so sorry," she said, barely holding back her laughter. "I warned you."

"I'm sure it will improve my hearing greatly, not having those pesky curls in the way."

"Oh, you hate it, don't you? I'm sure you're sorry you ever asked."

"I wouldn't go that far, but perhaps some form of punishment is in order." He gazed at her in the mirror, a look that made her stomach flip.

"Now you have me worried."

"As you should be. How about this? On our next day off, you are required to accompany me to the ruin of my choosing."

She quickly agreed.

But to Charlotte's dismay, Leon invited himself along to their field trip to the Temple of Karnak. Although he and Henry were childhood friends, they couldn't be more different. Where Henry was easygoing, Leon found fault wherever he could, complaining that the food was overcooked, his bed too soft, or the servants lazy. It would be a long day in his company.

Karnak spanned two hundred acres, more than they could possibly explore in one visit. Its vast complex consisted of temples, chapels, pylons, a sacred lake. Outside the entrance, they stopped in front of a single eighty-foot-tall obelisk.

"Its twin was given to France in the early 1800s and now looms over the Place de la Concorde," said Henry.

Charlotte tilted her head back. "It's a shame they handed it over. It belongs here. This other one looks slightly lost without it, don't you think?"

"The French have been very helpful in finding lost tombs and antiquities, shouldn't they get some of the spoils?" Leon countered. "Otherwise, what's the point?"

"The point is to preserve what's here and learn about the ancient history."

"Someone has to pay for it, and who would do that without getting something in return?" He cast Charlotte a sidelong glance. "Maybe some New York rich kid?"

Charlotte resented the implication that she was wealthy just because she came from New York. "Or perhaps some pompous British viscount?"

Leon laughed, then shrugged. "I may have a title, but there's nothing left of the family money. What was once a grand estate now looks a little like this." He looked out across the ruins. "Actually, worse. Everything burned to the ground, and my father couldn't afford to rebuild, so it's basically a pile of rubble. Which wouldn't be so terrible, I suppose, if my parents had found a way to cope with the loss instead of collapsing along with the walls and ceilings."

Henry placed a sympathetic hand on his friend's shoulder. They were all silent for a moment until Charlotte said, "I'm sorry to hear that." And she was sorry. That explained a lot about his sour behavior, and she promised herself that she would take it easier on him going forward, the way Henry did. "What will you do when the dig is closed down? Where will you go?"

"I'm not going anywhere," said Leon. "I'll attach myself to another group, maybe the French or the Polish. Zimmerman's already promised to make introductions."

"I'm sure they'll welcome your insights."

As the day wore on, Leon drifted away to check out the Festival Hall, while Henry and Charlotte lost themselves in the Hypostyle Hall, a large gallery consisting of 134 giant columns that soared almost seventy feet high, like a sandstone forest. The clerestory roof was no more, but inscriptions and reliefs covered almost every surface, carved by artisans under the reigns of multiple pharaohs.

Charlotte marveled at the quiet beauty of the ruins. "Imagine what this was like back then, with the walls and columns painted in bright colors. I could stay here all day just admiring the hieroglyphs and carvings. Each one tells a story. I mean, here's a relief of Sauke-met II leading an attack in battle, while over here he's offering incense to the gods during a festival."

"Quite a sight." But Henry wasn't looking at the temple; he was watching Charlotte. He cleared his throat when she caught him and stared absently about, as if he'd only just noticed the artwork. "The festivals must have left quite an impression on the average Egyptian."

She ducked behind a column and he followed her. "The people of ancient Egypt sure knew how to have a good time." She glanced back at him with a smile. "My favorite would be the festival of Bast."

"Ah, right. Honoring the birth of the cat goddess. Is it because she's the protector of women and children?"

"Sure. I love that women were free to do whatever they pleased during Bast. They drank, danced wildly, played music, became loud and boisterous." She suddenly remembered that the festival also famously included the "raising of the skirts"—where women flashed men as a way of celebrating fertility and female sexuality. Mortified, Charlotte pretended to be absorbed in a bas-relief sculpture.

"Wait a minute, there was something else involved in the celebrations," Henry said, tapping his cheek with his index finger. "Hmm. I can't think what it is."

"Is that so?" she teased back, daring him to say it out loud. He was as shy as she was, when it came down to it. She loved that she knew that about him. "And what would that be?"

Henry turned bright red, and they both burst out laughing.

They were usually surrounded by other people, and to be alone with Henry in this magical space was lovely. Over the past few weeks, Charlotte hadn't realized how much she ached to be seen by him, to be near him. When he sat next to her at meals or caught up with her as she walked back to the Metropolitan House after a long day at work, she reveled in the fact that he had sought out her company.

Henry took a step over to her and touched her hand with his. "The Egyptians certainly knew how to enjoy life."

"I envy them." They were deep in the shadows of the temple's walls.

26

Slowly, as if Charlotte might dissolve into the earth if he wasn't careful, Henry leaned forward and kissed her lightly on the mouth. She took hold of the lapels of his jacket and pulled him close, drawing courage from the women of the past who weren't afraid of desire. As the kiss grew deeper, his breath became ragged and a delicious tremor ran through Charlotte. They stayed there, swaying slightly, only pulling apart when the sound of Leon calling their names echoed through the columns and up into the African sky.

The next morning, Mr. Zimmerman took Charlotte aside and told her the time had come for her to dig, and she eagerly headed to her assigned spot, a vault where several fertility statuettes had been already found. The Valley of the Kings had been chosen by the ancient Egyptians as a burial ground due to its secluded location in the dusty hills east of the Nile, and Charlotte knew the geography of the place well, having ventured deep inside the most famous tombs, from the brightly decorated one belonging to King Tut to Seti I's final resting place, with its mesmerizing hieroglyphs.

After just a few minutes of digging, Mr. Zimmerman came over, looking sheepish.

"I have a favor to ask you, Charlotte," he said.

"Yes?"

"As you know, Leon hasn't had a find yet this season. He asked if he could work at your site instead. Do you mind switching? I feel bad for the guy."

Charlotte was certain Leon wouldn't have made the request if she had been a man. But she hated to put Mr. Zimmerman in a bind. He'd been so kind to her.

"Of course."

Leon's spot was located on the eastern side of the cliffs, near the mouth of a tomb that had already been thoroughly examined by the French, which meant there probably wasn't much to discover. After several hours of fruitless labor, the lunch bell rang. Charlotte's back was sore, her shoulders ached, and the rays of the sun burned feverishly on any exposed skin. But she stayed on, determined to make the most of her one opportunity, which meant she was alone when her spade hit something hard. Her fatigue faded away at the sight of a smooth surface, one that had been purposefully laid down, most likely thousands of years ago. She worked faster, her breath catching in her throat, and eventually uncovered what was unmistakably a stone step situated only a few feet from the entrance to the other tomb. An odd placement, but not unheard of. She let out a small cry of triumph, one that came out strangled as she hadn't stopped to drink water in ages.

She breathlessly informed Mr. Zimmerman of her find. He brought over two of the strongest Egyptians, who used pickaxes to carve out the space around the step, which led to another. And then another. By the end of the day, the stairway had been cleared and part of a door was visible.

A door to a previously undiscovered tomb.

While the excavation season had yielded several important artifacts such as oil lamps, wine jars, and the fertility statuettes, unearthing a new tomb was a remarkable feat. And what if it was another Tutankhamun—an unspoiled tomb full of riches?

It would take another day to fully clear the entrance. That evening at dinner, Charlotte buzzed with excitement, as did the rest of the team, and she was treated like an equal, with Henry insisting on clearing the dirty dishes so she could continue answering everyone's questions. The only sourpuss was Leon, of course, who sulked in the corner.

The next morning, even though Charlotte could tell Mr. Zimmerman was as eager as she was to get inside, they first had to wait for the arrival of an inspector from the Department of Antiquities, as a representative was required to be present for any new discoveries. The man arrived after an excruciating hour-long wait, and then he and Mr. Zimmerman spoke quietly with each other before the man gave a nod and they were allowed to proceed.

Outside the entrance, Mr. Zimmerman held out his hand. "After you, Miss Cross. Let's see what we've got here."

CHAPTER THREE

Annie

NEW YORK CITY, 1978

It was never a good sign when Annie's mother played the Rolling Stones on the dusty turntable in their basement apartment. While the dulcet tenor of Jackson Browne or the harmonies of Styx signified that Joyce was more or less content, Mick Jagger yowling about being shattered meant Joyce was as well.

Annie heard the music blasting as she closed the front door of the brownstone firmly behind her. She'd been cleaning their landlady's apartment—which consisted of the three floors above their own—the entire afternoon, and her back ached as she maneuvered down the steep steps that led to the sidewalk. Thank goodness Mrs. Hollingsworth was up in her bedroom on the second floor recovering from a twisted knee, or she'd have been stomping around her parlor in a fury at the bass droning through her parquet floor. Annie did a quick U-turn, closed the small metal gate behind her, and turned the stiff doorknob that led to the basement apartment's front door, tucked directly beneath the steps she'd just descended.

When she and Joyce first moved in, six-year-old Annie had imagined their hideaway as a fairy's cave, a place where they could be safe. At nineteen, she recognized that they lived in a hovel of sorts, with rats scurrying outside the barred windows late at night and the damp smell of mold seeping through the brick walls in the spring. Joyce still insisted on calling it a "garden flat" when speaking to others, even though the garden out back consisted of a series of uneven bluestone squares edged with desolate tufts of ragweed.

On top of her job waitressing at a diner on Lexington Avenue, a few days a week Annie scoured Mrs. Hollingsworth's apartment in exchange for discounted rent. Her duties included scrubbing Mrs. Hollingsworth's toilets and dusting the floor moldings of every room, dragging a cloth along the top edge like some hunchbacked servant girl. Right now, all she wanted was to make herself some macaroni and cheese and curl up on the couch with the latest issue of *Vogue*. But her respite wasn't coming any time soon. She walked over to the record player and carefully lifted the needle before turning it off. Blouses were piled up on the one armchair, and several skirts were draped over the couch.

Joyce flew out of the bedroom in a silk slip, eyes wide. "Where have you been?"

Even in an agitated state, her mother was a beautiful woman. At thirty-nine, she was often mistaken for being in her late twenties, and it was no surprise that her face, with its with baby-smooth skin and upturned nose, had at one time been celebrated by top fashion photographers.

"I was cleaning."

"Brad's due in an hour and nothing fits. Nothing. We're supposed to be going to Mortimer's and then Régine's for dancing, and I can't look like some frumpy nun. You have to help me."

"Not all nuns are frumpy. Julie Andrews wasn't."

"She was a novitiate, not a nun. And she didn't last very long."

Annie pointed to a brushed-silk dress in a grayish silver. "What about that one? It'll look great on the dance floor."

"The color is boring. I can't look old. I simply can't."

Annie sighed. "How about if I play around with it? Maybe lift the hem a few inches?" She'd seen a similar design in last month's *Bazaar*, with dolman sleeves. Annie's love for fashion had begun when she'd gotten a set of paper dolls for Christmas one year. She'd created dresses, coats, and hats for each one in bright colors and then gotten sucked into the glossy pages of *Mademoiselle*, working her way up to the serious, grown-up styles of *Bazaar* and *Vogue*. Clothes protected; clothes were armor. Clothes were a distraction when things got difficult.

"Could you? And maybe lower the neckline as well?"

Annie grabbed the dress and headed to the bedroom, where her sewing machine sat in a corner. On the bed was a Macy's bag.

Annie's stomach dropped. "What did you buy?"

Joyce ran into the room and clutched it to her chest like it was a crying baby. "I needed makeup."

"The medicine cabinet is practically exploding with makeup. We won't have rent if you keep on buying things you don't need."

"It's an investment in our future. Once Brad and I are married, we'll never have to worry about this again. And don't tell me what to do. I'm the mother here."

"Then act like one."

She'd pushed it too far. Joyce's eyes welled up, and she plopped on the bed, letting the bag fall onto the floor. "Fine. Take it all back. I thought, after the week I've had, that I deserved a little treat. A pick-me-up."

A few days earlier, Joyce had announced that her agency had dumped her. Not that she worked much at all anymore, only catalog ads for JCPenney and Sears. But now Joyce was too old even for that type of job, and Annie knew her mother was gutted. The only bright spot was this burgeoning relationship with Brad. Annie had seen her mother cycle through a number of Brad types after her father died when she was five, precipitating the move to the garden flat. But Joyce's eyes lit up whenever she mentioned Brad's name, which was often. They'd met at the local watering hole on Lexington a few weeks ago, Joyce brimming with excitement after he'd bought her a daiquiri and they'd talked for hours.

"Maybe you'd be better off without me." Joyce eyed the bedside table that sat between their twin beds. Annie knew a bottle of sleeping pills lay in the top drawer. It wasn't an idle threat.

Annie sat beside her. "Go put on your face while I play with your outfit."

Joyce hugged her close, smelling like Anaïs Anaïs. Annie breathed in deeply. She loved her mother, even when she was a mess. Joyce needed Annie to maneuver in the world, and most of the time it was lovely to be needed.

Forty-five minutes later, Joyce had a new outfit that she twirled around in with delight. Annie began cleaning up the scattered clothes. Her fingers were sore, her eyes hurt, and her stomach growled.

"No, there's no time," said Joyce. "Just stick them under the bed or something."

"Then they'll need to be ironed." A task that would surely fall to Annie.

"No, it's time."

A silence fell between them.

"But it was starting to rain when I walked in," said Annie.

"Then you should take an umbrella. Annie. Please."

Annie eyed the darkness outside the windows and sighed. Her

mother needed this to work out so badly, and Annie most definitely didn't want to be blamed if—or when—it went wrong. There was no point in putting up a fuss.

The fact was that Joyce wasn't ready for Brad to meet Annie. And it wasn't just that Brad didn't know Joyce had a nineteen-year-old daughter. It was a matter of aesthetics.

Whenever Joyce was forced to introduce Annie as her daughter, Annie steeled herself for the expected look of confusion. The person would stare at Annie a beat too long, taking in her round face and lackluster light brown hair, then look over at Joyce, with her blonde updo and perfect bow lips. Their gaze would travel back to Annie, noting the way she towered over her mother, her shoulders and arms muscular from carrying trays of food at the diner and scrubbing floors, before taking in Joyce's cinched, twenty-three-inch waist.

"How nice," they'd say as Annie slowly faded into the background.

Joyce loved to compare their hands, her lacquered nails and long fingers a stark contrast to Annie's substantial grip and ragged cuticles. "You have your father's build," she would say. "He was a big guy, but so graceful on the dance floor."

Annie didn't remember much about her father, but she'd been so young when he died. She still remembered the smell of his aftershave and the feel of his rough cheek on her own, as well as the fact that he'd take her to the Met Museum on Saturdays while Joyce slept in, where she'd scamper around the Egyptian Art collection, pointing out the blue hippo, which was her favorite object. Before they left to return home, he'd pick her up so she could get a good look at the Cerulean Queen, which was his favorite.

Joyce marched to the coatrack near the front door and grabbed Annie's red coat and an umbrella. "It won't be that long. Brad and I will be on our way in no time. Two loops around the block and the place is all yours. Hey, maybe before long, we'll be living in luxury. Brad's in sales, you know."

Whatever that meant.

Annie didn't have much choice. She put on her coat and headed out into the cold November air.

Annie wandered the familiar streets of the Upper East Side in a hungry, exhausted daze. She wanted more than anything to settle in for the night with her macaroni and cheese and a long, hot bath, which would take the chill from her bones. She passed her old high school, which looked uglier than ever in the gloom of the evening, the Brutalist architecture slightly improved by colorful graffiti. Five years ago, she'd been a freshman, eager to move on from the impenetrable cliques of middle school. Nothing much had changed for her, though.

That year her geography teacher, Mr. Williams, asked the class to write an essay about where they would travel if they each had $1,000. The boy sitting next to her immediately chose Rome, for the Colosseum and the pizza, while it took Annie a while to wrap her head around the very idea of making such a huge decision, especially one that didn't involve her mother. She finally settled on Paris, for the fashion. She worked hard on her essay and got an A.

Annie brought it home to show Joyce, but her mother had been harshly rejected during a bathing suit go-see that day and was in no mood to read it. When Annie gently suggested they each get part-time jobs to lessen their dependency on the income from the modeling gigs, Joyce surprised her by considering the idea. Joyce looked through the classifieds and, right then and there, called to answer an ad for a receptionist position in a midtown law firm. The very next day, she went to the interview and, to Annie's delight, was offered the job. Meanwhile, Mrs. Hollingsworth had just inquired about Annie taking over for her maid, and Annie had accepted, hoping to do her part.

As Mrs. H's cleaner, Annie was paid $170 a week, along with a discount on rent. To Annie's surprise, Mrs. H added that, every week, she'd put ten dollars into a cookie jar that sat on the kitchen counter. "That money is yours, not your mother's," said Mrs. H. "Do you understand? I suggest you forget it exists entirely."

Annie had nodded, embarrassed that Mrs. H was aware of the upside-down mother-daughter dynamic in the basement apartment.

When Annie came home from school the first day of her mother's new job, excited to have the place all to herself for once, Joyce was lying on the living room couch in a bathrobe, a cool compress over her forehead. The work had been too much, too demanding. Joyce couldn't possibly answer all those phones, and, after mixing up the senior partners' calls one too many times, she had been summarily let go.

"Great, you can take the cleaning job, then," Annie said.

Joyce weakly lifted up one arm without removing the compress from her eyes. "It would damage my hands, darling."

Annie let loose a stream of complaints about Joyce's maternal deficiencies before storming off. When she finally cooled down enough to return home, her mother was sleeping heavily in her bed, and when Annie leaned over to check on her, still angry, she discovered an empty bottle of pills on the quilt. Annie called for an ambulance and, sick with worry, rode in it to the hospital, where Joyce had her stomach pumped. After, Joyce insisted to the doctor and to Annie that it had all been a silly mix-up; she'd completely forgotten how many she'd taken because Annie's harsh words had "burned into my soul." She promised to be a better mother and begged Annie's forgiveness, and the doctor, thoroughly disarmed by her allure and charm, had

36

discharged her. The shock of that awful night had stayed with Annie long after. Her mother was delicate, and it was Annie's job to protect her from the world.

After Annie graduated from high school, while many of the other students were heading to college, she picked up the waitressing job. It didn't seem fair that others had the freedom to dream of the future while Annie was stuck in the present, hoping the check for the phone bill didn't bounce and making sure to tell Joyce how beautiful she looked before she left for a go-see.

Annie checked her watch. She'd given her mother plenty of time to head off on her date with Brad. She reached their building and opened the door to the basement apartment, feeling the blast of heat that the overactive radiators emitted during the cooler months. However, as she set her keys down on the tiny table beside the coatrack, she heard a peal of laughter from the bedroom. Joyce and Brad were still here.

Annie picked up her keys and backed out the door, closing it behind her. She considered heading to the diner where she worked and ordering a hamburger and fries, but then she remembered the shopping bag filled with makeup. They couldn't afford any more unnecessary expenses, even with her employee discount.

At least the rain had stopped. She sat on the steps to Mrs. H's front door, tucking her raincoat under her. Neighbors passed wordlessly by, matronly women with little dogs out for their evening walk, men with briefcases returning from a work dinner.

"What are you doing out here, for goodness' sake?"

The voice came from over Annie's right shoulder. She twisted around to find Mrs. H peering out of one of her parlor windows, a silk scarf loosely covering the large pink rollers in her hair. She looked like one of those marionettes with huge heads and skinny bodies Annie had seen in a puppet show as a child.

Annie rose to her feet. "Shouldn't you be upstairs? What about your knee?"

Mrs. H waved a pale hand in the air. "I had the nurse help me downstairs before she left. I'm sick and tired of staring at the same four walls. Are you locked out of the apartment?"

She considered lying and saying yes, but Mrs. H had an extra key. "My mom has someone over."

"I see." The woman's lips pursed. "Come inside. You look like a drowned rat."

Annie let herself in. Mrs. H was already halfway down the front hallway, leaning heavily on her cane as she made her way to the kitchen at the back of the brownstone. Annie knew every inch of the apartment by now, from the coffin corners on the stairway to the parlor adorned with European etchings and porcelain vases, and couldn't help but notice a stark difference between the public areas and the ones where visitors didn't venture, like the kitchen. There, a small sink stood next to a chipped countertop, a line of drunkenly crooked cabinets just above it. In one corner was a linoleum table covered by a stained tablecloth. Mrs. H often declared she was one of the "faded rich," ladies who had lunched in style at the Russian Tea Room twenty years ago but were now trapped in their decaying, depreciating townhouses in a dangerous city.

Annie's gaze was drawn to a large pot of spaghetti on the stovetop that Mrs. H's cook had made.

"You want some pasta?" asked Mrs. H as she settled into one of the kitchen chairs. "Help yourself."

Annie took a bowl from the cabinet and ladled a knot of spaghetti into it. She didn't care that it was cold; anything would do at this point. She joined Mrs. H at the table, aware that they'd never been in such close proximity before. Mr. H had died a decade or so ago, although Mrs. H still constantly invoked the first-person plural when speaking of him, saying "We loved that restaurant until it closed," or "We prefer the silverware polished weekly." It was sad but also sort of sweet.

"So tell me, who's the latest swain?"

Annie hadn't realized how close an eye Mrs. H kept on their comings and goings. Lately, the men Joyce dated didn't tend to stick around very long, which only made her clingier with the next one, accelerating the downward spiral. Instead of getting wiser with age, her mother was becoming more desperate, regressing into a lovelorn teen.

Annie jumped to her mother's defense. "She's very serious with Brad. He's in sales."

"What kind of sales?"

"Yachts."

Annie had no idea what the man sold, nor did Joyce, probably, but it was the first thing that came to mind.

Mrs. H let out a small, disappointed sigh. "Tell me, girl, what are you going to do with your life?"

Annie was unprepared for the change in subject. "I'm not sure."

"What do you want to do?"

For so long, Annie's goal had been the same as her mother's: help Joyce find a man so that they could live the life they deserved, with a nice apartment in one of the new white-brick high-rises and vacations to Florida. When Annie turned twelve, she'd taken over managing their money by necessity, but living on the edge financially had kept her focus on the here and now—mainly whether or not they could afford next month's rent. She was too tired to imagine a life beyond the one she currently lived.

Before Annie could come up with an answer that might satisfy Mrs. H and allow her to eat more than two forkfuls of pasta, the phone hanging on the wall just above Mrs. Hollingsworth's head let out a shrill ring. Mrs. H lifted the receiver and twirled the cord around her finger. "Hollingsworth residence."

Annie got in another two bites before Mrs. H hung up. "I need you to run an errand for me."

"Now?"

"Yes. Go upstairs into my closet and take out the feather boa that's hanging in there. Somewhere on the right side, I think."

Reluctantly, Annie did as she was told. It was almost worse to have had a few bites of food than none at all. Her stomach craved to be filled. Mrs. H's closet bloomed with gowns and dresses from another era, ones that the widow probably would never wear again. While the designs were out of date, some of the fabrics would be perfect turned into tunics or skirts. Annie took down the feather boa, which had been dyed a strange pea green color, and sneezed.

Back downstairs, Mrs. H placed the boa into a shopping bag. "Now take it to the Met Museum."

Annie must have heard her wrong. Or maybe Mrs. H was losing her marbles.

"I'm sorry, you want me to take this to the Met. Now?"

"Yes. They're waiting. Go in the side entrance on 84th Street. Tell them it's for Diana, and make sure she gets it and knows who sent it." She pronounced the name in a fancy way, *Dee-AH-nah.*

"Diana who?"

"For goodness' sake, enough with the questions. Go on, and I'll have the spaghetti heated up for you by the time you get back. I even have some ice cream for dessert."

"What flavor?"

"Strawberry."

Annie's favorite.

CHAPTER FOUR

Charlotte

NEW YORK CITY, 1978

All afternoon, Charlotte considered canceling her meeting with Frederick about her Hathorkare research. After the shock of seeing the broad collar, she was in no state to present such a complicated proposition to her boss. The museum system had very clear hierarchies that could not be circumvented, and without Frederick's backing, she wouldn't be able to get her article published. So much rode on this one conversation.

Just before six o'clock, she came upon Frederick outside the door to the staff offices, watching a group of women assembled around the Cerulean Queen.

"Docent drama time." He nodded in the direction of one of the docents in training who stood nervously beside the sculpture. She had blonde hair heavily sprayed into place as if a gale might blow through at any minute, and opened and closed her mouth like a guppy. "How wrong do you think the poor dear will get it?"

Charlotte didn't envy her; the rigid pedagogy of the docent

program was probably more difficult than graduate school, in many ways. After ten months of intense training in art history, replete with exams, papers, and practice tours, qualified docents became the face of the museum, leading adults and school groups on tours and subjected to frequent peer reviews. Those who slacked off were asked to leave—even though the position was unpaid.

Early in the docent-training course, each applicant was randomly assigned an artifact or artwork and expected to offer up a presentation, no prior research allowed.

"I think she's actually quaking," Charlotte said, trying to match Frederick's bonhomie. "I still don't understand the point of putting them through this kind of torture."

"It makes them see the piece with fresh eyes, the way our visitors do."

"I suppose."

"This is an Egyptian statue," the woman began, studying the piece intently, as if the lips might open and tell her what else to say.

"So far, so good," said Frederick under his breath, giddy with delight.

"It helps that this *is* the Egyptian wing," answered Charlotte.

The woman cleared her throat. "It was, unfortunately, not intact when it was discovered."

"As evidenced by the fact that half her head is missing." Frederick chuckled. He was in a good mood; maybe, in spite of Charlotte's unease, this evening would be the perfect time to approach him about her Hathorkare theory.

"How long do they have to present?" asked Charlotte.

"Three minutes."

A stout woman with gray hair stood planted on the spot like a sphinx, a stopwatch in one hand. As the docent continued speaking, mumbling about the piece being "very old" and "made from polished

42

cerulean," the educator shook her head. "Go deeper, Priscilla. Really *look* at it."

"Um. Back when it was made, it would be displayed in a home. Or maybe a temple or a pyramid—I'm not sure—and the woman who this represents was very beautiful and wealthy." The trainee continued talking in circles, but was slowly losing momentum, like a toy with a dying battery. She locked eyes with a dark-haired woman in a Chanel suit who stood a few feet away from Charlotte. Another docent in training, Charlotte guessed. The dark-haired woman was mouthing something, trying to help out her friend.

"It's from the New Kingdom," said Priscilla proudly.

"She got that last bit right," said Frederick. "I'm almost impressed."

"Looks like she has a prompter." Charlotte gestured with one elbow in the dark-haired woman's direction.

"I take it back."

Just as it was becoming too painful for Charlotte to watch the history of her favorite statue get mangled by Priscilla the wannabe docent, the educator pocketed the watch and clapped her hands together. "I've heard worse," she said, "but you have a long way to go, Priscilla. Why would you describe this piece as 'old'? That's boring, not to mention redundant."

Charlotte didn't wait to hear the answer. "Frederick, I believe your next appointment is with me."

He stiffened. "Is this about the loan?"

"No. It's not about the loan." She swallowed the wave of panic that threatened and reminded herself to breathe. "I have something interesting to show you."

"In that case, show away."

In her cubicle, she laid out the photographs from Luxor on her desk in order and launched into her pitch. "It's common knowledge among historians that Saukemet II ordered the erasures of Hathorkare's name and image in anger, shortly after he came to power. But I think the timing is off."

"You do, do you?" Frederick raised his eyebrows in amusement, as if she were a child who was unsuccessfully trying fit a piece into a jigsaw puzzle.

"Yes. Way off. By studying the dates when certain of her temples were dismantled—which, of course, was common at the time—and then reassembled by successive pharaohs, I can prove that the erasures occurred at least twenty years later—which takes all the air out of the revenge theory."

Frederick studied the photos for a minute before glancing back at Charlotte. He had written his dissertation on Saukemet II and was considered the topmost scholar of the pharaoh's reign. Just Charlotte's luck. "Why on earth would he order the erasures, then?" he asked. "That doesn't make any sense."

"My theory is that, as an older man, Saukemet II expected his son to become pharaoh after his death. However, the daughter of another royal family enjoyed a more direct line to the dynasty's founder, which made her a potential threat to Saukemet II's plans. It didn't help matters that his predecessor was Hathorkare, whose depictions sometimes contained male traits—like a reddish tint to the skin, a headdress, or a beard—presumably to reinforce the idea that she was as powerful as a man. As far as I can tell, only *those* types of images of Hathorkare were vandalized. If Saukemet II was so angry at his stepmother, why would he carefully pick and choose which ones to remove?"

"Why indeed?"

"My guess is he didn't want his subjects to be reminded of Hathorkare's appropriation of male divinity. Furthermore, the proscription against images of Hathorkare was lifted not long after it had been firmly established that his son—and not the daughter of the rival clan—would inherit the throne, which backs up my theory that he was more concerned about his legacy than some personal grudge against Hathorkare."

Frederick stared hard at her documentation as she pointed out specific examples of the erasures.

"If I'm right," she continued, "it means that Hathorkare was not universally reviled, as we've long thought. Instead, she should be considered one of the top pharaohs of ancient Egypt in terms of her longevity and her artistic and economic contributions, a woman who successfully ruled both as regent and in her own right, guiding her successor on how to lead a country."

Frederick didn't speak for a moment after she finished. "How long have you been working on this?"

She pointed to the thick manila folder on her desk, filled with her references, sources, notes, and journal research. "I started looking into it a few years ago. But I wanted to wait to say anything until I was sure I had it right."

"That's a long time to keep secrets." He ran his hand through his hair and gave a little shake of his head. Frederick didn't like to be surprised. "Well, I have to admit I'm quite impressed. Your premise would turn history on its ear. After all, it was the Met's own curators who called her a vixen."

"Not quite. They called her a 'vain, ambitious, and unscrupulous woman' who was unloved by her people and by her successor. These photos prove them wrong. Wrong about the timeline, wrong about the reason for the erasures, and wrong about her character."

"I'm guessing you want to write a journal article about this?" said Frederick.

Charlotte's pulse quickened. "I do. I know we have a lot going on with the Tut exhibition, but I think I can get it done by early next year."

"That won't work."

She'd figured he'd push back, and was prepared. "I'll do it in my spare time, on weekends, at night. I promise it won't interfere with Tut."

"It's not that. It's a lovely premise, and very modern with women's lib and all that craziness. Almost a little too on the nose, you might say."

"I'm dealing with what happened in the past, not what's going on now."

"Well, it still won't work."

"Why not?"

"You don't have proof. Your theory is all well and good, but it's just a theory. You need something specific, something that proves *why* the erasures were executed. Knowing *when* isn't enough."

As much as she hated to admit it, Frederick had a point. Charlotte's throat tightened as she guessed what was coming next. "I see."

Frederick tapped the folder with his index finger. "Unfortunately, the only way to present this properly is by going back to Egypt and doing the fieldwork yourself. You'd have to ensure your 'selective erasure' theory holds firm, as well as find some proof of motive."

"But you know I can't—"

"Then I'm afraid I can't help you." Frederick's expression toggled back and forth between relief and pity. Relief that his expertise would not be questioned, and pity for Charlotte for being so weak.

But when Charlotte thought of returning to Egypt, her insides recoiled. She couldn't go back, not after what had happened. Not after the night that she'd screamed so hard her throat had burned for days, making it impossible to speak. Not after Egypt had taken away her soul.

CHAPTER FIVE

Charlotte

EGYPT, 1936

Charlotte's excitement at possibly finding an untouched tomb plummeted when she noticed that the door at the bottom of the steps had a broken seal. Someone else had been inside after the priests had closed it up. Still, it would be a new addition to the Valley of the Kings, and her name would be listed in the history books as the one who discovered it.

Mr. Zimmerman held up his lantern as he, Charlotte, and the inspector walked through the doorway and found themselves in a narrow tunnel. They all had to stoop, as the ceiling was only about five feet high. The hallway's walls were covered in hieroglyphics, but most were so faded as to be unintelligible. The only exceptions were the two wedjat eyes painted across from each other about halfway down the incline. Charlotte had always loved the design: an almond eye with an elegantly raised eyebrow, a mark like a teardrop below, and a swirl that curved along the upper cheek that represented well-being, healing, and protection. It thrilled her to think that an ancient

Egyptian artist had stood on the very spot where she was right now and carefully traced the outline before filling it in with a mixture of ocher and soot.

They continued deeper into the tomb, and she heard the voices of the other team members following behind, including those of Henry and Leon. The end of the tunnel opened to a burial chamber that Charlotte guessed to be around twenty feet square. She'd seen photographs of Tut's burial chamber after it was discovered, a jumble of treasures from floor to ceiling, and this couldn't be more different, completely bare except for a large object at the far end of the chamber and a long bundle that lay in the middle of the floor.

As light filled the space and her eyes adjusted, she let out a soft cry.

The large item was a sarcophagus, and the bundle lying beside it, a mummified corpse.

They drew closer. The mummy on the floor was wrapped in strips of linen, but the left thumb poked through the cloth, the thumbnail intact. After thousands of years, a perfect thumbnail. The Egyptian mummification process was a long one, lasting seventy days, but by removing all the moisture from the body, the embalmers were able to preserve it so well that, other than a natural darkening of the skin, the result was incredibly lifelike—even strands of hair were preserved.

The process was rather ghastly, in Charlotte's opinion. All the internal organs were removed, including the brain, which was pulled out through the nostrils in pieces. The heart was left behind, while other organs—the lungs, liver, stomach, intestines—were placed in canopic jars, to be interred with the deceased. Then the body was covered in a type of salt and left to dry out, before being wrapped in hundreds of yards of linen and finally placed in a coffin.

And now she was looking at the result.

"Interesting," said Mr. Zimmerman, kneeling down.

"What's that?"

"One of the mummy's arms is crossed over the chest, a sign of royalty in the Eighteenth Dynasty."

"Do you think someone took it out of the sarcophagus?"

"Perhaps. Tomb raiders were certainly here at some point, looking for any amulets and jewels that the priests left in the wrappings of the body. Wonder what else they made off with." He rose and together they approached the sarcophagus. "Will you look at that?" Mr. Zimmerman said, pointing at the side.

Charlotte translated the marking. "'Great Royal Wet Nurse Bennu.'"

"The royal nurse of Hathorkare," said Mr. Zimmerman.

Charlotte had heard of Hathorkare and the supposed curse associated with her, along with the accusation that she had stolen the throne from her stepson. Her mummy had never been found.

After another consultation with the inspector, Mr. Zimmerman called for two of the stronger workers to help lift the lid of the sarcophagus.

It turned out that the mummy on the floor had not been entombed alone. Inside lay another wrapped figure, arms straight along its sides. Which meant the mummy with the bent arm had had its sarcophagus stolen and been abandoned on the dirt floor, a terrible injustice.

"If the arm is crossed, could she possibly be Hathorkare, buried with the mummy of her former nurse to keep her company?" asked Charlotte.

Mr. Zimmerman threw the mummy on the floor a quick glance— he was more interested in studying the sarcophagus's markings. "Perhaps. In any event, she's a minor player in Egyptian history, one who stole the throne in a blatant power grab from the true pharaoh, whose tomb has already been picked through. I'm afraid there's nothing new here to add to the canon."

His lack of excitement dimmed Charlotte's, but she continued exploring. In one corner lay several mummified animals that resembled geese, most likely left for the deceased to dine on. The Egyptians expected their afterlife to be as satisfying as their actual one, which was why King Tut had a chariot placed in his tomb, along with containers for food and drink, several pairs of underwear, and even a couple of board games.

How sad, if this *was* Hathorkare's final resting place, that she was stuck with only fowl to eat and nothing to play with? What else had been inside before the plunderers had struck?

After the tomb had been thoroughly examined and explored, Charlotte reluctantly followed Mr. Zimmerman back along the tunnel that led to the opening. While the discovery was important, the tomb itself was fairly unremarkable, with its faded walls and almost empty chambers. She paused in front of one of the wedjat eyes in the tunnel. Just below it, level with the dirt floor, was a tiny hole, large enough for a mouse. Charlotte reached down and poked her finger inside. To her surprise, the wall there was quite thin, and there was space behind it.

"Mr. Zimmerman, come quick!"

Mr. Zimmerman joined her, with Henry close behind.

"What is it?" asked Mr. Zimmerman.

"I noticed a hole, and the stone crumbles easily." She pointed to the gap near the floor. "I think there might be a niche."

Mr. Zimmerman crouched down and called out for some tools. Leon appeared out of nowhere and edged his way in front of Charlotte, holding a pointing trowel in one hand. He knelt and followed Mr. Zimmerman's instructions to delicately expand the hole. "Give us some room," said Mr. Zimmerman.

Charlotte held her ground, resenting Leon for taking her place. Henry stood right behind her and touched her waist lightly with one hand, sensing her irritation. Ever since their kiss at Karnak, they'd done their best to keep their affection for each other a secret from their colleagues, stealing a kiss or two only when the coast was clear.

Slowly, Leon extricated what looked like a chain of sorts, covered in dust, which Mr. Zimmerman carefully brushed off. It was around two feet long and involved some kind of intricate webbing.

Henry pointed a flashlight at the piece as Mr. Zimmerman held it up for examination. The reflected light burned Charlotte's eyes, and she was forced to squint.

The chain was made of metal, and not just any metal.

Gold.

And it wasn't a chain at all. Charlotte immediately recognized it as a broad collar, a wide, layered necklace made up of several rows of connected amulets. An important find, for certain.

The thieves hadn't gotten everything after all.

The next day was Sunday—the team's day off—and, still buzzing from her discovery, Charlotte agreed to accompany Henry on a trip into Luxor right after breakfast. The air was crisp and clear, the sky blue, which rarely happened in Egypt. The constant swirl of sand tended to cast a yellow glow instead, as if they were on some planet other than Earth.

The city of Luxor lay along the east bank of the Nile, and Henry helped Charlotte into one of the small boats that made the crossing and sat next to her on the bench, their legs touching. Together, they watched as water buffalo grazed in the tall marshes and young boys splashed each other and shouted as the boat pulled away from the shore.

Luxor brimmed with life, the open-air bazaar filled with the cries of vendors selling mangoes and figs, as well as the cackle of hens. The aromas of exotic spices mingled with the colorful tapestries of local craftsmen, while children raced around their mothers' skirts and skinny dogs lolled in the shade panting. Not long into their stroll, Charlotte and Henry were mistaken for tourists and beset by men in robes offering antiquities. "True antiquities, sir, I promise you," they insisted.

Charlotte had been warned early on about the forgery trade that flourished in the city, but Henry became engaged in conversation with a tall man in black. When Charlotte shot him a look, Henry just shrugged. "I'm curious. Let's see what he has to offer, shall we?"

They followed him into a house where hundreds of supposed antiquities were displayed in a small room off the salon. Limestone tablets carved with crude hieroglyphs, amulets, and dozens of scarabs littered a large table.

Henry picked up a scarab and studied it. "I still find it odd that a beetle best known for rolling its dung into a ball is one of the great symbols of ancient Egypt."

"Because their young are hatched in the ball, and the rolling of it resembles the journey of the sun across the sky," said Charlotte.

"That's still something of a stretch."

"Renewal, my dear. They offer protection." Charlotte took it from him and studied its crude markings. It was a fake, but a decent one.

"Would you like one? A magical charm?"

At this, the seller's face brightened. "I have a wonderful one in carnelian for your wife, you will find it perfect. It's upstairs, I'll be right back."

Charlotte blushed at the man's mistake.

Henry drew near. "Mrs. Henry Smith. I rather like that."

"You're going to buy your fake wife a fake scarab?" teased Charlotte.

Henry stood only a foot away, looking down at Charlotte as if she were made of gold. Her breath caught in her chest.

"I'll buy my wife anything she likes," said Henry quietly. "I read somewhere that the forgers roll the fake scarabs in chewed food and have geese swallow them whole. Apparently, the fowl's digestive system adds to the patina."

Charlotte made a face and dropped the scarab, and they both laughed.

Henry wandered around the room, eventually opening a door near the back. "Look!" he whispered.

Charlotte joined him. The room was dominated by a workman's bench with tools strewn about: brushes, saws, a magnifying glass, files, and gravers. In one corner lay a large sycamore mummy case that had been chopped in half, the wood used for fake funerary statues, no doubt. They'd stumbled into a forger's workshop.

"What are you doing?"

The man had returned, carrying several amber-colored scarabs.

Henry quickly made excuses, and soon they were back out on the street, the man scowling at them from the doorway.

"You're going to get us both in deep trouble one of these days," said Charlotte. "You know that, don't you?"

"I liked being mistaken for your husband, so that made it all worth it. Besides, it's not as if he can call the police to complain."

"It doesn't seem right, to sell these fake wares to unsuspecting tourists. Some of those replicas were quite good, you'd need to be an expert to spot them."

"They're just making a living; I don't blame them."

"But it diminishes what ends up in museums, what we go to great lengths to excavate."

"Think of it like this," said Henry. "If an unsuspecting tourist brings home a fake scarab or a pottery bowl and that gets their friends interested in ancient Egyptian culture, the better for the Met Museum or archaeologists like us. They, in turn, might bring their children to the museum, or donate to the Egyptian Art collection, or even fund a dig."

Charlotte wasn't so sure. "You don't think forgeries diminish the artistry of the ancient workers? Shouldn't they be the ones to get all the acclaim?"

"I hate to break it to you, but those workers are all long gone. I doubt they have an opinion either way."

"Unless the Egyptian view of the afterlife is correct. In that case, you might be struck by lightning any day now."

"Oh, I think that's already happened."

The way Henry looked at Charlotte made her forget all about the long-dead artisans or the angry forger. By the time they got back to the Metropolitan House, Charlotte wanted nothing more than to disappear into Henry's room for the afternoon. She was still buzzing from the high of finding an undiscovered tomb; for the first time, the idea of being an archaeologist here in Egypt didn't seem so crazy. In Egypt, she could make her own rules and lead the life she chose, not the one her parents expected of her. And if ancient Egyptian women got to enjoy the pleasures of the body without censure, it was only fair that she should as well.

As they neared his room, Charlotte took Henry's hand in hers. Henry fumbled with his key and, once he finally got the door open, pulled her inside, where Charlotte eagerly melted into his embrace, losing herself to the cadences of their movements and the contours of his body.

After, Henry told her he loved her, and she said it back, without any hesitation. He was charming and kind, and they made a perfect match with their love of archaeology and this wonderful, wild, mysterious country. What the future held for the two of them was opaque, but she didn't want to worry about that right now.

That evening, after dinner, ten or so of the team gathered on the veranda. Charlotte would miss this terrace when she was back in New York, as it was the perfect place to have coffee first thing in the morning while the desert turned pink with the sunrise, or to enjoy a glass of wine in the starry darkness, Henry by her side. She wanted to savor every minute of the time she had left in Egypt. Being in this exotic country, far from her parents, made Charlotte understand how small her life in New York City was, with its rules and social mores.

The conversation turned to the wet nurse's tomb, and she stopped her ruminating to pay attention.

"You did good work excavating that piece, Leon," said Mr. Zimmerman. "We'll be including it in our journal submission early next year."

"I'm sorry, what?" asked Charlotte.

"We're talking about the discovery of the broad collar. From your tomb."

Charlotte had eagerly examined the artifact after it had been properly cleaned. The broad collar was indeed made of gold, exquisite and in almost perfect condition, missing only one tiny amulet on the bottom row. What made it most intriguing was the name inscribed on the clasp: Hathorkare. Mr. Zimmerman had surmised that it had once belonged to the pharaoh, but was unwilling to jump to any conclusions as to what that meant regarding the exposed mummy. The team had looked around for any other hidden niches, including under the wedjat eye opposite, but had come up empty.

Leon tipped his chair back on two legs. "Shouldn't it be *our* tomb? After all, I was assigned it in the first place, and I helped uncover the treasure."

The afternoon of lovemaking, followed by a large glass of wine, made Charlotte more assertive than she normally would have been. "You gave up your dig site because you didn't think it was any good. And then, once inside the tomb that *I* discovered, you practically pushed me out of the way to get to the niche, which—may I remind you—I also discovered."

One of the other archaeologists spoke up. "Enough with the squabbling. Be happy you're a footnote, as that's all you'll be getting. The Met Museum, and our esteemed leader, Mr. Zimmerman, should get all the credit for putting us here in the first place."

"Of course," Charlotte conceded. Leon said nothing.

"In any event, half of everything we find goes to the Egyptian government, don't forget," said Henry. "Let's hope we can hold onto the broad collar."

"I heard from the Department of Antiquities inspector today," said Mr. Zimmerman. "I'm afraid it's bad news. They *will* be taking the broad collar."

Leon let his chair crash down onto the porch loudly. "That's not fair!"

For once, Charlotte and Leon were united in their reaction.

"In return, we have a number of more important items from another dig that will be sent back to the States," said Mr. Zimmerman. "And don't forget the Hathorkare curse. I might have saved you both from certain death." He held out his drink with a laugh. "You're welcome, my friends."

"What's the point of even bothering," whined Leon, "only to have the antiquities end up in the Egyptian Museum? They might as well toss them into the trash."

"How so?" asked Charlotte.

"The museum isn't well-run," explained Henry. "There's not much money, which means the works don't get the treatment they deserve."

"It'll end up covered in as much dust as when it was in the tomb," added Leon.

"What about the mummies?" asked Charlotte. "What happens to them?"

"They're still there," said Mr. Zimmerman. "The door will be locked and gated so no one else can gain entry."

Charlotte found that strange, and said so. "Why are they left behind? I mean, they're actual people, not things. No one wants the mummies?"

Leon sniffed. "Why would you? There's nothing valuable about a pile of bones and tendons."

Charlotte begged to differ, and his cavalier attitude rankled her. "They were once as alive as we are, and might have wielded great power, even. The one with the crossed arm could have been royalty."

"We'll never know that for sure," corrected Mr. Zimmerman. "Not without a sarcophagus. For now, they'll both remain on-site."

Charlotte pulled her shawl tighter around her shoulders. It seemed wrong, to have gone into the tomb and extricated the last of the riches, leaving the possible queen and her nurse with nothing but a few mummified geese. The conversation turned to the international situation, what would happen to the other excavation teams in the Valley of the Kings as uncertainty clouded Europe, with Hitler's forces reoccupying the Rhineland against the terms of the Treaty of Versailles. Dark clouds were gathering.

That night, she dreamed of the mummies wandering around the tomb, bemoaning the loss of the necklace in the darkness of their burial chamber. Who had these women loved in their lifetimes? What had they accomplished? Why were they forgotten? Charlotte got up and splashed water on her face, and then she and Henry made love once more.

After, she dreamed of a little girl with thick eyelashes and alabaster skin, and a month later, she discovered she was pregnant.

CHAPTER SIX

Annie

NEW YORK CITY, 1978

The Met Museum loomed in the night sky, its expanse so wide that it would be almost impossible to capture the entire building in a single photograph. A sprawling staircase in the shape of a stunted pyramid crawled up the limestone exterior, guarded by four imposing pairs of Corinthian columns. To either side of the main entrance, a trio of more restrained additions stretched out like the wings of some magnificent creature.

A few taxis glided past, but the sidewalks were empty of pedestrians, a fact that made Annie nervous. In the past couple of years, as the city fell apart financially and resources became scarce, the general mood of its citizens had turned feral. Stabbing, muggings, and murders were climbing. She figured if she was attacked, she could run to the nearest Fifth Avenue doorman for help.

The entrance was on the north side of the building, and beyond it, Central Park yawned into blackness. The security guard at the door didn't seem surprised by her request, just told another guard to escort her and went back to reading his *New York Post*. Annie had spent countless hours on the other floors of the museum, but she'd never been to the basement level. She followed the security guard down a wide white hallway with signs reading "Yield to Art in Transit" posted at regular intervals. Overhead, exposed pipes and conduit ran along the ceiling.

Finally, they reached a set of double doors. "In there," the guard said.

Annie pushed the doors open. Inside was an anteroom with a couple of desks that led to a vast room with large tables where a dozen or so women were at work, sewing colorful appliqués on layers of tulle, ironing black and white tunics, and sewing flounces onto dark velvet drapery. Other than the vibrant fabrics, everything else—the walls, the cabinets, and even the floor—was white, so that it resembled some kind of fashion laboratory. The workers even wore white gloves on their hands.

No one had noticed her entrance. Annie approached the woman working closest to the door. "Excuse me, Mrs. Hollingsworth asked that I give this to Diana," she said.

The woman's eyes widened in horror.

"Dee-AH-nah," Annie quickly corrected. She pulled the boa out of the shopping bag and held it out.

"Right." The woman exchanged a worried glance with the worker sitting next to her. "Do you want to take it in, Mona?"

"Um. No, thank you."

Just then, a wisp of a girl rushed by. The woman named Mona grabbed the girl's arm. "Wanda, this just came in." She took the boa from Annie and handed it to Wanda, who accepted it with a trembling lip. What on earth was going on down here in the bowels of the museum late at night that made everyone so worried? Annie couldn't help but think of the sweatshops from the 1910s she'd read about in history class, where young girls slaved for hours making shirtsleeves.

Wanda disappeared through a closed door.

"What is this?" she asked the woman named Mona.

"It's the Costume Institute workroom."

"You work here?"

Mona let out a loud scoff. "God, no, we're docent trainees."

"Docents? Like you give tours?"

"One day we will," said the other woman, who didn't seem as offended as her fellow worker by Annie's gaffes. "I'm Priscilla, by the way. And this is Mona. We volunteer our time to the museum."

Priscilla's vowels were those of New York City's upper class, ladies who lunched at expensive bistros and summered on the East End of Long Island. On second glance, the occupants of the room were all over forty, with styled hair and diamond studs in their ears. This was no sweatshop.

"What are you working on?"

"The exhibition for the Met Gala," answered Mona in a vague European accent.

Of course Annie had heard of the Met Gala, a big party for high society that was held once a year. With a start, she realized that this Diana everyone was talking about was, in fact, Diana Vreeland, the former editor of *Vogue* and *Harper's Bazaar*, who now worked at the Met as some kind of consultant. She'd read her editorial letters with glee month after month.

"When is the gala?" asked Annie.

"November twentieth, which is why we're here into the late hours of the night." Mona seemed more proud than upset by the idea of working late. "The theme this year is *Diaghilev: Costumes and Designs of the Ballets Russes.*"

Annie had no idea what she was talking about. Annie looked around the room and noticed several mannequins dressed in bright outfits that were not at all like the ballet costumes worn today.

"These are for dancing in?"

"Diaghilev was a choreographer from the early 1900s who formed a dance company called the Ballets Russes," explained Priscilla. Her delivery was rote, as if she was recalling a series of memorized facts. "His sets, costumes, and choreography revolutionized art, fashion, and dance. On the fiftieth anniversary of his death, we're celebrating the vital design and vibrant colors he brought into the world."

"Well done, Priscilla," Mona said dryly. Priscilla gave her a wide grin in response, missing Mona's patronizing tone entirely. The two women were a study in contrasts: Mona with her dark hair and aquiline nose versus Priscilla's blonde curls and blue eyes. Priscilla's lids were brushed with eye shadow that matched the exact shade of her irises, which had the unfortunate effect of making her look permanently stunned.

"How does one become a docent?" asked Annie.

"First, you have to apply, and then you have to go through the training, which is quite extensive," said Mona. "We come every Monday when the museum is closed and spend hours with the curators and other staff members, learning everything about the Met, from the layout to the provenance of the artwork. 'Museum fluency,' it's called."

"We have to know our way around," offered Priscilla.

"That sounds fun," said Annie.

"It's hard work," said Mona.

"It's more difficult than getting into an Ivy League school," added

Priscilla. "For example, today I had to talk about a randomly chosen piece of art for three minutes straight. I did fairly well, considering, right, Mona?"

"Sure you did."

Priscilla's enthusiasm dipped ever so slightly. "The critiques can be quite withering. But eventually you're allowed to do research and present to the staff. If you pass, you're considered 'floor ready.' If not, you're out."

Being a docent sounded like a dream job to Annie. But then again, it wasn't a job. "You're volunteering your time?"

"Of course," said Priscilla. "It's an honor to be here—and most of us are already involved in the museum in some way, anyway. As donors and whatnot. The past few weeks, on top of our regular studies and classes, we've been lucky enough to assist Mrs. Vreeland with the gala."

As if summoned by the very mention of her name, a door opened and the woman herself appeared. She held the boa high in one hand, the ends draping down, her other hand resting on her hip. She appeared to be in her seventies and was exceedingly narrow everywhere: hips, bust; even her face was long and thin. At first, Annie would have described her as horsey, but when she moved, it was with an air of authority that rendered traditional ideas of beauty or ugliness irrelevant. Thick black hair rose high above her forehead, and her cheeks were slashed with red blush that extended all the way to her earlobes.

Diana Vreeland. The most fashionable woman in New York City.

"Listen up, girls," said Vreeland in a low growl. "I had Wanda reach out to docents old and new for ideas to adorn the neckline of the Zobeida costume from *Scheherazade*. I explained that the dancer who wore it was known for posing in a photograph with a snake from the Bronx Zoo, which I thought made my intentions quite clear. Not a half hour later, I'm handed a boa the color of pickles. So now, I have one question: Who brought this disastrous object into my lair?"

Priscilla and Mona both turned to look at Annie. She could run from the room, but Mrs. H would ask about the boa. She had no choice.

Trembling, she lifted her arm into the air.

"Um, that was me."

In the bright lights of the Costume Institute workshop, Diana Vreeland stared at Annie like she was from another planet.

Annie lowered her hand down by her side. She'd never felt so conspicuous, so out of her element as she did in this room of well-coiffed Upper East Side doyennes. Not only was she twice the size of most of them, her hair hung limply down her shoulders from the damp mist outside, and her skin was shiny and pasty. Her very presence in this pristine, select environment was like a pustule, and now all eyes were on her.

"Mrs. Hollingsworth sent me with the boa," Annie explained weakly. "She wanted to help."

At the mention of Mrs. H's name, it was as if the entire room let out its breath. Mrs. Vreeland threw back her head with a throaty laugh. "Ah, that Nora. Always putting me on, a gag gift for a giggle, I suppose. How is the darling's hip? Or is it her arm?"

"Her knee," said Annie with relief, although she was fairly certain Mrs. H had sent over the boa in a sincere attempt to help out, not as a joke. "She's getting around much better now."

"Wanda!" called out Mrs. Vreeland.

The girl came running. "Yes."

"Why didn't you *tell* me that this was from Mrs. Hollingsworth? I can't possibly manage without the *full* information, you see."

"I'm so sorry, Mrs. Vreeland." At that, Wanda burst into tears.

Mrs. Vreeland stared at her, unbothered. "I can't have simpering around me, not now. It's too close to our deadline for tears. Off you go, thank you, dear, that's all we'll need from you." She handed Wanda the boa. "And give this to that young lady on your way out."

Wanda scampered away, throwing the boa at Annie as she exited the room, bursting into heaving sobs before the door to the Costume Institute had even closed. Annie felt terrible for her, but at the same time, she didn't quite see what was so upsetting. Mrs. Vreeland wasn't yelling, wasn't throwing things.

"Listen, everyone," said Mrs. Vreeland, clapping her hands twice. "I'm going to try again." She trotted over to a mannequin wearing a pearl-encrusted leotard in white and dark blue, with poufy silk leggings that cascaded down to the ankle. "You must keep in mind that *Scheherazade*'s Zobeida is the favorite wife of the king. But she's also a sensuous woman who desperately needs love. She's still young, and I imagine she has a peacock and loves cinnamon and flowers. It's important we get this right. Fashion must be the most intoxicating release from the banality of the world." She paused. "*Now* do you understand what I'm looking for?"

Annie looked around in astonishment as the other women nodded their heads knowingly. She'd mentioned snakes earlier, and now peacocks, and something about banality.

But what on earth did that have to do with the neckline of the costume?

Strangely enough, Annie was dying to know the answer.

CHAPTER SEVEN

Charlotte

NEW YORK CITY, 1978

When Charlotte finally made it home that evening, she was greeted by the rich scent of Indian spices.

"I thought we were ordering in," she called out to Mark as she tossed her keys on the small table in the foyer. "Are you cooking?"

"Wait, don't come into the kitchen yet," Mark answered.

Charlotte patiently stood on the other side of the swinging door that opened into the kitchen of the Central Park West apartment she shared with Mark. In many ways, it was still his apartment, or his parents' apartment, more precisely. He'd grown up here, stayed on after his parents passed away, married and had a daughter, got divorced, and then roamed the oversized prewar rooms in mourning after his ex-wife and four-year-old child moved to Los Angeles. After all those upheavals, the place still had the same dining room table, rugs, and sofas as when he'd been a child. His ex-wife, Beverly, had redone the kitchen a sickly avocado green, but they'd separated before she could get her hands on the rest of the rooms, which was probably a good thing.

Charlotte had met Mark twelve years ago, when her friend Helen—who worked as a conservator at the museum—dragged her to an awful off-Broadway play in the West Village. At the time, Charlotte lived in a studio apartment on Charles Street, sleeping in a loft bed left behind by a former tenant and having her morning coffee on a small balcony that looked out on a surprisingly healthy magnolia tree, considering the backyard was hemmed in by brownstones. She'd only gone to the play because it was within walking distance, and she was looking forward to having a glass of wine with Helen after.

When a man walked up to Charlotte during intermission and asked what she thought of the play, she'd immediately replied "Ghastly." Why that particular word came to mind was beyond her, as it wasn't a word she'd ever used before. The play was about a bunch of shipwrecked intellectuals discussing obscure philosophies, and their elevated language had unintentionally slipped into her vocabulary.

The man was almost too handsome, with a prominent nose, high cheekbones, and hair that was just beginning to gray. He started laughing, a genuine, hearty laugh that made everyone turn around and smile. At which point Helen returned from the bar with a couple glasses of wine and promptly introduced Charlotte to Mark Schrader, the evening's playwright.

When the play won an Obie the next week, Mark reached out—he'd gotten her number from Helen—and insisted Charlotte owed him a drink. He was charming and not pushy, and soon enough they were meeting regularly for meals, and then it just seemed natural that she sleep over at his place. He was ten years younger than Charlotte, which at first she thought was risqué before realizing that it really didn't matter, not at their age, anyway.

Mark had introduced her to the downtown theater scene, which featured fresh voices like Sam Shepard and avant-garde theater companies like Mabou Mines and the Wooster Group. Although there were times Charlotte was flummoxed by whatever was happening onstage, she'd learned to appreciate the effort. Her work was grounded in the past, and it was refreshing to get a sense of the future, of forward movement. Maybe that was why she and Mark were such a good fit. They came at life from very different starting points, which kept their interactions fresh and fulfilling. Even after a dozen years, they could still talk for hours about books or plays, politics or art. He never ceased to surprise her, or make her laugh.

"Okay, you may enter," Mark finally said.

She pushed open the door to find him standing at the oven wearing an apron. A vase of fresh flowers sat on the kitchen table, which was already laid out with his mother's fine china.

"Wow, you're ambitious tonight," she said. Mark was a great cook, but he usually went all out on Sundays, when his fellow professors at Columbia's theater department dropped by, along with a handful of students. "Do I smell curry?"

"You do. I wanted to make your favorite dish."

It was almost as if he'd known she'd had a tough day. But then again, there had been several times when she was struggling when he'd called her out of the blue, offering a sympathetic ear. They were in tune with each other, in that way.

"Really? To what do I owe this honor?" she asked.

"I figured we deserved a quiet night at home together."

The way he answered made her suspicious. Then again, they'd had a difficult month, as his daughter, Lori, had unexpectedly shown up at their apartment from California and announced she was quitting college and would be acting instead. She was out tonight, with friends, and it was a relief to have the place to themselves. Mark was probably trying to make up for the imposition. "Did the photos arrive?" he asked.

"Yes, they did."

"And what did Frederick say?"

She didn't want to talk about Frederick's reaction to her finding, or the shock of seeing the broad collar earlier that morning. Mark knew very little of her time in Egypt; Charlotte had learned the hard way that that particular time in her life was better left unspoken. "He said he'd think about it."

Mark put the lid back on the pot of rice and came over to her. He was a good five inches taller than her and still lanky. She wrapped her hands around his waist as they kissed. "I'm sorry he's not as enthusiastic as you would've liked," he said.

"I imagine part of him doesn't want me to go public with the information, as it negates his own work."

"Sounds like Frederick. I hope he comes to his senses soon."

"Me too."

Charlotte went into their bedroom to change into jeans. The building was slightly run-down and filled with old-timers, but it'd been built during the 1920s and the ceilings were high, the windows large. Lori hadn't spent much time here growing up. During school months, she was in Los Angeles, and come June, Mark rented a bungalow in Laurel Canyon and happily assumed the role of full-time dad for the summer. After Charlotte came into the picture, she would join them for a week or two before heading back to New York, mock-complaining about how unfair it was the two of them had summers off, while secretly delighted to be returning to her desk at the Met. It wasn't that she felt left out, more that she didn't want to interfere with their established dynamic as father and child.

And now Lori lived with them, full-time. It hadn't been an easy adjustment.

Charlotte removed her earrings and placed them in the small sau-cer that sat on their bureau, next to several photos in silver frames. A few were of her and Mark, with several others of Lori as a young girl. One showed Lori as an infant, her head softly traced with hair. Char-lotte adjusted it slightly, so it faced toward the door.

In the kitchen, she began dressing the salad, lost in thought.

"Charlotte, did you hear me?"

Mark was looking at her strangely. God, maybe the kids at work were right; maybe there was something off about her.

"Sorry, what were you saying?"

"I was saying that this was a special night, for a lot of reasons."

She was about to ask what they were but was stopped by the sound of the front door opening.

"Dad? Where are you?"

"Back here, in the kitchen." Mark threw Charlotte an apologetic look. She poured more wine into her glass in response.

Lori appeared in the doorway. Her long straight hair fell into her face, and her jeans were torn and ragged at the cuffs.

"I thought you were out with friends," said Mark.

"No." Lori grabbed a wineglass and held it out to Charlotte, who poured out what was left in the bottle. "Thanks. I have some great news. I got an agent."

Mark gave her a hug while Charlotte congratulated Lori. "Not bad for only being in New York for a month," she said.

"Let me jump in the shower and, hey, is that Indian food? I'm starving. I'll tell you all about it over dinner. I knew you'd be excited."

She started down the hallway that led to the three bedrooms. One was their bedroom, a smaller one Mark's study, and the last one, which had once been Lori's bedroom, was now Charlotte's study. However, these days Lori was crashing on the study's pull-out sofa, staying up late and sleeping in even later, which left Charlotte toiling away at the dining room table whenever she brought work home with her. Mark had assured her it was only temporary, but so far Lori showed no interest in moving out.

Then again, Mark and Lori hadn't lived together since Lori was a little girl, and Charlotte didn't want to get in the way of their re-union, nor did she relish the idea of becoming the evil stepmother. She'd tried hard to make a connection since Lori arrived, inviting her for walks in the park or bringing home her favorite cookies, but Lori continued to treat Charlotte with polite disdain.

"Sorry about this," said Mark once Lori had left the room. "I'll explain that we're having a quiet evening alone. She'll understand."

"No, don't be silly. It's great she has an agent. Maybe she'll book a job, make some money of her own." She left unsaid that the money could be used to pay rent on her own place.

"Dad!" Lori let out an anguished screech that rang across the length of the apartment.

"What is it?"

"There's a cockroach in the bathtub. You have to kill it! Ewwww!"

Mark whipped off the apron and tossed it on the foyer table, where it landed with a strange clunk.

It was going to be a long night.

Charlotte picked up the apron, curious. It had an unusual heft to it. Something was in the front pocket.

She slid her hand inside and pulled out a black box.

Inside lay a ring. Not a diamond, but a yellow topaz, her favor-ite stone.

That explained his nerves, the home-cooked dinner: Mark had planned to ask Charlotte to marry him tonight.

Charlotte placed the ring in the apron pocket where she'd found it, put on her coat, and walked out the door.

The next morning, Charlotte stumbled into the kitchen after a restless sleep, eager to make coffee, but first she cleaned up the small pond of melted ice cream that had collected on the counter around an empty carton of mint chocolate chip. Nearby, a loaf of bread sat on a cutting board, going stale in the morning sun next to an open jar of peanut butter. Lori had enjoyed a midnight snack or two, apparently.

After finding the ring, Charlotte had circled the block a few times before returning home. As she'd walked, she tried to figure out what Mark was thinking by proposing to her now, after so long together. They often joked about having a "European partnership," with no need to sanctify their love for each other in a church or some kind of ceremony in front of friends. What was the point? Charlotte had done it once and vowed never to again. Everything could change in a minute, even if you were careful. The fact that he was even considering such an act made Charlotte wonder if she'd read him all wrong.

She ran the coffee beans in the grinder, putting a towel over the top as she did so to try to muffle the sound. As the coffee machine began to drip, Lori appeared wearing a T-shirt and a pair of stained gray sweatpants.

"Sorry to wake you," said Charlotte. "Do you want a cup of coffee?"

"Sure."

The girl plopped into one of the chairs at the kitchen table.

"Did you sleep all right?" Charlotte asked, pouring out a cup.

"No. I swear the upstairs neighbor was running a marathon all night right above me."

"Sorry to hear it."

"Hey, where did all my posters go? Did you throw them out?"

"No. The posters are in the storage unit in the basement."

"Okay. Good." She picked up her coffee and walked out of the room.

It looked as if Lori was planning on making her sleeping arrangements permanent. Charlotte cringed at the idea of the study's rose-gray walls being jabbed with thumbtacks for Lori's posters of the Doors and the Beach Boys. But she reminded herself that Lori had entered Mark's life first; it was Charlotte who was the interloper.

Five minutes later, Mark appeared, rubbing the stubble on his chin. "Hey, again, I'm sorry about last night. I thought she was out for the evening."

"Right, about that." Charlotte took a deep breath. "When I picked up your apron, I noticed what was in the pocket."

"Oh, God." All signs of sleepiness disappeared. He sat down at the table and she joined him. "I wanted it to be a surprise."

She placed a hand on his arm. "I thought we agreed that marriage wasn't for us?"

"We did. But I'm worried that we're pulling apart, and part of me wants to make sure you're in it for the long haul. That you'll hang on through the tough times. And trust me, I don't blame you for pulling away. When I finally convinced you to move in with me, I didn't think we'd have a third party involved."

She lifted her arm and brushed away the crumbs stuck to her skin. "A third party who doesn't know how to clean up after herself."

"I'll talk to her."

That wasn't the point she was trying to make. "I'm sorry if you feel like you're caught between us, but to be honest, getting engaged right now would not help one bit with the family dynamic."

"Of course, of course. Pretend that you never saw it. I don't know what I was thinking."

"You're getting sentimental in your old age."

He gave her a mischievous smile. "Probably. I can't help but notice that you said 'getting engaged *right now*.' Does that mean you might consider it later?"

She stiffened. "I don't know what it means."

"Sorry, I was trying to be funny."

"Right."

His eyes searched hers. "Charlotte, sometimes I have no idea what you're thinking and it scares me."

Part of her wanted to pull him to her, tell him that he was the man of her dreams and they didn't need a ring to prove that. But the moment she considered the possibility, it was as if a deadbolt slid over her heart, pinning it deep inside her chest.

Instead, she reassured him with hollow words. That they were fine, that they'd be fine.

It was the best she could do.

"Meet me in Musical Instruments."

Charlotte knew that her best friend, Helen, would drop everything with that directive. The Musical Instruments collection at the Met was up on the second floor, behind a set of double doors. Not the sort of gallery that folks randomly strolled into, which gave the two of them a modicum of privacy.

Charlotte's favorite instrument was an Indian lute from the nineteenth century that extended out from the back of a brilliantly blue carved peacock, complete with real tail feathers, while Helen's was a late seventeenth-century Italian harpsichord with a mermaid carved between the front legs and a lush landscape of a hunter and his dog painted on the underside of the lid.

Helen strolled in, still wearing her white conservator's coat. She spent most of her day in the basement of the building restoring Old Masters, a painstaking job that required a deep knowledge of the sciences as well as an artistic eye, a rare combination. Helen was in her early fifties, and the two had been friends since she'd come over from the Gardner Museum in Boston fourteen years ago. Her parents had immigrated from Hong Kong when she was a baby, and she spoke with a Boston accent that thickened like chowder when she got riled up. "What's the buzz?" she asked.

"Mark was planning to propose last night."

"Wow. Have you ever discussed it?"

"No. I thought I'd made it very clear I wasn't interested in marriage. But he had a ring hidden in a pocket of the apron he was wearing. While he was cooking my favorite meal."

"That's so sweet. I swear, you should consider it. He's a good guy, he's in love with you. Married life isn't all that bad, you know."

"Easy for you to say. You and Brian are the perfect couple." Brian was a civil engineer, working for the city. Helen and Brian's parents had been best friends back in Boston, and there was never any doubt they belonged together. Their children were off at college, one at Johns Hopkins and the other at Yale.

"What do you mean he was *planning* to propose?" asked Helen.

"Lori interrupted our quiet evening at home."

"Kids have a tendency to do that."

"Not yours, I'm guessing."

Helen wandered over to an ebony oboe. "Sometimes I wish they would."

"What do you mean?"

"We're such a serene, calm family, doing what's expected of us. That's what my parents hammered into me, and same with Brian's. I hope we're not doing them a disservice."

"Enjoy it, trust me."

"I think you have to keep in mind that Lori is Mark's problem, not yours. She's not your daughter."

"Yes, I know."

"She's only eighteen, after all."

"When I was her age, I was working hours a day at a dig in Egypt, not leaving ice cream out for someone else to clean up."

"It's a different time. But I get it."

"I'm trying so hard to connect with her, but she wants nothing to do with me. No matter what I do, I still come off as the wicked step-mother."

"Is there any other kind?"

Charlotte laughed. She'd complained enough for one day. "How's the altarpiece going?"

Helen had spent months working on a series of panels from the 1400s. The gilded finish was covered with centuries of grime, which she'd painstakingly cleaned inch by inch with a Q-tip. Now it was Helen's turn to complain. She moaned about the travails of replacing the bare sections with twenty-four-karat gold leaf, which was both expensive and difficult to work with.

"What about your lady pharaoh?" asked Helen as they wandered by an installation of lutes. "Have you spoken with Frederick yet?"

"I did. Yesterday."

"Talk about burying the lede. What did he say?"

"He says I need to go to Egypt myself to find proof of my theory."

Helen let out a hoot. "That's great!"

"I just don't see why I need to go. I know I'm right. Why waste the Met's money?"

"Hold on." Helen faced her. "You're saying you'd refuse an all-expenses trip to Egypt? This is about that stupid curse, isn't it?"

Charlotte knew she couldn't hide the truth from Helen. "Of course it is."

Twice, Charlotte had tried to return to Egypt, and both times she was certain Hathorkare's curse had come back to haunt her, stemming from her time there as a young woman.

The first time Charlotte attempted the trip, early in her career at the Met, her mother passed away the day before she was supposed to leave. The second, sixteen years ago, a plane had crashed taking off from Idlewild Airport, just as Charlotte was waiting at the gate for her own flight. She'd watched in horror with her fellow passengers as the smoke and fire rose up from the marshland where it plummeted. Everyone on board had been killed, and Charlotte was convinced it was her own fault.

"I can't risk it," she said.

Helen stopped short. "So you think that you were responsible for your mother's death, as well as all of those passengers'? The plane had a mechanical short circuit, and your mother had been ill for years, right? Those weren't your fault."

If only Charlotte could be as certain as Helen. But after the second attempt, she'd given up.

She carried the curse with her, and simply couldn't risk it.

CHAPTER EIGHT

Charlotte

EGYPT, 1937

Charlotte wore the one nice dress she'd brought with her from New York for her wedding to Henry, which took place in the salon of the Metropolitan House. There had been a surprising number of dinner parties thrown by the various excavation teams working in and around Luxor over the past month, which meant by now her frock was looking quite tired—the neckline frayed and a few drops of red wine staining the hem—but she didn't have much of a choice. It was either that or her breeches.

Henry had insisted they marry as soon as the French doctor summoned by Mr. Zimmerman, at Charlotte's request, confirmed the pregnancy. They'd planned on performing the ceremony on the veranda, but a sandstorm had whipped up at the last minute, so instead everyone crowded in the salon, the air oppressive and the champagne warm. The members of the dig team knew what was going on, of course, and she was annoyed by the stolen glances at her belly, the jovial slaps on the back the other archaeologists kept giving Henry, as if she were one of Ramses II's concubines carrying the heir to the throne.

As the party carried on late into the evening, she retreated to a chair on the dark veranda. So far, being pregnant didn't feel any different from before. She wasn't sick in the mornings, she ate just as voraciously, and her stomach was still flat. But she was no longer allowed to excavate or explore, only to document the artifacts uncovered by the other members of the team. Leon was thrilled, she was sure, to have his competition sidelined. Although she'd never admit it to Henry, a part of her couldn't help but resent this tiny creature who was getting in the way of her reason for coming to Egypt in the first place.

Mr. Zimmerman had already offered Henry a position at the Met when they got back to the States. But she knew he would miss Egypt as much as she would. The only comfort, although it certainly was a selfish one, was that it wasn't just Charlotte and Henry who were leaving. The entire American team was pulling out of Egypt and heading home at the end of the month. The French and Polish crews staying on would be the recipients of the spoils instead.

"Are you feeling all right?"

Mr. Zimmerman spoke from the doorway where light spilled around his silhouette.

"Just fine," she said, begrudging the fact that she was now considered a delicate female as opposed to one of the crew.

Mr. Zimmerman took a seat in one of the rocking chairs, sand crunching underneath the runners. "I'm glad you and Henry found each other. My wife was a huge help to me in the field."

"I don't want to be a help." She knew she sounded churlish, but couldn't stay quiet. "I want to be an archaeologist."

"You're already one, in my book. You've got great instincts, and you're smarter than anyone else out there. Your time will come, I promise."

"Did you and your wife ever have children?"

He shook his head. "We put it off, and then she passed away. My one regret."

"I'm so sorry." All her pique vanished. She was lucky in so many ways. Lucky to have Henry by her side; lucky to be having a baby, even if it was a surprise.

"Will you be going back to school when you return?" asked Mr. Zimmerman.

"I'm hoping I can get through one more semester, but after the baby comes in the summer, I'll have to drop out anyway, so I don't know if it's even worth it."

"You'll figure it out. You have many years ahead of you."

Many years as a wife and mother. She trusted Henry and knew he'd do everything possible to take care of their family, but what would she have to offer at the end of the day, other than a list of the baby's latest achievements? Would she be able to hear all about Henry's work at the Met without feeling some resentment? Lately, Henry had been distracted, probably due to the stress of having a wife and baby thrust upon him. Charlotte loved him dearly, and was certain he felt the same, but wished they'd had a little more time just the two of them before facing parenthood.

It was hard to tell how old Mr. Zimmerman was; his face was etched with wrinkles from the blazing desert sun. He'd been a brilliant teacher and guide to Charlotte the last few months. "Henry is so grateful for the job at the Met. Thank you again for that."

"If it means I'll be seeing you at gallery openings and staff dinners, it is well worth it. Don't fret, Charlotte. I'll be keeping my eye on you; don't think I'll let you off the hook so easily."

Charlotte's heart warmed. Maybe all was not lost. Maybe there would be a way to make this work, just not as quickly as she'd like.

Mr. Zimmerman shifted in his chair. "I was sorry to hear Henry turned down the offer from the Polish team. Of course it's under-standable, under the circumstances. However, I promise I'll keep him busy in New York."

"I'm sorry?"

"The overseer position." Mr. Zimmerman paused. "Didn't he tell you?"

That explained Henry's mood. He'd been given the opportunity to stay on, keep working, finish the fieldwork required for his degree. And he'd not bothered to tell her.

She smothered her confusion under a wide smile. "Of course, I'd forgotten. No, we're very excited for New York, both of us."

"Why didn't you tell me about the offer?"

The wedding reception finally wound down around three in the morning, and Charlotte and Henry had retreated to their quarters. She hated that they were spending their first night as a married cou-ple arguing, but there was no way she could make love with Henry and pretend everything was all right.

"Because it didn't matter either way." Henry's eyes were bloodshot, and he swayed slightly as he took off his linen suit jacket. "We're go-ing back to New York."

"But it *does* matter. I hate that you're giving up an opportunity like this. Why are we starting out our marriage with secrets and re-sentment?"

He took her hand and led her to the bed, where they sat side by side like strangers waiting for a bus. "There's no resentment, I prom-ise you. I'll get back here and finish my fieldwork eventually. Right now, you come first, and I have absolutely no problem with that."

"Then why have you been so distant?" Her face was hot and she tried not to cry. Maybe it was the baby that was making her so emotional, but she had to be honest with him.

He put his arm around her and kissed the top of her head. "The job offer is not at all why I've been distant. And I admit, I have. But I had no problem telling Mr. Jankowski that I wasn't interested in the position."

"Then tell me why."

"I guess it's because I'm worried about being able to take care of you. I mean, I don't have much saved up, and New York is expensive. I hate the thought of meeting your parents and immediately being indebted to them. Are you sure they don't mind us staying with them until we get on our feet?"

"They don't mind at all."

In fact, Charlotte hadn't yet mailed the letter telling them about Henry, the marriage, or the baby. She kept meaning to, but day after day she'd forget, and it remained in the drawer of her desk. Her parents were expecting her to return to them the same fresh-faced, innocent girl she'd been when she left. Instead, she'd gotten herself knocked up by a poor Englishman, her college career cut short. It was everything they feared might happen to their little girl if they allowed her to travel across the world and work in a dangerous foreign country. She'd begged them for the opportunity, convinced them that she was mature enough to handle herself, and then confirmed their worst fears.

"Look," she said finally, "you are a brilliant Egyptologist. They'll love you once they meet you, and of course they'll love the baby. We may be doing things out of order, but that doesn't mean all is lost." She wondered who she was trying to convince.

"You're right. I'm silly to worry. We'll figure it all out."

He didn't sound very certain, though, and they listlessly undressed and crawled into bed, too tired from the festivities and the discussion of the uncertain future ahead to do more than kiss each other good night.

Charlotte woke up before Henry and went to the window. Outside, the desert shimmered in the sunrise, where a group of workers trooped out to the Valley of the Kings to begin work. There was so much still hidden in that desolate array of hills, where a maze of tunnels ran deep into the earth, representing thousands of years of burial ceremonies. That was what was so alluring about being here. Not only the potential for treasure, but the unfolding of information about a civilization that was so advanced that its art, politics, science, and beliefs rebounded around the world even today.

In comparison, even though Henry said he was grateful for the Met Museum job offer, she knew, for him, working at a museum would be no better than being locked in a mausoleum. He'd be far away from where the true work was being done, stuck all day writing seventy-five-word descriptions of limestone reliefs, when this was where he belonged. This was where they both belonged.

The idea came to her in a flash as the sun's rays poured in through the window. She took that as a good sign. The Egyptians' most powerful god was Ra, patron of the sun, heaven, power, and light, and maybe he was guiding her just as he had the ancient people of the Nile.

She woke Henry with soft kisses on his ear.

He smiled and pretended to swat her away, then pulled her on top of him.

"Hold on," she said. "I have an announcement."

"You're pregnant?"

They both laughed.

"No. We're staying here. You're taking the overseer's job."

"What about New York?"

"I dread seeing my parents as much as you do. Why should we have to give up doing what we love and scandalize my parents and their friends when we don't have to? You have a job here, I feel perfectly well, so let's stay."

He pushed himself up on one elbow. "You'll be having a baby come August. There's no way I'm allowing you to give birth out here in the desert."

She'd thought it all through before waking him. "First of all, women have babies here all the time, if you haven't noticed by the scrum of children running around everywhere we go. Second, Mr. Jankowski's wife is a doctor, so I'll have excellent medical care while we're in the field. Third, we'll be heading to Cairo in early June anyway, once the digging season's over, and I'll have the baby in one of the fancy hospitals there."

Henry grew serious. "The Polish team aren't as well funded as the Americans or the French. It will be a big step down from this," he said, gesturing around the room.

"When we met, we were both living in caves, may I remind you."

"That's true."

"Will Mr. Zimmerman be upset?" That was the only hiccup Charlotte could come up with.

Henry considered it. "He'll be happy for me to finish my degree; then he can hire me as a curator instead of a research associate. Although he may question my sanity, allowing my pregnant wife to prance about digs instead of staying home with her feet up in America."

"Tell him it's my idea. After all, it is."

Henry kissed her and let out a laugh, his boyishness reappearing. "You are a dream come true. I promise I'll take care of you, my love. I know right now it's my turn, but one day it will be yours."

She laid her head on his chest. One day was a long time from now, she was certain. Maybe this was madness, and she was just avoiding confrontation with her parents. But no, she loved Henry and wanted him to be happy, and she had faith all would be well.

This was the right decision for both of them, and made for the right reasons.

She'd tear up the letter to her parents and write a new one, telling of her husband, her baby, and her plans to remain in Egypt.

As Charlotte's belly turned from flat to convex, she craved honey more than anything else. She would tear off a chunk of pita bread and dip it into a jar, savoring the way it tickled her throat on the way down. The Polish team had settled in Edfu, just upriver from Luxor, working on a recently discovered tomb of a chief government minister's wife. Most days Charlotte stayed indoors feasting on whatever honey cakes or halva threads Henry brought back from the market.

Henry had been right; the dig houses where they lived were a far cry from the refined, cool rooms of the Metropolitan House. Instead, they crammed their belongings into what was basically a tar-paper-roofed shack consisting of a bedroom with two uncomfortable cots squeezed together and a small living area with a kitchenette, a table, and a rock-hard settee that smelled of rust. In another week they'd all head to Cairo to wait out the summer—and for Charlotte to wait out the baby—and she looked forward to being back in civilization once again, although she was content with their decision to stay in Egypt.

The baby was no longer a theoretical creature, as he or she had been for the first three or four months, when Charlotte had been fired up with surges of energy and lust that Henry enjoyed to no end. Now, her body was simply a vessel for this creature who bumped around in her belly like a fish in a bucket, poking and kicking and making itself known, waking her up in the middle of the night as it stretched its limbs. Mrs. Jankowski had been incredibly helpful, answering Charlotte's questions and calming her fears, patiently reassuring Charlotte that all would be well.

Even though their living conditions were miserable, Charlotte and Henry were not. When a swarm of pink locusts landed in their small garden, chewing up everything she'd planted, Henry jokingly suggested she fry them and slather them with honey. Even when the intense heat caused the tar paper roof to melt, dripping black specks onto the tablecloth, Charlotte insisted that polka dots were all the rage back in the States.

The only time her spirits flagged was when she received a letter from her parents. They were livid that she'd made such a rash decision without consulting them, and assumed she'd been seduced and ruined. They begged, pleaded, and finally demanded that she return home. In response, she'd penned flowery letters about her exciting, exotic life in the desert, with no mention of pink locusts or melting roofs.

Meanwhile, in the greater world, Japanese and Chinese troops were clashing, and the new prime minister of England, Neville Chamberlain, had inexplicably congratulated Hitler on his military restraint. Mrs. Jankowski was worried that Hitler would violate the nonaggression pact between Poland and Germany, while Mr. Jankowski assured them all he would not. Charlotte avoided reading the papers, preferring to lose herself rereading Amelia Edwards's memoir of Egypt, comparing the descriptions of the temples and landmarks from sixty years ago to Charlotte's real-life encounters with them. She missed being out in the field, but Henry enjoyed his role as overseer of the group, sharing stories of their finds each evening over dinner. Even surly Leon flourished under Henry's leadership, softening and becoming friendlier. One evening he'd surprised her with a toy dragon that he'd carved out of acacia for the baby.

Once in Cairo, Henry and Charlotte rented an apartment with delicate Italianate balconies not far from the Egyptian Museum, where both Leon and Henry took jobs to tide them over during the offseason. Their duties included helping the overwhelmed curators and staff organize the flood of incoming antiquities, documenting each one, and designating accession numbers, using the same methods as the Met. It was monotonous but provided a steady income.

Finally, in August, the baby arrived. The delivery was even more terrifying than Charlotte had expected. When her labor pains began in the middle of the night, she and Henry raced to the Anglo-American Hospital in the Zamalek district of Cairo, a tony part of town located on an island on the Nile. There, she was spirited away to the maternity ward while Henry waited with the men in the reception area. The next morning, with no baby in sight, Henry was told to go to work, which meant he wasn't present when the doctor decided to puncture the amniotic sac in an effort to advance the delivery. By then, several other pregnant women had come in and successfully delivered, and Charlotte was weak with exhaustion, still waiting, unsure where she was or what she was doing anymore, feeling completely alone. The doctor dismissed her cries during the procedure and told her to stop being so emotional, which made her want to take the amnihook and perform a similar procedure on him. When she finally delivered, Henry was still at work and had to be summoned to return. The worst moment, though, came right before he arrived, when she'd been propped up in bed and presented with her new baby girl, and Charlotte discovered she was too weak to even hold up her arms. The nurse gave her a look like she was an utter failure as a mother and placed the child in the bassinet, where Charlotte stared at her helplessly until Henry finally arrived to take charge. After harshly reprimanding the nurse for her lack of empathy, Henry lifted the child and carried her over to Charlotte with tears in his eyes.

Layla, they called her.

A beautiful name, in both Arabic and English, for a beautiful child.

CHAPTER NINE

Annie

NEW YORK CITY, 1978

The day after her late-night visit to the Costume Institute, Annie was still thinking about Mrs. Vreeland's hazy directive as she cleaned Mrs. Hollingsworth's bedroom. When she'd returned with the boa, she'd told Mrs. H that Mrs. Vreeland said it wasn't exactly right and left it at that, and luckily Mrs. H had just shrugged and put it aside. Now, staring into the woman's vast closet, Annie couldn't help but wonder what would work instead. The scarves were all predictably Hermès and would look silly over the costume on the mannequin. She let out a small sigh.

"What is it, Annie? Are you done straightening out the shelves in there?"

She'd completely forgotten Mrs. H's presence on the divan by the window. "Yes. They're all set." She shut the closet doors. "How do you know Diana Vreeland? Were you a docent?"

"I was, for a good ten years. Enjoyed every minute." Mrs. H took a sip of her tea. "It's the best decision I ever made, other than marrying Mr. Hollingsworth. You're with other people who possess a love for the art world, a dedication to passing on knowledge. I came into my own as a docent, after years of playing second fiddle. Suddenly I was thrust in front of strangers, sharing my passion for my favorite painters and sculptors. I had studied art history in college, but this was as if I were part of history, carrying on the legacy."

"I'd love to work for the Costume Institute," Annie shyly admitted.

"You'll have to marry rich, then. Or hope your mother does. There's no pay. All those women toil away for the sheer glory of it."

So that was out. Disappointed, Annie did what she always did when life grew dark: She pulled on her cowboy boots and headed straight for the Met. The Great Hall was crowded with visitors, babies in their mothers' arms and old folks in wheelchairs, a medley of different languages drifting up to the mezzanine balcony.

She wandered through the Arms and Armor section, wondering how on earth anyone could fight wearing so much gear, followed by the Western European Arts section, which took up two floors and included her favorite painting, Bastien-Lepage's *Joan of Arc*, which depicted the saint as a poor, disheveled girl standing in an unkempt garden. Annie recognized herself in the jut of the girl's chin and the wondering eyes.

In the Greek and Roman Art section, she came upon a Greek bronze chest plate from the fourth century BC, which had been forged to fit perfectly against the body it protected, replete with rippling muscles and a belly button. When she'd visited with her father as a young girl, they'd speculated about the soldier who'd worn it, whether he lived to old age or died in battle. That was the fun of exploring the Met: stumbling upon surprises that made you realize how small your problems were in the grand scheme of things, how many centuries the human race had been in existence. She found it reassuring.

Just beyond that section was a restaurant where sculptures rose out of a huge pool of water in the center of the room and the walls were painted the color of blackberries. It was fancy, not the sort of place Annie would ever feel comfortable in.

The layout of the museum had changed only slightly since she was a little girl. A big glass room had recently been added to the north side of the building for the Temple of Dendur. Annie had dragged Joyce to see it two months ago: an Egyptian temple that had been granted to the Met as a gift, in order to protect it from flooding from the construction of the Aswan Dam on the Nile. The Nubian sandstone building had been disassembled, shipped to New York, and reassembled, and, at eight hundred tons, weighed three times more than the Statue of Liberty. When Annie first saw it, she couldn't help but wonder if the temple was a little disappointed at its new home. Instead of gazing out over the Nile and the Egyptian desert, as it had for almost two millennia, it was tucked away in a kind of oversized greenhouse, its only view this time of year a line of leafless trees. Joyce had looked at Annie like she was mad when she'd voiced this concern out loud.

Over in the other galleries of the Egyptian Art collection, the Cerulean Queen beckoned. Annie's father had loved this strange half face, so she loved it as well. She drew close, puffing up her lips so they resembled that of the queen, just as an older woman with a close-cropped hairstyle and cool blue eyes walked by. Annie stepped back, blushing, but the woman didn't seem fazed by the fact that a patron was making faces at an inanimate object. Instead, she offered a brief nod and a smile before disappearing behind an unmarked door.

Part of the collection was cordoned off, as the museum prepared for the King Tut exhibition due to open next month. But Annie was still able to visit her other favorites, like the blue hippo that had become the unofficial mascot of the Met. It was a tiny thing, and had been buried in the tomb of some Egyptian steward. The description next to it said that hippos were feared for their ferocity, and that three of the figurine's legs had been broken before it was placed into the tomb, so that in the afterlife it couldn't harm the steward. She liked to imagine that at night the creature escaped from its vitrine and limped around the Met roaring its displeasure.

Her attention was drawn to the far side of the gallery, where several members of the museum staff had gathered in front of an open display case as a man wearing white gloves handled whatever was being placed inside. Annie stepped closer to get a better look and let out a small breath: The object was a gold necklace, but this was more than a necklace. Six rows of what looked like tiny spoons formed a foot-wide arc, like an upside-down rainbow. It was intricate and intriguing, and must have been quite heavy to wear. As the technician with the gloves lifted one side to adjust it, the tinkling of gold against gold filled the air.

Annie stared at the necklace sparkling under the bright lights. What a beautiful piece of art. And jewelry. A perfect mix of the two.

What had Diana Vreeland said the other night? An *intoxicating release from the banality of the world*. This was certainly that. The madness of the design definitely intoxicated Annie's senses.

It would be perfect for the neckline of the mannequin.

The gallery for the Costume Institute was right below the Egyptian Art collection. Annie swerved around the sign that read "Exhibition Closed" and flew down the stairs before one of the security guards saw her. To her delight, Mrs. Vreeland and half a dozen members of her entourage were gathered around one of the platforms where the mannequins were to be displayed. Mrs. Vreeland was holding several yards of velvet drapery in her arms while the others nodded their heads enthusiastically.

Annie stopped short a few feet away. "Um, excuse me, Mrs. Vreeland?"

The entire group turned and stared.

"Mrs. Hollingsworth's minion?" said Mrs. Vreeland. Annie was surprised she remembered her, although the word "minion" was off-putting.

"I found something for the *Scheherazade* costume. The zebra one."

A couple of women in the group tittered.

"Zobeida, you mean," said Mrs. Vreeland. "Is that so?" Her eyelids were shiny, as if she'd rubbed Vaseline on them after putting on her makeup. An unusual choice, but it made her brown eyes pop. Her lips and cheeks were red slashes again today, her hair styled to curl around her ears so it was hard to tell if the lobes were rouged as well.

"Zobeida," repeated Annie carefully. "It's just upstairs from here. I think you'll love it."

"Do we have time for that? We really must decide about the drapery," said a woman to Mrs. Vreeland's left. Her eyebrows danced as she spoke, lifting with the question and pulling together in consternation at the statement. "We need your preference today."

"Let's make it extreme, Marta. I want flouncing, not draping. Everything interesting is a little extreme. Understatement is just pitter-patter."

"What's upstairs is extreme," ventured Annie.

Mrs. Vreeland waved one hand in the air. "Oh, why not, I'm on my way out anyway. Come along, Marta, shall we see what this boa bearer is all worked up about? Let's get crackin'."

Annie led the two women upstairs to the display case, which the workers were in the process of locking. The necklace beckoned, twinkling under the bright lights.

Mrs. Vreeland peered over the vitrine, one hand on her neck.

"Frederick!" she yelled out.

The workers, as well as the visitors in the room, swiveled their heads in her direction with alarm.

"Get me Frederick right now!" she said to one of the workers. He took off running as Mrs. Vreeland wrapped her skinny arm around Annie's shoulders. "This is the piece, *of course*. You have an eye, my dear."

"It reminded me of Cartier's Art Deco period," Annie said, beaming.

"That's a girl who knows her stuff." She stepped back and studied her. "Nice boots, by the way."

Before Annie could respond, a tall man—supposedly Frederick—approached them with an air of authority. He was followed by the same woman with the short hair Annie had seen by the Cerulean Queen not ten minutes ago.

"Mrs. Vreeland, how lovely to see you," said the man. "May I introduce Charlotte Cross, the associate curator here in the Egyptian Art collection?"

The two women shook hands, Mrs. Vreeland doing so with an enthusiastic fervor that wasn't matched by the associate curator.

"Frederick, you know Marta Meyer, the curator for the Costume Institute."

More hands were shaken.

"You are admiring our new acquisitions?" said Frederick.

"It appears that you have been keeping secrets from us. Tell me about this necklace," she answered.

"We call it a broad collar, made of gold, crizzled glass, and a pigment known as Egyptian blue. It's composed of hundreds of small nefer hieroglyphs, which resemble tiny spoons. 'Nefer' is the Egyptian word for 'good' or 'beautiful,' and the craftsmanship and size imply that it belonged to a member of royalty. The piece was discovered in the Valley of the Kings in 1936, and the back is inscribed with the name of the female pharaoh Hathorkare, who ruled during the early period of the New Kingdom. It's one of a kind."

"A female pharaoh, you say?"

"Indeed."

"That settles it. I want the broad collar for my exhibition."

The woman named Charlotte stepped in before Frederick could answer. "Absolutely not. This is not a bauble for some fashion show. We're still determining whether it should be displayed at all, as I have questions about the provenance." She glared at Frederick.

Mrs. Vreeland made a graceful flicking motion with one hand, her polished nails shining like rubies. "As far as I'm concerned, fashion is not to be so casually insulted. Fashion is part of the daily air; you can see the approach of a revolution in clothes."

Charlotte ran her hand through her short hair, making it stand up on end. While her part was streaked with gray, the rest was a dark chocolate color. "What does that even mean?"

Mrs. Vreeland was undeterred. "Not to mention the Costume Institute is part of this great museum for a good reason. I'm sure we don't need to remind the board how much money the Met Gala brings in each year."

Charlotte began to speak, but Frederick interrupted her. "That's enough. Let me handle this. We all must work together."

"I knew you'd understand, Frederick," said Mrs. Vreeland.

But Charlotte refused to be ignored. "We don't need the money. I assure you, the Tut exhibition is going to shower the Egyptian Art collection in riches. You can't put the collar at risk—it's too valuable. There are no barriers in the costume exhibition, nothing to keep it safe from the public."

The woman named Marta spoke up. "I also worry about putting something like this into the exhibition, Diana. It's not original to the costume or Diaghilev's vision."

"You could say the same about the Rodin sculpture that we're using in the show," answered Mrs. Vreeland. "I love the idea of integrating two different mediums, and this calls out to me in the same way the Rodin does. I'm simply *mad* about it."

"But it's not historically accurate," said Marta.

"Don't worry about that. I prefer to blend fiction and fact. I call it *faction*."

Charlotte threw her hands in the air. "Now she's making up words?"

"Enough, Charlotte," barked Frederick. "My goodness." He turned to Mrs. Vreeland. "Diana, let's talk about this over coffee, shall we?"

Mrs. Vreeland took his arm but at the last minute looked back over her shoulder at Annie. "Well done, girl. Show up tomorrow at noon in my office. I'm thinking I could use a new assistant, someone with verve. It's hard work and long hours, but I think we might make a good match."

Annie barely stopped herself from jumping up and down, her entire body sizzling with excitement and pride. She'd taken a risk and it had paid off.

Starting tomorrow, if all went well, she would be working for Diana Vreeland, the leader of the fashion world. Certainly, the pay had to be decent, the wages better than those of a maid. She might never have to clean houses or waitress again.

She watched as Frederick and Mrs. Vreeland sauntered out and the others slowly dispersed, all except for Charlotte, who stood staring into the display case, inexplicably shaking with rage.

Annie burst into the apartment and yelled for her mother.

Joyce came running in from the kitchen, one hand on her heart. "What is it? Is everything all right?"

"Everything is wonderful. Guess what, I got a job!"

"Oh." Her mother deflated slightly. "I thought you were hurt. You gave me a terrible scare." She pulled away from Annie and walked back to the kitchen. She wasn't wearing any makeup, which was odd. Without her thick mascara and glossy lips, Joyce was a ghostly version of herself, wan skin over sharp cheekbones. "I was just pouring myself a drink."

Annie followed her. It was only four o'clock in the afternoon.

"Are you all right?"

"Sure. What were you talking about? A job?"

"Yes. I was asked to be Diana Vreeland's assistant at the Met Museum. She's working on the Met Gala for the Costume Institute."

Joyce's mouth dropped open. "*The* Diana Vreeland?"

"The one and only." Annie explained about Mrs. Hollingsworth's errand, and how Annie had returned today and ingratiated herself with her discovery of the broad collar.

Joyce took a slug of her drink. "What about your job waitressing? What about Mrs. Hollingsworth?"

"I'll let them know that I've got a real job. Mrs. H can hire someone else. I'll go up and tell her now."

"Hold on. She's bound to be upset, you know how picky she is about people coming into her home. How much will you get paid?"

That was a good question. "I don't know all of the details just yet, but I'll find out tomorrow."

"You don't even know the salary? What were you thinking? And we can't upset Mrs. Hollingsworth, not now."

"Why not?"

"Brad wants to meet and have a talk when he's back from his business trip to Sausalito."

A talk. That was never a good sign, and explained why Joyce was barefaced and boozing it up.

"What if Mrs. Hollingsworth gets angry and kicks us out?" slurred Joyce. "You understand that she gives us a discount on the rent? She could probably get double if she wanted to. You need to think of us, not yourself at a time like this. Sure, you might make a little more money, but then she'll raise our rent and we'll be in big trouble. I'm not saying you can't do it, but I think it would be better to wait."

"But that's crazy. How can I tell Diana Vreeland to wait? For me? The Met Gala is coming up, they need me there now. Here I have a dream job at my fingertips and you want me to keep on doing Mrs. H's laundry so we can stay in this rattrap?"

She'd never spoke so forcefully to her mother before. The glass trembled in Joyce's hands and fell to the floor, shattering on the linoleum. Her mother sobbed as Annie found the broom and cleaned the mess up, dumping the glass into the dustbin and wiping up the spilled alcohol with a cloth.

Joyce wiped her eyes. "You've got so much going on. You're just starting out, and I'm on my way to the loony bin for aged models. I hate my life."

While Annie knew that this was her mother's way of manipulating her, she also knew there was a real chance that her mother might do something tragic if pushed. "I'm sorry," said Annie. "I didn't mean to upset you. Hey, maybe I can get you a ticket to the Met Gala this year? Would you like that? You can dress up and have a night on the town, on me. What do you think?"

"Really?" There was a hint of hope in her voice. "The Met Gala? There are so many fancy people who go to that. Well-off people. What would I wear?"

"I'll remake one of your old dresses."

"Oh, darling." A tentative smile broke out on Joyce's lips. "What would I do without you?"

While Annie's manager at the diner was spitting angry when Annie announced that she was quitting, Mrs. H's face lit up with a huge grin when she gave her the news. "There you go, my girl. That's what I'm talking about. Good for you."

"You're not mad that I can't give you any notice?"

"Why would I be mad? Anyone can clean my bathtub, it's not rocket science."

"But the discount on the rent—I don't know how much I'll be making yet, so I don't know how it'll all work out. Or *if* it will all work out."

"Your mother seems to be home a lot these days. Why don't we have her take over?"

Annie couldn't tell if Mrs. H was kidding or not. "Um, she's very busy, in fact."

"I'm sure she is."

Luckily, Mrs. H didn't pursue that idea any further.

A little before noon, Annie approached the security guard at the side entrance of the Met. He checked her name off in a book and let her inside. She found her way back to the Costume Institute workroom, where the women were all still hard at work, as if they'd never left, and she gave Mona and Priscilla a quick wave before knocking on the door to Mrs. Vreeland's office.

"Come in!" Mrs. Vreeland was sitting behind a large desk, looking impeccably stylish in jersey pants and scarlet python boots. Roger Vivier, Annie guessed. The bag on top was a classic cordovan leather Gucci. Her desk was covered in papers and photos, as well as a galley of the exhibition catalog, and behind her a square window looked out onto Fifth Avenue. Mrs. Vreeland opened a yellow legal pad, picked up a pencil, and gestured for Annie to take a seat.

As she did, a waft of Opium perfume tickled her nose.

"Tell me your full name, please."

"Ann Michele Jenkins. Everyone calls me Annie."

Mrs. Vreeland scribbled Annie's name down on the pad and underlined it twice. "Well, Annie, you're my new helper." Even in the small room, Mrs. Vreeland's voice bellowed out like a foghorn. "As the special consultant to the Costume Institute, it is my job to make this exhibition shine, it must be *to die*. Come in every day at nine and be prepared to stay late."

"I will. My schedule is wide open." Annie swallowed. "May I ask, how much do I get paid?"

"Money? A tiresome subject."

"Only if you have too much of it."

Mrs. Vreeland regarded Annie with delight. "*Excellent* point. I'm allowed to pay you twelve thousand dollars a year. Will that do?"

Twelve thousand was much more than Annie currently made. She was moving up in the world, all right. "Of course. Thank you."

"Let's do an inspection, shall we? See how our ladies are managing."

Annie followed her new boss into the workroom, and together they walked from mannequin to mannequin, Mrs. Vreeland stopping at each one to assess, adjust, and critique as the docents stood by nervously.

"Sergei Pavlovich Diaghilev was a genius," said Mrs. Vreeland as she wandered the floor. "He took the boring pastels of the fin de siècle and replaced them with bright reds, oranges, and purples. His strong personality attracted all kinds of five-star artists to the Ballets Russes, from Stravinsky to Picasso. He had flair, taste, and he transformed the art of ballet. In our exhibition, we have some of the best of his costumes from seminal ballets such as *Swan Lake* and *The Sleeping Princess*. Just look at this diaphanous dress from *Narcisse*," said Mrs. Vreeland to Annie. "Couldn't you see it at Studio 54?"

Annie nodded, her head spinning. She'd never been to Studio 54.

"But we have a big problem," said Mrs. Vreeland.

"What's that?"

"The bosoms on these mannequins are not right, and because of that, the line of the costumes is all wrong."

"But they're the mannequins you specified, from Bergdorf's," ventured one of the docents.

"They simply will not do as is. Annie, your first job is to cut off the bosoms from all the female mannequins. I'm off to meet Jackie O for tea. Ta-ta, ladies."

And she was gone.

Annie had figured that cleaning for Mrs. Hollingsworth was backbreaking, but her arm was practically numb by the time she finished sawing sixty-six breasts off thirty-three mannequins. After that, she was tasked with picking up two stuffed peacocks from a man named Bill who lived atop Carnegie Hall. Annie spent a good hour wandering the two floors of studios that perched over the storied concert hall—she'd never even known that they existed until today—before she located someone who said, "Of course, Bill Cunningham," and directed her to the correct studio. Then she had to wrestle the birds into a cab without damaging their tails and get them safely back up to the Met. At that point, Mrs. Vreeland had decided that feather fans would make perfect gifts for all the guests at the gala ("Choose a yellow that vibrates"), and so Annie flew down to the garment district to source them. And when the examples she brought back weren't the exact color Mrs. Vreeland had in mind, Annie barely stopped herself from rolling her eyes before heading downtown once again.

She returned with several shopping bags filled with feathers, but the office was empty. A note on Annie's desk asked Annie to "coordinate with the Egyptian gadabouts regarding Zobeida's special trinket," signed by Mrs. Vreeland. The handwriting was flowery, but every letter *t* contained a powerful slash that ran the length of the entire word.

Annie was let into the Egyptian Art staff offices by the curator, Frederick, who was on his way out and breezily pointed across the room. "Speak with Charlotte."

Charlotte, the woman who was dead set against the whole idea of the Costume Institute using the necklace in the first place. Annie straightened her shoulders and walked over. Charlotte was using a loupe to examine a photograph of some ancient building, and didn't sense her presence until Annie cleared her throat.

She jumped in surprise and the loupe fell onto the floor.

"I'm so sorry," said Annie, getting down on all fours. "I'll get it."

At the same time, Charlotte leaned over, and they just barely avoided knocking their heads together. "Please," said Charlotte in a curt tone. "I'll pick it up."

Annie looked up at her, still on her hands and knees, and nodded.

"Give me a little room," directed Charlotte.

Annie scooted back and sat on her heels. "Just there. No, a little to the right," she said as Charlotte groped and finally got hold of the loupe.

Charlotte placed it on her desk and swiveled her chair around to face Annie, who rose to a standing position with as much grace as she could muster.

"Yes?" Charlotte said, wrinkling her forehead. It was hard to guess her age. She wore no makeup or jewelry, and her jawline was sharp. Her eyes had heavy lids that lent her an air of elegant detachment. "Are you here to purloin more of our antiquities?"

"Um, just the one. Mrs. Vreeland asked that I come here to coordinate the transfer."

"Coordinate the transfer?"

"Yes, of the necklace."

"Broad collar."

"Broad collar. Right." She refused to let Charlotte know how in-timidated she was. After all, she had Mrs. Vreeland's backing, and had seen firsthand the woman's power. If Mrs. Vreeland wanted the broad collar, she got it. If Charlotte wanted to be all business, Annie would comply. "I'm happy to bring any paperwork you have to Mrs. Vreeland for her signature."

"There's no paperwork. It's not a formal loan. I do have to let the technician know, and the earlier, the better."

"Okay, then. When should I pick it up?"

"You won't be picking up anything. I'll have one of the technicians bring it to the exhibition hall. When do you need it by?"

"Well, the gala is on Monday, and they're moving the mannequins in today. So tomorrow?"

"Is that a question?"

"Tomorrow. Yes. Tomorrow would be fine."

"Very well." Charlotte jotted it down on the calendar on her desk. "I'll be in touch."

Annie didn't move. "I think it's beautiful."

"Sorry?"

"The broad collar. I think it's beautiful. I promise we'll take good care of it, as it obviously means a lot to you."

For the first time in their conversation, Charlotte's expression softened. Annie held her gaze as something—fear, maybe pain—flitted across Charlotte's face.

"You're Little Red Riding Hood," Charlotte finally said.

Annie wondered if she'd misheard. "I'm sorry?"

"You have a red coat. I've seen you here before."

"Sure, I'm in the museum a lot. I loved the Met even before I got hired. My dad, before he died, used to bring me to the museum, and so sometimes when I'm nervous or upset, I come and stare at these super-old things and it calms me down."

Super-old things? Why was she babbling on about what a mess she was? This wasn't professional at all.

"I do that as well." Charlotte spoke so softly Annie almost didn't hear her.

Several of the other staff members flew in through the door, talking loudly and laughing, and the moment was broken. Charlotte gave a curt nod and turned back to her photo, and Annie slipped out, relieved she'd at least accomplished what she'd set out to do.

By eight o'clock that night, Annie was exhausted but also exhilarated. She stepped into Mrs. Vreeland's office to ask if she was done for the day.

Mrs. Vreeland took a long drag on her cigarette. "The yellow is wrong for the fans." She held up one offending feather. "You don't understand yellow. Only Matisse and I understand yellow. First thing tomorrow, you must return and get it right."

Annie's heart sank. Maybe she wasn't as adept at reading Mrs. Vreeland's cryptic orders as she'd hoped.

"And as for those . . ."

Annie followed Mrs. Vreeland's gaze down to the floor. She'd worn a pair of Mary Janes in the hopes that they would be fashionable yet walkable, but they were scuffed up and dirty after seven hours of wrangling stuffed peacocks and tromping through puddles.

"I shouldn't have to say this, Annie Jenkins"—Mrs. Vreeland paused for effect—"but everyone knows that unshined shoes are the end of civilization."

CHAPTER TEN

Charlotte

NEW YORK CITY, 1978

The director of the Met Museum, Mr. Lavigne, sat behind his desk in his expansive office overlooking Fifth Avenue and offered Charlotte a patient smile. He was well-liked by the staff, considered to be fair and approachable. He moved about the museum with a catlike efficiency and was known to appear out of the blue when you least expected him, a quality that Charlotte found unnerving.

She hadn't spent much one-on-one time with Mr. Lavigne before today, although they'd mingled at several of the Met's social events and openings and spoken on the phone briefly about his friend's daughter's reference. Charlotte had brought it up when she'd first arrived, and Mr. Lavigne had thanked her profusely, but when she'd changed the subject to the loan, his cordiality had dissolved.

"I can't reveal that," he told her. "Anonymous donors must remain exactly that. I'm sure you understand."

She'd been waiting for days to have this conversation, and immediately pushed back. "I have firsthand knowledge that the broad collar belongs to the Egyptian Museum, so it makes no sense at all that some private owner is lending it to the Met."

"What exactly is that firsthand knowledge?"

Charlotte tried not to get distracted by her rich surroundings. Underneath her feet was a Savonnerie knotted-pile carpet; oversized tomes on art history were neatly arranged on the bookshelves. The paneled walls featured first-rate artwork by the masters, including several small Goyas, and a Roman statue of young boy stood beside the doorway. She wondered if Mr. Lavigne rotated the art depending on his mood. "I was there when it was found, in December 1936, in a tomb in the Valley of the Kings."

"And you say it was destined for the Egyptian Museum after that?"

"Yes. But my guess is the broad collar never made it that far. It was stolen."

"It may be as simple as the Egyptian Museum sold it but never kept a record. We both know the Egyptian authorities had a difficult time keeping track of the riches they acquired from the American and European excavations."

"Maybe in the early '20s, but by then they'd straightened up and were more careful, at least in terms of what they let leave the country and what they kept for themselves. Egyptian inspectors from the Department of Antiquities were present at every tomb opening, documenting exactly what was discovered."

"Still, I assure you, we vetted the broad collar carefully before accepting the loan."

"I'd love to take a look at the documentation. I'm curious to see if the Egyptian Museum is missing on the provenance papers. That's a big red flag, I would say."

Even though Mr. Lavigne kept his expression neutral, his nostrils flared slightly. She was pushing him too far. "I can't show the papers to you, I'm sorry," he said. "Doing so would reveal the names of the donors. However, I can assure you that the Met Museum follows the guidelines of the Association of Art Museum Directors."

Designed to curb the import of stolen items, the guidelines discouraged the acquisition of any object without a documented trail of provenance before 1970. "Does that apply to objects loaned by thieves?"

"We are not allowed to be in possession of any objects that are stolen."

"That wasn't always true." She couldn't help needling him. "It's amazing to think that Luigi Palma di Cesnola personally stole over thirty-five thousand objects from the island of Cyprus, handed them over to the fledgling Met Museum, and was made director in return."

"Not the most auspicious start, I agree." Mr. Lavigne cleared his throat. "But times have changed, and best practices have as well, for the better. May I ask, why is this piece of such interest to you? We've had many items on loan to the Egyptian Art collection over the years, and none have warranted such a strong response."

Once again, there was no way to explain what it meant to her. Why she so desperately needed to know where it had been for the past forty-one years. "I was there," she said weakly. She could still recall the smell of the interior of the tomb—of sandstone and stale air—years later.

"Yes, you mentioned that already."

She'd wasted her time coming here. Even worse, now Mr. Lavigne thought she was some silly, emotional woman making vague accusations. Which, when she looked at it from his perspective, she was.

"Charlotte, I admire everything you're doing in the Egyptian Art collection, and Frederick speaks very highly of you. Please, let the curators and board handle the legal matters of the museum. They know what they're doing, I assure you. After all, you certainly have enough on your plate these days with the King Tut exhibition opening."

The meaning behind his statement was clear: She should stop causing trouble and stay in her own lane. "Can I make one request?" she asked, stopping at the doorway.

"You may."

"The broad collar has been snapped up by Diana Vreeland for the upcoming Costume Institute exhibition, where it will be unprotected and unmonitored. I'm very worried." Annie Jenkins's awkward appearance at Charlotte's desk yesterday hadn't done anything to calm her fears.

"I have great faith in our security team. You should as well. No one's going to steal the necklace from the Costume Institute exhibition, I assure you." He lifted his chin. "I have an idea. Why don't you write an essay about the discovery of the broad collar for the museum's newsletter? It would make a marvelous piece. 'Recollections of a Woman Egyptologist,' or something like that. What do you think?"

She thought that was a terrible idea, but knew enough not to say so.

Charlotte wasn't about to give up. She knew museums sometimes used specialized detective agencies to track down missing works, but she was pretty certain they couldn't be found in the phone book. Instead of going back to her office, she stopped on the mezzanine floor. An unmarked door led to the small office space where the Met's chief security officer and his assistants worked. A floor plan of the museum was tacked up on one wall, and the room smelled of tobacco and aftershave.

Charlotte had last spoken with Mr. Fantoni earlier in the year during the preparations for the Tut exhibition. He was an ex-cop, fast-talking but smart, and under his command, the treasures of the Met had been kept safe and sound.

"Ms. Cross, to what do we owe this pleasure?"

If she told the truth—that she was inquiring about a possibly suspicious loan—Mr. Fantoni would no doubt go straight to Mr. Lavigne, which wouldn't help her case at all. "I'm here because a friend of mine is writing a book on art provenance, and she was trying to find out who is the top expert on art theft, tracking down stolen items, that sort of thing."

"Well, that's what we do here. I'm happy to chat with your friend."

"Right, well, I know you're so busy with the Tut exhibition, and I hate to distract you. I can't imagine what it's going to be like when you'll have five hundred people stomping through the gallery every half hour."

"Tell me about it." He scratched his cheek. "On top of that, can you believe that I have security guards telling me they'll resign before they do night duty in the exhibition? Afraid of the King Tut curse and all that. But not everyone, thank goodness." He looked over at a young man who was emptying out the trash cans beside each desk. "Billy, you're not afraid, are you?"

The kid rose up full height, and Charlotte was certain he was about to salute. "No, sir!"

"Anyway," she continued, "is there some kind of private agency that devotes itself to hunting down stolen treasures, particularly those that have been smuggled out of the country of origin? I figured if anyone would know, you would."

Mr. Fantoni pulled a business card from his desk drawer. "I'd recommend Tenny Woods. Tell your friend he's the guy when it comes to international art theft. He's over on Lexington, right here in the city."

Charlotte called the number, but no one picked up. She figured she'd show up in person, but before she did, she had one more matter to take care of.

Joseph was waiting by the vitrine in the Egyptian Art collection that held the broad collar, talking with Annie Jenkins, who waved as Charlotte approached. Charlotte unlocked the case and waited as Joseph slid on a pair of gloves before carefully lifting out the broad collar and placing it onto a soft foam form covered by a Tyvek skin. He stuck pins into the form to keep the broad collar from shifting and then placed the form onto a cart for transportation.

Charlotte checked that it was intact, which it was, other than the one missing amulet. The last time she'd seen the broad collar, before it turned up again at the Met, it was in the hands of the man she had loved most in the world, at a time when she'd never been so scared and helpless. He'd touched it, and then he was gone. Without thinking, she reached toward the very edge of it with her bare finger, hoping that maybe she'd receive some sign of him if she ran her finger over the same gleaming strands of gold.

"Charlotte, what are you doing?"

Joseph was looking at her strangely. She pulled her hand away and nodded. "Sorry. Let's go."

The three of them took the elevator down to the Costume Institute's exhibition hall, which was busy. Too busy for Charlotte's taste. The mannequins were in place, but there were lampers on ladders focusing lights and troops of well-dressed women adjusting sleeves and pulling on hems.

"I know it looks like chaos," said Annie with an apologetic smile, "but Mrs. Vreeland has things well in hand. It will be safe."

"Where do you want it?" asked Joseph.

Annie led the way to a mannequin dressed in the strangest outfit Charlotte had ever seen, some kind of dance leotard featuring large pantaloons and studded with pearls. In fact, all the clothes were odd, each one crazier than the next. She'd expected a froth of dainty tulle confections upon hearing that this year's exhibition featured a ballet impresario, but these were loud, bordering on obnoxious. And captivating. She hated to admit it, but the effect was intriguing.

The overhead lights hid nothing; Charlotte could see where colors had faded, or where a collar that was supposed to be white was, in fact, stained with sweat. It was obvious that the harem skirts and embroidered jackets had been worn by actual dancers, ones who leaped across stages and entertained audiences. She thought of Mark and how these costumes wouldn't be out of place in some of the avant-garde shows they'd seen downtown; they still came off as fresh and modern.

Annie must have caught the amazed expression on Charlotte's face. "Incredible, right?"

They watched as Joseph delicately arranged the broad collar around the mannequin's thin neck and secured it in place. It wasn't at all what Charlotte would've chosen to pair with the costume, but it also wasn't completely out of place.

"You have to assure me that this will be safe," said Charlotte to Annie. "This is your responsibility."

Annie nodded solemnly. "I will, even if I have to give my life in order to do so."

The statement was so absurd that Joseph burst out laughing. "You two are out of your minds," he said, walking away, shaking his head, pulling the cart behind him.

Charlotte and Annie exchanged a brief look, and Charlotte shrugged. "He's probably right." She wandered over to a flamboyant watercolor of a set design by Léon Bakst, which would feel right at home in a modern-day East Village theater. "My boyfriend is going to love this exhibition."

"You have a boyfriend?" asked Annie.

"Yes." Charlotte winced.

"What?"

"I hate that word."

"What word?"

"'Boyfriend.' But nothing else is much better. 'Partner,' 'significant other,' they're all terrible."

"Have you considered 'swain'?"

Charlotte laughed in spite of herself.

Even though Annie Jenkins was part of this ludicrous exhibition and had convinced Diana Vreeland to take the broad collar out of the safety of its vitrine, there was something refreshing about the girl. Annie had spoken of her father in their last meeting, and Charlotte wondered how many years ago he'd passed away. No doubt her devotion to the Met, however misguided, was Annie's way of keeping her absent loved one close.

And Charlotte knew exactly how that felt.

CHAPTER ELEVEN

Charlotte

EGYPT, 1937

While Charlotte was sorry her parents couldn't meet the new baby, she didn't regret her decision to stay in Egypt. She and Henry were living in the middle of a bustling, cosmopolitan city, surrounded by fellow Egyptologists, and she had a baby who hardly fussed, just looked up at her with golden-brown eyes bordered by thick lashes. Henry was a very hands-on father, although he had his own unique approach to child-rearing, preferring to soothe Layla to sleep with a chronological recitation of the pharaohs of the Middle Kingdom. Most of the time, Charlotte had to admit, Layla fell asleep much faster on his watch.

As the weather finally cooled, though, Henry became fidgety again, his attention less focused. One night he came home and absent-mindedly kissed Layla before rifling through his briefcase, as if Charlotte weren't even in the room.

"Did you forget something?" she asked.

"Yes. I meant to bring back a description of a stela that needs to be reworked. I swore I put it in here."

She grabbed his arm and pulled him toward her. "No, dummy. Me."

Henry dropped the bag and enveloped her in his arms. "I'm sorry, my love. It's a mess at the museum. I can barely stand it anymore."

She knew it was more than that. Soon, the digging season would start back up, and the scholars, researchers, and archaeologists would descend upon the ancient sites like ants trailing each other to the anthill. "You want to get back out in the field." It was a statement, not a question.

He released Charlotte and sat at the kitchen table. "Of course. I was thinking, maybe I could go until Christmas, then come back to Cairo."

"You'd leave me behind?" The highlight of Charlotte's day was hearing Henry talk about what had gone on at the museum, what objects he was documenting, the latest news from the other archaeologists. As it was, her brain felt underused, mired in a lethargic stupor of feedings and naps. If he went away, she'd completely lose her connection with that world.

"I won't subject you to locusts and tar, not with a child."

"We can live right in Luxor. You'll have longer to travel each day, but at least we'll be together."

He hesitated. "I'll think about, all right?"

"Maybe I can work as well, if we find a baby nurse."

His face settled into a frown. "No. Layla needs you right now."

She didn't want to push too hard. "Is Leon going back?"

"Of course."

Henry and Leon had been meeting after work for some time now. When she was pregnant, Henry's movements were a hazy part of her life, as her focus was on the child growing inside her. But now she noticed he had dinner meetings or late hours several times a week, always with Leon.

"How's Leon doing? He's not trying to one-up you all the time, is he?"

"No. We're working well as a team these days. He's tempered in his old age."

"Or the fact that you're not a woman, showing him up." She still held on to her distrust of the man, but maybe Leon had changed.

Or, now that she was a mother, Charlotte was probably no longer seen as a threat.

Which made her want to get back to work even more.

In the end, Charlotte got her way. By November, they had settled in a small house just across the river from Luxor, surrounded by palm trees and a garden full of jasmine, deep within the green oasis that spread out from either side of the Nile, a stark contrast to the sandy rock cliffs in the Valley of the Kings less than two miles away.

Most mornings Charlotte nursed Layla outside in the garden to the sound of doves cooing. While Charlotte was utterly exhausted from waking every four hours to feed the hungry child, the baby was growing quickly. Henry had been right; there was no way she could have left her behind to go to the dig, and no way she could bring her along. Instead, she sat in the garden and marveled over the baby she and Henry had created and tried to be content with all that she had.

Her body had changed since the birth. Her hips were wider, her feet half a size larger. Henry was still acting distracted, and they hadn't slept together since the baby's birth. One afternoon, Charlotte left the baby with Mrs. Jankowski for an hour and wandered the town's center. She found a shop selling cotton dresses and bought one in a deep lavender. That evening, she planned to make a fancy dinner and seduce Henry, let him know that she was still his wife, not just the mother of his child. But when she returned home, Mrs. Jankowski was pacing the living room.

"What is it? Did something happen to Layla?" Charlotte should never have left her alone. She dropped her tote bag and began to race to the nursery, but Mrs. Jankowski stopped her.

"No, the baby's fine, she's sleeping," said Mrs. Jankowski. "I just heard the news that we're leaving."

"Who?"

"The entire team. Things in Poland are getting worse; we should be with our families."

"Of course." Charlotte was ashamed at how relieved she was that it was Hitler's aggression that had Mrs. Jankowski so upset, not Layla's well-being. "What happens to the excavation?"

"When we come back, we'll start where we left off."

Just then, Henry burst through the front door. He and Mrs. Jankowski spoke quickly to each other, and then the woman left.

"What's going on?" asked Charlotte. Her plans for a quiet dinner for two dissipated.

"We're leaving. Now."

"Where?"

"America."

"We're not Polish. Our families aren't threatened." It wasn't like Henry to get caught up in a panic, but the logic didn't make sense, either. The thought of getting from Luxor to New York with only a moment's notice seemed as crazy as heading to the moon.

"Trust me, it's time."

"Why, though? What's the rush?"

Henry began gathering up papers on his desk, refusing to meet her eyes. "I don't have time to explain. We're taking a steamer from

Luxor to Cairo, leaving tonight. From there we'll board a ship to New York."

"I really think you're overreacting."

"Leon will meet us at the dock. Grab what you can and leave the rest in the trunk. I've arranged to have it picked up and shipped separately. There's a cart and donkey waiting outside."

Henry's panic came across as way out of proportion. It wasn't as if Hitler was going to invade Egypt tomorrow; their lives weren't at stake. He was keeping something from her. Or maybe she was still wrapped up in the dream world of being a mother and had lost her perspective. Reluctantly, she did what he asked.

The ship was long and narrow, with two floors of accommodations and public rooms and a sundeck on top. Their room was small but comfortable, dominated by a bed with a copper frame. She placed Layla in the center of the bed and began unpacking. The trip would take a few days, and maybe, by the time they arrived, she'd have gotten to the bottom of whatever was going on with Henry. Once they reached Alexandria, she'd send a telegram to her parents with the news they were returning home. She worried about the reception they'd receive, but there was no going back now.

As the ship pulled away from the dock, Charlotte stayed in the cabin with the baby. Henry arranged for their dinner to be brought to the room, and the food was decent, if bland. Layla fell into a deep slumber, aided by the gentle rocking of the ship and the vibration of the steam engine.

But as she and Henry got ready for bed, a crackle of thunder made Charlotte jump. It rarely rained in Egypt, and at first she wasn't sure what the sound was. Soon after, the wind picked up, howling outside their cabin door like a clan of hyenas. Charlotte eventually fell into an uneasy sleep beside Henry.

At some point in the night, a loud crunching sound jolted her awake. She wasn't sure where she was for a moment, in Cairo, or maybe the house in Luxor? No, she was on a boat. And there was screaming coming from the promenade outside their cabin. The sound of doors opening and slamming shut was followed by footsteps and men's voices, the wind howling over the chaos. Henry leaped out of bed and put on his trousers. "Stay here, let me see what's going on."

The baby woke and let out a soft cry. Charlotte picked her up and held her to her chest, hoping the pounding of her heart would soothe rather than upset the girl.

Henry was back in a flash.

"We've hit something. Another ship, it looks like. Get dressed now."

Charlotte's mind whirled with confusion and fear. If she got dressed and went outside, it would mean she'd have to face the expanse of water that separated her and Layla from dry land. Better to stay here and pretend that everything was fine. She couldn't do it; she couldn't. She imagined the water reaching her feet, and then her waist, before finally enveloping her in its suffocating kiss.

"Charlotte. Now."

She blinked away the darkness. If she followed Henry's commands, they would stay safe. Charlotte gently placed the baby on the bed and pulled on her dress and shoes as Henry reached into the closet and grabbed an unfamiliar suitcase.

"Do we need the luggage?" asked Charlotte. "Won't that just get in the way?"

"Only this one," he said.

Charlotte didn't recognize it. "Whose bag is that?"

"Leon's. I said I'd store it for him."

That made little sense. Surely Leon had more room in his cabin than the three of them did in this one. But there wasn't time to ask questions. She bundled Layla in a blanket and followed Henry outside.

The darkness was like nothing she'd ever experienced. No stars, no moon, just pouring rain and infinite black.

The ship was listing, and the shoreline had disappeared in the storm. Someone shouted that there were too few lifeboats. No one knew where to go or what to do. Leon appeared, holding two life jackets. He handed one to Charlotte and one to Henry, but Henry insisted Leon keep it for himself. Henry held Layla while Charlotte lifted the orange vest over her head and fastened the straps with shaky fingers. She took the baby back into her arms—the bulk of the vest made holding her awkward—and followed the men to the ship's stern. The wind whipped rain into their faces as the baby's cries grew louder.

"The lifeboats here are full up," said Henry. "Quick, let's go up a level to the top deck."

But as they approached the stairs, the ship gave another violent shudder, sending a crew member who was coming the opposite way hurtling into Henry. The suitcase fell from his grasp and spilled open. Inside were several objects wrapped in cloth. A few had come loose of their wrapping as they fell onto the wooden deck, including some small statues in ivory and faience and several pieces of jewelry.

One Charlotte recognized immediately. A broad collar.

The same one from the tomb that she'd discovered. She picked it up and checked the back for the cartouche of Hathorkare.

She looked up at Henry in shock. "What are you doing with this? Shouldn't it be in Cairo?"

The baby yowled, and she kissed Layla's soft head.

Henry grabbed the necklace and stuffed it into his pocket. Leon bent down to help, and Charlotte was almost certain she saw him surreptitiously stuff a handful of the items into his jacket pocket as well. They were like a pair of street urchins fighting for pennies. Henry closed the suitcase and clicked the clasps firmly shut. "I'll explain later."

Another shudder.

"We have to get off the ship!" yelled Leon.

Everything began to tilt, and Charlotte dropped to the floor so she wouldn't fall with Layla in her arms. The child looked up with large, worried eyes, and Charlotte understood how stupid she'd been to put her baby in harm's way by remaining in Egypt. They should be in New York, safe and sound. The passengers around them were screaming, the women crying. Charlotte thought of the crocodiles of the Nile. There weren't that many anymore, she'd been told. But even so, the currents were swift, deadly.

A heavy wooden lounge chair slid along the deck, almost in slow motion, headed directly for Charlotte. She lifted Layla into the air and took the brunt force of the chair to her torso, moaning from the pain. "Take the baby," she screamed to Henry. He crawled over and tucked Layla under one arm, still holding the damn suitcase in the other.

Meanwhile, Leon scrambled to get the chair off Charlotte, but gravity and the tilting of the ship worked against him. "Go up to the top deck with Layla," yelled Charlotte to Henry. "We'll meet you there!"

"No, I won't leave you," he yelled back.

Leon fought in vain to free the deck chair, which was now entangled with two others. Charlotte was penned in, trapped, her ribs aching with every breath.

"Go," said Leon. "I'll get her out."

The baby wailed harder. Charlotte knew every one of her baby's sounds: of delight, of hunger, of fear. This particular cry meant that her mother's arms were the only thing that could calm her.

"Please, go!"

The boat gave yet another groan. The last thing Charlotte saw before a wall of water swept over her was Henry's retreating back and her child's chubby, sweet hand stretched out over his shoulder, palm open wide, reaching for her mother.

CHAPTER TWELVE

Annie

NEW YORK CITY, 1978

After Annie's strange conversation with Charlotte in the exhibition hall, she made her way to the staff cafeteria in the basement—she'd overheard Priscilla call it the "staff caf"—and stood in line to get a cup of tea and a cranberry scone.

The cafeteria consisted of a series of low-ceilinged rooms and several stations where Met employees could get hot or cold food. She poured milk into her tea and picked out the largest scone in the basket before paying at the cash register and settling down at a table near the back, where a few security guards dozed in chairs. On the other side of the room a half dozen pretty young women around Annie's age sat at a large table, laughing uproariously.

Their lives were so different from her own. Sometimes she wondered what it would have been like if her father hadn't died. Joyce would've found the adoration she craved in her husband's eyes, while Annie would've been free to live a normal teenager's life, joining clubs that met after school and sleeping over at friends' apartments.

She took a sip of her tea and decided it needed more milk. But as she rose and turned to head back to the hot-drinks station, she rammed straight into a man or, more specifically, his tray of food. Annie caught the bowl of pasta just before it slid to the floor but at the expense of her tea, which splattered over the table.

All eyes turned to Annie. She was an oaf; the last place she should be working was a museum. She'd probably be fired before the week was over.

"I'm so sorry," she whispered, grabbing her napkin and futilely dabbing at the lake of liquid that was forming on the tabletop.

The man with the tray let out a laugh. "It's my fault, I'm so hungry I was walking way too fast."

He wore a navy blue security guard uniform. She guessed he was only a few years older than she was, with long arms and skinny wrists that extended a few inches out from the hems of his jacket sleeves.

"That'll teach me," he said cheerily. The *th* sound came out as a *d*, an accent particular to the outer boroughs.

He put his tray down on a nearby table and jogged off to get a large pile of napkins. Once he returned and they'd cleaned up the mess, he pulled out the chair opposite hers, his pasta still steaming, and sat. "Wait a minute, can I get you another drink?" he asked, holding his fork in the air. "Tea, was it?"

"Oh, no, it's fine."

But he ran off again, this time coming back with a tea with exactly the right amount of milk.

She took it from him gratefully.

"Thank you," she said. "Again, I'm sorry for bumping into you."

"I was going to have to sit and eat dinner alone, so I consider it an opportunity. Wait a minute, is it okay if I sit here? I'll be done fast; I only have ten minutes before I start my shift."

"Of course, it's fine."

"What do you do here?" he asked.

"I'm the assistant to Diana Vreeland in the Costume Institute," she said proudly.

"Dee-what?"

"*Diahna*," repeated Annie. "Like the regular name Diana, but fancy."

"The Costume Institute. Right. I've never worked one of the Met Galas before, but I signed up this year. I hear the toughest part is telling Mick Jagger not to smoke in the bathroom."

Annie laughed. "I imagine he'd just ignore you. Or tell you off and have his bodyguards throw you into the fountain."

Her dinner companion got a slightly panicked look in his eyes.

"I'm kidding, I'm sure he's a sweetheart. I'm Annie, by the way."

"Billy." They shook hands.

"Where are you from, Billy?"

"Brooklyn, like pretty much every other guard in this place. It's basically a huge, connected network of us, a union job, so it's a good one. I started a month ago, got it through my uncle Marco."

"Do you like it?"

"At first, all that standing around for twelve hours at a time did me in. I had sore feet, a sore back. But now I'm used to it."

"Do you get bored?"

"Nah. There's always some interesting person to watch, wonder who they are, where they're from. Or, if it's quiet, I'll stare at the paintings or the suits of armor and let my mind wander. Imagine some poor dope riding a horse wearing all that metal while trying to poke someone else with a lance. There are so many galleries and so many objects, I don't think it's possible to get bored." He held up one finger. "Actually, I take that back. It gets boring when you're asked the same question over and over."

"What question is that?"

"'Where's the whale?' Then I have to let some poor family down gently that it's all the way across the park at the Museum of Natural History. I've seen kids melt down fast when they hear that. But then I tell them about the mummies and they perk back up. My favorite assignment is the Great Hall because it's nonstop busy and time flies by. The worst is when you get Section D."

"What's that?"

"Cleaning duty. You spend the shift mopping floors and picking up trash."

The table of pretty girls erupted in laughter. Billy gave them a cursory glance. "The development staffers. They always leave tons of scuff marks from their high heels, drives us nuts."

"What's your favorite painting?" she asked.

"Oh, that's a tough one." He glanced down at his watch. "Shoot, I better be heading off."

"But you barely touched your food."

"That's okay. It was fun talking to you."

"It was." Annie was thrilled to have made a friend. "Where are you off to?"

"Nineteenth Century American Paintings, up on the second floor." Billy gave a shy smile. "I'll tell you what? Why don't you walk with me and I'll show you one of my favorites."

Annie finished the last piece of her scone. "You bet."

They tossed their trash and walked through to the Great Hall before climbing the sweeping staircase that led to the second floor.

Billy, as a security guard, probably knew more about the ins and outs of the building than anyone. "I know you've only been here a month, but have you ever had anyone try to steal anything while you've been guarding?" asked Annie as they ascended the shallow steps.

"No, thank goodness. I mean, it's not as if we have guns or anything to stop them. A year ago, a couple of teenagers stole a ring from one of the vitrines in the Egyptian Art collection."

"Aren't they locked?"

"This particular one had a quarter-inch crack in between the door panels, as well as some space at the very bottom. The kids noticed the cracks, and then came back with a wire hanger and a museum floor plan. One acted as a lookout as the other fished into the vitrine with the hanger, knocked the ring onto the museum map, and pulled it out. Easy enough when you think about it."

"It seems almost too simple. Where was the guard?"

"We can't be in every room, and they timed it just right."

"There aren't any alarms or anything?"

"No. Not yet, anyway. That kind of technology is still a long way off. Luckily, the dopey kids went straight to a jeweler right on Lexington Avenue, who recognized the ring and called the museum asking for eighty thousand dollars for his trouble."

She paused at the top of the staircase. "Wait a minute, the jeweler tried to blackmail the museum?"

"Stupid, right? The security head nabbed him as well as the kids."

"What happened to the kids?"

Billy led her along the mezzanine balcony and into the American Paintings and Sculpture galleries. "It was their first offense, so they didn't get any jail time. The jeweler got a light sentence, I think." He smiled. "This place is full of crazy stories. I love it."

"You should write a book about it."

"Nah. My plan is to save enough money and get my undergrad degree, eventually be a technician here. They get to spend time with the art, make sure it's in its optimal climate, create mounts, that kind of thing. Can you imagine being able to touch a Michelangelo? With gloves on, of course."

"I can't. I'd be terrified."

He stopped in front of the enormous oil painting of George Washington crossing an icy Delaware River. "This is one of the most popular paintings in the museum."

"I can see why."

"But over here's my favorite. Winslow Homer's *Northeaster.*"

He guided her farther into the gallery, to an oil painting that showed a great wave smashing onto dark, craggy rocks, the water spraying up almost like smoke on one side and curling over in a massive breaker on the other.

"It's almost like the water's about to splash down on you," said Annie.

"Exactly right. In an earlier version, Homer had two figures crouching on the rocks, but he later removed them. Whenever I'm posted to this gallery, I pretend that it's a window, not a painting. I swear sometimes I can hear the rush of water if I listen hard enough."

The security guard on duty came over and shook Billy's hand, and then Billy took up his position, standing tall with his hands behind his back. A few tourists wandered by speaking French to each other. With its parquet floors and beautiful artwork, the gallery invited a sense of hushed awe upon its visitors, almost like a place of worship.

"I hope I'm not too chatty," Billy said. "My dad says it's like my brain never turns off, that my head is filled with words that just have to come out, like some kind of overstuffed ravioli."

Annie giggled. "My dad used to say I was a magpie. I thought that was some kind of pie until he explained it was a bird who could talk."

"You know, the magpie is a symbol of good luck in East Asia, you can find them all over Chinese artworks."

He knew so much, it was a little intimidating.

"Cool." What a stupid reply. But she couldn't think of anything else to say.

"You seem like a quiet type to me," said Billy. "Or maybe that's because I take up all the oxygen in the room."

"No, that's not true at all. After my dad died, I didn't talk as much." Annie would never forget the day she answered the door to their apartment to find two men in suits staring down at her. They asked for her mother, and then Joyce was crying, and Annie heard them say her father had tried to stop some kids from harassing a woman on the subway and been shot. The men in suits offered empty platitudes and handed over her father's bloodstained wallet and his set of keys before eventually letting themselves out.

Billy lightly touched Annie's shoulder. "I'm sorry."

"It was a long time ago. It's funny, we used to come to the museum at least once a week when I was a kid, and now I wonder what he would think if he knew I was working here."

"He'd probably be very proud."

Annie blushed and thanked Billy for the chat and the tour. "I should let you get to work."

"I hope we bump into each other soon," said Billy. "Although maybe not so violently the next time."

Annie giggled and agreed.

"You must come to me right away." Mrs. Vreeland's voice sailed through the phone receiver as if she were standing in Annie's kitchen. Annie had just finished cleaning the dinner dishes from the night before when it rang. "I'm at 550 Park. Right away, I tell you."

"Right away? Of course." Annie hung up the phone and dried her hands on her jeans. Her mother was still asleep and probably would be until noon. Now that the modeling work had dried up and Brad was still away on business, she had little motivation to rise.

Annie left her mother a note and jumped on a bus to 62nd Street.

Mrs. Vreeland's building was the fancy prewar kind with an awning that extended the width of the sidewalk. The doormen wore white gloves yet treated Annie, in her jeans and messy ponytail, as if she were a high-society debutante. She appreciated their kindness.

She took the elevator up and knocked on Mrs. Vreeland's door.

"Come in!"

Annie opened the door and stood there, gaping. Everything was done in vibrant shades of red: the boldly floral wallpaper, the dozens of patterned throw pillows, the floor-to-ceiling chintz drapes, the shag carpeting, even the floral arrangements. It shouldn't have worked, but somehow it did, the electrifying shock of color accented with tall Venetian screens and dark wood side tables.

Mrs. Vreeland lay sideways on the couch wearing a red dressing gown, a turban on her head. "It's ravishing, isn't it?" she said, lifting her arms wide. "I'm mad about red. I wanted my apartment to look like a garden in hell. All my life I've pursued the perfect red—I can never get painters to mix it for me. I'd tell them, 'I want rococo with a spot of gothic in it and a bit of Buddhist temple,' and they'd look at me like they had no idea what I'm *talking* about! Sit there."

Annie perched on a Georgian easy chair, unsure why she'd been summoned. The coffee table in front of her was covered with spiral shells of different sizes. "That's quite a collection."

"In this room you'll find many small gifts from friends, including a collection of Scottish horn snuffboxes and Himalayan snow leopard throw pillows. I'm very lucky to have been surrounded by some of the best of people. Not growing up, unfortunately. My mother rejected me thoroughly, called me an 'ugly little monster.' But I was exposed to such artistry when we lived in Paris. I mean, Nijinsky and Diaghilev visited our apartment on avenue du Bois de Boulogne, if you can imagine such a thing. That more than made up for not being wanted. France taught me so much. How to *dance*, how to *dress*."

Annie looked down at her jeans. "I'm sorry, I wasn't expecting your call."

"Don't apologize, dear. I love blue jeans. Blue jeans are the most beautiful thing since the gondola. They have fit and dash and *line*."

Annie took a moment to consider the pronouncement. It made sense, in a weird way. "I remember you did an entire shoot featuring denim."

"You know my work, then?" Mrs. Vreeland said, pleased.

"Of course. While all the other women's magazines were writing about how to take care of your husband or how to please your mother-in-law, you filled the pages with women striding across the African desert."

"Those were magical days, but life goes on. Now, Annie, I know this job is difficult, being my helper, and it's only going to be messier the closer we get to the big night. But it's the way I work, and if you're able to put up with my many eccentricities, I assure you, you'll go far. My *former* former helper, a lovely Southern gentleman named André, has gone on to write for *Women's Wear Daily*."

"I'm just happy to be part of the team."

"We *are* a team. And I can tell you love clothes as much as I do. The beautiful thing about working at the Costume Institute is the reverence with which the clothes in the collection are treated. Wrapped in acid-free tissue paper, nothing stored on hangers, which after three months simply *ruin* the shoulders. Drawer after drawer of soft treasures. It's a dream, one that I did not expect after my years toiling away for the magazine world before being fired at the ripe old age of seventy. Now I'm in my element, and few can keep up with me, but I knew right away you could. We *understand* each other, don't we?"

"Of course." Annie nodded her head enthusiastically.

"The next few days, I'll need you to check the spelling of every name, every exhibition label, and, the evening of, treat every donor with respect and gratitude. I like to think of this exhibition as a three-dimensional fashion magazine layout, and it must be properly grouped and accessorized. I choose the music, the lighting, the perfume—"

"Perfume?"

"Oh, yes. We have it infused into the exhibition hall. This year it's Mitsouko, by Guerlain of Paris, which was originally created for Diaghilev. Isn't that to die?"

"Incredible." Although Annie had to wonder what kind of damage the perfume did to the costumes.

"I say, there are days I wake up and pinch myself." Mrs. Vreeland swung her legs around and placed her feet delicately on the floor. "I love working with beautiful things and beautiful people."

"What I most admire is how you hire women who break the rules of what a fashion model should look like," offered Annie. "Cher, Lauren Hutton, Anjelica Huston."

"I've always appreciated women who were interesting rather than beautiful. Probably to prove my mother wrong. You don't need beauty, but you must have style. Embrace what you have, I say. If you're tall, wear high heels. If you have big hands, wear chunky rings. The models I've had the pleasure to discover and work with were never boring." Her eyes twinkled. "It's not about the dress, it's about the life you're living in the dress. Now, pick up that notepad and I'll dictate some memos."

Annie gathered up the pen and notebook from a side table and they began, Mrs. Vreeland reeling off missives to fashion-world luminaries like Oscar de la Renta, Kenneth Jay Lane, and Richard Avedon. After the last one, Mrs. Vreeland glanced at her wristwatch. "Off you go, now. I'll see you at the museum in an hour."

Annie rose to her feet, still reeling from the tornado of words.

"I just had a *splendid* idea," said Mrs. Vreeland. "Butterflies."

"I'm sorry?" Annie waited for an explanation, but the woman was lost in thought, one hand under her chin, the other fluttering in front of her.

"Butterflies. Hundreds of them."

"When? For the exhibition?"

"Of course for the exhibition! This year I'm inviting a group of VIPs to a special walk-through, conducted by me, while the rest of the guests are off dancing. And there simply *must* be butterflies for the VIP tour! I imagine a dizzying kaleidoscope of shape, pattern, and color. The room must feel as if it's taking off in flight, just like the dancers once did on the stage of the Théâtre du Châtelet. I know you will come up with something marvelous."

The phone rang, and Mrs. Vreeland pounced on it with glee, motioning Annie to let herself out.

"Misha, my darling. How are you getting along with Mr. B? Now tell me *everything*."

The day before the "Party of the Year," as the Met Gala was often called, Mrs. Vreeland went into overdrive, which meant Annie did as well. Annie loved the feeling of taking ownership of the Metropolitan Museum, stomping after Mrs. Vreeland through the restaurant behind the Greek and Roman wing where dinner would be held after guests had streamed through the exhibition, followed by dancing in front of the Temple of Dendur. She made checklists and did her best to translate Mrs. Vreeland's off-the-cuff, enigmatic commands into English. And then there was the exhibition itself, which Mrs. Vreeland fussed with until poor Marta looked like she was about to scream. Mrs. Vreeland had no qualms about climbing onto the platforms where the mannequins were displayed, adjusting the way the dresses fell, or objecting to the lighting. ("Shine it on the *costumes*, not the mannequin's face; this isn't some razzmatazz Broadway show!")

That afternoon, Annie and Mona were sent off to the Temple of Dendur to oversee the placement of the bars and tall cocktail tables. The men setting up knew what they were doing, so she and Mona stood along the far wall and kept an eye on things as the gallery was transformed into a disco, replete with a neon dance floor.

"I stopped by the restaurant earlier, it looks very festive," said Annie. She'd been pleased to see that the yellow feather fans at each place setting worked wonderfully with the floral centerpieces.

"There's not much you can do with the Dorotheum," sniffed Mona.

"Is that the name of the restaurant?"

"It was designed by a woman named Dorothy Draper, and no one likes it, hence the nickname. Those awful coral banquettes and the birdcage chandeliers? Even worse, the frolicking sprites that rise out of the fountain. Just terrible."

There appeared to be a fine line between stylish and garish, thought Annie. A week ago, if asked, she would've deemed the restaurant to be elegant and Mrs. Vreeland's apartment garish. But it was actually the opposite.

"I can't believe the temple came all the way from Egypt," said Annie.

"Did you know there's graffiti on it?" asked Mona. She was skinny, but her voice was deep, a startling incongruity. Priscilla, meanwhile, spoke in a breathy Marilyn Monroe voice, which annoyed Mona but Annie found sweet. The two docent trainees were so different from each other, but both deeply devoted to the Met. "Here, I'll show you."

Mona led Annie around to the far side of the temple's gate, where "Leonardo 1820" was carved into the sandstone.

Annie sighed. "I guess some things never change. Like spray paint on the subway cars, people love to leave their mark."

"You take the subway?" said Mona. "Don't you worry about getting mugged? My husband won't allow me. He says these days it's far too dangerous."

"I keep an eye out for trouble." And she had, ever since her dad had been killed. If something seemed off in the subway car she was sitting in, she got out.

"It's so much easier to just jump into a cab."

And much more expensive. "I suppose."

"Although I must say, the traffic lights in New York City leave something to be desired. You can hardly go for one block before the next one's changed to red. Drives me insane every time I get in a taxi. I seriously don't know how you can stand it."

Annie shrugged. Having never lived anywhere other than New York, she had nothing to compare it with.

"Annie!"

Billy the guard was loping their way, arms pumping, legs striding. She heard Mona stifle a laugh next to her.

"Billy," said Annie warmly to make up for Mona's rudeness. "You on Egyptian duty today?"

"I was. I'm about to take a break and then head to the Greek and Roman wing. You ready for the big night?"

Annie introduced Mona, who gave him a weak nod of the head.

"I suppose we're ready," said Annie. "Although there's still a million things to be done."

"I bet. You work for Dee-*ah*-nah, too?" he asked Mona, stressing the middle syllable and throwing a grin Annie's way.

"I'm a docent trainee," answered Mona. "And no, I don't work directly for Mrs. Vreeland. I volunteer for the museum."

Annie was only realizing now how cliquey the museum was, with its many factions: the director, the curators, the development staff, the art handlers, the conservators, the docents, and the docents in training. And then there was Mrs. Vreeland, floating above the fray as the "special consultant" to the Costume Institute.

"Huh. Okay," said Billy. "Well, I'll see you tomorrow night. Since you're both with the Costume Institute, I have to ask, does my outfit meet with your approval?" He held out the bottom of his suit jacket and did an awkward curtsy.

Annie laughed. "You look just fine."

After he left, Mona turned to Annie with a smug look. "He likes you, you know."

"Do you think?" The idea made her smile. He was a sweet, boyish kid.

"But you can do much better than a guard," offered Mona. "They're a dime a dozen. Don't settle, whatever you do."

"I think he's nice."

Before Mona could respond, Priscilla appeared, saying they were needed in the workroom. There, the trio unpacked dozens of boxes of perfume, taking care not to break any of the bottles. The butterfly question had been solved only the day before, when Annie had confided to Priscilla that she was panicked about Mrs. Vreeland's strange request. Priscilla consulted with a friend who was a volunteer at the Museum of Natural History, and after several phone calls, Annie was all set. She'd arranged to pick up a box of butterflies right before the exhibition opened.

For her last project of the day, she addressed the invitations to the private VIP gathering. The list was a who's who of New York City's rich and famous, including Lee Radziwill, Betsy Bloomingdale, Mick Jagger, Diana Ross, and Steve Rubell.

Back at the apartment, although Annie's back hurt and her eyes were red, she put the finishing touches on the dress she'd be wearing to the Met Gala. Taking Mrs. Vreeland's advice, she'd decided to accent her more "interesting" features. Annie had chosen a plissé fabric that shimmered in the light and sewn in shoulder pads, hoping they would give her a nice line without making her look like a football player. From there, the gown dropped straight to the floor and swished around her legs—no waistline, just like her own sturdy torso. She'd borrow some of her mother's chunky rings to wear on her fingers, just as Mrs. Vreeland suggested.

Annie had been lucky enough to secure a ticket for her mother as well. She couldn't wait for Joyce to watch her thriving at her new job, escorting the VIPs through the Great Hall and acting as Mrs. Vreeland's favorite helper. Maybe Joyce would meet someone wonderful there to take her mind off Brad. For Joyce's dress, Annie had taken a simple wine-colored sheath and added a fantastical collar, ruffles trimmed in gold. Her mother would be the center of attention once again.

It was sure to be a magical, perfect night.

CHAPTER THIRTEEN

Charlotte

NEW YORK CITY, 1978

The office of the art theft investigator was located above a hair salon, up a set of creaky, narrow stairs that rose between walls of peeling yellow paint. The sign on the second-floor door read "Tenny Woods, Art Recovery Expert."

Charlotte turned the doorknob and entered a small antechamber with a secretary's desk that had a towering stack of files on top and an empty wooden chair behind it. More files were scattered on the floor by a narrow bookshelf, and what looked like several days of mail were piled on a chair in the corner. In contrast to the mess, the walls were bare other than a couple of framed prints by Jacob Lawrence and Charles White. Intrigued, she stepped closer, only to realize that they were originals, not prints.

"Finally!"

She spun around. A man who looked to be in his sixties stood in the adjoining room, rifling through the top drawer of a file cabinet. Tenny Woods, she presumed.

"I'm sorry?"

"I've been waiting. I need you to go through the files out there and find me all that mention Benin or Nigeria." Mr. Woods's voice was low and growly.

"I'm sorry?"

He shifted his weight impatiently, hands resting on the drawer. "You're from the temp agency, right?"

"No. I'm an associate curator at the Met Museum, Charlotte Cross." She walked into his office. "I was hoping I could have a minute of your time."

Mr. Woods's office was filled with thick art books, like Mr. Lavigne's, but instead of being carefully lined up on antique bookshelves, Mr. Woods's were stacked on chairs, lying on the floor, many splayed open, others riddled with bookmarks.

The man slowly made his way behind his desk. "Sorry about that. My mistake." He was tall and skinny with graying temples and large hands. He wore a navy blue jacket with a handkerchief neatly arranged in the breast pocket and gestured for her to take a seat. "So, what is it you're here for, then, Miss Cross?"

Where to begin? "There is an antiquity on loan at the museum that I believe is stolen, and I want to find out who owns it."

"Isn't this something you should take up with Mr. Lavigne?"

"I tried. But he won't tell me who it is. Apparently, they prefer to remain anonymous."

"That's their right, of course."

"I realize that. But it's important I find out the answer."

"I see. Let me ask you, why would the owner lend something out in the first place if it's stolen? Seems rather risky."

He had a point.

"It was so long ago that the theft occurred, maybe they think enough time has passed."

"Usually it takes about a decade before a stolen antiquity hits the market. How long has it been in this case?"

"Forty-one years."

He let out a long whistle. "I see."

"Are those originals in your foyer?" she asked.

"They are. My parents lived in Harlem during the Renaissance and became patrons for several artists. Lucky for me, they had a good eye and passed on not only their collection, but also their interest in art."

"How did you become an investigator of art?"

"My thesis in grad school was on repatriation of stolen African art, and eventually I began to wonder why I was writing about it instead of doing something about it." He checked his watch. "Tell me more about your particular case."

She took a deep breath and steeled herself. If she wanted Tenny Woods to look into her case, she'd have to fill him in on the details. It helped that he was a stranger, and she reminded herself that this was just another story to add to his files. Whatever pity or judgment she saw behind his eyes was not anything she had to fix. It was all business. "Back in 1936, when I was working in Egypt at the Valley of the Kings, we uncovered a tomb and found two mummies and a broad collar. The broad collar was destined for the Egyptian Museum at that time. This week, the broad collar showed up at the Met as the anonymous donation I told you about." After Charlotte had realized it was the same one, she'd stopped by the Met library and looked through the Egyptian Museum's most recent catalog. "It's listed in the index in the Egyptian Museum's catalog, still, to this day, even though it's clearly not in the museum's possession."

"Interesting. But then why are *you* here, instead of a representative from the Egyptian Museum? It wasn't stolen from you."

"I don't think it ever made it into the Egyptian Museum in the first place. The two men who I believe took the broad collar happened to oversee the museum's documentation at that time. They could have made a false entry to cover their tracks."

Mr. Woods eyed her warily. "The antiquity you describe isn't the only one of its kind out there. Are you sure it's the exact same item you found?"

"Yes, because the markings on it were unique. It had the cartouche of Hathorkare on the clasp and was missing one of its amulets."

He rubbed his chin with one hand. "Well, I suggest you contact the Egyptian Museum first. If you're right, it's their theft to follow up with. Not yours."

"We both know the Egyptian Museum is having trouble just keeping the lights on these days. I'm not sure what kind of resources they have on hand to start this kind of inquiry."

He didn't disagree. "So you're going to lead the charge? Why?"

"Because I knew the two men personally. Quite well."

"Tell me more."

Charlotte swallowed hard. "I was in Egypt with my husband, a man named Henry Smith. The last I saw the collar, it had fallen out of a suitcase that Henry was carrying, onto the deck of a ship that was about to sink into the Nile. He stuffed it into one of his pockets. I had no idea it was even in his possession at the time."

Now she had Mr. Woods's full attention. "I see. What happened to Henry, if I may ask?"

"He was presumed dead, drowned. I assumed the collar was lost as well."

"But here it is."

"You can imagine my surprise."

"You say 'presumed dead,' Miss Cross. Do you think there's a chance he survived?"

"I don't know, I don't know what to think." But she wasn't thinking of Henry; she was thinking of Layla. The not knowing was the worst of all. Not knowing where Layla's tiny body had ended up, what terrifying impressions might have gone through her mind. The fact that their last touch was fraught with fear and panic. She coughed, erasing the dark thoughts under the guise of clearing her throat. "Henry's body was never found. But I don't know anything for sure. I was in the hospital for several weeks after, so I don't know what happened."

"I'm sorry for your loss." Mr. Woods was still and quiet.

"Thank you, it was many years ago. But I have to know why the broad collar resurfaced, and who it belongs to. Do you understand?"

"You think your husband might still be alive, that somehow he escaped with the stolen goods?"

"It's important I find that out." No doubt Mr. Woods thought her a distraught widow, which was better than knowing she was a destroyed mother. As long as he looked into it.

"Unfortunately, Henry Smith is a very common name, and as this occurred many decades ago, I don't think there's much for me to go on."

"What about making Mr. Lavigne disclose the name of the current owner? You could work backward from whomever that is, follow the chain of custody."

"There's no reason for Mr. Lavigne to tell me that information. It would only lead to a headache for him, and besides, he's signed a contract."

"Is it legal if the goods are stolen?"

"Now we're back to square one."

He was right.

She paused. "There's another name, an associate of my husband's who was on the ship with us. At the time, Henry said it was his suitcase."

"What's the name?" Mr. Woods picked up a pen.

"Leon," she answered. "Leon Pitcairn."

Charlotte studied her reflection in the full-length mirror in the bedroom. She had chosen to wear a vintage black georgette gown to this year's Met Gala, one she'd first seen in the window of a Greenwich Village thrift store twenty years ago and that luckily still fit. It wasn't on trend, by any means, with tulip sleeves and an unfashionable lack of embellishment, but Charlotte had always liked the way it gently draped around her hips, providing a subtle sense of curves to her thin frame.

Mark stepped up behind her and slipped his hands around her waist.

"You look ravishing."

She turned around and adjusted his bow tie. "You clean up well yourself."

The plan was to meet Helen and her husband for drinks at an East Side bar an hour before the gala officially began, partly to engage in some pre-gala gossip, as well as provide lubrication for what was sure to be a long night ahead.

The phone rang and Mark grabbed the receiver from the bedside table. Charlotte assumed it was Mark's ex-wife again. She'd called twice a day since Lori had arrived in New York, although Lori rarely wanted to speak with her. When she did, her answers were short and curt, bordering on rude, which made Charlotte both relieved and annoyed: relieved that Charlotte wasn't the only person Lori treated that way, and annoyed that Lori was able to get away with it in the first place.

But instead of yelling for Lori, Mark handed the receiver to Charlotte.

"It's for you."

She lifted it to her ear. "Hello?"

"Miss Cross, it's Tenny Woods."

Charlotte's heart began to pound. He wouldn't have rung her at this hour, at home, unless he had something to report. For a second, she regretted going to see him. Did she really want to know the answer to what had gone on all those years ago? Why dig up the past now?

Mark was studying her closely. She couldn't have this conversation in front of him.

Charlotte told Mr. Woods to hold for a moment. "I'll just be a minute," she said to Mark.

He grabbed his cuff links from the bureau, adjusted the baby photo of Lori so it was even with the other framed photos around it, and closed the door behind him.

"Yes, Mr. Woods, I'm here."

"Please, call me Tenny."

"Very well, please call me Charlotte. What did you find out?" she said, barely breathing.

"The identity of whoever recently loaned the antiquities to the Met is tightly sealed. The best I could get was that the items are owned by a husband and wife."

"No names, no nationalities?"

"I'm afraid not."

She was disappointed but not surprised. Most serious collectors tended to be private, operating on the principle of mutual discretion between buyer and seller, with the goal of owning a rare piece of history. The obnoxious collectors—the ones who splashed their names across multiple galleries—were usually angling for something less refined, like trying to buy goodwill for their progeny or acceptance into the inner circles of a social elite that would never have them.

"Well, thank you for looking into it. Let me know how much I owe you for your time."

"That's not all, though."

Charlotte closed her eyes tight and waited.

"Back in 1937, there were Egyptian warrants out for the arrests of Henry Smith and Leon Pitcairn on charges of smuggling."

"What? Are you sure?" Even though all the evidence—the secretive talks with Leon, the suitcase filled with antiquities—now added up, she still couldn't believe Henry would have been capable of such a thing.

"The warrant was dated November of that year."

The same month they fled.

"Henry Smith was never located, but the other man was. Leon Pitcairn."

Charlotte's mouth went dry. "You're sure? The same Leon Pitcairn?"

"I believe so. The Egyptian authorities caught up with him a few years later, and he spent some time in prison in Cairo."

"Is he still alive?"

"He is."

"Where?"

"Luxor, Egypt. He's a guide in the Valley of the Kings."

Charlotte's mind raced as she strapped on her high heels.

Tomorrow, she'd meet with Tenny to discuss next steps. She had to find out how Leon escaped from the sinking boat. Tenny said he had an associate in Egypt who could possibly help. The provenance of the loaned broad collar was her way into the truth of what happened that night, she was certain. The stories were linked, and she had to know more.

Out in the foyer, Mark held Charlotte's cashmere coat over his arm. "Who was that?"

"Someone from work. A technician needing advice on moving something."

"At this hour?"

"It's all hands on deck for Tut the golden boy."

She hated to lie, but she needed time to process what Tenny had told her. That Leon was still alive, had survived the shipwreck, and was now a guide at Luxor. There were two tiers of guides at the Valley of the Kings: those who were affiliated with well-established companies and made a steady income and those who hovered around the entrance, offering their dubious services to unsuspecting tourists. According to Tenny, Leon was one of the latter, no longer able to work as an archaeologist after being caught selling antiquities on the black market.

He must be in his mid-sixties, she figured. What had happened to him between that night on the ship and now? And if he *had* survived, what about Henry?

What about—

"You look like you've seen a ghost," said Mark. "Are you all right?"

"I'm fine."

As he slipped the coat over her shoulders, a wail rose from Charlotte's office. Lori stomped out not long after, holding some typed pages in her hand. "I need help."

"What is it?" asked Mark.

"I can't remember any of the lines for my audition, it's like they just fly out of my head." She looked like she was about to cry.

Earlier that day, Lori's new agent had called to say that she'd finagled her an audition for one of the popular soap operas. Charlotte had made a point of bringing home cupcakes to celebrate, but Lori had refused to take one, saying she had to watch her weight from now on.

"Can we work on it tomorrow morning, before I teach class?" offered Mark.

"The audition is at eleven in the morning. I won't be able to learn it that fast. Please, it's my big chance."

Never mind the fact that Charlotte and Mark were dressed to the nines, obviously about to go out. Mark looked over at Charlotte. She knew that expression; it meant that he was going to ask her something he knew she wouldn't like.

She gave a subtle shake of her head. It was bad enough having to watch as the partygoers oohed and aahed over a bunch of clothes, but she was also required to sit at Frederick's table and help woo the big donors, a talent she'd never quite mastered. She tended to get overwhelmed by the noise and the crowds, shrinking into herself as Frederick regaled and dazzled. Mark somehow always managed to make a personal connection with whoever was seated next to him and then wrangle Charlotte into the conversation with an easy grace.

He nodded and turned back to Lori. "You'll figure it out, sweetheart. I'll work with you when I'm back."

"No! You've always said that you only have one chance to make a good first impression. If I take a nosedive on this audition, word will get around that I suck and I'll never get another chance again."

The drama of the young, thought Charlotte. Yet not all of them. Annie Jenkins didn't seem to have any diva-like tendencies. She was innocent and doe-eyed, but possessed a seriousness that came from having been knocked down a few times. Although it really wasn't fair to compare.

She checked her watch and looked over at Mark. "We should go."

At which point Lori burst into tears. Mark held out his arms and pulled his daughter to him, giving Charlotte that same look.

He didn't want to go. Which meant the table would have an empty seat, which would upset Frederick to no end. She rarely asked

Mark to work events, only the big openings and the Met Gala, while she went to dress rehearsals, previews, and opening nights for every show he worked on, not to mention those of his Columbia students.

"You might as well stay," she said curtly, buttoning up her coat. If things went south during the audition, no doubt she'd get the blame, which would make home life even more difficult than it already was.

There was no point in pressing Mark further. Tonight, she was on her own.

CHAPTER FOURTEEN

Charlotte

NEW YORK CITY, 1938

After Charlotte returned to New York from Egypt, she had nightmares that sent her mother running into her room in the middle of the night. While her other friends had gotten married and moved out of their parents' homes, Charlotte was still in her childhood bedroom, and needing her mother's comfort when she awoke screaming about storms and Layla only made her feel more ashamed. Her mother never asked what had caused her to lash out in her sleep; she preferred to offer a cup of tea or a glass of water instead, and, once Charlotte had calmed down enough, slip back to the bedroom she shared with Charlotte's father just down the hall.

At home, Charlotte was discouraged from mentioning her lost husband and baby. She didn't speak of the days after the ship sank when, soaking wet and shaking with cold and confusion, two ribs broken, she'd been transported to a hospital and then, when she fought the nurses and refused to stop yelling no matter how much it hurt, she was given a shot and woke up in what turned out to be a women's psychiatric hospital. She could still remember the pungent smell of disinfectant that permeated every surface. Finally, once she was considered to be reasonably subdued, it was arranged for her to return to New York. By then, she had given up hope. If Henry was alive, surely he would have found her.

Perhaps it was for the best that she not discuss the horrifying end to her time in Egypt, because otherwise she would've never engaged in small talk with visitors, instead preferring to relive the way her child had barely been able to catch a breath in between screams as she was carried up to the top deck of the steamer, or how the raindrops on the baby's cheeks were indistinguishable from her tears.

Charlotte, in her madness, would have been subjected to the concerned looks of her parents' friends when they stopped by or, worse, the subtle disapproval of the fact that she had lived her life wildly and chosen recklessly. Mothers would point her out to their daughters in church, whisper warnings about what might happen if a young girl roamed too far out of sight.

Ruin and destruction.

One day, in her grief-laden haze, she heard the doorbell ring and recognized the voice of Mr. Zimmerman speaking to her mother down on the front landing. She crept unsteadily into the hallway to eavesdrop, still wearing her nightgown. Her mother curtly informed him that Charlotte had come down with a tropical fever and was unable to have visitors. That there was no telling when she'd be well, and it was best to let her recover.

Mr. Zimmerman told her mother that he would be happy to offer Charlotte a position at the Met once she did, and handed her a letter to pass on to Charlotte. That letter never made it to Charlotte's hands, but she'd spied the remains of it in the parlor fireplace later that day.

Not long after, she dressed for the first time in weeks and left the house while her mother was out running errands. Inside the Met

Museum, she told Mr. Zimmerman that she'd made a swift recovery and requested a position that didn't require much public interaction. He suggested she join the team as a part-time researcher, working in the Met's library. When he started to offer his condolences on her loss, she cut him off, explaining that she would prefer not to speak of the past, only the present, and he respected her wishes. On nights that she worked late, she would venture into the Egyptian Art collection, drawn to the Cerulean Queen, where she'd stand and stare at the statue for a good five minutes before moving on.

Hathorkare's tranquil expression, even with most of her face missing, seemed to convey that Charlotte wasn't alone, that other women had suffered over the centuries before her and continued living, even if what was scarred and shattered was invisible to the outside world.

For a long time, Charlotte kept herself busy working part-time at the museum while finishing up her undergraduate degree. Most of her friends were occupied with babies and family life that Charlotte had no wish to witness—though every year on Layla's birthday, she forced herself to walk to the elementary school playground on West 11th Street and observe the girls who were around the same age that Layla would have been as a kind of bittersweet punishment for her sins. If only she and Henry had returned to New York, they might have been here with Layla, pushing her on the swing set. All three of them would be safe. Her parents would have fawned over Layla and accepted Henry within days. Charlotte had been young and stupid, her perspective skewed.

But whenever she spiraled into shame and bitterness, she remembered that there had been extenuating circumstances. Henry and Leon had gotten mixed up in something nefarious, and it was very possible they were in a rush to leave because they were close to getting caught. Which would explain why Henry had become short and distracted around Charlotte and Layla during the last few weeks of their time there. But there was no way to get answers, no way to punish Henry as she desperately wished she could. Rail at him, make him bleed. Even worse, she was alone in her grief. He was the only other person who'd been an integral part of Layla's short life.

In the meantime, Charlotte began her graduate studies at the Institute of Fine Arts and rose quickly in the museum's hierarchy despite the fact that she was a woman, mainly due to her industriousness and single-minded focus. When the war finally came to an end, she worried she'd lose her position to a returning veteran, as had happened to several of her female colleagues, but Mr. Zimmerman kept her on staff.

Around the same time, her parents began holding dinner parties at home every week in an obvious effort to pair Charlotte up with an eligible bachelor, and to make her ailing father happy, Charlotte reluctantly obliged, although she still refused to dye her gray streak, despite her mother's haranguing. At one such party, she was seated next to a former Yale quarterback and current Wall Street banker named Everett, who insisted she expound on the mummification rituals of the ancient Egyptians over the soup course, which turned everyone at the table green except him. They laughed later at the fact that it was his strong stomach that first caught her fancy.

Everett delighted in being surrounded by other vivacious, outgoing sorts, where Charlotte barely tolerated it, but he didn't seem to mind when her mood darkened and she turned inward, refusing to see him for several days in a row. No doubt Charlotte's mother had told Everett that Charlotte suffered from some sort of womanly hysteria; he never asked, and Charlotte never volunteered the reason for her capriciousness. In fact, her unavailability probably intrigued Everett, who was considered a top catch in their social circles and had mothers shoving their daughters in his path regularly.

He was intelligent and fun to be around, which was why Charlotte said yes when he proposed to her during dinner at Fraunces Tavern, which he'd chosen because it was the longest-running restaurant in New York City and he knew she appreciated "old things." They spent the next week up at his family's house in Maine, where the snow was deep and the fireplaces enormous. His family accepted Charlotte easily, happy to have Everett's wild days as a single fellow finally curtailed. She enjoyed most the daily sleigh rides. The bitter cold on her cheeks—so different from the furnace-like climate of Egypt—kept the bad memories at bay.

Like many of his generation, Everett had been sent to Europe during the war and fought in terrible battles, but he shared a camaraderie with the other surviving soldiers he'd served with that appeared to soften the worst of the memories. For Charlotte, the frightening wartime years had put her own travails in perspective: Her tragedy was just one of many horrors that existed in the world. Not that the pain eased in any way, but instead of eating away at her insides like an ulcer, it had hardened into a cyst.

Two and a half months before the wedding, when she and her mother were at the dining room table sorting through the guest list prior to sending out invitations, Charlotte mentioned that she was going to tell Everett about Henry and Layla. Of course she didn't say their names out loud. "I want to tell Everett about what happened in Egypt," she said instead.

"I don't think that's a good idea," answered her mother quickly. "There's no need to bring all that up."

"But he should know I was married before. It's only right."

"You were on the other side of the world. It doesn't really count. And it wasn't even for one year."

Charlotte was surprised that her mother even knew the length of the marriage, as she'd been averse to hearing any details.

Her mother continued. "Consider it the same as having a marriage annulled, like the Catholics do. *Poof,* never happened. Now, where did I put those stamps?" She bustled off into another room, unwilling to discuss the matter further.

But as Everett escorted Charlotte home a week later, after a party they'd attended at an apartment overlooking Gramercy Park, he announced that they would stop by Egypt after their honeymoon in Greece. "You can take me to all your old haunts," he said. "After all, if I'm the husband of a curator in the Egyptian Art collection, I ought to have visited at least once."

"I'm not the curator," she said, pulling her hand out of his.

"Assistant curator, then. You'll be curator soon enough."

"There's no need to stop in Egypt. Besides, I'll have to get back to work. And you will as well."

She tried switching the subject to the groomsmen's tuxedos, which she couldn't have cared less about, but Everett wasn't deterred, insisting he'd change their itinerary first thing the next morning.

So she began to tell him about Egypt. At Fifth Avenue, she spoke of the Met dig team and meeting Henry. By Sixth Avenue, she'd covered their shotgun wedding at the Metropolitan House. By Seventh Avenue, Layla was born. By Eighth Avenue, Henry and Layla were lost to the Nile. Charlotte didn't explain the accident in detail, as it was too painful. However, the joy of being able to say their names out loud and speak of a time that had been tucked away in the dark recesses of her brain made her almost giddy, like she'd drunk several glasses of champagne.

When they reached the doorstep of her parents' brownstone, Everett assured Charlotte that he understood why she hadn't told him, and said he loved her no matter what. But then he didn't call for two days, which was unusual, and when he finally did, he said he was off to Boston for a work trip.

A week later, just before the invitations were to be mailed, the wedding was called off in a hurried telephone call between their two fathers. Less than a year later, Charlotte's father died, and her mother began to fail soon after, taking to her bed, uninterested in drink or food. It was right around the time Charlotte had decided to attempt to travel to Egypt with several PhD candidates from her department, a trip that she never made. One night, as Charlotte sat vigil by her bedside, her mother reached up and grabbed Charlotte's hand.

"I'm sorry," she said, her voice hoarse.

"There's nothing to be sorry for."

"No, there is. He was looking for you."

"Who?"

"We shouldn't have interfered."

She closed her eyes, and by the next morning, she was gone. Charlotte figured her last words were those of a confused, frail woman.

Not long after, Charlotte moved out of the brownstone and into the small Greenwich Village apartment on Barrow Street, and fitted her life tightly around her job at the Met.

And that worked, for a time.

CHAPTER FIFTEEN

Annie

NEW YORK CITY, 1978

Annie raced home to get dressed for the Met Gala. She'd spent most of the day dealing with Mrs. Vreeland's last-minute adjustments to the exhibition and still had to pick up the butterflies at the Museum of Natural History. Joyce was supposed to help Annie with her updo, but she wasn't home yet.

Annie slid into her dress and gave a little shimmy. It had come out perfectly, and she loved the way the material subtly suggested the shape of her body as she moved. While she waited for Joyce, she applied her own makeup, but instead of heavy foundation and lots of color, she opted for a minimal look, emphasizing her eyebrows and lips only. In the mirror, the color of her eyes, hair, and dress became one soft, golden hue. Just as Mrs. Vreeland had said, by focusing on what made her unique—in this case her natural glow—she'd turned it into something interesting. Same with the rings on her fingers— she wore two chunky rings on one hand and three on the other, and the jewelry provided a nice balance. She'd created a look that worked with her own body type and personality.

The last time she'd gotten this dressed up had been a disaster, and she was determined not to repeat it. Her junior year of high school, everyone went to the prom, whether they had a date or not, and Annie spent a good month working on her dress. She found a pattern that was similar to a maxi dress she'd seen in a magazine: navy with long sleeves, a ruffled collar, and a mix of large and small polka dots. It was from the Dior 1970 spring/summer haute couture collection, perfectly accessorized with a wide black leather belt.

"It's smart to keep your arms and legs covered, and I like the high neck as well," her mother had said as Annie modeled it the night of the prom. "How about I do your makeup and hair?"

Annie had sat in the kitchen chair as her mother spread the contents of her professional makeup kit—which was the size of a small suitcase—across the table. "We'll go with a bright pink lipstick and tan foundation," Joyce said. "That will take care of the ruddiness of your skin, and we don't want to accent those chubby cheeks of yours. For the eyes, I have a navy shadow that perfectly matches the dress."

When Annie looked in the mirror after she'd finished, she had mixed feelings. Her skin tone was far from her natural one, veering toward orange, and her eyes practically disappeared into her skull. The cascade of curls in her hair was already going limp, but Joyce sprayed them with a generous layer of Aqua Net that made Annie's eyes water.

Joyce was a professional model; Annie just had to trust her.

Annie had walked into the gym where the prom was being held to discover all the other girls wearing layers of lacy pastels with empire waists, like a flock of Bo-Peeps missing their sheep, and long, straight hair with little or no makeup. In comparison, Annie looked like a Mack Truck wearing lipstick. No one spoke to her other than the geography teacher, Mr. Williams. She'd held out for twenty-five minutes before fleeing.

Tonight, at the Party of the Year, it would be different.

The front door opened and slammed shut.

"Mom?" Annie called out. "Where have you been? I have to be out of here in ten minutes."

Joyce came up from behind Annie in the bathroom. She stared intently into the mirror. "Wow. That's some look you've got going there."

The vagueness of the statement made Annie uneasy. Maybe she had no idea what she was doing, and this was going to be another debacle where she'd be laughed out of the museum and find herself out of a job.

"I like it," she said weakly.

"Do you want me to do your eyes?"

"No. I'm going to leave them like this."

She diverted her mother's attention, worried that she'd insist on doing it her way. "Do you want to try on your dress before I go? We'll meet in the Great Hall, okay? I'll introduce you to Mrs. Vreeland, and I made sure you're sitting at a good table for dinner. Your hair looks nice. Were you just at the salon?" With Annie's new salary, the thought of spending money on a hairdresser didn't set off financial alarm bells in her head the way it used to.

Joyce patted her coiffure. "Thanks. But I'm afraid I can't make it tonight."

Annie spun around. "What? You're not going? Why not?"

"Brad called. He wants to meet."

After everything that Annie had done to finagle a ticket and alter one of Joyce's dresses to her exact specifications, she couldn't even be bothered to go? Annie had even fought to get her an invitation to the

VIP tour. Until now, she hadn't understood how desperately she wanted her mother to see her in a new light, not as her homely daughter but as an integral part of the team behind the Met Gala.

"He's just going to break up with you, Mom," said Annie, not caring how mean she sounded. "Are you really going to skip this amazing event, which anyone in their right mind would be dying to attend, in order to get dumped by Brad?"

Joyce's eyes began to water, and she twisted the wishbone necklace that lay in the hollow of her throat. The necklace had been Annie's father's last Christmas gift to Joyce, and she never took it off. "You're a cruel child, do you know that?"

"I'm not. I just think you're making a mistake. Can't you put him off for one night?"

"He leaves for the West Coast tomorrow. And I want to see this through. I *have* to see this through, for my own sanity."

Sanity would be not getting involved with a stranger from Nashville in the first place. "He's probably married. Why do you allow him to treat you like this? You deserve better."

"Watch it. Remember who you're talking to, Annie."

Annie threw up her hands. "Fine. Do what you like. I don't care."

"Is that how you're wearing that dress?" asked Joyce. "Don't you want to belt it?"

Annie stifled a scream. "I really don't want to talk to you right now. I'm very disappointed." She grabbed a clip that lay on top of the sink and hastily put her hair up in a messy bun.

Joyce sat on the bed, working herself up to a good weep. "Please don't be mad at me. I really like Brad, and maybe I can change his mind."

"I'm leaving." Annie grabbed her handbag and coat. "You are unbelievable."

Normally Annie wouldn't even consider leaving her mother when she was crying or upset. In the past, she'd drop everything to comfort her, do whatever it took to make everything okay between them. But not this time. She was too angry.

Outside, Mrs. H called out from her window. "Girl! Let me see that dress."

Annie opened her coat, letting it fall to her elbows.

"It's smashing. I see Mrs. Vreeland is rubbing off on you."

Annie pulled her coat back up and smiled. That was exactly the boost she needed. "Thank you." She gave a quick salute and was gone.

Outside the Metropolitan Museum, a red carpet spilled down the front steps like a river of merlot, and the first of the limos was pulling up to the curb, where a clique of photographers waited patiently for their prey.

Annie watched with bated breath as Lee Radziwill alighted from the back of a limo wearing an ivory silk dress that was fitted at the waist, with an enormous white stole slung over her shoulders that threatened to swallow her whole. Diana Ross turned heads in a long-sleeved black gown that shimmered with sequins and sported a plunging neckline as well as a matching veil. The dress was stunning, but Annie wasn't so sure about the choice of a veil. She'd have to ask Mrs. Vreeland her thoughts on the subject tomorrow.

They were followed by fashion photographer Mary Ann Miller and model Dymphna Kerrigan. Mary Ann, a petite redhead, wore a sparkling pink toga dress with a large bow over one shoulder, while Dymphna was squeezed into in a bright red sheath that accentuated her curves. Her wrists and neck glittered with diamonds.

The crowd of bystanders gasped as the downtown artist Jenny Pyle spilled out of her limo in a beaded jumpsuit and platform heels, her famous curls dyed jet-black.

Annie could've stood there for hours, marveling at the stylishness of each celebrity. Instead, she marched over to the employee entrance, where the security guard greeted her with a scowl.

"You'll have to open the box."

"If I open it, it'll be ruined," she explained. "This is a very special package for Mrs. Vreeland, and she needs it tonight, right away."

After the argument with Joyce about the gala, she'd taken the bus across the park to the Museum of Natural History and spent far more time than she'd expected running from office to office in search of the entomologist who'd promised her butterflies. Finally, she was handed a box that was ungainly in size but light in weight and caught a taxi to the Met, setting the box gently on the seat beside her and steadying it with one hand as the driver raced along the 79th Street Transverse.

The exhibition was about to open, and she should be by Mrs. Vreeland's side, but now the security guard was insisting she open the box, which would not do at all. Her feet hurt from running in heels and a drop of sweat slid down her chest. Just her luck, it was an unusually warm day for late November.

The security guard appeared to be unimpressed by her fancy outfit and her association with Mrs. Vreeland.

"Nope. Open it up."

"Hey, Carl. She's okay. I'll vouch for her."

Annie looked to her right, where Billy was signing in for his shift. Carl gave her the once-over and then nodded. "All right. Go ahead."

"You saved the day," said Annie as she and Billy walked down the hall together. "Thank you so much. I'm late and this is crucial to the evening. Just *crucial.*"

She was speaking in the same cadence as Mrs. Vreeland, and the thought made her smile.

"I can only imagine," said Billy. "You must be excited for tonight."

"Excited. And nervous." And disappointed that Joyce wouldn't be waiting for her upstairs. But she didn't say that out loud.

"You look terrific."

"Well, thanks. All the heavyweights of New York high society are here, I figure I should look the part."

"You look better than any of them, I'm sure."

Annie blushed and couldn't think of what to say back. In many ways, Billy came off as younger than Annie. He lacked the weight of the world that she carried around with her; his attitude was always positive. She envied that about him.

"Hey," said Billy. "At some point, we should meet up for a pizza or something. That way you can see me in my natural state."

"Natural state?"

Billy slapped the side of his face. "What am I saying? I'm such a dolt. I mean, not wearing a blue suit. Wearing normal clothes."

He was asking her out on a date. She thought that was an excellent idea and said so.

"Great," he said. "I'll find you tomorrow and we'll figure something out."

In Mrs. Vreeland's office, Annie took a moment to collect herself. She was about to attend the Party of the Year, and Billy the adorable security guard had just asked her out. Life couldn't get better than this. She turned off the light and closed the door and prayed that the butterflies would be safe until the big reveal later in the evening. Leave it to Mrs. Vreeland to come up with the craziest ideas.

But the woman knew what she was doing—that much was clear as soon as Annie stepped into the exhibition, where a bevy of society ladies with white teeth and skinny arms wandered the space. Annie had only seen the exhibition with the harsh overhead lights on; under the designer's lighting, each costume seemed like it was lit from within, as if one of the mannequins might at any moment come to life and dance up the stairs, join in on the cocktail party raging in the Great Hall. Diaghilev's bold use of color and style made each tableau unique, but Mrs. Vreeland's extra touches—like the peacocks perched on the shoulders of the peacock bearers from *Le Dieu Bleu*, the classical music playing in the background, and the subtle bouquet of perfume that tickled the nose—elevated what was ostensibly a textile display to a joyous celebration. Annie could just imagine what it had been like in Paris back in 1909, when Diaghilev founded the Ballets Russes. As the curtain rose, the audience must have gasped in shock at the staggering strangeness and beauty of it all.

Mrs. Vreeland had magically re-created a moment long past.

Annie knew she should find her boss and see what needed to be done, but she took a few moments to wander the exhibition first, stifling a yelp when she spotted the Egyptian broad collar sparkling on the chest of the mannequin wearing the Zobeida costume. Annie felt as proud as the archaeologist who first pulled it up from the Saharan sand or wherever these things came from.

The biggest draws were the Nijinsky costume from *Swan Lake* and the ones by Matisse from the Stravinsky ballet whose name Annie didn't dare try to pronounce. She had learned so much in such a short amount of time. The sting of disappointment over her mother's absence faded, replaced by a sense of purpose and pride.

In the Great Hall, Annie spotted Mrs. Vreeland standing at the center of a crowd, wearing a flowery velvet dress by Givenchy. Velvet seemed to be a trend, as Pat Buckley, one of the gala's co-chairs, wore a similar design but in brown. Mrs. Vreeland smiled at Annie from across the way but then turned her attention to Bill Blass, tucking her arm into his as they headed into the restaurant for the dinner portion of the evening. The rest of the crowd followed, including

Priscilla and Mona with their husbands. Priscilla looked stunning in an embroidered, wine-colored sheath, and Mona's aqua gown contrasted beautifully with her dark hair.

Annie hovered along the edges of the room during dinner, too nervous to be hungry. A feathered fan in the perfect shade of yellow lay lightly on each place setting, and the guests appeared to enjoy the three courses. Mrs. Vreeland barely touched her plate, and near the end of the meal she stood and surveyed the room.

"May I have your attention, please." She waited with her head thrown back, one arm raised as the murmuring subsided, holding her champagne flute as if it were an Olympic torch. "On May 19, 1909, at the Théâtre du Châtelet in Paris, Russian genius Sergei Pavlovich Diaghilev astounded the audience with a performance by his Ballets Russes, one that dance critic John Percival wrote 'transformed ballet and sparked off a flamboyant revolution in fashion and interior design.' Diaghilev's career was one of collaboration with some of the greats of that century, including Debussy, Stravinsky, Cocteau, Ravel, Picasso, Prokofiev, and Balanchine, and my hope is that tonight you've gotten a sense of this man, a self-described cheeky charmer and unprincipled charlatan who radically changed the course of cultural history. I thank all the dedicated workers who helped us mount this show, and all of you for your support of this wonderful institution. And now, I encourage you to join us for dessert and dancing at the Temple of Dendur."

Mrs. Vreeland led the way, taking tiny steps like a Japanese geisha because she disliked the sound of women's heels hitting the floor. Annie had learned that fact only two days ago, when Mrs. Vreeland had admonished her for "galumphing like a heathen." At the entrance to the Temple of Dendur gallery Annie paused, taking in the scene. In the darkness of night, it was as if the temple floated above the shallow pools of water surrounding the ancient structure on three sides. The crowd had grown in size, and the music was loud; the pounding of the bass made Annie's head spin. Everyone appeared to be having a great time except the security guards, who were busy asking guests not to lean on the black stone statues that lined the near wall. She saw no sign of Billy.

"It's time for the VIP tour." Mrs. Vreeland appeared at Annie's side. "I'll see you in the exhibition hall—just wait for my signal. I can't wait to see what you've conjured."

"Of course."

"And you look *smashing*, by the way."

Annie stammered her thanks and began to express her gratitude for the opportunity to be her assistant, but Mrs. Vreeland was gone before she could get the words out.

She sprinted down to the exhibition hall and out the door that led to the basement hallway. She was gathering up the butterfly box from Mrs. Vreeland's desk when she heard footsteps.

She froze. "Hello? Mrs. Vreeland?"

There was no answer. She hadn't bothered to turn on the lights or close the door to the Costume Institute behind her when she came in. Yet the door was now shut, the expanse pitch-black.

"Hello?" Annie's voice came out wobbly. "Is anyone there?"

She stood still, listening intently, but the only sound was her own breath and the gentle fluttering of the butterflies in the box in her arms, like baby heartbeats.

One of the guards must have come by and closed the door. She put her head down and charged out of the room, relieved when she reached the well-lit hallway.

Back in the exhibition hall, Annie made her way to one corner and crouched down with the box, trying not to be seen. The VIP tour had already begun, and Annie recognized the mayor and the museum director, along with a dozen or so others who were admiring the brightly printed tunics and shorts by the painter Léon Bakst. They listened intently as Mrs. Vreeland expounded on the design. "I can already see these diaphanous dresses being a big hit at the Hamptons next summer, can't you?" she boomed in her imperious way.

As Mrs. Vreeland led the group to the next display, she spotted Annie and, for a moment, a look of confusion crossed her face. But then she gave her a quick nod of the head.

It was time.

Annie pulled open the flaps. At first, nothing happened, so she gave the box a little shake. In a rush, a cloud of small, winged insects flew out of the box and up into the air. It occurred to her that she had no idea how she'd get the butterflies back in the box. Of course Mrs. Vreeland didn't concern herself with such logistics; that was Annie's job. She'd figure something out.

Annie looked up, expecting to see a mass of orange wings—a "dizzying kaleidoscope of shape, pattern, and color," as Mrs. Vreeland had explained when she'd first come up with the idea.

But something was off. These butterflies were small and dark. There were hundreds of them. Maybe thousands.

They swarmed the hot spotlights and flitted recklessly around the heads of the guests, who swatted at them and cried out in shock.

"Oh my God!" Marta's voice came out strangled. "It's moths! An invasion of moths!"

Annie stared, her mouth open, at the ugly little monsters she'd just set free, as mayhem broke all around her.

"Where did they come from?" cried the director of the museum.

Mrs. Vreeland smashed one between her two hands and glared in Annie's direction.

There must've been some kind of mix-up. But Annie had been perfectly clear with the person at the Museum of Natural History. Butterflies. Not moths. Who would want a box of moths? How could they have made such a terrible mistake? Annie checked the box. It was the same one she'd picked up, the word "Butterflies" clearly printed on the side.

"The clothes!"

Mrs. Vreeland was pointing at one of the more fragile costumes, a silk number, that a couple of moths had already descended upon. The piece had been carefully stored for decades, only to be in danger of being destroyed in minutes because of Annie's mistake.

She ran to the mannequin, trying to flick them away, but the insects easily dodged her efforts. All around her they were spreading throughout the room like a plague.

Annie had to find help.

She ran to the basement hallway, yelling for security, for anyone, but got no answer. The technicians and conservators who might normally be working late stayed as far away from the building as possible during the Party of the Year.

Tears of frustration and fear pricked her eyes. She'd be fired, certainly, for this mishap. Annie would be just like the former assistant Wanda, running for the door after being publicly axed.

But for far greater a mistake.

CHAPTER SIXTEEN

Charlotte

After an endless dinner in the Dorotheum, Charlotte was finally able to slip away. She had a blister on one heel from the ridiculous shoes she was wearing and needed a break from the cacophony, so she cut through the Great Hall to seek refuge—and a Band-Aid—at her desk. Frederick hadn't been pleased at Mark's empty seat at their table, but Charlotte had asked the waiters to clear it away and then made a point of smiling and chatting with the donors on either side of her, even though she was still seething at Mark for staying home.

She'd gone straight to the museum from home, having canceled on drinks with Helen and Brian, knowing she wouldn't be very good company. When she'd first arrived, she'd spotted a tall girl in a long, shimmering dress watching the proceedings. Charlotte's first thought was that she resembled an Egyptian queen, but then she realized it was Annie Jenkins. Quite the transformation from the girl in the red coat with curved shoulders and a hangdog look on her face who she'd seen wandering the galleries of the Egyptian Art collection not long ago. The job agreed with her.

Even though her heel was aching, Charlotte took a moment to

soak in the grandeur: the security guards in their uniforms, the staff dressed to the nines, and the guests swanning about in the latest fashions. For once, the inhabitants of the hall matched the formality of the architecture, as opposed to regular visiting hours when shaggy-haired kids in jeans and sneakers wandered about. Tonight, Charlotte could almost imagine what the museum had been like when it opened its doors in 1880, back when women wore bustles and men sported frock coats.

The staff offices were empty, as to be expected. A pink interoffice envelope lay on her chair, and she picked it up and placed it on the top of her black metal inbox. Sitting down, she rifled through her drawer for a Band-Aid. After she stuck the plaster on her heel and slipped her shoe back on, she absent-mindedly picked up the interoffice envelope and unwound the string closure. She figured it was yet another random missive from accounting, but instead it was a blank piece of paper.

Strange.

Until she turned it over. This wasn't an interoffice memorandum. A message had been scribbled in thick block letters with a black Magic Marker:

**IF YOU WANT YOUR RESEARCH BACK,
YOU BETTER MIND YOUR OWN BUSINESS.**

Charlotte dropped the paper like it was on fire and immediately patted the top of her desk. Her colleagues always joked about how neat Charlotte's desk was—she preferred to keep what she was working on front and center, with everything else tucked away in the drawers. Front and center was exactly where she'd left her Hathor-kare file. But it wasn't there. She yanked open the bottom drawer of her desk and leafed through the tabs: "Tut Exhibition," "Budget,"

"Staff," "Inquiries." Everything was accounted for except for the one file she was looking for. The thick, worn manila folder that contained the photos, her notes, the geographical surveys, everything to do with her findings. All the work she'd done the past three years.

She glanced around, her hands shaking, throat dry. She checked the trash bin under her desk, thinking maybe the cleaning staff had tossed it out. But that was empty. She looked around her colleagues' desks on the off chance someone had picked it up by mistake, not that any of them would ever do such a thing.

Still nothing.

Three years of work.

Gone.

Shaking, she checked the desk drawers again, the trash can, the floor around her desk. Who would take her research? And why?

Mind your own business. It must have something to do with the fact that she was questioning the provenance of the loaned broad collar.

Whoever had taken the file knew how important it was to her. No doubt someone didn't like her inquiring about the collar, wanted her to keep quiet, not cause a fuss. Which meant her hunch about the shady provenance was correct. In her head, Charlotte ran through a list of who had known about her research project. She'd kept mum about it on purpose, knowing that her theory might be wrong, and also because she didn't want anyone else to steal the idea and publish it before she had a chance to. Frederick knew, of course, and Mark and Helen. She'd enlisted the help of one of the museum's librarians several times, but she hadn't gone into detail as to why she was requesting the particular materials. Her head spun with the possibilities.

If only Mark were with her now, to help her think it through.

The bass notes of the music pounded away, making it hard to concentrate. But then her ears picked up another sound, something shrill, not in tempo with the beat.

Like people were screaming.

Something was wrong.

Forgetting the lost file for a moment, Charlotte ventured back out into the galleries, cocking her head. The noise wasn't coming from the Temple of Dendur, where the crowd was. It was coming from below, rising from the basement level, where the exhibition hall was located.

"Guards! Is anyone up here?" she shouted. There was no answer. Whatever was going on, she had to see if she could help.

But as she turned to go, something caught her eye. Just to her right was the gallery where she'd hidden from the gossiping technicians, where her favorite statue was located.

And where an empty pedestal now stood.

The Cerulean Queen was gone.

Charlotte approached the empty pedestal. Maybe it had been taken away for cleaning, or for research purposes, although surely she would have been informed of that. Then again, she'd been so busy and distracted lately. As she grew closer, she gave a silent prayer that a small card reading "Object temporarily removed" would be sitting in place of the statue, which would mean it was somewhere safe in the basement, being studied or polished. But there was no card.

The Cerulean Queen had been plucked right off its stand.

The Queen was one of the most well-known and loved pieces in their collection, and to have it go missing was a nightmare, for the museum and for anyone who loved ancient art. The statue was delicate and, in the wrong hands, could be irreparably damaged. Even more damaged than it already was.

In the dim light, a sudden movement caught her eye. A shadowy figure slipped out of one of the galleries to her left, a man in a dark suit.

Thinking it was a security guard, Charlotte yelled for help. He stopped for a moment, without turning around. The way his body stiffened at the sound of her voice was not normal. And he held some kind of bag in his right hand.

This was no guard. It was the thief.

Charlotte flew at him, not thinking, yelling as loudly as she could. He took off, running north before taking a sharp right turn, down the stairs to the exhibition hall, Charlotte following as fast as she could. On the landing she spied him weaving through the crush of people who were making their way up to the main floor, yelling and tripping over each other to get away from whatever terrible thing was going on down there.

Every instinct told her not to follow the man into the crush of bodies, but she couldn't let him escape.

Charlotte took a deep breath and dove straight into the advancing crowd.

When Charlotte entered the exhibition hall of the Costume Institute, her first thought was that maybe a bomb had gone off, as the air was filled with bits of debris. Only when she looked up at the spotlights did she comprehend that whatever was in the air wasn't falling; it was flying. The room was filled with insects of some sort.

It brought to mind the locust plague she'd experienced in Egypt, when they'd been inundated by millions of them for days on end. But these weren't locusts. They were small and dark, attracted by the spotlights. The creatures cast erratic shadows around the entire room, making it feel like it was vibrating.

Annie Jenkins was helping an older woman with a cane toward the stairs while the remaining staff members scurried around helplessly swatting the air. A security guard tried to kill one of the insects after it landed on a costume, but the strength of his smack ended up knocking the mannequin over, which, in turn, fell into the mannequin next to it, creating a domino effect and causing even more screeches. Diana Vreeland stood with her hands on her cheeks, shaking her head. No one knew what to do.

Over in one corner was a large open box with the words "Live Butterflies—Handle with Care" printed on one side. God knew what was going on down here, but whatever it was, it had turned into a total disaster. What utter insanity, to bring live insects into a museum. No doubt it was one of Diana Vreeland's crazy notions, like the infused perfume that tickled Charlotte's nose and made her want to sneeze.

She scanned the room for the man from the Egyptian wing, but the layout of the hall made it difficult to find him. He could be hiding behind any of the velvet curtains that draped the displays, or maybe he had squeezed back into the crush of people waiting to get up the stairs. It was utter chaos. Luckily, a clutch of guards had just arrived at the back entrance of the room, reinforcements for the ones who were already there and were doing their best to assist the attendees.

Their focus, rightly so, was on getting the crowd upstairs safely. Which left all the costumes and other artwork unattended.

Including the broad collar.

In the craziness of the moment, she'd forgotten it was down here. She spun around and located the mannequin, which stood intact, including the broad collar. It was safe, at least.

Charlotte sprinted over to the guards at the back. "There's been a theft. The Cerulean Queen is missing from the Egyptian Art collection. I followed the thief—he ran down here. Did you pass a man in a dark suit?"

One of the security guards shook his head. "I can't hear you."

"The Cerulean Queen has been stolen," she shouted.

Now she had his full attention. "You said the Cerulean Queen is missing?" he yelled back, his eyes wide.

"Yes. And I think the thief may be in this room somewhere."

It occurred to Charlotte that this moth debacle made the perfect distraction for a thief, drawing the security guards from the Egyptian galleries down to the basement and away from their posts. But it was impossible to communicate that clearly with all the noise. She pointed to one of the guards. "You, find out where they control the music and shut it off." She pointed to another. "Turn on all of the overhead lights and close the door to the stairway once everyone's out." She recognized one of the guards as the young kid who had been cleaning up in the head of security's office when she'd stopped by. "Have every exit to the museum closed until we find the thief." The kid took off running.

Soon, the overhead lights blinked on and the music faded. Charlotte continued issuing orders. "Get some netting from the conservators' workshop and use it to block one doorway. Then turn off the lights in the room but keep the light in the hallway on. The moths will be attracted by the light and fly into the netting." Even as she spoke, she knew they were wasting valuable time.

"Did anyone see a man holding some kind of a bag come through here?" But her question fell on empty ears as the guards scrambled into action to corral the moths.

Annie Jenkins was suddenly by Charlotte's side. "You mean a bowling-ball bag?"

"What?"

"I saw a man with a bowling-ball bag run past me a little while ago."

"In a dark suit?"

"Yes."

"What way did he go?"

She pointed to the door to the back hallway. "Through there. Why are you after him?"

A pulse pounded in Charlotte's temple as she answered. "He's stolen the Cerulean Queen."

CHAPTER SEVENTEEN

Annie

He turned to the right," said Annie, following Charlotte down the main basement hallway.

Annie knew she shouldn't be running away from the mayhem she'd just unleashed, but the distraught look in Charlotte's expression overrode Annie's sense of duty to Mrs. Vreeland. Something terrible had happened, and she preferred to jump into action rather than face what was sure to be the wrath of everyone who had worked so hard to make the exhibition a success. Her chest heaved with effort as they sprinted down the long hall. The man could have gone anywhere.

"There must be more guards down here," said Charlotte. "We'll round up some help and see if we can track this guy down. What did he look like?"

"Dark suit, tall," answered Annie, panting hard. "I didn't see his face, but I noticed the bowling-ball bag because my dad used to have one just like it. He stood out because he didn't seem upset by the moths the way everyone else was, it was like he expected them."

Charlotte nodded, like she wasn't surprised by that fact. "What exactly happened in there?"

Annie's insides twisted. She'd been so stupid—why hadn't she checked the box before she set them all free? "Mrs. Vreeland wanted butterflies released for the VIP tour. But something got mixed up and instead the box was filled with moths."

"Which are attracted to fabrics. Genius, really."

"I'm sorry?"

"Who gave you the box?"

"I picked it up from the Museum of Natural History before I arrived."

Charlotte gave Annie a quick sideways glance. "Is that right?"

"You don't think I was part of this, do you?" Annie's face burned. "I swear, I was just doing what I was told." She grabbed Charlotte's arm. "Is the broad collar safe?"

"It is. I checked on it."

"Thank goodness. Do you think that the moths and the theft are related? Like I said, the guy didn't seem overwhelmed by the pandemonium. Not in the way everyone else was."

"Maybe."

They ventured farther down the bright hallway, the only sound their footsteps and the buzz of the fluorescent lights overhead.

"This is crazy," said Charlotte. "Everyone's upstairs. We shouldn't be doing this alone."

"But we can't let the man escape," countered Annie. A rush of cool air made her stop in her tracks. "What is that?" She pointed to what looked like an old-fashioned tunnel with an arched brick ceiling that branched off to the left. Padlocked metal cages lined the sides, bursting with a mishmash of antiquities, including marble sculptures, fluted columns, and coats of armor. The handle of a dagger poked through the gap between one of the cage doors.

"It's an obsolete storm drain for the park's reservoir, built back in the mid-1800s. It runs diagonally north to south the entire length of the building."

"And they use it for storage?"

"There are over two million pieces of art in the museum's collection; we can only exhibit a fraction at any one time. We need all the storage space we can get."

A wave of sadness ran through Annie at the thought of so much art tucked away in a cold, dark hole in the ground, pieces that were deemed extraneous and locked away in an art jailhouse because they didn't make the cut anymore, or never had.

"I can't believe it," said Charlotte, swearing under her breath. "I was right there when he took it."

"You saw him steal the Cerulean Queen?"

"Not exactly. But I came upon him right after and followed him down the stairs to the Costume Institute exhibition. If only I'd been a few seconds earlier, I might have caught him in the act and stopped him."

"That's terrible. But it's not your fault."

"It's someone's." Charlotte didn't meet Annie's eyes.

Annie shrank back, stung. Did Charlotte mean it was *her* fault? Maybe it was. If the moths were some kind of diversion for the theft—and it was too much of a coincidence to think they weren't— then she was definitely at fault. She'd probably be put in jail, or at the very least fired for her actions.

Charlotte turned to walk back from where they came from, but Annie stayed put, staring hard into the darkness of the tunnel. "Wait, I think I heard something."

"It's probably a rat scurrying around. The man is long gone by now."

Annie ventured forward a couple of steps. "I'll wait here, you go get the guards."

"I'm not leaving you here alone, Annie. Don't be ridiculous."

Annie stared into the darkness, her eyes refusing to adjust. "I swear—"

Suddenly, a figure emerged like a rocket out of the pitch black. A man. He swung a bowling-ball bag at Annie's head, but she ducked in time, falling back against one of the cages. With his other hand, he shoved Charlotte hard and sent her sprawling to the ground, face-first.

As the adrenaline surged through Annie's body, it was as if time slowed down. She scanned him from head to toe: His shirt collar was open, and a silver pendant around his neck blinked in the light. His eyes were dark brown and almost lashless; his hair dark, curly, and short. He gave off a musky, animal scent, and the look on his face was one of fury and violence.

He stared at Annie, breathing heavily. She was trapped and he was twice her size. But then Annie's hand fell upon the handle of the dagger that poked out of the cage. As he began moving toward her, she yanked it hard, and to her surprise, the blade slid out easily.

The man registered the weapon with wide eyes, taken off guard. Annie did the only thing she could think of.

The scream came from deep in her belly, a terrifying, massive sound that she'd never made before in her life. It sounded like something a cornered animal made, ungodly in its pitch, echoing against the tunnel walls and hurting her own ears.

The man took a step back, turned away, and disappeared into the darkness.

Charlotte was shuttled off to be seen by the museum's medical staff after Annie scared off the attacker, insisting to the guards who led her away that she was fine, just bruised. Annie, meanwhile, was marched upstairs to the mezzanine level and planted in a chair in the security office under the watchful eye of a man who introduced himself as Mr. Fantoni, the Met's chief security officer.

"The fence barrier deep inside the tunnel had been clipped," reported one of the guards to Mr. Fantoni. "It appears that's how the thief escaped."

"We need to check the entire tunnel system under the building and make sure it is fully secure," said Mr. Fantoni. "There's no excuse for this, absolutely none. We'll also need to perform a search of the entire museum. It's going to take all night, so let's get all hands on deck. It's possible the thief left the statue in a public area and plans on returning later for retrieval, so keep your eyes peeled. First and foremost, make sure that fencing is secured."

Billy stood in one of the far corners of the room, his face ashen. It was awful that they were going after him, too, that Annie had dragged him into this nightmare. He'd only been trying to help when he let her go through security with the box. And now his job was probably on the line, just for being a nice guy. When she caught his eye, Annie mouthed, "I'm so sorry." He gave her a wan smile in return.

"In the meantime," continued Mr. Fantoni, "no one is allowed to leave the building without a thorough search of their belongings. What are the approximate dimensions of the statue?"

The guards looked at each other, unsure.

"The Cerulean Queen is around five inches in width, height, and depth," answered Annie. "About the size of a large grapefruit."

"Don't you work for the Costume Institute?" asked Mr. Fantoni, checking his notes.

"I do, but I visit the Egyptian Art collection all the time. The Cerulean Queen is one of my favorites."

Mr. Fantoni looked up at his staff. "It may be that the two events of this evening—the stolen statue and the moth incident—are related. That one was a diversion for the other."

"Charlotte and I had the same thought," said Annie. "About the events being related." Maybe if she was as helpful as possible, she wouldn't get in trouble for her part in releasing the moths. "That the moths pulled the guards away from the gallery with the statue so the thief could steal it."

"Where is Miss Cross now?"

"Getting examined by the medics."

Mr. Fantoni studied Annie closely, like he was trying to decide something. Maybe being helpful wasn't the best idea. "How long have you worked here at the museum, Miss Jenkins?"

"I started last week."

"I see. A recent hire. And how did you get the moths in the building in the first place?"

Billy stepped forward. "It was me. I'm sorry, sir. I let Annie take the box in. I was told they were butterflies. But she'd never do anything like this on purpose."

"Billy, I'm disappointed in you," said Mr. Fantoni. "Did you inspect the box? Or even question why it would be a good idea to bring a flock of butterflies into a museum?"

"A kaleidoscope."

The tall figure of Mrs. Vreeland breezed into the room. Annie turned around in her chair and offered up a hopeful smile. At the very least, now Annie had someone who could attest to the fact that Annie had been just doing her job.

"Sorry?" said Mr. Fantoni.

"That's what a collective of butterflies is called," Mrs. Vreeland declared. "A *kaleidoscope*."

"Thank you, Mrs. Vreeland, for that."

Mrs. Vreeland turned to Annie. "What on earth were you thinking?

I simply don't *understand* how this could have happened. An absolute travesty, that's what it is, an absolute travesty."

Annie squirmed in her chair. "I did what you told me to do. Not moths, of course. But butterflies. For the VIP tour."

"I never told you anything of the sort."

Annie's heart turned to lead and she struggled to speak. How could Mrs. Vreeland deny it? Had she forgotten their conversation in her apartment? Or was she trying to dodge being blamed? But Mrs. Vreeland was forthright to a fault and known for her trap-like memory. "You did," said Annie. "You said, 'There simply *must* be butterflies! Hundreds of them, a dizzying kaleidoscope of shape, pattern, and color.' You wanted the room to feel like it was taking off, flying, like the dancers on the stage." Annie had memorized the wording scribbled in her notebook.

"For God's sake, that doesn't mean *literal* butterflies, Annie. I meant for the lighting effects to *mimic* butterflies." Mrs. Vreeland looked around the room, her small dark eyes scrutinizing the faces of those assembled. "Does anyone here think I meant literal butterflies?"

The security officers shrugged their shoulders in response.

"But that's what you said . . ." Annie's voice trailed off. Nothing was going right.

Mr. Fantoni came around from behind his desk and sat on the edge of it, staring down at Annie. "Even if you did misinterpret what was asked of you, you brought moths instead."

"I didn't know, I swear," replied Annie. "The box said butterflies. There must've been a mix-up."

Mrs. Vreeland threw up her hands. "But I didn't want real butterflies, just the *illusion*."

"Yes, we get that," said Mr. Fantoni. "Please, let me finish with my questions."

Mrs. Vreeland crossed her skinny arms over her chest. "Fine."

"Now, Annie, where exactly did you get these insects from?" asked Mr. Fantoni.

"The Museum of Natural History. The curator's name is Jonathan Scarborough."

"I know Jonathan, let's get him on the phone right now!" demanded Mrs. Vreeland. "Call the operator, ring him at home." One of the security officers disappeared into the other room.

Annie glanced over at Billy, who looked like he was about to be sick. Her dream job had turned into a nightmare, and she was dragging Billy down with her.

Mr. Fantoni was quickly connected to Jonathan Scarborough. They spoke briefly before Mr. Fantoni hung up the phone. "It turns out someone called Mr. Scarborough this afternoon and asked for moths instead of butterflies. They had already rounded up the butterflies, so they switched them out and put the moths into the same box. He said it was a woman who called." He paused. "She identified herself as Annie Jenkins."

Annie blanched. "But it wasn't me! It was someone pretending to be me. I wasn't any part of the theft, not on purpose, at least. If I was, why would I stick around long enough to get caught?"

What little fortitude she had left began to ebb. They were going to charge her with being part of a crime, and she had no way to prove the truth, that she wasn't involved.

The attacker's menacing expression loomed in her mind's eye. Even though Annie lived in New York, where muggings were commonplace, she had never been assaulted before. It was probably because she was tall and broad-shouldered, making her a less compelling victim. Tonight, for the first time in her life, Annie had been physically threatened, certain that she and Charlotte were about to be killed, but no one cared at all. She remembered the horrible look on the man's face as he lunged at her, and tried not to cry.

"Enough!"

Charlotte sailed into the room, followed by Frederick. "Why are your harassing this poor girl?" she said.

"We aren't harassing anyone," said Mr. Fantoni. "We're trying to find out the facts."

"The facts are that you ought to be scouring the streets of New York for a man carrying a bowling-ball bag with a valuable antiquity inside. Not making some poor kid cry."

She was standing up for Annie, which no one ever did. She believed in her.

"I have to explore all of the possibilities, Miss Cross," protested Mr. Fantoni.

"I was there. I saw him right after he stole it and followed him all the way to the storm drain. That's the man you want."

"Of course, and we're in the process of doing exactly that. But Miss Jenkins here sure made it easy for him to escape." He paused, looking at Annie again, as if by staring at her long enough, she'd break and admit to whatever it was he suspected her of. "And I want to know why."

CHAPTER EIGHTEEN

Charlotte

The security department of the Met reeked of perfume, aftershave, and cigarettes. The perfume came from the wiry figure of Mrs. Vreeland, and the other odors from the dozen or so security officers squeezed into Mr. Fantoni's office. Annie was crouched in a wooden chair surrounded by interrogators, her pretty dress wrinkled and dirty and her face blotchy and tearstained.

Charlotte glared at the assembled crew. "I was there, I saw how she reacted. We were in fear for our lives. She somehow got her hands on a seventeenth-century Indian dagger from the storage bin—you might want to check and make sure the other caged artifacts aren't as easy to gain access to while you're at it—and scared him away. If it wasn't for her bravery, I don't know what might have happened."

"Are you all right, Charlotte?" asked Mr. Fantoni. "You weren't hurt?"

"I'm fine." Her palms still stung from landing face-down, but that was the only lingering effect. She'd told the medical staff that she was slightly bruised from the fall. They'd shone lights in her eyes and checked her pulse before letting her go. She'd come upon Frederick in the Great Hall, where lines of exiting partygoers snaked all the way around the information desk as security guards painstakingly inspected each guest and their belongings on their way out.

Mrs. Vreeland excused herself. "I must see to my remaining guests. Apology letters must go out first thing in the morning, and it appears that I will be writing them all myself." She frowned at Annie.

Annie squeaked out "I'm sorry" before the woman stepped out of the room like a Russian tsarina heading to the firing squad.

Mr. Fantoni turned back to Charlotte. "Charlotte, can you tell us what the man looked like?"

Charlotte's mind went blank. She could envision his hulking figure, but when she tried to imagine his face, it was all a haze. "I didn't get a good look at him, unfortunately. He pushed me from behind and then I fell to the ground."

"He was tall," said Annie, "with dark eyes and thick brown hair, cut short. He wore a dark suit, no tie, the collar open. There was a funny silver necklace around his neck. Like a cross, but with a small circle at the top."

Charlotte recognized the shape immediately. "An ankh. The Egyptian symbol of eternal life. Which means he might be Egyptian."

Charlotte caught Annie's eye. It was all connected: the missing file, the missing statue, and the broad collar—she was sure of it.

If only she had a way to prove it.

Charlotte stood at the top of the steps to the Met, looking out into the black night. Around her, party attendees were still filing out, chattering to each other about what had happened, looking shocked and slightly weary.

"Charlotte."

Mark was halfway up the steps, his tux peeking out from beneath his trench coat. She let him fold her into his arms and buried her head in his chest. Her stupidity—leaving her file on her desk where it could be easily snatched up, allowing the Cerulean Queen to be plucked from under her nose, going after the thief and putting not only herself but also Annie in danger—flooded back. It had been a disastrous evening.

"What's wrong?" he asked. "And why is everyone leaving? I thought this thing carried on late into the night. I was hoping to surprise you."

She brushed away her tears and looked up at him. "It was a nightmare. A thief stole one of our most important pieces, and when I confronted him with another employee, he went after us."

"What? Are you all right? Did you get hurt?" Mark held her arms and looked into her face, then glared up at the building as if he were going to run inside and punch someone.

"I'm fine. We're both fine."

"Who's 'we'?"

"A young girl who works for the Met Gala." She blinked back tears. "And my Hathorkare folder was stolen. Three years of research. Gone."

"Stolen? By who?" A vein in Mark's forehead pulsed.

"The same thief, I'm guessing, took the file and left a threatening note for me to stay out of his business."

"What business is that?"

"I was looking into the provenance of a new piece that's on display. A loan. I believe it was stolen."

"Are the police involved?"

"The security team is working on it, along with the director."

"Why didn't you tell me about this?"

His questions were becoming overwhelming. All Charlotte wanted was to go home, get out of her dress and into sweatpants, and curl up on the sofa. She needed time to think about what had just happened and what she should do next. Tonight, in the basement, it was as if the Hathorkare curse had arisen once again to punish her for being part of the discovery of the broad collar, for having held it in her hands. For having loved the man who tried to take it away from the land of its origin. Her head spun with long-lost memories.

Mark sighed. "I'm sorry for not being here. I should've been."

Charlotte stayed silent for an extra beat. "How is Lori doing?"

"We worked on the audition, and she was excellent, a natural. I think she has a chance at this, believe it or not."

"Great." The word came out flat, bordering on sarcastic, even though she hadn't meant to say it that way.

"Look, I understand it's been a tough week," said Mark. "But I assure you, Lori is a good kid. I'm willing to give her a little slack and I hope you will as well."

"It seems to me you're giving her a lot of slack."

"How do you mean?"

Charlotte's rage from the events of the past hour funneled into her resentment of Lori, the words tumbling out as if of their own accord. "She's not accountable to anyone. She throws her laundry in the washing machine and leaves it there for two days. She's rude to me and her mother, but then gets super sweet when you're around."

"It's hard to explain, Charlotte, but she needs some room to express herself right now, even if it's not in a way that we approve of." He was speaking in his professorial voice, as if she were one of his Theater Arts 101 students. "Maybe because you aren't a parent, you don't understand what it's like."

If she'd been a dog, she would've snarled. "Be careful, Mark."

"What? I'm doing everything I can to make peace between these two women I love very much. I know this isn't what we expected when you moved in with me, but Lori is my daughter, she is part of the package, which maybe you don't understand having never had a child of your own. I'm just asking you to ease up a little."

For years, people had looked at Charlotte with a polite sympathy after asking if she had any children and learning she did not. As if they were the keepers of some secret that she would never be privy to, as if she were less than them because she didn't have a son or daughter in her life. Or they'd make a patronizing show of being jealous of her independence and freedom, a cover for the fact that she did not fit into the world as they saw it. A single woman, especially back in the 1940s and 1950s, was an aberration, considered barren. With the onset of the '70s, conventional wisdom had eased slightly, but that was mainly for the younger set. At the age of sixty, Charlotte was past redemption.

It was time. She was tired of keeping secrets from the people close to her, especially Mark. Mark, who only wanted the best for her and who didn't give up when she pushed him away or closed down.

"You're wrong there," she said.

"I'm wrong about what?" asked Mark.

"I *was* a parent. For three months."

Mark went white. "When was this?"

"In Egypt. I was married as well."

She studied his face as he ran through the expected emotions: shock, then pity, then confusion. "Why didn't you ever tell me this?"

"I never told anyone. My parents knew, but they didn't want it getting out, and so once I was home, we acted as if it never happened." She paused, remembering Everett's abandonment. "I did tell someone close to me, once, but it was the wrong thing to do. I learned from my mistakes, I guess."

She wobbled slightly. Mark put his hands on her shoulders. "Let's sit down."

As the full moon slid behind the clouds, like it was seeking cover from the harsh stare of the earth, Charlotte told Mark about meeting Henry, their rushed marriage, and their delight at the birth of Layla. She glanced over at him once as she spoke, but the pain reflected in his face forced her to look away, keeping her eyes trained on the plaza in front of them. She spoke of Layla's sweet nature and how she'd enjoyed being a mother, even if it came at the expense of her ambitions. How Layla's mouth formed a surprised O whenever Henry sneezed. About how hot it was in the Valley of the Kings but how cool the interiors of the tombs were. She spoke of her last night as a mother and a wife, of the ship's sinking, and the surprise she felt when the broad collar tumbled out of Leon's suitcase. Of Layla crying for her in Henry's arms.

"I never saw either of them again. Presumed drowned. I should've never gone to the Valley of the Kings, I should've stayed in Cairo. Or I should've gone back to New York earlier, for God's sake. What on earth was I thinking?"

"You were in love. And you loved your work."

"I put my baby in terrible danger."

"You couldn't have known. And it sounds like Henry put you both in danger, to be honest, that last night."

"It didn't make sense, our leaving in such a rush. I remember wondering why Henry was so anxious to get out. Looking back, I can see that he and Leon were up to something suspicious, and maybe they used the Polish withdrawal as an excuse to get out of the country themselves. Or perhaps he was covering for Leon. No matter what, inside one of Leon's suitcases was the broad collar that was supposed to be in the Egyptian Museum. The same one that just turned up at the Met."

"Are you sure?"

"Absolutely."

"How did you escape the ship?"

They were dancing around the true tragedy. But it was all connected.

"I was trapped, stuck under these heavy wooden deck chairs, and I insisted that Henry take the baby to the top deck. Leon had stayed to help free me when suddenly the ship tilted the other way and the chairs slid away, but at the same time the water came at us so fast I couldn't grab on to anything." She took a couple of deep breaths, steadying herself. "The next thing I knew I was enveloped by dark water. Without the life vest, I would've drowned for sure. I yelled for Henry, over and over, but the ship had disappeared, and after ages the captain of a nearby boat heard me and picked me up. My voice was almost gone by then, I didn't want to leave the water in case they were still out there, but they dragged me back to land."

"Thank God. What happened once you were at shore?"

"To be honest, I went mad. To the point where I did nothing but cry and sleep. They took me to a hospital and held me there. I tried to ask about Henry and Layla, but there were very few survivors. Their bodies were never found. They said the Nile is unforgiving, in that way."

"I'm so sorry, Char." Mark's eyes were red. "I had no idea."

"My parents insisted I not speak about it. It was easier that way."

"But that's terrible. You had a baby, you are a mother."

"When I got back to New York, Mr. Zimmerman took me on at the Met part-time, I reenrolled at college, got my degree. It was easier to pretend none of it happened, that it was simply a nightmare I left behind when I left Egypt."

"Yet the broad collar survived."

"Yes. Which makes me wonder about everything else I was told. If Leon survived, maybe Henry did, too? What if . . ."

She couldn't finish the sentence.

"Who was the man on the phone earlier?" asked Mark.

"His name is Tenny Woods. I hired him to track down the current owner of the broad collar."

Mark regarded Charlotte as if he were staring at a stranger. Which, in a way, she was.

"I'm sorry for not telling you," she offered.

"No, that was your past, your history, to honor as you needed to. I'm not mad or upset that you didn't tell me, I hope you understand that."

"I do." He was saying all the right things and handling the news quite well, so far. But Charlotte knew from experience that the initial response didn't always stick.

He made a small sound and tapped his knee with his hand. "Lori's baby picture. Of course."

"Sorry?"

"The one on our bedroom bureau. You always angle it in a particular way, and then I adjust it back. But you move it so you can't see it when you're in bed, is that right?"

She'd just confided in Mark the biggest secret of her life, shocked him to no end, and broken his trust by withholding her past. And yet he'd recognized that she'd moved the silver frame ever so slightly so as to avoid seeing Lori as a three-month-old baby because it reminded her too much of Layla at that age.

He understood that the smallest act revealed the most.

With that, she began to sob. Whatever happened in a week or a month or a year was out of her control, but for now, she wept the tears of a newly grieving mother in his arms.

CHAPTER NINETEEN

Annie

Annie took a few deep breaths of cold air to steady herself as she exited the museum. The guards had searched her handbag on the way out even though the act was futile; the man with the Cerulean Queen was somewhere far away by now. It hurt to think of the empty pedestal, and she knew that Charlotte Cross was one of only a few people in the world who felt the loss as much as she did. Maybe that was why they'd both taken off after the man, fueled by their mutual outrage.

Charlotte had tried to stand up for Annie, but in the end, Mr. Fantoni refused to back down. "The thief got away unharmed, dagger or no dagger. Depending on where we go from here, the NYPD or the FBI may want to question you," he'd said to Annie before finally dismissing her. "You are not to set foot in the museum in the meantime, and trust me, I'm keeping my eye on you."

Annie was in big trouble. Until they caught the thief, she would be under suspicion. She began to make her way down the steps but stopped when she noticed Charlotte huddled in conversation with a man about halfway down. Their heads were almost touching, and the man's arm was around her shoulders. Whatever was going on was intimate and she didn't want to encroach. Instead, she stayed to the far left side, concentrating on each step so she didn't fall.

"Oh, I'm sorry."

In the darkness, she'd almost run right into someone else sitting on the stairway. With a start, she recognized Billy, his blazer carefully folded across his lap, his slicked-back hair shining in the dim lamplight. She imagined him carefully combing it back earlier that day, knowing that it would be a big night, wanting to look his best, and her heart broke for him. For both of them.

"Annie. Hey." He looked up and gave her cheerless smile.

"Not in any rush to get home?" she asked.

"Nah." He stared out at the taxis surfing down Fifth Avenue. "I don't really want to have to tell my parents and my uncle that I'll be losing my job any day now."

She turned to him. "I'm so sorry, it's all my fault. If only I'd understood what Mrs. Vreeland meant in the first place. Or didn't mean. I'm an idiot."

"Hey, I didn't get half of what she was talking about up there. It was like listening to another language. Maybe I'm too stupid for this job."

"No, you're not. You were only helping me out. And keep in mind the real villain is whoever switched my request from butterflies to moths. Someone was out to get me. You got caught in the cross fire, and I'm sorry for that."

"The guard's job is to inspect all packages going in and out. I screwed up."

"Because I distracted you."

When he turned to look at her, she expected his eyes to be filled with anger and blame, but he just looked tired. "Yeah. Because you looked so pretty."

Her insides melted. No one had ever said that to her before. That kind of compliment was usually reserved for her mother, not Annie. They looked at each other for a moment; then Annie broke the silence. "Will they definitely fire you for this? It seems drastic."

"The security guards are part of a union, so I do have some protection. It will take them a few weeks to sort it all out. Or not."

"What would you do instead?"

"Well, I'm not going to apply to get my bachelor's degree anymore. What's the point?"

"You mean you won't try to be a technician?"

"Who would hire me, after this?"

"Maybe the union will help you explain everything and you'll be able to stay on at the Met."

"That would be great. I guess we'll see."

Annie wondered what would happen next for her. She imagined herself locked in a jail cell, barraged with questions from the FBI that she couldn't answer.

On top of that, she wasn't allowed back in the museum, and the thought devastated her. To no longer be able to wander the halls and revel in its history lessons would be a bitter loss. None of the other New York museums, grand as they were, even came close. But then again, having to pass by the empty pedestal for the Cerulean Queen and be reminded of her part in its theft, even if it was unintentional, would be awful enough.

She said goodbye to Billy, looked up at the glorious facade one last time, and headed out into the dark night.

Annie steeled herself before opening the front door to the apartment. The lights inside were blazing, which was odd. She'd expected it to be pitch dark, the only sound her mother's sobs from the bedroom.

What a pair they made: Annie, unable to keep a job for more than a week, and Joyce, unable to keep a man for more than a month. How did other people in the world manage to keep up the momentum? They got jobs, got promoted, met someone, got married. She and her mother were stuck in some loop where they would never be free from each other. In twenty years, nothing would have changed. Joyce would be making the rounds of the local bars like some washed-out Tennessee Williams heroine, and Annie would be making ends meet by cleaning the townhouse upstairs for whoever bought it after Mrs. H died. It was pathetic.

She'd been given the chance of a lifetime and blown it. Not only for herself, but she'd brought Billy down with her, which made it so much worse. She should've known a job like that of assistant to Diana Vreeland was beyond her capabilities. Her education was lackluster, her knowledge of the wider world even worse. It was amazing she'd lasted a day. Still, she hadn't imagined the fact that she'd been able to do well, for a time. Maybe if she'd gone to one of the fancy private schools on the Upper East Side, she'd have known right away that the butterflies were a metaphor, and not done such a stupid thing as letting loose fabric-eating insects in a clothing exhibition. She flushed in embarrassment, just as she had when Mrs. Vreeland rebuked her in the security office.

Inside the apartment, the radio softly played classical music and there was a strange aroma in the air. She found Joyce in the kitchen wearing an apron over her dress, removing something from the oven.

"Mom?"

"Ah, Annie. Move the kettle, will you?"

Annie lifted it off the stove and Joyce carefully set down a baking pan. Annie leaned in and sniffed. Joyce had made banana bread. The very idea left her speechless. Her mother hadn't done anything like that in ages.

"When I got home, I noticed there were some bananas that had turned, so I threw this together," said Joyce with a wink. "I figured you might want a bite after running around all evening after Diana Vreeland. Are you hungry?"

She was. Starving, in fact. She hadn't eaten a thing since breakfast.

She sat down at the counter and watched her mother as she peeled off the oven mitts and carefully cut a slice. The bread hadn't had enough time to cool and fell apart on the plate. Normally, that would have sent Joyce into a sea of tears at her incompetence, but she only laughed as she passed the clumpy mess over to Annie. "It's too hot, wait a minute for it to cool down. How was the gala?"

"Um, fine." Annie didn't trust this version of Joyce one bit. There was a chance she was overplaying the mother role, holding herself together in the face of another breakup as long as she could before the mask disintegrated and she either threw the entire tin of banana bread across the room or crumpled to the floor in sobs.

"Tell me, who was there I would know?"

"Diana Ross. The mayor." Annie's mind went blank. Not that it mattered, as her mother was barely listening to her, instead softly humming along with the music. "How was your night?"

"Oh, grand."

Joyce reached around the back of her apron and untied it, then folded it carefully into a square. She laid it on the countertop, one hand lingering on top of it. Only then did Annie understand what was going on.

A large opal sat atop her mother's ring finger, the milky white stone glinting with hints of iridescence.

"What is this?" she asked, looking from the ring to her mother's face and back to the ring.

"Brad proposed!" Joyce jumped up and down like a child and held out her arms. Annie slid from behind the counter and gave her a hug, jumping a little bit with her, as that was what Joyce seemed to want them to do. "We had dinner, and I was waiting for him to tell me the bad news—that his mother was sick and he had to fly home, or his job was sending him to Timbuktu—all the kinds of things I've heard before. But he just kept talking about how he'd never met anyone like me before. How much he loved New York and that he was going to quit his job and come live here. And then he got on one knee and the waiters brought over champagne. You should have seen it, it was glorious! Everyone clapped and congratulated us, and they even gave us a free dessert!"

"Wow."

"Brad gets me like no one else does. We just understand each other, it's hard to explain."

"Wait, you said that he's moving here?"

"That's the best part. He's flying to Nashville tomorrow, getting his things, and driving back. He'll be here by the weekend."

"What about his job?"

Joyce waved her ringed hand in the air. "He said he can get a job anywhere. He's in sales, it's no big deal."

"Where will he live?"

Joyce turned to the sink and began running the water. "Oh, you know, wherever makes the most sense." She put on a pair of plastic gloves and poured dish soap into the mixing bowl.

"What does that mean?" Annie didn't mean to be firing off so many questions, but none of this sat right.

Joyce scrubbed the bowl with a sponge, a dreamy smile on her face. "Here, I figured. I mean, why not? He said he doesn't have many things, so it'll be an easy transition."

Annie squeezed into the tight corner of the kitchen near the sink so her mother couldn't avoid her eyes. "How are the three of us going to live here? The two of us barely fit as it is. Am I supposed to sleep on the couch? And what about his clothes? We don't have enough closet space. I can't believe you've done this without talking to me beforehand."

Joyce tossed the sponge in the bowl and yanked off the gloves. "I knew you couldn't be happy for me. Now that I finally have what I wanted, you're jealous."

"Jealous? Of the fact that some stranger is going to quit his job and move in with us? How much do you really know about him? He sounds like a freeloader if you ask me." She glanced down at the ring. "An opal? Aren't you worth more than that?"

"I love opals, and he knew it. That's why he chose it."

Annie had never heard her mother profess a love of opals. She was so desperate to have a husband that she was willing to twist herself into whatever version of herself he wanted her to be. "I can't believe you're okay with him moving in with us."

"Well, he's not, not really."

"You just said he was. By next weekend, no less."

"Not with *us*. With me."

Annie was too shocked to speak at first. "What about me?"

Joyce sucked in her cheeks. "You're a big girl now. You've got a job, you're making a decent salary. I figured you'd want to be like other girls your age and find some roommates, share a place downtown. That's what I did when I first started modeling, and it was great fun. You've been taking care of me for ages, now's the time for you to stretch your wings. You're free, finally. I thought you'd be excited."

"Excited to be tossed out of my home with less than a week's notice?"

"Sure." She didn't meet Annie's eyes.

All the resentments that Annie had kept shoved down so that she didn't set her mother off on one of her moods began to rumble to the surface. The way Joyce twisted around the reality of the past stung.

"For years I've been making sure we had enough to eat, taking care of you through your moods and your men. I thought the plan was for your boyfriend to buy an apartment where we could all live together?"

"Things change. Please, Annie, I have to make this work."

"Why? Why can't we stay the way we are? He can move here, get his own place, and you can take it slow. Why trust a guy who's willing to quit his job so fast? Makes me wonder if he had one in the first place."

"I don't know how you can say that since you've never even met him."

All the signs pointed to a disastrous end. No doubt this Brad was a deadbeat who wanted a free place to stay in New York while he figured out his next move. Little did he know what he was getting into. The two of them would sink into an abyss that would leave Joyce helpless and vulnerable, and Annie wouldn't be around to save her. "I've never met him because you refused to introduce me. Because you didn't want him to know that you had a grown daughter."

"A grown daughter who should be out of the house by now, living on her own."

"If I'd left, how would you have been able to manage?"

"That's not the point," Joyce dodged. "You have a job, there must be coworkers from your fancy museum job that you can reach out to for a place to crash, even if it's temporary. Or friends from school. You really should be with people your own age."

"I don't have any friends, and you know why? Because I was working two jobs to keep us afloat."

"I did my best—"

Annie cut her off. "And let's be honest, the real reason you don't want me here is I'm a reminder of how old you really are."

She wasn't expecting the slap across the face. Her mother had never hit her before, not even when she was a young girl. Joyce recoiled in horror as soon as her hand left Annie's cheek. "I'm sorry, darling."

Annie should've known this day would come, when her mother would toss her out on the streets all in the name of setting her free. Not to mention the fact that she didn't even have the fancy museum job anymore. But there was no way she was going to confess that to Joyce and watch her try to conjure up the appropriately sympathetic expression when underneath she'd be panicking at the thought of Brad arriving to find Annie planted on the couch.

Annie had nowhere to go, and no landlord would take her in if she was jobless.

For years she'd thought she was being a good daughter by propping up Joyce on her down days, when in fact she'd lost valuable time, thrown it away, by being her caretaker.

In the bedroom, she filled a suitcase with clothes and toiletries. If her mother wanted her out, she'd go, and let Joyce live with the consequences.

Annie quietly let herself in to Mrs. H's front door using her key. What she needed to do would only take a few minutes. A lamp burned on the narrow table in the front hallway, the one Mrs. H always left on to deter burglars.

But as soon as Annie closed the front door behind her, footsteps sounded on the creaky second-floor landing.

"Mrs. H, it's just me, Annie," she said quickly. "I'm sorry to wake you."

From the top of the stairs, Mrs. H pulled her glasses down her nose. She wore a high-necked Victorian nightgown, and her gray hair was tied up in a ribbon.

"What are you doing here? What time is it?"

"I'm sorry. I need to get the money I saved up. I wouldn't bother you if it wasn't an emergency."

Mrs. H slowly made her way down the stairs, clutching the banister. "What could you possibly need it for this late?"

"I need a hotel room, I guess. And then I need money for food and stuff."

"You and your mother had another row?"

"Something like that. I'm on my own, now."

After Annie had stormed out of the basement apartment, she'd waited for a moment on the sidewalk, hoping in vain her mother would follow and usher her back inside, apologize for the squabble. But she was no longer her mother's focus. Not that she ever was.

"At least wait until morning," said Mrs. H. "Your mother will come around."

Annie's skin prickled with shame. "Please. I need the money now, or I wouldn't be here."

Mrs. H ushered her inside and waved her into the kitchen, where Annie settled into the same chair she had last time. Mrs. H put on the kettle. "Now tell me what's going on."

"There was a mix-up at the Met Gala tonight. I won't be working there anymore."

"Well, I'm sorry about the job. I can only imagine what it's like being at Diana's beck and call."

No matter how much of a mess it turned out to be, Annie didn't regret that she'd taken the job. The joy of rushing around town, doing errands and being part of a team, was like nothing she'd ever experienced before. "It was wonderful, for a time. But on top of that, my mother got engaged and so I have to find a new place to live."

"How about this? You stay here for a bit. You can take the spare room on the third floor."

"I couldn't impose on you."

"I'm not letting you out this late, it's not safe, and you're dressed in a way that will garner the wrong kind of attention."

Annie looked down at her dress, the one that she'd put on not five hours ago with such hope. The hem was dirty and her feet hurt and her mother had just chosen a man over her own daughter. Tears streamed down her face at her predicament, as well as the unexpected kindness that Mrs. H had shown her.

"Now, don't cry. Think of it this way: You're free."

She wiped her eyes. "Free to do what?"

Mrs. H waved her hand in the air. "Anything. You're healthy and young, go out there and make some noise."

"But I don't know what to do, or how to go about it."

"Excuses. Tonight, you'll take the spare room and get some rest. Tomorrow, you can make me breakfast and start fresh. Think about what you want to do next."

"I want to fix what I screwed up. I screwed up badly. And not just my life, other people's lives as well."

"Now, now. Stop being dramatic. You're just a kid. You're *supposed* to screw up at your age. You still have plenty of time to make things right. When you're my age, it's too late. Too late to apologize because the people you screwed over are dead."

Annie had never heard Mrs. H speak so bluntly, and she couldn't help but laugh. "Oops. Sorry."

Mrs. H let out a giggle. "That's terrible of me, isn't it? Well, it's true. Then, and only then, is it really over. So stop grousing about how tough you have it. When you're eighty, you can grouse."

She rose, picked up the cookie jar filled with Annie's money that sat on the counter, and planted it on the table. "Until then, get the hell on with it."

CHAPTER TWENTY

Charlotte

Look, Charlotte, I can't just show up at the Met and offer to pitch in to help recover the Cerulean Queen. That's not the way it works."

Tenny Woods placed his coffee on his desk as he removed his coat, eyeing Charlotte warily.

She'd turned up at his office at eight thirty after a sleepless night. Once she and Mark had returned from the Met, he'd gone straight to bed while she'd retreated into the dining room to try to piece together the strange series of events from the evening, eventually crashing on the living room couch, her mind whirling. She knew Mark had wanted her to join him, but his need to protect and understand her, while comforting at first, was also suffocating. She didn't have all the answers to his questions, and before she could help it, her natural evasiveness kicked in.

At the same time, she couldn't figure this out alone. She hoped Tenny Woods might be able to help. Right now she needed to do something material. Take action.

"I would think the Met would want as much assistance as they can get," she said. "The Cerulean Queen is a major piece in the collection." Her explanation of last night's events was disjointed and confusing, no doubt, but Tenny appeared to understand the basics: Charlotte had received a threatening note and one of her important files had gone missing, possibly taken to stop her from asking any more questions about the loan's provenance. On top of that, a valuable statue had been stolen, possibly by using a diversionary tactic involving moths. A lot of "possiblys." It all sounded as insane to her as it probably did to Tenny, who took multiple swigs of his coffee as she spoke.

"The Met has its own security team, they'll reach out if they need me," he said.

"What happens next? Do they go to the press?"

"What happens next is they'll notify the New York Police Department and the NYPD's Property and Recovery Squad. They may contact the FBI as well."

"What would you do, if you were in charge?"

He considered the question. "If my priority was to recover the statue, I'd go to the press, as well as alert the National Antique and Art Dealers Association. But there's no promise that will work. The rates of recovery for this kind of crime are less than ten percent."

Less than ten percent. The more often the statue changed hands—as the thief pawned it off to an unscrupulous dealer, who then sold it to a discreet client, who sold it to some unsuspecting collector—the less the chance of tracking it down. The odds weren't good.

Tenny looked through the notes he'd been taking. "This girl, Annie Jenkins, the one who set off the moths, do they suspect she's part of the crime ring?"

"They do, but I disagree. She was terrified, and I don't think she was pretending."

"What makes you believe the missing file and the threat are related to the theft?"

Now that she was asked that question point-blank, Charlotte had a hard time coming up with an answer. "It's just too strange that it all happened at the same time. I'm convinced that it has something to do with the events in Egypt in '37. With Leon and Henry."

He tapped a couple of fingers on the desk. "Huh."

No doubt Tenny thought she was projecting her own tragedies onto what was happening today, and maybe he was right. But if Leon was still alive, anything was possible. Charlotte's past was threatening to swallow her up whole and ruin everything she'd worked for and accomplished. There was one concrete clue that Charlotte had gleaned from the evening's events, though. "Annie Jenkins said the man who attacked us wore a pendant with a cross with a small circle at the top."

"An ankh?"

"Yes."

Tenny straightened. "Interesting." He shuffled the papers on his desk, looking for something. "The past few years I've been following the movements of an underground organization that's focused on repatriating Egyptian art that it believes has been illegally acquired by other countries."

"Right. I've read about them. They're known as Ma'at, named after the Egyptian goddess of justice."

"Exactly. No one knows who they are, but so far they've 'repatriated' two minor antiquities from a couple of smaller museums. If this latest job is one of theirs, it means they've learned from their past crimes and are upping their game." He found what he was looking for. "These are some of the newspaper articles that were written about the crimes." He handed her a small stack of clippings, stapled together.

"Do you mind if I take these with me, look through them?"

"Go right ahead."

"Do you think Mr. Fantoni is familiar with Ma'at?"

"I would hope so."

"What else is known about them?"

"I was curious, so I did some more digging, and your former colleague Leon Pitcairn has bragged about being associated with Ma'at. It can't be confirmed, of course."

Her theory that all the recent events were connected wasn't inconceivable. Then again, she wouldn't put it past Leon to brag about something that was completely untrue. That was the kind of man he was. "I see. Anything else I should know about Ma'at?"

"They're based in Cairo. No one knows the size of the organization, or who exactly is involved. But there is one thing we do know." Tenny paused. "They're dedicated to their cause and very, very dangerous."

Charlotte wasn't even sure where to begin when she returned from her meeting with Tenny and sat down at her desk at work. There were budgets to be reviewed, memos and letters to be responded to. In the meantime, rumors about last night's insect invasion and theft were making the rounds of the staff offices, and the murmurs and whispers threw off Charlotte's focus.

Instead of tackling her inbox, she took Tenny's newspaper clippings from her handbag and read through them. The international theft ring known as Ma'at had hit two European museums in the past couple of years: the Petrie in London and the Kunsthistorisches in Vienna. Neither was as famous as the Met, but both held an extensive array of objects from the time of the pharaohs, many of which could be considered the rightful property of Egypt, having been spirited away before any kind of governmental regulations were in place. The robbers had used diversionary tactics to lure the guards away from their posts before striking, and in one instance, a guard had been killed. As Tenny had warned her, this was a dangerous crew. A crew that Leon was possibly involved with.

Charlotte set down the clippings and stared at the empty space where her research file on Hathorkare would normally be. The loss was more than academic; it tore at her heart, and now she was off-balance. The article was supposed to have been the pinnacle of her life's work in the field of Egyptology, but that wasn't the only reason she had spent countless hours on the project. She'd wanted to give Hathorkare the acclaim she deserved, show the world what a woman could do when she was given a chance. How thousands of years ago a female had led an enormous, complicated country through an era of artistic creativity and economic prosperity, ordering ambitious building projects—including a sprawling memorial temple and a pair of ninety-seven-foot obelisks—and enriching its citizens with gold, incense, and ebony by expanding Egypt's trade network.

If the file wasn't returned, would Charlotte have the energy to spend another three years gathering up evidence to make her case? The threatening note implied that she would get her research back if she stood down. But why would they even bother? It was nothing to them but a pile of photographs, papers, and scribblings. Her precious file was probably in the back of some garbage truck by now, on the way to a landfill where it would decay in the sun next to oily pizza boxes and crumpled soda cans.

Hathorkare deserved to be celebrated, and Charlotte was the one to have led that celebration, to have their names linked together. Not anymore.

What if her uneasiness from last night—that this was all related to the Hathorkare curse—was true? While Charlotte hadn't been directly responsible for taking the broad collar out of Egypt forty-one years ago, she had associated with those who had attempted to. Maybe instead of being killed like Henry, she was being toyed with, the one project she was most excited about—the one that might finally put her on the same level as, if not higher than, the other Egyptologists of her generation—vanishing before her eyes. Could an ancient pharaoh do such a thing? Charlotte rubbed her temples with her fingers, doubting her sanity.

Tenny had advised her to wait and see how the Met handled the case, but she didn't have the patience.

Frederick was hanging up the phone when she entered his office.

"What's the museum going to do?" she asked without any preamble.

"I just spoke with Mr. Lavigne, and for now we're going to sit tight, see if a ransom note shows up."

The worst possible decision, in her opinion. Charlotte dug her fingernails into her palms to keep her voice even. "Is this coming from Mr. Fantoni? He didn't seem like the wait-and-see type."

"It comes from the board. They had an emergency meeting earlier this morning, and I assure you, they're connected with the best security and legal minds around."

It was hard to tell if the board was following protocol, or if they preferred to keep the news mum for now. Especially as the theft had happened on the same night as they were throwing a massive party, the place bursting with drunken strangers—not a great look. The moth incident was all over the papers, which was bad enough, but so far the theft hadn't hit the news.

"I understand their rationale, but do you worry that they're wasting valuable time?" asked Charlotte. "That piece is on its way back to Cairo right now, I'd bet on it. Whoever took it didn't do so for money."

"We can't know that."

"What about the threatening note I received? It was left by someone with access to our offices, someone who knew what would hit me the hardest, keep me quiet. That's not a long list."

Which included Frederick.

Frederick, whose renowned expertise on Saukemet II would have been repudiated by Charlotte's revelations about Hathorkare.

Frederick held up his hand. "At the moment, the focus is on recovering the Cerulean Queen, so keep your composure and take a back seat for now. I know you don't want to hear that, and I know how hard you worked on the Hathorkare project, but I beg you to let the experts do their job."

"What experts? Did you know there's a ring of thieves focused on repatriating Egyptian antiquities?"

"Ma'at? Yes, I know of them."

"The Cerulean Queen would be the perfect target for one of their heists, and they used diversionary tactics in their first two thefts. Does the board know about that?"

"I have no doubt they do. But my hands are tied, Charlotte. I have to let this play out with the board and Mr. Lavigne, no matter how frustrating it is to the rest of us. There's a methodical and thoughtful approach that we simply must follow. They may have information we don't, and we have to respect that."

Charlotte was being constrained, and she hated that feeling more than anything. She worried that everyone was stalling right when they ought to be taking action, doing something bold.

Deep down, though, she knew that the thefts of the Cerulean Queen and her file, while devastating, were not the true reasons for her edginess.

The truth was out there. The truth about how the broad collar necklace ended up in New York, and the truth about what really happened the night the steamship went down. Charlotte had survived. Leon had survived. She had to know for certain what happened to Henry and Layla. That came first.

Which meant, for now, Charlotte wanted out. Out of the politics of the Met. Out of the gutting loss of her research and the missing Cerulean Queen. Out of New York.

And there was only one place she needed to be right now. The country that had swallowed her innocence and spit her out, breaking her heart and her spirit. For so long she'd been trying to ignore the past, to move on from it. But the events of the past twenty-four hours changed all that.

It only took her a few seconds to make up her mind. "I'm going to Egypt," she said. The words came out gravelly, like she had sand in her throat.

"I'm sorry. What did you say?"

"I have to go. To Egypt."

Frederick gave a small half smile, like she must be joking. "Don't be silly."

"I'm sorry to leave you with so much going on, but it's important to me for personal reasons."

Frederick's half smile turned to a panicked grimace. "Well, it's important for me for personal *and* professional reasons that you stay right here and help me manage the Tut opening. This is no time to travel to the other side of the world; in fact, it couldn't be a worse time. This is your job, Charlotte."

She rose to go. "I'm sorry."

Frederick's face had gone bright red. As he became more irate, she grew more composed, more confident in what she'd decided.

"If you go now," he said, "I can't promise what will be here when you get back. Including your position."

Charlotte would be jeopardizing everything. But there was no other choice.

It had to be now.

Charlotte walked out of the museum, still stewing over her conversation with Frederick.

No doubt part of the reason he was so upset was that he recognized how integral Charlotte was to getting anything accomplished in the Egyptian Art collection. Frederick tended to be more concerned with wining and dining possible donors than managing the staff, and her absence would only make that more obvious. But maybe it was time for him to learn the hard way how often she covered for him.

She decided to walk across the park instead of taking the bus, as she needed time to think before she shared her plans with Mark.

"Um, hi, Charlotte."

She looked up to see Annie Jenkins in her red jacket. She had deep circles under her eyes, and her shoulders were hunched as if she might crumple to the ground at any moment. She stood awkwardly in front of Charlotte in the weak November sun, shifting her weight from foot to foot.

"Hi, Annie. What are you doing here?"

"I was waiting for you. Since I'm not allowed inside." She looked forlornly up at the building like it was a lover who'd jilted her.

"I'm heading west. You can walk with me if you like."

"Okay." They started off. "Is there any news about the thief?" Annie asked.

Charlotte shook her head. "Nothing new from last night."

"Thanks for standing up for me. I really appreciate that."

"Sure. It was a scary experience, and I didn't like the way they were hounding you."

"That meant a lot." She matched her strides to Charlotte's. "The man with the necklace, you think he's Egyptian?" Annie asked.

"I really don't know. There have been some thefts by an Egyptian organization called Ma'at, and that may be who's behind this one as well." Charlotte explained briefly what Tenny had told her about the group.

"What will they do with the things they stole?"

"That's a good question. If their goal is to bring them back to their homeland, to Egyptian soil, they'll have to keep them hidden for a long time before they can be displayed. That is, if they could ever be displayed at all, without the authorities being summoned and an international law tribunal ultimately deciding their fate." It curdled Charlotte's insides to imagine the Cerulean Queen, which had reigned gloriously in the Met galleries for over fifty years, locked away in some dark storeroom, hidden from the eyes of the public and the study of researchers. If that was the case, what did it matter whether it even existed or not?

A heartless question.

"If there's anything I can do to help, let me know," said Annie. "I want to clear my name."

"I'm leaving the country, actually. On my way to my travel agent now."

Annie's face fell. "Where are you going?"

"Egypt."

Her mouth opened to a wide circle. It was extraordinary, the way her expression revealed exactly what she was thinking. The kid was an open book. "To track down the thief?"

"No, for personal reasons."

Charlotte's plan was to locate Leon and speak with him in person. That was the only way to get answers, by catching him off guard and forcing him to tell her how he was alive, how the broad collar ended up at the Met instead of at the bottom of the Nile, and what he knew about what happened to Henry and Layla.

"Is that safe?" asked Annie. "What if the thief is back in Egypt as well?"

Charlotte remembered Tenny's remark about Leon, that he might be associated with Ma'at. It was a risk she was willing to take. "It's a big country."

"Are you going alone?"

"That's my plan, yes."

"Do you need an assistant? I can come. I have money saved, so I can pay my own airfare." The girl was like a puppy that had been yelled at too many times, cowed and desperate for connection.

"I really don't think that's necessary. But thank you for offering."

Annie was quiet for a moment. "When were you last there?"

"Ages ago."

"When exactly?" Annie spoke in earnest; she actually wanted to know the answer.

"I was last there in 1937."

Charlotte might as well have said it was the 1500s, from the shock on Annie's face. "Wow. I'm sure it's changed a lot. You might want someone like me on hand to be there for you, you know, because . . ." She trailed off.

"Because I'm old?" Charlotte laughed. "Sixty isn't old. I'm just getting started, believe me. You're what, twenty?"

"Nineteen."

"When's the last time you've been abroad?"

"Never."

"Seems to me you're the one who would need assistance, in that case. Cairo would eat you alive."

"Then it's settled, we'll go together."

Charlotte had to give Annie credit: She was an obstinate one. "No. That's not what I said. Let me put it this way: Do you have any experience with antiquity theft? Any familiarity with Arabic?"

Annie stopped and faced her. She was a few inches taller than Charlotte, and her cheeks were pink from the cold. "The jobs I had before working for Mrs. Vreeland were waitressing and housecleaning. So no, on both counts. But I'm the only one who can identify the thief. What if you run into him?"

Charlotte was about to launch into an explanation when she remembered she didn't owe Annie Jenkins anything. After all, Annie Jenkins was the one who'd convinced Diana Vreeland to use the broad collar. At least Frederick had had the sense to secure it in a locked vitrine in the Egyptian Art collection first thing this morning.

"Look, you've been through a lot," said Charlotte. "We both have. But we're not in this together. What happened last night was terrible, and I'm sorry you got caught up in it, but let's let the police and the museum's security team do their job."

Annie began to speak, but Charlotte cut her off. "Thank you, but I think you should head home now."

Then she turned and walked away. She had enough to deal with, and taking care of Annie Jenkins was not part of her plan.

"You've got to be kidding."

Mark paced along the length of the dining table as Charlotte collected a notebook and pens, as well as her camera, and stuffed them into her carry-on bag. On the way home, she'd stopped by the travel agency and booked a ticket on a flight to Luxor connecting in Cairo that left the next evening, knowing if she waited too long her resolve might falter.

"I'm dead serious," she replied. "I have to find out for myself what happened, how Leon survived, and how the broad collar was recovered."

"Thanksgiving is in two days. What about our Thanksgiving plans?"

They usually hosted Thanksgiving for any of Mark's students who couldn't go home. It was always a merry crew; she wouldn't be missed. "I'm sorry about Thanksgiving, I really am, but you'll have Lori here to help out."

"What about the art theft expert you've been talking to? Why can't you send him?"

"Tenny? Because this isn't about the theft. It's about what happened to me back then. Leon could lie and Tenny wouldn't know it. I know how to confront Leon, what to say and how to say it."

"I'm coming with you, then. We'll cancel Thanksgiving."

Charlotte shook her head. This was something she needed to do alone. "You have to stay here with Lori. How did her audition go, by the way?"

Mark's tone brightened slightly. "She got a callback."

"That's great. When's the next audition?"

"Don't try to change the subject. What if you wait until Christmas break and we both go then?"

"I can't wait that long."

He let out a long, frustrated sigh. "You're not telling me everything, are you? I thought we'd had a breakthrough last night, on the steps of the Met. But you're already putting up walls. Your evasiveness is going to be the end of us."

"Please, Mark." She hated leaving him like this, but he'd never understand her reasoning. He'd never lost a child. "I promise I'll be careful, and I'm sorry I can't explain it to your satisfaction. I need you to trust me on this, that I know what I'm doing and that I'll be back and it'll be just like it was before."

"Where you keep secrets and I'm wondering what you're thinking half the time?"

She was disappointing him. Again. Maybe it was better for her to be alone than to be with a generous, kind, smart man who wanted nothing more than to connect with her in a way that she couldn't reciprocate. It was doing neither of them any good, and he deserved better. The thought made her heartsick.

"What does Frederick say about this?" he asked.

"He's not happy."

"So you're putting your job at risk by heading to Egypt on a whim? Look, you've just been through a traumatic experience. Now's not the time to be making rash decisions."

She zipped up her bag. "Now's exactly the time. For too long I've been pretending the past never happened. I have to face it or I'll go mad, and I have to do it now."

Lori appeared at the doorway, looking concerned. "Is everything all right?"

"Hey there," said Charlotte. "I'm going abroad for a while, so you'll have to be second-in-command over Thanksgiving. I understand you got a callback, is that right?"

Lori's face brightened into a smile, perhaps one of the first smiles Charlotte had seen her make since she'd arrived. "I did. It's right after Thanksgiving."

"I'm sure you'll do well," said Charlotte. "Break a leg, kid."

Thanksgiving Eve, Charlotte settled herself into her window seat on the flight to Cairo, hoping she'd be able to get some sleep. As the last of the other passengers filed onto the plane, she leafed through the articles Tenny had given her as a way to calm herself down.

She couldn't believe she was on a plane to Egypt, that she'd made it this far without the trip being thwarted by a loved one dying or some terrible aviation tragedy. It was very possible she was putting herself in harm's way by flirting with the curse so brazenly, testing whether or not it existed. Helen might think it was superstitious nonsense, but Charlotte knew better. Anything could go wrong, she had to be prepared for the worst.

"Um, hi."

Charlotte looked up and froze.

A young woman smiled nervously down at Charlotte, hitching the strap of a backpack over one shoulder as a flight attendant slammed shut the last of the overhead bins.

Annie Jenkins was coming to Egypt after all.

CHAPTER TWENTY-ONE

Annie

After Charlotte walked away from Annie in Central Park, Annie had waited a little and then followed her from a safe distance. On Broadway, she loitered inside a doughnut shop until Charlotte finished up her business at the travel agency, and then darted in, saying she was Charlotte's assistant at the Met and that Charlotte had asked her to reconfirm the date and flight number.

Armed with that information, she collected her money from the jar in Mrs. H's kitchen, grabbed her passport from the small desk in the basement apartment where her mother stored their important papers, and then, for the second time in her life, walked into a travel agency, where she paid in cash for an economy-class ticket on a flight to Luxor that connected in Cairo, leaving the next evening.

Charlotte needed her; she was certain of that. Just as her mother had needed Annie, and Mrs. Vreeland had as well, for a short while. Annie would make herself indispensable to Charlotte, who was far too old to be flitting off to a foreign country alone. While Charlotte said she was going for personal reasons, the timing was too convenient. Surely she was hoping to retrieve the Cerulean Queen, and since she had no idea what the thief looked like, Annie would be able to help in that regard. Then, Annie could clear her name and be allowed to return to the Met, even if it was only as a visitor and not as Mrs. Vreeland's assistant.

She was taking a huge risk, and when she saw Charlotte's shocked expression on the plane, the recklessness of her decision hit with full force. She quickly slid into her seat, in the row just in front of Charlotte.

"What on earth are you doing?" hissed Charlotte, leaning forward.

Annie twisted around so she could see a sliver of Charlotte's face between the seats. "I thought I might be able to help?" she answered, her voice rising with doubt.

She didn't mention that yesterday a pair of men in suits had shown up at the door of the basement apartment. Joyce had been out, and Annie began to shake as she watched from behind the curtain of Mrs. H's living room as they waited for someone to answer. It reminded her of the night the men in suits brought the devastating news of her father's death: the solemn looks on their faces, the way they spoke to each other in hushed tones.

Eventually, the two men left, but Annie knew they'd be returning soon. Just as Mr. Fantoni predicted, Annie was wanted for further questioning. The thought terrified her.

As the jetliner rose into the air, Annie gripped her armrests and closed her eyes tight, overwhelmed by the loud piercing screech a huge metal tube filled with people made as it strained to fight gravity. She was grateful that Charlotte was seated a row behind and so didn't have to witness her panic at being on a plane for the first time. When the aircraft gave a strange shudder during their ascent, she yelped.

"It's just the wheels retracting," said the man seated next to her. "No cause for alarm."

She whispered a thank-you and spent the entire flight distracting herself with the travel guidebook and the history of ancient Egypt that she'd bought earlier that day, figuring she should learn everything she could if she was going to be of help.

When they finally landed in Cairo, Annie's relief at being back on the ground was short-lived. They had to run to make the flight to Luxor, which left no time for conversation, and the smaller plane turned out to be even louder than the one they'd just taken, more skittish in the air, but at least the flight only lasted an hour and a half. By then, her mouth was dry and her eyelids drooping. The jet lag was like nothing she'd experienced before; thoughts floated into her head a few beats behind their normal speed, and her body felt vulnerable and weak. Charlotte, meanwhile, read through some archaeological journals the entire flight and, after they landed, headed to the exit at a brisk pace.

"I'm sorry for showing up unexpectedly," said Annie as Charlotte tried in vain to hail a taxi.

Charlotte spoke without looking at her. "I don't know how you figured out where I was going and when, but I don't appreciate you sneaking around like that. When I said you weren't invited on the trip, I meant it."

Taxi after empty taxi passed by them, instead pulling over for male passengers who were waiting a little farther up the curb.

"What on earth is going on?" said Charlotte under her breath.

"They don't want to pick up two women," said Annie. She marched off the curb and stood in the middle of the road, one hand outstretched, palm out. The next cabbie who approached honked his horn and waved for her to move, but Charlotte was quick to the punch, opening the back door and sliding in before Annie joined her as well.

"Well done," Charlotte murmured. "We're going to the Winter Palace Hotel," she said to the driver.

The cabbie stared at them in the rearview mirror before nudging the gear shift into drive. "You wives of archaeologists?"

"No," answered Charlotte. "Why would you think that?"

"All the foreign archaeologists stay at the Winter Palace. When their wives visit, they stay there as well."

Annie couldn't help herself. "She's not a wife, she *is* an archaeologist. A curator for the Met Museum's Egyptian collection, in fact. In New York City."

Charlotte gave Annie a curt shake of the head.

"Ah, I see. Good for you, then." The driver didn't speak for the rest of the trip.

Annie settled into her seat, amazed she was over five thousand miles from New York. Her queasiness began to wear off as a dry wind blew through the open windows. They passed fields green with clover before entering the city, situated alongside the eastern edge of the Nile. Somewhere nearby was the Valley of the Kings, where King Tut was discovered.

"Thank you for agreeing to let me stay," she said. "I'm ready to help out."

"I haven't agreed to anything. I may dump you at the airport tomorrow. And I'm not sure you're qualified to do much of anything." Charlotte fiddled with the crank for the window. "Do I remember you telling me you cleaned toilets before working for Diana Vreeland?"

"I worked as a maid, yes. But I've been taking care of myself and my mother for the past decade or so. She's—ill." It wasn't exactly untrue.

Charlotte looked at Annie square in the face for the first time since they'd landed. "I'm sorry to hear that."

"She's better now. Which is why I'm ready to try new things." Like find whoever stole the Cerulean Queen and clear her name, and Billy's. But Annie didn't say that part out loud.

"As I said. We'll see how it goes."

The Winter Palace, located right on the Nile, exuded a nineteenth-century charm and was where Agatha Christie penned *Death on the Nile*, according to Annie's guidebook. The hotel's cavernous lobby looked out onto a beautifully manicured garden and a large pool.

A woman wearing a headscarf and a badge that read "Fatima" welcomed them from behind the check-in desk. "How may I help you?"

"I'm checking in, and we'll need another room as well." Charlotte gave their names and handed over their passports. The clerk checked the hotel registry and studied the documentation, taking her time leafing through Charlotte's passport and then Annie's, comparing their faces against the photographs. Annie could feel her eyelids getting heavy, and wanted nothing more than to take a long nap.

"You are from New York?" asked Fatima.

Charlotte nodded, and Fatima made a note in the registry.

"What do you do there?"

"I work at the Met Museum, Annie was recently employed there."

"Are you here for business or pleasure?"

"Pleasure," said Charlotte. "Seeing the sights."

"How lovely. We have many sights to see. Have you been to Egypt before?" The clerk didn't seem to understand that the last thing they were interested in was chitchat.

"Yes, many years ago," answered Charlotte.

Finally, they were handed two sets of keys for adjoining rooms, and the bellman rushed over to take their bags.

"Enjoy your stay," said the clerk. "If there's anything I can do to help, please reach out."

Charlotte gave Annie a room key and told her to get some rest. Outside Annie's window, the Nile lazed by on the other side of a street where old cars whizzed by donkeys pulling carts. On the sidewalk, a pack of skinny dogs sat panting in the midday heat under a palm tree. The air was suddenly filled with a rhythmic chanting, which Annie assumed must be the call to prayer. The guidebook had said to expect it five times a day, that observant Muslims would head to the nearest mosque or roll out a small rug at the sound of the call.

She had no sooner lain down on the lumpy bed and closed her eyes than she heard a very soft click, like someone was closing a door very carefully. Annie looked out the peephole of her door just in time to catch Charlotte walking by. She opened her hotel room door and stuck her head out into the hallway. "Charlotte?"

Charlotte jumped at the sound of Annie's voice, and her face was red when she turned around. She was obviously trying to ditch her. While every fiber of Annie's being wished to go back and crawl under the sheets to sleep off the fog of jet lag, if she didn't tag along, the only view of Egypt Annie would get was of the inside of her own hotel room. If she was going to clear her name, she'd have to make the effort.

"I'll come with you," she said brightly.

"You really don't have to."

"I insist." She grabbed her small travel bag from the table just inside her room and ran back out. "Where are we off to?"

Charlotte's mouth was a thin line. "I need to track down someone I used to know."

"An old friend?"

"Something like that. But I'll need to speak with him privately."

Annie agreed, and together they walked for about ten minutes until they reached a decrepit apartment building on a narrow street. Charlotte pulled out a piece of paper with an address scribbled on it—at the top was written "From the desk of Tenny Woods"—and double-checked that they were in the right place. Laundry hung from the balconies, and a gang of small children watched as Charlotte rang the bell on the front door. A shriveled woman opened it, looking annoyed, holding a broom in one hand.

Charlotte spoke to her in Arabic. Annie could only pick up the name "Leon Pitcairn" from the string of foreign-sounding words.

The old woman scowled and shook her head and slammed the door hard.

"Is Leon Pitcairn who you're looking for?" asked Annie.

"He is, and apparently, he's not home. But I'm not giving up that easily."

"Where to next?"

"The Valley of the Kings."

They took a ferry across the river, then a taxi that climbed up into the sandy hills marking the beginning of the Sahara Desert and the Valley of the Kings. Neither a tree nor a bush dotted the landscape; the sand whirled about; the sun was white and the sky yellow.

After passing through a rustic ticket office, they walked up the main artery of the Valley of the Kings, along with hundreds of sightseers. A peaked mountain rose in the distance, but instead of sloping gradually down, the bottom section dropped away in a series of cream-colored cliffs. According to her guidebook, these provided a natural barrier for the tombs, protecting them from the harsh desert environment. The only places offering shelter from the sun were the gaping tomb entrances, which had been slashed into the bellies of the limestone mounds with surgical precision.

"There are so many people," said Charlotte as a pair of tourists jostled their way between her and Annie. "The place is overrun with tourists, and the damage must be immeasurable. I would think they'd take measures to protect the tombs."

"The entry fees must help pay for the explorations, though," ventured Annie. "Are they still exploring?"

"Of course. The underground tunnels located so far are only the tip of the iceberg. Who knows what else is buried under our feet?"

A man selling water stood over by one of the tomb entrances. He offered up a bottle, and Charlotte took it, handing it over to Annie. As she counted out the coins to pay, she asked if he knew a man named Leon Pitcairn.

The man nodded.

"I believe he's a guide?" Charlotte added.

He nodded again.

"Is he here today?"

"No. Leon's taken some tourists to Abu Simbel," the man said. "He'll be back in two days."

"*Shukran.*" Charlotte handed over some more coins. From his smile, she'd tipped well. "Don't tell him I was asking for him, I want it to be a surprise," she said.

"Of course."

Charlotte turned and headed for the exit.

"What, we're leaving already?" said Annie. "We just got here. Isn't this where the broad collar was discovered?"

Charlotte paused. "Yes. It was here. I doubt the tomb's open, though, as it was pretty bare-bones."

"Is that a mummy joke?"

Charlotte almost smiled. "I can show you where it is," she said with what Annie detected was a hint of pride. "Follow me."

Charlotte stopped in front of a pair of tomb entrances located close together. Both were blocked with locked metal gates and solid-looking doors. She explained how when she first discovered it, the entrance had been completely hidden by rocks and debris, and how she'd come upon the first stone step, which led to another and another, until she realized what she'd found was an entirely new tomb.

Charlotte's strong reaction to the broad collar being included in the Costume Institute's exhibition now made sense. It wasn't just a pretty piece of jewelry; it was a part of history, and a hard-won part of history, at that.

"Excuse me, miss?"

A large man in a white robe approached. He nodded to Charlotte and pointed to the far side of the pathway. "My grandfather, over there, said he knows you and wanted to say hello. Pay his respects."

Annie and Charlotte turned to see where he was pointing. Four old men, also wearing robes, sat in chairs underneath a pair of umbrellas. One rose and beckoned them to come closer.

When the old man and Charlotte were only a few feet apart, he held out one hand, palm up. There was a large scar in the fleshy part between his thumb and forefinger. When Charlotte caught sight of it, her expression changed from suspicion to delight.

"Of course!" she said. "It's you."

"I recognized you even though it's been many years," said the old man.

Annie looked at Charlotte. "You know each other?"

"We met briefly, back in the '30s, when I was working on my first dig."

"This woman," said the old man, bowing his head, "saved my life after I'd been bitten by a cobra."

"I'm happy you're doing well, Mehedi," Charlotte said.

"Better than well. This is my grandson Jabari," he said, pointing to the younger man. "He's part of the council that oversees the running of the Valley of the Kings."

"It's all very different from when I was here last."

The two of them spoke for a few minutes, and then the man asked Charlotte if there was anything he could do for her.

Charlotte glanced over at Annie. "Can we see the tomb with the sarcophagus of Hathorkare's wet nurse?"

"It hasn't been opened in many years," said the old man. "But for you, of course. Jabari here will take you."

Annie tried to imagine coming to this strange country alone, working in the desert with snakes and scorpions lurking around every rock. Charlotte's steely nature made sense now, but whether it had been honed during her time here or she'd been born with it, Annie wasn't sure.

As Jabari fiddled with the lock to the tomb, Charlotte asked about Leon Pitcairn.

"No good, that man," Jabari said. "Charming, though. The tourists love him."

Once Jabari opened the doorway, he led the way, bending low, holding an industrial flashlight that illuminated two scary-looking eyes painted on either side of the otherwise bare walls. Eventually, the narrow hallway opened up into a larger room, the interior decorated with faded hieroglyphics.

"Jabari, would you mind shining the flashlight on that wall?" asked Charlotte, taking the lens cap off the camera that hung around her neck. He did so, and she snapped several photos, even though the paint on the wall was barely legible.

Charlotte took more photos, Jabari lighting the way. "I wish I'd taken more time to study these back in 1936," she said. "We were all so drawn to the broad collar that we missed the literal writing on the wall."

"What does it say?" asked Annie.

"I can't make it out, but I'm wondering if that's a depiction of Hathorkare," she said, pointing to a relief of a reddish figure wearing a headdress and kilt.

Annie had read about Hathorkare in her travel guide, a rare female leader who stole the throne from her stepson. "My guidebook says that the figures with red skin tones are men."

"Hathorkare was something of a chameleon. Several years into her reign, she began ordering the artists who carved or sculpted her image to add masculine traits to their depictions—reddening her skin tone, dressing her in a man's kilt, adding a false beard."

"Why would she do that?"

"So the public would be more inclined to accept her role as their divine leader. With every stone carving, every sculpture, she cemented her hold on the populace. Unfortunately, I doubt my camera will pick up any of this clearly, not without proper lighting."

"We can arrange that for another day," said Jabari.

As Charlotte took more photos, Annie looked around, amazed and slightly claustrophobic. Over by the far wall was a sarcophagus, and beside that some kind of bundle. Annie let out a loud squeal as a beam from the flashlight passed over it.

"Is that a mummy?"

The wrappings had partially come undone, so Annie could see the head—with actual hairs on it—as well as a thumb poking out of a skinny arm that lay across its chest. She backed away, one hand covering her mouth.

Charlotte, ignoring Annie's reaction, moved closer and knelt down beside it. She stayed there a moment, unmoving, like she was offering some kind of prayer.

Eventually, she looked up at Jabari. "I always believed this was Hathorkare."

"It's hard to say," answered Jabari. "They moved the mummies around all the time, trying to keep two steps ahead of the plunderers. You can't be sure, there's simply no way to prove it."

Annie's curiosity got the better of her. "Why is the mummy outside the sarcophagus?" she asked quietly.

"There's another one already inside," said Charlotte. "The markings on the exterior of the sarcophagus indicate that it contains Hathorkare's wet nurse. The pharaohs and their wet nurses were often buried together, as wet nurses were held in high regard. It was an honor."

"So they were killed and buried with their charge? Some honor."

"They were already dead at that point. And yes, it was an honor. This one's sarcophagus was probably stolen, the mummy inside unceremoniously dumped on the floor."

"The queen Hathorkare was the one who usurped her stepson, right?" Annie said brightly, proud that she'd remembered what she'd read in the guidebook, as well as the fact that she'd used "usurped" in a sentence for the first time in her life.

"Enough chatter. This is a place of respect."

Embarrassed, Annie swallowed hard and stepped backward, toward the exit. She didn't want to be in this room full of death and decay anymore.

Her foot landed on something soft and crunchy. Looking down, she recognized it as some kind of animal, maybe a bird, with a long neck. She fell sideways, sticking out her hand to catch herself but still landing hard on her bottom. Jabari was there in a flash, but she waved him away, embarrassed and slightly sick, as a sprinkling of dust fell down from the ceiling. She coughed.

Charlotte pulled a tissue from her bag and handed it to Annie. "That's a mummified goose you stepped on. We prefer it if the objects in the tomb remain intact, going forward. You need to be more careful."

Charlotte's reprimand was the last straw, and Annie didn't have the strength to fight the wave of self-pity that washed over her. She was a tired, confused, and unemployable nineteen-year-old, without a home or a job, who had just fallen over a mummified dead goose in a scary hole in the ground. She'd been an idiot to follow Charlotte to Egypt, as she was completely out of her element, just like at the Met. Wherever she went, she left a trail of damage and destruction.

"Fine, I'll leave you to it," said Annie, wiping her face and shaking the dust out of her hair as she rose to her feet.

"Hold on a second." Jabari pointed to the place on the wall where Annie had made contact as she fell. "What's that?" A square stone had come loose.

Charlotte dropped to her knees and began gently pulling the stone out. "The other object we found in here was in a hidden niche. This might be another, it's definitely loose. I thought we checked every inch of the walls back then, but over the years this one must've eroded."

"Maybe we should get someone to come and look at this?" Jabari suggested. "Someone with the proper tools?"

"No, I've got it," said Charlotte.

Jabari crouched beside Charlotte and shone the light as she worked. Behind the rock was an opening about the size of a milk crate. Inside, Annie spied several pieces of broken pottery and a dilapidated wooden box about twenty inches tall that appeared to be intact.

"A canopic box," said Charlotte.

"What's that?" asked Annie.

"Canopic boxes and jars were where the organs of the mummies were stored. They were entombed with the mummy." She gasped as the flashlight picked up a row of symbols roughly carved into the wood. "This is Hathorkare's cartouche. Her name is on it, clear as day. Which means . . ."

"That this might actually be her," finished Annie, looking back at the mummy lying on the floor.

Jabari spoke up. "Nothing else must be touched or moved, not until we've alerted the Egyptian authorities."

Just then, more dust began to fall from the ceiling. Jabari rose to his feet, looking up, his eyebrows knit together. "We should probably get out of here."

"But the niche," said Charlotte. "There might be more inside."

"We don't have time for that. Let's go." He began herding Annie and Charlotte out. Annie was just about to step into the long hallway that led to the exit when she heard a rumble, not in the tomb itself, but on the other side of the wall, right above where the niche was located. Something had come loose, was about to collapse. She noticed Charlotte glance back at the box sitting in the niche, tears in her eyes. Without thinking, Annie darted back, reached inside the niche, and grabbed the box with both hands as Charlotte cried out for her to stop.

A second later, several large stones fell right where the box had been sitting, obliterating the shards of pottery that had been scattered on the ground and creating a massive cloud of dust.

The three of them sprinted for the exit, the dust storm following close behind.

Annie eagerly gulped in the fresh air outside the tomb. As she'd run, she'd tucked the box under one arm and used the other to cover her nose and mouth, not that it had done much good. She was coated with dust, as were Charlotte and Jabari. Annie handed Charlotte the canopic box, and they both paced back and forth, coughing, while Jabari called out in Arabic to the staff nearby; some ran over with bottles of water, and others scattered, presumably to get more help.

"What about the mummies?" said Charlotte once she'd taken a few swigs of water. "We have to get them out, make sure they're safe."

"We'll need to make sure the tomb is secure first," answered Jabari. "The change of air pressure when a tomb is reopened or a new section discovered can make it unstable."

Charlotte turned to Annie, her face full of concern. "If you hadn't grabbed the canopic box, it would have been demolished. Why did you do it? You put yourself in danger."

"I could see how badly you wanted it. Are you going to look inside?"

Charlotte shook her head. "It's sealed. They'll need to run it through a CT scan machine."

"What's that?"

"A new technology, only been in use for about five years. With it, they can see inside something without having to open it. Like X-rays."

"That's cool. Does the fact that the box has Hathorkare's name on it prove that the mummy with the crossed arm is your lady pharaoh?"

"I'm afraid not. But it's better than nothing. If the mummy is still intact, that is."

By now, several men in hard hats had ventured into the cave to assess the damage as Charlotte and Annie, as well as a group of tourists, watched. They eventually reemerged and spoke with Jabari, who turned to Charlotte with a smile. "The only damage was in the niche. The rest of the tomb is stable, for now, but we'll be extracting everything that's inside over the next couple of days. We don't know how long it will hold up."

"Can I get inside to take more photos?" asked Charlotte.

"I'm afraid not. Only trained personnel allowed."

"Damn." She looked longingly over at the tomb entrance. "Everything else will go straight to the Egyptian Museum?"

"Of course."

Charlotte handed him the canopic box. "This needs to be sent there as well."

"Who exactly was this Hathorkare lady?" asked Annie as they walked away.

Charlotte looked up at Annie with a huge grin on her face. "Come with me. I'll show you who this Hathorkare lady was."

They left the Valley of the Kings, winding around the hills until they reached a massive temple three stories high. The limestone cliffs behind it had eroded into irregular shapes, so that in the late-afternoon sun it appeared as if dozens of crudely carved, ghostly figures looked down on the temple, watching over it, protecting it. Charlotte and Annie followed a ramp to the second level, where Charlotte explained that this memorial temple had been built by Hathorkare, who it turned out wasn't a nasty usurper at all, according to Charlotte's research, but a smart, savvy leader who didn't get nearly enough credit for her contributions to Egyptian culture and government.

Annie turned in a slow circle, taking in the terraces and porticos and the hundreds of columns, many of which still had the likeness of the female leader carved into them. As Charlotte spoke, the macabre creature in the tomb was transformed into a woman with eyes lined with kohl, dressed in white linen, her arms covered in gold bracelets and her fingers adorned with rings, striding across the promenade, giving orders and overseeing the construction of her grand temple.

With Charlotte's words, a long-dead, long-disdained woman was brought to life.

"Thank you, Annie, for going back for the canopic box. I know I've been a beast, but I'm glad you're here with me."

"I'm glad I'm here as well." It had been the most exciting, surprising day of Annie's life.

Then, in a low voice, Charlotte confided to Annie the true reason for her trip to Egypt. That she'd been married before. That she thought her husband had been killed in a boating accident on the Nile, which she herself had narrowly escaped. That a colleague— Leon Pitcairn—had been with them and was also thought drowned, lost, along with the broad collar. Which was why Charlotte had been so stunned to see it on display at the Met, and why she had decided to come to Egypt to track down Leon, who was rumored to have ties to a criminal organization called Ma'at.

There was more to the story, Annie could tell, from the way Charlotte's voice cracked as she spoke.

But Charlotte didn't offer and Annie knew better than to press.

CHAPTER TWENTY-TWO

Charlotte

Charlotte hadn't expected to confide in Annie. She also hadn't expected the crazy swells of emotion that arose in her as they drove in the cab from the airport. She was stunned that she'd made it all the way to Egypt, having been convinced for the entire length of the transatlantic plane ride that they might plummet into the ocean any minute, or that the pilot would have to turn around and return to the New York airport due to a technical difficulty. As the sun had swept up from the horizon and painted the buildings of Luxor a soft pink, she'd found herself inhaling sharply, remembering all the times she and Henry had walked these streets. The spice store stood on the same corner; the vegetable market was opening for business, same as it had four decades ago. Probably the same as it had four centuries ago. The city was infused with her past, the way a lover's scent lingers on a pillow.

She remembered vividly what it had been like to arrive here as a nineteen-year-old. Confused, uncertain of her place in the world. But eager to please. So eager to please. While her skin might be more wrinkled and her stamina not what it was, being back on Egyptian soil made it impossible for her to deny that she still was that same raw, vulnerable person, and the thought rattled her deeply.

Maybe that was why she hadn't walked away from Annie after they landed at the Cairo airport. Annie's desperate act was no different from Charlotte's. The haunted look in her eyes was perhaps partly from the trauma of being attacked in the basement of the Met—an attack that Charlotte could have avoided if she'd been thinking straight—but also something else, something deeper. They both wanted to escape the web of pain that New York represented.

The shock of being back in the tomb with the two mummies, and the near miss as the ceiling rumbled and the rocks began to fall, made Charlotte once again worry about the sanity of her decisions, as well as the possibility that the curse was still in play. But they'd made it safely out and rescued the canopic box with the cartouche, all thanks to Annie. Even if the box didn't prove a thing about the mummy on the floor and Charlotte's photographs turned out to be indecipherable, it was something to add to the story of Hathorkare.

As the sun set over the Valley of the Kings, it had been a relief to tell Annie of her prior time in Luxor, to say the name of the man she'd loved out loud. With each retelling, the painful memories subsided—ever so slightly—and Charlotte was able to cautiously acknowledge the harsh series of events that had shaped her life as a young woman. If only her mother had encouraged her to speak about her experiences in Egypt, maybe she wouldn't have lived the ensuing years in such terrible fear of losing someone else. It had been awful of her parents to insist she shut away that time of her life, but, looking back now, she understood that they were products of their era and had been frightened and shocked by her brash decisions. They'd done the best they could.

After an unexpectedly solid night's sleep, bolstered by the lingering effects of jet lag, Charlotte and Annie met up in the hotel restaurant the next morning for breakfast. Leon wouldn't be back until tomorrow, which meant the day stretched ahead of them. Charlotte dropped the film off at a nearby camera shop and returned to the lobby, where Annie was waiting, dressed in a white linen blouse and khaki-colored, wide-legged linen pants belted at the waist, looking as though she'd just walked off a film set about Egyptian explorers. Charlotte stopped herself from asking Annie where her pith helmet was.

"Last night I reread what my ancient Egyptian history book says about Hathorkare, and it's really dismissive," said Annie in between bites of toast. "Why don't they know what you do?"

"Because it's new information. Which unfortunately is no longer in my hands."

"What do you mean?"

"The night of the theft, someone took my file containing all the research I'd done. They left behind a threatening note, and I'm guessing it's related to the broad collar's provenance and the fact that I was asking about it."

"That's horrible." Annie straightened in her chair, her eyes sparking with anger. "Do you think it was taken by the same man we chased?"

"The timing would suggest it. But it doesn't explain how he got into the locked offices."

"An inside job."

"Hopefully the security team will figure that out."

"Yesterday, you said that Leon was associated with the thieves who stole the Cerulean Queen, is that right?"

"That's what I've been told. Of course, we don't have any proof that it's Ma'at that stole it, although the theft is similar to others they have committed."

"It's worth digging around, right?"

"I do think the stolen Queen and the reappearance of the broad collar are related. But we have to be careful. I've been warned that Ma'at is a dangerous organization, and no one knows exactly who's involved or how widespread their reach is. In any event, the first step is to talk to Leon, which we can't do until tomorrow, unfortunately."

The waiter poured them more coffee. "Well, what should we do today, then?" asked Annie. "My guidebook said that the Temple of Karnak is pretty cool."

"Funny you say that."

"Why?"

"The Temple of Karnak is where my Hathorkare theory begins." Charlotte described the destruction of the images of Hathorkare, and how the precise timing of the vandalization could be calculated by studying the subsequent pharaoh's renovations at Karnak. "In the file that was stolen, I had photographs from Karnak that backed up my theory."

"Then we have to go. You can start over."

Starting over. All those hours, lost. It hurt to think about. "That's futile. It took me three years to get to this point."

"So what? Instead of proving it now, you do it three years later."

"I'll be sixty-three then."

"And three years after that you'll be sixty-six. What does that matter?"

How nice to be young, thought Charlotte, with decades stretching ahead of you. But exploring Karnak was better than sitting around waiting for Leon to return.

They headed out into the bright morning sun. Outside the temple, they walked along the Avenue of the Rams, which was lined with over one thousand statues, a troop of sphinxes, rams, and ram-headed lions.

"When will the mummies and artifacts from the tomb be taken to Cairo?" asked Annie.

"*Bukra fil mish mish*," answered Charlotte.

"Mish what?"

"It means 'Tomorrow, when the apricots bloom.' Basically, it's the Egyptian way of saying they'll get there when they get there, don't hold your breath."

"But they'll eventually go on display at the Egyptian Museum?"

"Hopefully, yes."

"Why hopefully?"

"It's something of a shambles, the Egyptian Museum. To be honest, they'd be much better off at the Met. At least we have electricity, we can keep the temperature and humidity stable and ensure they don't get damaged."

"Last week, I heard some of the docents talking about the Benin bronzes in the same way. That they're better off at the Met instead of being returned to Africa."

"Right. Truly gorgeous pieces. Stolen from the kingdom of Benin by British troops in the 1800s and now scattered in museums around the world."

"But now the ruler of Benin wants them back. The docents were very upset that the Met's collection of bronzes might be spirited away."

"They're safer at the Met, for certain."

"But they were stolen. Shouldn't we give them back? Just like when we find the Cerulean Queen, we'll want it back, since it was stolen from the Met?"

"You can't compare the two. Benin doesn't even *have* a museum. What then, the bronzes get put into storage, completely out of the public's view?"

"What about all of the things in storage at the Met?"

Charlotte caught herself bristling. Why was she becoming so defensive? "We can't exhibit everything," she explained. "There wouldn't be a building large enough. And in any event, the question of the Benin bronzes is moot, as it looks like they'll have a deal in place to return them very soon."

A conversation from long ago drifted into Charlotte's memory, back when she and Leon had been on this very site, arguing about the obelisks, one of which had ended up in Paris. Charlotte had rued the fact that it had been taken away. It was strange how, after so many years working at the Met, her viewpoint had changed 180 degrees. Had she been just an innocent kid, like Annie was now, unable to understand the nuances of antiquity preservation and ownership as they existed in the real world? Or had she become jaded over time, developed an unwarranted proprietorship over the objects in her galleries?

Her galleries. That really said it all.

Charlotte spent a moment among the columns in the Hypostyle Hall, remembering her first kiss with Henry, before getting to work. The more she studied the erasures and compared them with the dates of reconstruction, the more a hesitant excitement crept through her. Hesitance because this was only the beginning, not the end of the project now, and she still didn't have the solid proof that Frederick was looking for, the reason why the erasures occurred in the first place.

But excitement because, even without the proof, she was even more certain she was correct.

The next day, it was time to track down Leon.

As Charlotte and Annie headed back to Leon Pitcairn's apartment building, they passed a grungy-looking open-air restaurant with mismatched tables and chairs spilling onto the sidewalk. The customers, all men, stared hard at the pair of women as they walked by. Charlotte doubted tourists often ventured this way. But one of the men glanced up and then quickly turned away, lifting a cup of coffee to his mouth. He wore khakis and a white button-down shirt, and Charlotte caught a glint of yellow on the pinky finger of his left hand. A ring made of yellow jasper, a ring Charlotte had seen before.

"This way," she said to Annie, maneuvering in between the tables to where Leon Pitcairn sat.

He put down his coffee and did a terrible double take. "Charlotte Cross? My God, is that you?"

She'd last seen Leon on a sinking ship, yet here he was, drinking coffee and walking the streets of Luxor like nothing had ever happened. Seeing him in the flesh was astonishing and strange, and she knew her face reflected that. Leon's professed shock, though, had an air of showmanship about it, as he loudly exclaimed his surprise and wrapped his arms around her before giving her a European-style double-cheek kiss. Charlotte introduced Annie as her assistant and took up his invitation to join him, gesturing for Annie to do so as well.

Leon's youthful good looks were gone. His high forehead was now a bald pate, the skin sagged under his eyes, and his nose looked like it had been broken a few times over.

"I thought you were dead," he said, twisting the ring on his finger. "I can't believe it's actually you."

"Imagine my own surprise when I heard you were still alive, kicking around the Valley of the Kings."

He regarded her with wary eyes.

"Let's stop with the games," she said. "I know what was going on back in '37. That you and Henry were smuggling antiquities from the digs out of Luxor, out of Egypt. Is that why we had to leave so quickly? It wasn't because of world politics, like Henry said."

For a moment it looked as if Leon was going to try to deny it, but Charlotte cocked her head at him in warning. "I'm sorry for what happened," he finally said. "It was a terrible night, a terrible time. And yes, Henry convinced me to set some things aside. We'd worked at the Egyptian Museum that summer, we knew what a mess the place was, that no one would notice. Why not get a little cash for all the trouble we took to pull these things out of the earth, digging away in the hot sun, melting day after day? You remember what it was like."

"From what I recall, it was the local Egyptian workers who did most of the hard labor. I don't remember seeing you lift a pickax."

"Henry said he wanted to take care of you and . . ."

As he trailed off, Charlotte spoke up fast, not wanting to hear the baby's name come out of his mouth. "You survived. How did you survive?"

"All those years swimming for Cambridge paid off and I made it to shore, somehow. I assumed you and Henry had perished, as hardly anyone escaped. It's truly astonishing to see you, really. In any event, I took it as an opportunity to turn my life around, eventually becoming a guide."

"After a stint in jail for smuggling."

Leon shifted in his seat. "You've done your homework."

"I have."

"Well, you've got me there. When I first got to Cairo, I changed my name to get the authorities off my back, did what I could to get by. But yes, I eventually got caught and paid the price. An Egyptian prison is not something you want to ever be inside, trust me on that. I learned my lesson, and now I take tourists around, charm the ladies, make the men think they're getting a look at the 'real Egypt,' collect my fee. It's not much, but it keeps me going."

"I know you and Henry took the broad collar that I found."

"That *we* found."

She ignored his correction. "It ended up in New York, on loan to the Met. How did that happen?"

Leon shrugged. "All I know is that it was in the suitcase that Henry was carrying. What happened next is anyone's guess."

"He's still alive." It was a statement, not a question. "Where is he?" She'd avoided this question until the last moment, knowing the answer could send her reeling. To anyone walking by, they looked like two people having a pleasant enough conversation, when in fact she would have enjoyed clawing the smug look off his face.

Leon licked his lips. "I have no idea. I assumed he died as well. Never heard from him again. Heck, maybe the broad collar washed up on shore and someone else nicked it. The curse lives on, it seems." He checked his watch. "I have to get to work, there's a dozen Swiss tourists waiting for me to reveal the wonders of the ancient world. It was nice catching up, best of luck to you, Charlotte. And to your pretty assistant."

Charlotte rose to go and Annie did as well. "You're despicable," said Charlotte. "Zimmerman trusted you, we all trusted you."

"I didn't work alone. Maybe you don't know the man you married."

The accusation cut to the quick, but there was something else to it, something that didn't fit.

Charlotte and Annie walked back to the main road, where Charlotte ducked into a store selling tunics and pulled Annie in with her. "Let's just make sure he's not following us," she said.

They pretended to peruse the offerings, and a minute or so later Leon hurried by, looking haggard, and boarded a bus headed to the ferry.

"He's lying about Henry," said Annie.

"You noticed that, too?"

"Instead of saying, 'Maybe you *didn't* know the man you married,' he said, 'Maybe you *don't*.' Present tense."

"I caught that as well."

The truth had come out, even with all of Leon's denials and evasions. Henry was alive, and her heart soared with hope that maybe, just maybe, their daughter was also alive. But that line of thinking would get Charlotte nowhere without tracking down Henry, and she wasn't any closer to the answer than she'd been before ambushing Leon.

"What curse was he referring to?" asked Annie.

"It's said that if you take something that was dear to Hathorkare out of the kingdom, you'll face the wrath of the gods."

"Then the shipwreck was Hathorkare trying to stop them?"

"I'm not sure what it was." She explained how the curse first came to light in the early 1900s, with the tragic deaths of the earl and his wife not long after they brought the Cerulean Queen to England. She also mentioned her aborted attempts to return to Egypt, which both times had ended in disaster. Charlotte waited, expecting Annie to offer some kind of platitude or repudiation, as Helen had done when she'd brought up the curse.

But Annie didn't question it. "That's awful. I'm so sorry."

In spite of the heat, a chill ran down Charlotte's spine. "Let's go back to Leon's apartment building, speak to some of his neighbors."

The landlady answered the door, scowling as she'd done the day before, but her reticence fell away when Charlotte offered her fifty Egyptian pounds. Charlotte's Arabic was rusty and the photo she'd brought of Henry from their wedding day was faded and wrinkled, but the old woman studied it carefully. The photo had been shipped separately in a trunk the day after she and Henry left Luxor, along with some hastily packed clothes and possessions, and was waiting for Charlotte when she arrived in New York. It had taken her six months before she could even summon up the courage to open the lid and look inside.

"Have you ever seen this man before, with Mr. Pitcairn, perhaps?" she said to the landlady. "He would be around the same age as Mr. Pitcairn."

The landlady pointed to Henry's face and nodded. "Big ears," she said in English. "It was a few years ago, I can't remember how many, a man with big ears like that and hair like that came looking for Mr. Pitcairn. I can't say if it was the same man."

A mixture of joy, fear, and confusion threaded through Charlotte. Henry had been here. But before she could ask another question, Annie began coughing. Charlotte turned to her. "Are you okay?"

Annie shook her head and leaned over, hands on her knees. The cough grew worse. "I need water," she finally said, her voice cracking. "The desert air, it's too much."

The landlady pointed behind her to a small room off to the left, where Annie disappeared from view. Charlotte found herself irritated at Annie for distracting the old lady at such a crucial moment.

She held up the photo again. "What was his name? Was it Henry?"

The woman shrugged. "I only saw him that one time. Mr. Pitcairn, he pays his rent on time, but I don't like him. I told my dear husband when he was still alive that I didn't trust Mr. Pitcairn one bit."

"What happened when you saw Mr. Pitcairn and this man?"

"They were shouting, making a terrible noise. The man was English, like Mr. Pitcairn." She wrinkled her nose, her disdain for the country obvious.

"What were they fighting about?"

"I don't know. My husband told them to stop yelling in the hallway, that they were disturbing the other residents, but Mr. Pitcairn refused to let the man inside his apartment."

Annie returned, her face red but the coughing fit over. "Sorry about that."

Charlotte ignored her. "What were they saying?"

"The man with the ears was warning Mr. Pitcairn." The landlady looked up at Charlotte with rheumy eyes and a determined look on her face. "He was telling him to stay away from his daughter."

After the landlady closed the heavy wooden door, the world spun around in circles, as if Charlotte were caught in a tornado. She looked up and saw a swirl of skinny palm trees and a grainy sky and tried to catch her breath.

Annie, whose coughing fit had immediately abated, guided her to a bench set back from the road. "Put your head down, try to breathe."

The landlady had spoken of a daughter. Where was Layla now? Why had Henry not tried to find Charlotte after the shipwreck? He had to have assumed she was dead, as Leon had. Perhaps he was ashamed of what he'd done, at the peril he'd put them all in. But she could have forgiven him; they could have been a family again.

Charlotte had always been reluctant to imagine Layla as a fully grown woman. In her head, she'd kept her as a baby or at best a young girl. Now she had to reconfigure everything. Including the fact that she was alive.

The questions kept coming. What was her daughter doing with Leon a few years ago that Henry was so worried about? Leon Pitcairn was sickly looking, his teeth stained and his breath foul—Charlotte couldn't imagine her beautiful daughter being romantically involved with a man like that, if that was what Henry's warning was about. The landlady could have been wrong, of course. Her eyesight wasn't very good, and there had to be more than one Englishman with big ears out in the great wide world.

Right before Charlotte and Annie had stepped off the stoop of Leon's apartment building, the landlady had added that the Englishman finished with a threat for Leon to stay far away from Cairo.

Perhaps Layla was only visiting Luxor when she saw Leon, and she lived in Cairo.

Charlotte had so many questions. She closed her eyes, trying in vain to shut out the madness and frustration, as the world spun once again.

CHAPTER TWENTY-THREE

Annie

After her conversation with the landlady, Charlotte had become alarmingly fragile. She took a few deep breaths as she rose to her feet, and Annie stayed close by her side as they walked back to the hotel, in case she had another spell.

Charlotte approached the front desk to see if there were any messages. The clerk was the same one they'd met on their arrival—Fatima—and she handed over an envelope from the director of the Egyptian Museum. Charlotte opened it right away. "He says congratulations for the discovery of the canopic box, and requests my assistance in overseeing the transfer of the canopic box as well as the mummies to Cairo," she said to Annie.

"When?" asked Annie.

"Tomorrow. Off to Cairo we go." Charlotte put the director's letter back in the envelope and turned to Annie. "I'll head up to my room and confirm the arrangements. Can you go to the camera store and see if the Kodachrome slides are ready to be picked up? I could use some aspirin as well, if you don't mind."

"Of course." Annie was pleased to be of service. She asked Fatima where the camera store was, and the clerk led Annie outside onto the hotel steps to best explain.

"Do you see the fruit stand on the next block?" she asked, pointing. The wind caught her headscarf, almost pulling it right off, but she readjusted it quickly. Judging from the gray traced through her hair, Fatima was older than Annie had first guessed. "Not the first fruit stand, but the one right after."

"I see it."

"Just beyond that is a narrow alley, and the shop's in there. If you blink, you'll miss it."

"Great. And is there anywhere to get some aspirin?"

"Further up the street, you'll see a pharmacy. It's not far." Fatima paused. "Is everything all right? Your mother didn't look well when she came in."

Annie almost corrected her, but then stopped. It was nice imagining a mother who would take her to faraway places and stand up for her the way Charlotte had done after the Met Gala. "She's fine."

"Is there anything I can do to help? Anything at all?"

Annie remembered Charlotte's warning about Ma'at, that they could be anywhere. No one was to be trusted, and even though it was Fatima's job to take care of hotel guests, Annie didn't want to attract undue attention. "It's jet lag, that's all."

Annie brought the slides and aspirin with her when she met Charlotte for dinner in the hotel restaurant, a hushed room with thick carpets and widely spaced tables. Charlotte's color had returned, but there was a weariness in her eyes.

"How are you feeling?" Annie asked.

Charlotte flicked her napkin and laid it on her lap. "Better, thanks." She took several minutes studying the slides, holding them up to the light of the chandelier, before letting out a sigh. "It's hard to tell without a projector, but I'm worried they didn't come out very well."

"You can always go back and try again, with better lighting. Jabari said he could arrange it."

Charlotte shook her head. "Unfortunately, I was informed by the director of the Egyptian Museum that the surveyors concluded the tomb would have to be closed permanently, as the damage was too severe."

They fell into silence, staring out at the other diners and watching the waiters come and go. "Does your guidebook tell you anything about the goddess Hathor?" asked Charlotte out of the blue.

Annie shook her head.

"The name 'Hathorkare' means 'The goddess of Hathor is the life force of Ra, the sun god.' Hathor was a powerful deity of many things, including fertility, childbirth, motherhood, music, dance, drunkenness. The list goes on and on."

"Sounds fun."

"Not at first. Initially, she was sent to earth by the sun god, Ra, to destroy humanity, punish rebellious humans for their selfishness and ingratitude. She swooped down and destroyed everything in her path: people murdered, houses crushed, cities toppled, crops wiped out, gone in an instant. Eventually, Ra realized there would be no one left if she kept this up, but by then she was out of control, so he called upon the goddess of beer to create a huge batch of ale and dyed it red. Hathor drank it, thinking it was blood—she was quite vampirish by that point—and passed out cold. When she woke up, she was transformed into a kind, benevolent goddess. The mother of all mothers."

"That's quite a story." Annie worked up the courage to ask the question that had been nagging her since their conversation with the landlady. "If you don't mind me asking, what was the name of your daughter?" she said softly.

Their main courses arrived. Charlotte took a sip of white wine and looked Annie in the eyes. "Layla," she answered.

"And that's really why we're here, right?"

Charlotte nodded. "We were all on the ship together. Henry, Leon, Layla, and myself. She was barely three months old. When I saw the broad collar and realized it hadn't gone down with the ship, I hoped that Layla had survived as well, and I thought by tracking down Leon, I'd be able to find out the truth."

The enigma that was Charlotte Cross finally made some sense to Annie. The child was the main reason for their trip to Egypt; the Cerulean Queen and the missing file were secondary. Although Annie wished she'd known from the beginning, she understood why it would be a difficult subject to bring up. "Leon lied, though."

"By his lying, I know there's something true out there. I just don't know what it is."

"Why would your husband keep her from you?"

"Because he didn't know I survived, I have to guess."

"He didn't even try to look for you?"

"As you know, he was involved with some kind of smuggling operation. Would that be enough to keep me from our daughter?" She frowned. "No. He wasn't like that. I have to believe he thought I was dead, just as I thought he was."

"So now we go to Cairo," said Annie. "Do you hope you'll find her there?"

"I do." Charlotte's eyes were bright and her mouth twitched. "I hope I can find out something about her, about Henry. But it's not like we have anything to go on, and Cairo is a huge city. I've spent all day trying to figure out what to do next, and I have no idea."

They ate in silence for a while.

"What about the Cerulean Queen?" said Annie.

"What about it?"

"Are you still interested in tracking it down?"

"Of course."

"What if I found something that could help?"

"And what would that be?" asked Charlotte, cutting into her lamb with a knife.

"When we were at Leon's apartment building, and I had that coughing fit, I didn't really have a coughing fit."

Charlotte looked up from her plate. "What do you mean?"

"From where I was standing, I could see a pitcher of water and what looked like a mail room, so I pretended to need water and found the slot for Leon Pitcairn's mail." Annie's heart had pounded like crazy as she rifled through the mail, and she was terrified the landlady might turn around at any moment and catch her.

"What did you find?"

"Nothing. His mail slot was empty."

"Okay."

"But the outgoing mail included this." Annie took an envelope from her lap and placed it on the table. The return address was Leon's, the mailing address a post office box in Cairo.

Charlotte looked up at her. "You went through the building's mail?"

"This was the only thing of interest."

"And you opened it?"

"I think that pales in comparison with smuggling ancient antiquities."

Charlotte didn't disagree. She picked it up and pulled out the note, handwritten on Leon's stationery, and read it out loud: "'I have confirmation that she is in the country, awaiting clearance from customs. Transfer to the unique location has been arranged and you will be notified once she reaches her final destination.—L.'"

FIONA DAVIS

Annie sat on the edge of her chair, not caring that she was smiling like a lunatic. "'She' has to refer to the Cerulean Queen. They're talking about an object, not a person."

Charlotte studied the note. "Maybe. It doesn't give us much information."

"So we go to the police. They can track down the owner of the post office box and arrest them."

"For what? There's nothing illegal about this note. They'd take one look at it and think we were mad."

"We could explain. You're an important person at the Met, surely you have some influence."

"I'm not as important as you think. Especially these days. Besides, the first thing they'd want to know is how you got your hands on it. The answer might get you into more trouble than Leon."

All of Annie's excitement drained away. "Right. Opening up someone else's mail."

"I'm sorry, Annie," said Charlotte, handing back the letter and envelope. "It's just not enough."

CHAPTER TWENTY-FOUR

Charlotte

Luxor Airport at dawn was filled with tourists pouring in from Cairo to see King Tut's resting place. Charlotte wondered how Frederick was doing with the exhibition preparations. While New York was the sixth and last stop on the tour, it was considered the biggest in terms of draw and excitement. King Tut mania had gripped the United States, and Charlotte couldn't help worrying about the effect its success would have on the fragile underground resting places in the Valley of the Kings. How many visitors was too many? How much exposure to the wet breaths and the surreptitious touches of tourists was too much?

Charlotte and an inspector from the Egyptian Antiquities Organization watched as two wooden crates containing the mummies from the crumbling tomb were carefully lifted into the storage hold of the plane, followed by a crate containing the sarcophagus and a smaller one with the canopic box.

The flight was smooth, and before long they were in Egypt's capital city. Annie had shaken off her disappointment at Charlotte's reaction to the stolen letter after Charlotte promised to bring up the theft with the director of the museum, in the hopes that he might be able to help. As their taxi followed the truck transporting the crates from the airport to the museum, Annie squirmed in her seat and braced herself at every intersection.

"How do they do this?" she said.

"Do what?" asked Charlotte, trying not to laugh.

"There are absolutely no traffic lights, no stop signs. Yet somehow all these cars, vans, motorcycles, and trucks race through the intersections without slamming into each other."

"The key," Charlotte explained, "is that the drivers rarely hit their brakes. As long as no one stops, the flow of the streets is like the flow of a river with multiple tributaries, one wave following another." She pointed out a bus sliding in behind a Mercedes as a motorcycle dodged both. "Lanes are theoretical, honking a given."

"It's insane."

Charlotte shrugged. "I suppose I got used to it."

The Egyptian Museum, which had been a second-rate institution when Charlotte lived in the city decades ago, had dropped even further down the scale. With scant electricity, the galleries were lit only by the ambient rays of sun from the windows. Yellow spots of paint dotted beautiful Hellenistic vases from when the walls and ceilings had been shoddily repainted, and many of the vitrines sported large cracks. In the lobby, a security guard stood in the corner, spitting tobacco onto the stained floor.

The director of the museum was a portly man who seemed to be made of circles—a round belly and a chubby round face with a pair of round spectacles perched on his nose. He came huffing up to where Charlotte and Annie waited in the lobby.

"Miss Cross, it's a pleasure to meet you," he said.

"Please, call me Charlotte." She shook his hand and introduced Annie, and then he led them up to his office on the second floor, which was dark and dusty, a far cry from the pristine, antique-filled domain of Mr. Lavigne at the Met. Frederick had met with Omar Abdullah multiple times as the terms of the King Tut exhibition were negotiated and had complained about how difficult it was to come to an agreement. But today Omar appeared quite at ease, leaning back in his chair with his hands crossed behind his head.

He explained that he'd arranged for the mummies and the canopic box to be transported to Cairo's top university hospital the next day, where a CT scan machine would examine both mummies and the box. They spoke of people they knew in common and the gossip of the museum world in general before Charlotte finally brought up Ma'at.

Omar sighed. "They're obviously trying to restock our coffers, but the methods are certainly dubious. There's no question a number of important antiquities were spirited out of Egypt before the authorities began to crack down, but I would prefer they go through international legal channels as opposed to stealing them back."

"Has anyone from Ma'at ever approached you with an artifact that was stolen?"

"No, and I couldn't accept it if they did. Is there something in particular you're referring to?"

Charlotte shook her head, not wanting to break Frederick's trust, but Annie spoke up before she could stop her.

"The Cerulean Queen was taken from the Met earlier this week," said Annie. "We think it was Ma'at that stole it."

Omar's eyes went wide. "That's terrible. Was anyone hurt?"

"Luckily, no," interjected Charlotte, sending Annie a sharp look.

"What makes you think it was Ma'at?" asked Omar.

"Well," ventured Charlotte, "we believe the man who ran off with it was Egyptian."

Omar let out a short snort. "Not every Egyptian is a member of Ma'at."

"Of course not," assured Charlotte. "But it's similar in certain ways to the previous two robberies they took credit for, which is why we're asking. The investigation is in the early stages and hasn't been made public."

"Please let them know if there's anything I can do to assist, I shall," offered Omar.

"I do have another question, if you don't mind," said Charlotte. "There's a broad collar currently on loan at the Met that was found in the 1930s, in the same tomb as the one we were in two days ago. The piece is privately owned, but I know for a fact that it was supposed to have been sent here, to the Egyptian Museum, after being excavated. Your records show it as being part of the collection, at least back then, and I'm curious if there's a record of it ever being sold."

"When was it discovered?"

"December 1936."

"Let me check." He walked over to a bookcase and pulled out an enormous ledger. As he leafed through the pages, the smell of mold and dust almost made Charlotte sneeze.

"That's odd, it's listed as part of our collection, but it looks like there's no record of it actually arriving. Are you sure it wasn't allowed to leave the country? Partage was still in practice then."

"I did the paperwork myself. It was meant to end up here."

"That's concerning. I'll have our legal department look into it."

While Charlotte would have preferred that the news of the Cerulean Queen stay private, she didn't mind throwing Frederick under the bus for putting the collar on display without properly vetting its provenance. And now she'd proved that it had never even made it to the Egyptian Museum. Hopefully, Omar would be able to ascertain who the owner was and force the Met to produce a proper record of sale, if one existed.

Finally, she asked Omar if he'd ever met an Egyptologist named Henry Smith. Omar smiled blandly and shook his head.

Yet another dead end.

The bazaar of Khan el-Khalili had been a hub for merchants and traders in Cairo since the fourteenth century. Many of the buildings lining the narrow streets and alleys featured stunningly intricate wood lattice screens called mashrabiya that let in indirect light while keeping the interiors cool. Charlotte had visited the area multiple times when she lived in Cairo, and it hadn't changed at all since then. The shops sold anything and everything—colored glass lamps, copper plates encrusted with silver, western desert rugs, cotton shirts and caftans, old coins, even leather camel saddles—and the bazaar teemed with international tourists.

"What's partage?" asked Annie as she and Charlotte neared the bazaar.

"A system set up where foreign archaeologists who discovered Egyptian antiquities received a share in the spoils," explained Charlotte. "Any finds were divided up fifty-fifty."

"Okay. What's the difference between antiques and antiquities?"

"'Antique' is French for 'old.' Anything that's at least one hundred years old is antique. Antiquities run from 5000 BC to about the fall of Rome, around 500 AD."

"That's really old."

Charlotte led Annie to a shop window filled with tapestries and alabaster vases. A bearded man welcomed them inside and offered to show them around. "My name is Babu. Anything special you're looking for? We have some beautiful, rare Islamic-era tiles that just came in."

Charlotte humored him, murmuring about how lovely they were. The phone rang, and Babu stepped way to answer it.

"These tiles are beautiful," said Annie, lightly running her finger over one.

"They should probably be in a museum."

Annie pulled her finger away. "Aren't there art police who go around and check what's being sold?"

"There are too many private dealers making shady sales outside of the commercial market. It would be impossible."

Babu returned, apologizing for the interruption. "Now tell me, what brings you to my humble store?"

"To be honest, I'm looking for someone." She took out the wedding photo and handed it to him. "His name is Henry Smith. Have you ever seen him before? He would be in his sixties by now."

"This is your husband?" asked Babu, looking back and forth at Charlotte and the image of her in the photograph.

"Yes. We lost track of each other ages ago, and it turns out he's come into some money that I'd like to get to him."

Charlotte had thought that up on the spot and was quite proud of herself, she had to admit. Annie gave a quick nod of approval.

"I don't know him." Babu handed back the photograph and wiped his mouth with the back of his hand. "It's unseemly, a wife looking for her husband. If he left you, I'm sure he had a good reason. Good day."

Charlotte held her tongue. It was infuriating to think that four thousand years ago, Egyptian women had more rights than they did today, when they could easily be supplanted by a second wife if their husband so desired.

Outside on the street, Charlotte unceremoniously ripped the photo in half as Annie gasped. "It'll be easier this way," she said, shoving the half with her image into her handbag.

Two days ago, she never would have dreamed of defacing the photograph, as she considered it a private keepsake of her first love, albeit one she always kept hidden. With Henry alive and walking the earth, that nostalgia was turning poisonous. He had survived without finding her, taking their daughter with him, and the viciousness of her actions that afternoon was nothing compared to the fury he would face if she ever found him.

They tried a few more shops, yet each time she produced Henry's image, the salesman shook his head, and her prompting of "He's an Englishman in his sixties with large ears" didn't jog any memories. She was wasting time. She'd hoped, incorrectly, it appeared, that if Henry was here in Cairo, he'd be well-known in the antiquities community and it would be an easy task to track him down.

"Why don't you try asking about your daughter directly?" said Annie.

"Unfortunately, in Egypt, 'Layla' is as common as 'Linda' in America."

"And the last name is Smith." Annie sighed. "Not helpful."

Annie paused outside a shop with a large window. The etched lettering on it read "Farid Gallery, Cairo + Geneva." "Should we try one more?"

Reluctantly, Charlotte agreed. Maybe she *should* have left it up to Tenny's contact to do the legwork. None of the shop owners or sales staff were even vaguely interested in helping her, whether because they'd never seen Henry, or his image in the photograph was drastically different from the way he appeared today and they didn't recognize him, or they just didn't like Charlotte asking questions. It was hard to say.

Inside, a woman with long red fingernails and a head of thick gray hair pulled back in a bun looked up from where she was unpacking merchandise at the checkout counter. "May I assist you?" she asked.

Charlotte surveyed the shop's wares as she and Annie approached the register. The antiques here were of a much better quality than the others that they'd seen earlier that day, the displays artful, including wooden boxes with intricate floral inlay and excellent reproductions of faience ushabti—small figurines representing servants that were buried with the pharaohs. The place was like a maze, with beautiful objects covering almost every surface of the many display cases and bookshelves. "What a gorgeous shop."

"Thank you."

Annie held up a pendant necklace of King Tut's funerary mask that the woman had just laid down on the countertop, next to a gold statue of the same. "He's everywhere," Annie remarked.

"He is, indeed. My name is Heba, by the way. I'm the owner." The woman smiled as Charlotte picked up the statue, which was already flaking bits of gold paint. "I'll give you a tip, don't waste your money. These are the trinkets we sell to street vendors." She took the piece from Charlotte and began wrapping it back up in newspaper. "It all goes straight to the tourist traps." She turned her head and yelled toward a door at the back of the store, "Nephi! Take this box off the floor, please," before turning back to Charlotte and Annie. "Is there anything special you're looking for?"

"I'm wondering if you've ever seen this man." Charlotte pulled out the photo. "His name is Henry Smith. He's English, has big ears, and would be in his sixties by now." She was done with small talk. It hadn't gotten her any closer to learning Henry's whereabouts.

The woman took a quick look. "Hold on a second," she said, raising her index finger in the air. "Let me get my glasses."

She disappeared into a back room.

"*I'm* tired of King Tut, and the exhibit hasn't even made it to New York yet," said Annie.

Charlotte understood the sentiment. "Back when the tomb was

first opened, in 1922, Tut-mania was all the rage. And now here we are again."

"It's not fair, it should be Hathorkare getting all of the attention."

"Maybe one day she will."

The woman returned wearing a pair of oversized eyeglasses. She took the photo and studied it, then shook her head. "I'm afraid I can't help you. Those ears are quite large, I'd remember them," she said with a smile.

"Thank you for taking a look."

"Sure. I take it the missing half of the photo is of you?"

Charlotte admitted as much.

"You obviously feel very passionately about this man. To rip it in half like that."

"I didn't have a pair of scissors."

"Of course." The woman offered a warm smile and patted her on the arm, the simple acknowledgment of another woman's pain. "Well, take a look around the store and let me know if there's anything I can help you with."

"Thank you."

They circled the floor once, just to be polite, before heading back to the hotel, defeated.

CHAPTER TWENTY-FIVE

Annie

Annie did her best to stay out of the way of the technicians and staff pressed into a small room in the basement of the hospital. Unlike the Egyptian Museum, the hospital very much belonged in the twentieth century, the floors pristinely clean, with walls the color of snow. She watched as Charlotte directed the positioning of the canopic box onto the bed of the CT scanner, which resembled some kind of space-age torture machine. Omar had promised it would give them a full picture of whatever was inside the box—as well as an "inside view" of the mummies—without having to pry open the lid or make any incisions.

Having spent several days practically glued to Charlotte's side, Annie had come to understand that the curator had two different dispositions. One was relentless and single-minded, insisting that the workers at Luxor who packed up the mummy support the bent arm with extra padding, barging into antiques stores and shoving that sad, ripped photograph into the salespeople's faces. Then there were times when Charlotte thought she wasn't being watched—like looking out at the city of Cairo from the taxi—that her face went soft and the hint of the young, vulnerable woman she once had been broke through her defenses.

Compared to Charlotte, Annie had barely lived at all. So far, this trip had been a lesson in pushing forward even when nothing was going your way, of being brave. Like the story of Charlotte and the Bedouin and the snakebite. What would Annie have done if someone with a cobra bite asked for her help? Fainted, most likely.

She wanted to be the type of person who didn't let the emotional craziness of others get in the way of her dreams. She wanted to be like Charlotte, striding along the streets of Luxor and Cairo, waving her arms and raising her voice when someone bumped into her or a waiter refused to give them a decent table. Sure, once Annie had gotten them a cab by stepping into traffic, but that was driven by a mix of jet lag and desperation.

Annie loved how physically expressive the Egyptians were, whether greeting an old friend or fighting over a parking spot. Or even deciding which way to place a canopic box on a stretcher to be scanned, which seemed to be a bone of contention at the moment. The technicians, Omar, and Charlotte all appeared to have strong opinions on the matter, and finally, after much discussion, they agreed to lay it on its back. Then they were all herded into an adjoining room where several monitors were set up behind a glass window.

Omar stood next to Annie.

"What happens now?" she asked.

"This will take a series of X-rays of the object, slices, if you will"— he made a motion with his hands to demonstrate—"and when they're all put together, they will give us a virtual three-dimensional view of the object."

"Why can't you just force the box open and look inside?"

"The viscera inside were preserved using a resin that ended up gluing the lid shut. This way we won't have to damage anything."

As the images began appearing on the monitors, Omar used a pen to point out what he believed was a liver. The grayish image reminded Annie of a cow's tongue. She was glad she hadn't eaten a big breakfast that morning.

Charlotte gestured to a small white object on the scan, near the bottom of the box. "What do you think that is?" she asked.

Omar studied it and conferred with the technicians. "Something solid. A bone, maybe?"

"It's a tooth." Annie didn't realize how loudly she'd spoken until everyone turned around to stare at her. Heat rushed to her face at having interrupted the experts' deliberations. She shrugged. "I had my wisdom teeth out earlier this year."

The technician turned back and nodded his head. "She could be right," he said in English.

"An oral surgeon!" cried Omar. "Get me an oral surgeon, right away!"

Not long after, one appeared. Omar and Charlotte explained to him what they were doing, and the man leaned in close to the monitor and studied the image. Using a pen, he pointed to a long tendril that extended from the object, and said something in Arabic that got everyone excited.

Charlotte waved Annie over. "You were right, it's a molar," she explained. "Do you know what this means?"

"That Hathorkare ate too many sweets?"

Charlotte rolled her eyes. "If the tooth in Hathorkare's canopic box matches a missing molar in one of the mummies' mouths, then it's more than likely that mummy is Hathorkare. It would be a way to definitively identify her, and the fact that this molar has only one root will help narrow the location down."

All this discussion of missing teeth was making Annie's own mouth ache.

"The other clue will be the size," continued Charlotte. "Right now, the technician is measuring the tooth, and then we'll scan each of the mummies' jaws and see what we find."

It was nice to see Charlotte distracted from her hunt for her daughter, even though Annie knew they'd be right back to it once the scan was over. And what a distraction. The box was removed from the scanner and then, very carefully, the mummy with the folded arm was lifted from the crate and laid gently on the scanner bed. Charlotte hovered over the handlers, urging them to take care, as if the mummy were a living human being. Its thin locks of reddish hair shone under the bright fluorescent lights. The neck was slim, the cheekbones jutted out, and the lips were slightly parted, as if the mummy were about to comment on the indignity of her current situation. Annie already considered the mummy a female, which she knew was a big assumption, but there was no question she emanated a grisly beauty, with her narrow chin and high cheekbones.

Once again, everyone waited as the CT scan was activated. The room remained silent the entire time, and Annie prayed that the tooth would prove Hathorkare's identity, for Charlotte's sake, since Charlotte's search for her husband and daughter so far had been fruitless. At least this way she could go back to New York with an archaeological triumph, and a major one at that.

Finally, the scan was completed. Annie made her way closer to Charlotte in order to be nearby in case the results were disappointing. She felt responsible, in a way. After all, she was the one who'd accidentally found the canopic box and stirred everything up.

Charlotte took her hand and gave her a quick smile. Annie squeezed her hand back. There was always the second mummy. If this one didn't match, then maybe the other would.

The technician zoomed in on the image of the mummy's jaw. Annie wasn't a dentist, but it sure looked like the mummy was missing more than a few teeth. On the screen, the technician's cursor blinked beside a whitish tendril that trailed down from a space at the back of the mummy's jaw, like the tentacle of a jellyfish. One tendril, not two. Annie held her breath. He pressed a bunch of keys on the computer that allowed him to measure the empty space above the tendril from many different angles, then murmured back and forth with the oral surgeon. Then they huddled with Omar.

The room remained perfectly silent.

Finally, Omar turned and addressed the assembled group. "That space"—he pointed to the scan—"is where a molar once was. You can see here that there is still one root remaining in the gum. The tooth that is in the canopic box was measured to be 1.74 millimeters wide. The space in the jaw of this mummy is 1.8 millimeters wide. According to Dr. Aziz, that can be considered a perfect match."

A perfect match.

They'd done it. Annie and Charlotte had discovered the mummy of the ancient Egyptian female pharaoh Hathorkare.

Applause and cheers broke out. Omar raised his voice to be heard.

"Ladies and gentlemen, may I present you with Hathorkare, the fifth pharaoh of the Eighteenth Dynasty of ancient Egypt."

A roar of excitement rose up from everyone present, but it was drowned out by the sound of something exploding. A blinding green-yellow light flashed from the examination room, as powerful as a beam from a lighthouse. Annie turned away, covering her face with her hands, certain that the CT scanner must have blown up. When she opened them, she noticed Charlotte staring into the examination room, her mouth slightly opened, eyes wide, as if she hadn't even blinked.

"What happened?" Annie asked.

Charlotte didn't answer, didn't even acknowledge Annie's question, as Omar and two members of the technical staff rushed into the room with the scanner. Luckily, all was in order. The mummies were safe; the equipment was intact. "Probably an electrical surge," Omar said.

Next to her, Charlotte shook her head slowly, as if she was still in shock.

"Are you okay?" asked Annie.

"I think I'm better than okay," she answered finally, a peculiar look on her face. "I think I'm going to be just fine."

The group in the CT scanning room finally dispersed after much backslapping and congratulations. Omar had a smile so wide Annie thought his face might break, and she understood why. They'd accomplished an enormous feat by identifying Hathorkare. Annie caught one last look at the queen as she was being lifted off the CT scan machine and placed back inside the packing crate. To think this was the woman who walked the earth thousands of years ago, ordering temples to be built and ruling all of Egypt. Her bent limb was like an act of defiance, as if she'd raised her arm to fight off the high priests who had wrapped her in linen before burying her in a gloomy tomb.

"You did it!" she said to Charlotte.

Charlotte shook her head as if to pull herself out of a trance. "Wow. Yes. Funny how you can stumble on to something that suddenly changes everything. Or should I say, *you* stumbled upon it."

"Tripping over mummified geese will do that. Will you write an article about this?"

"Omar and I already have discussed possibly coauthoring it. Now if only I could convince people that she was a real leader, not a 'usurper,' as you put it. I want to tell the whole story." She glanced over at the CT scanning machine again, as if looking for something. "Without that, she's still a woman who didn't know her place."

"Well, I hope she somehow knows that you've been fighting for her. Anyway, congrats. You deserve it."

"Thanks. You hungry?"

"Starving."

They found a small restaurant a few blocks away from the hospital, and Charlotte ordered for them both.

"We'll have the tahini, an order of the warak enab, and the baba ghanoush. With mangoes for dessert, please." Charlotte handed the waiter their menus and turned to Annie. "This is the end of the mango season in Egypt, you don't want to miss it."

Before they'd left, Annie had been worried that she wouldn't like Egyptian food, but she found the different tastes and textures delicious. Today's meal turned out to be a dip made of sesame paste that came with toasted bread chips, balls of rice that had been rolled up in grape leaves glistening with olive oil, and mashed eggplant seasoned with garlic and spices. Nothing like she'd ever tried before, but full of flavor. The fashion in Cairo surprised her as well. Many Egyptians wore Western clothes—the men in wide-collared shirts and women wearing skirts that hit right above the knee. Flared jeans were everywhere, just like back home.

Charlotte barely picked at her food, as if something was weighing on her.

"Is everything all right?" asked Annie. Living with Joyce had made her especially alert to the emotional temperatures of those around her.

"When that burst of light occurred in the CT scanning room, did you see anything?" Charlotte asked.

"No," said Annie. "Why, did you?"

Charlotte didn't meet her eyes.

"What? What did you see?"

"You're going to think I'm losing my marbles."

"Never."

Charlotte spoke slowly, softly, as if she didn't trust what she was saying. "After that bright flash, I saw a woman sort of hovering in the air, just above the scanning bed. She wore a nemes headdress with a golden cobra rising out from her forehead—the adornment of a male pharaoh—but she was unmistakably female: dressed in linen, her fingers ringed with golden scarabs, and the broad collar around her neck."

"It was Hathorkare," Annie said, leaning forward. "I'm sure of it. What happened then?"

"We stared at each other through the glass for what seemed like minutes. I felt like I was stuck in place, entranced by this spirit but terrified at what might come next. I didn't know why she was there. Was she angry at having been disturbed? Or was she finally free? Then the figure bowed its head slightly and disappeared. When the lights came back on, I looked around, expecting everyone else to be as shocked as I was. But no one else appeared to have even noticed. I realized I was alone in having the vision, but instead of being freaked out, a strange sense of calm came over me."

"It was definitely Hathorkare. That means the curse was lifted. You've been forgiven."

Charlotte gave a slight shiver. "You don't think I'm crazy, do you?"

"Not at all. You're free. And so is she."

As the waiter cleared their plates, Charlotte threw Annie a small smile. "Maybe you're right. I like the idea that she's finally at peace. That makes one of us."

"You'll find what you're looking for."

"I'm going to reach out to Tenny, ask if he knows anyone here I should talk to regarding Henry. Maybe one of his associates can help." Charlotte looked out into the street. "That's weird."

Annie followed her gaze. A couple of women walked down the sidewalk, holding shopping baskets. "What?"

"A man came around the corner and saw me, and then suddenly turned around and disappeared."

"Maybe he forgot his wallet at home."

"It's just that I think I noticed him earlier today as well. As we went into the hospital."

Annie pictured her attacker at the Met, the way his eyes bulged as he came at her, and shivered. "Was he tall, with dark hair?"

Charlotte pulled her gaze away from the street and rubbed her eyes. "That describes pretty much most of the men in Cairo. I'm tired, that's all. It's making me paranoid."

The mangoes arrived, and Annie bit into a slice, wiping the juice off her chin with her napkin. "What happens to the mummy now?"

"She'll be put on display here in Cairo."

"Does that bother you?"

"I do feel protective of her, somehow." Charlotte fiddled with her silverware. "I mean, is it right to stick her in a display case where the general public can wander by and ogle her? People who have no idea who she is, who are just satisfying their morbid desire to see a dead body?"

"I totally get that. But I meant would you prefer to have her at the Met?"

"Of course, if only for the research possibilities. But there's no way that's going to happen, even if it is a superior institution."

"I think she'd rather be with all her mummy friends here in Egypt," said Annie.

Charlotte laughed. "You raised some good points earlier, and a lot of museums are asking themselves the same questions these days, including the Met. Is the goal deaccession—sending everything back to its country of origin, no matter what—or is it better for an institution like the Met to hold on to the object and keep it safe? What if it gets sold by the country of origin to raise money—which happens all the time—and is placed in the private collection of some million-aire, where it's lost to both the public and academia?"

"But who are you to say that you know what's best? Not you, specifically—the Met, I mean," Annie added quickly. "What about the works of art stolen by the Nazis during World War II?"

"What about them?"

"Do the investigators who are tracking down the original owners or their descendants question the ability of those people to properly take care of the paintings?"

"Of course not."

"So why should museums make that kind of judgment call?"

Charlotte sat back in her chair. "I used to think the way you do, when I was younger. And now, to be honest, you're making me ques-tion my current position." She didn't seem upset, just thoughtful.

Annie had impressed Charlotte. She tried to play it cool, like she had this kind of back-and-forth every day. "Maybe Hathorkare would have preferred to have been left in the tomb." The woman was royalty, after all, and now, as Charlotte had brought up, she'd be gawked at like some exotic animal in the zoo, people filing by before heading to the gift shop to buy a postcard. "I know it's a huge discovery and all, but a part of me feels bad, like I was the reason for all this. I hope she doesn't curse me."

"I promise, you're not cursed. You were amazing."

"It's the first time my klutziness paid off, I guess."

"We were a great team, Annie. Thank you for all that."

"'Were'? Don't we still have work to do?"

Charlotte shook her head. "No. You're getting on a plane tomor-row and going back to New York. Our work here is done. Or, rather, *your* work is."

Panic shot through Annie. Right when everything was looking up, Charlotte was going to send her home? "But we only just got here. Are you going back as well?"

"No. I need to try to find Henry. I can't give up just yet."

"Don't forget the Cerulean Queen. I'm here to help identify the guy who stole it, remember? You still need me." Annie was embarrassed by the pleading tone in her voice, but she couldn't help it. Returning to New York was a dismal idea. She had nothing there anymore—no place to stay, no job, no life. She'd been a big asset; Charlotte had just admitted as much. "Look, I came here to try to fix the mess I made at the Costume Institute, to prove that I'm not an accessory to the crime or whatever it is they suspect me of."

"And I came here to find my daughter." Charlotte paid the check, and Annie followed her out onto the sidewalk, where half a dozen men sat behind cheap souvenirs laid out on blankets, calling out to passing tourists to inspect their wares.

"But we think the Cerulean Queen and your daughter are somehow related," said Annie. "Besides, I shouldn't have even left the country, I was told to stay in New York. When I go back, they might arrest me for fleeing or something, so I really need to have something to show for it."

"Trust me, they have bigger issues to deal with. I highly doubt they believe you're part of an international smuggling ring, the girl who opened a box of moths."

The insult stung.

Annie was all too familiar with this kind of rejection. First her mother, who she'd taken care of and worried over until Annie had been rendered moot by a new boyfriend. Then Diana Vreeland, who'd dismissed her after a misunderstanding. And now Charlotte. Why was Annie drawn again and again to women she hoped would help her, guide her, but who then discarded Annie like an old sock the minute she wasn't needed anymore? She was desperate for a mentor, someone to explain how the world worked, but instead she was repeatedly shown the door.

They had come to a stop in front of a man selling clumps of bracelets, Egyptian cat statues, and a King Tut mask statue—a match of the one they'd seen in the gallery the other day. Annie reached down and picked it up, stalling for time.

"This is one of a kind," the seller said, pointing at the statue. He had a long face and bushy eyebrows. "You won't find this anywhere else."

In spite of their argument, Annie and Charlotte exchanged a knowing smile. "Right," said Charlotte, taking it from Annie. "One of a kind." Instead of handing it back to the seller, Charlotte got a strange look on her face. "That's weird," she murmured.

"It's unique, I promise," said the seller. "Farid."

Annie froze. That word. "'Farid'?"

"Yes," he answered.

"'Farid' means unique?" she asked him.

"Yes, yes, I sell it to you for very cheap."

Annie turned to Charlotte. "The letter from Leon. He wrote: 'Transfer to the unique location has been arranged.' The last store we went to yesterday was called the Farid Gallery. The *Unique* Gallery."

But Charlotte didn't seem to even hear her; instead, she handed back the King Tut statue and pulled out some pounds from her wallet, pointing to a cheap glass perfume bottle. "I'll take that, no need to wrap it up."

"Why on earth are you buying souvenirs when I have just discovered something monumental?" said Annie.

But Charlotte just shoved the perfume bottle into her handbag and grabbed Annie's arm.

"Let's go."

CHAPTER TWENTY-SIX

Charlotte

Charlotte felt terrible about the argument she and Annie had back at the restaurant, especially after having divulged her strange vision and gratefully accepting Annie's reassurance that it was a blessing, not another curse. Over the past couple of days, Charlotte had become fond of Annie. Behind her loud laugh and lumbering gait was a fragile child who was desperate to please, yet she had an inner strength that she was only now beginning to tap into. It had been marvelous watching her transformation.

Annie was smart and pushed Charlotte out of her comfort zone, which was maybe why Charlotte found herself now keeping the girl at arm's length. She was resolutely proud of Annie one moment and then irritated the next.

Like a mother might feel.

But Charlotte already had a daughter.

Yet as they sped toward Khan el-Khalili, her protective side kicked in. Ever since she'd held the second King Tut statue in the palm of her hand and heard the word "farid" spill out of the seller's mouth, everything had become clear. She didn't want to put Annie in harm's way, but she couldn't do this without her.

The labyrinthian alleyways were packed. Once they reached the Farid Gallery, Charlotte peered into the front window, where several tourists lingered over a display of amulets. Nothing bad could happen to her and Annie if there were other people about, certainly. She took a deep breath and ventured in, Annie right on her heels.

The handsome woman from the other day, Heba, stood behind the cash register, looking over an invoice. She glanced up briefly but didn't acknowledge them, an unusually tepid response to a returning customer in a touristy neighborhood like this one. Two visits in two days surely would have signaled a probable sale, and any other salesperson would have come running. Could she possibly not have remembered them? It seemed unlikely.

Something was off.

The box of cheap souvenirs they'd seen the other day was no longer on the floor, but the back door to the office area was slightly ajar.

Annie nudged Charlotte. "Do you notice anything different?" she asked.

Charlotte looked around. "What do you mean?"

"The owner's not wearing glasses. Yesterday she had to go to the back room to get them to see the photograph. But today she's reading glasses-less."

"Maybe the writing is large enough for her to see. Or she's wearing contact lenses."

"Or maybe she needed time to gather herself together after seeing Henry's photo. Because she recognized him."

Charlotte hadn't considered that; she wasn't thinking about the photograph or Henry at all. She glanced at the door to the back room before pulling Annie down one of the narrow aisles near the front of the store.

"Where are we going?" asked Annie.

"Shhh. Play along." Charlotte reached into her pocketbook, lifted out the perfume bottle, and then dashed it onto the floor a few feet from where they stood, angling it slightly so the glass shards flew across the tiled floor toward the center of the shop, skidding like ice away from them.

Annie jumped and cried out. "What on earth!"

"Annie, how could you?" chided Charlotte. "I told you not to be so clumsy!"

Annie gave her a confused look, but Heba was already heading their way, holding a broom in one hand and a dustpan in the other. "What's going on?" she asked as she turned into the aisle.

Charlotte deftly slid by her, pointing at the mess. "I'm afraid she dropped something. I told her to be careful. Annie, help her clean up, please, it's the least you can do." She glanced toward the back of the shop, and Annie's eyes went wide with understanding.

"Right." Annie turned to Heba. "I'm like an elephant in a tea shop sometimes. Or what is that expression? A hippo in an egg shop. No, that's not it. A bull in a china shop. Yes! That's it. In any event, I promise I'll pay for it—here, let me take the broom."

Charlotte eased away, and Annie, in response, shifted slightly so Heba had her back to Charlotte. They instinctively knew what the other was doing, like dance partners in a ballroom.

As Annie and Heba tussled over the mess and who was going to clean it up, Charlotte slipped through the door at the back of the store. Inside were a couple of desks and several file cabinets and metal shelving, as well as a dozen or so boxes and crates tucked back in a corner.

Luckily, the box she'd seen yesterday was set apart from the others and sported a bright "Egyptian Customs" sticker. She opened it up and dug inside, feeling around for the right shape. It didn't take long for her to locate exactly what she was looking for: the statue of King Tut.

When she'd first held it in her hands in front of Heba, the weight of the piece hadn't made an impression. It was only when Charlotte took the same statue from Annie in front of the street vender and been surprised by its lightness that it registered: The one in the Farid Gallery was far too heavy to be made only of plaster.

If someone wanted to get a stolen antiquity out of one country and into another, a cheap plaster cast would be a great way to conceal it. Especially in the form of King Tut, which was manufactured in mass quantities and wouldn't attract attention from customs agents.

Charlotte didn't have much time. She turned the statue upside down and, using her nail, scraped at the bottom of it, directly on the seam. The plaster began to chip away.

She dug further, listening as Annie carried on with her apology monologue. The girl was creative. A large chip fell away as Charlotte's fingernail struck something hard. Underneath the plaster, a brilliant blue color appeared. It was polished, and the exact same hue as the Cerulean Queen.

"I'm sorry, where is your friend?" Heba's voice carried from the other room.

She was out of time.

Charlotte quickly wrapped the statue up and tucked it into the box as Heba strode into the room, followed by a panicked-looking Annie. "What are you doing back here?" asked Heba. She crossed her arms and shot Charlotte a look.

"Sorry, I was looking for the bathroom."

"The bathroom is not for customers."

What Charlotte really wanted to do was grab the Cerulean Queen and make a break for the door. But now was not the time. Heba herded them out onto the sales floor.

"Did you get the mess cleaned up?" Charlotte asked Annie as brightly as she could manage.

"Yes, we're all set," Annie answered.

Luckily, a new batch of tourists in the company of a guide entered the store, circling around Heba like a pack of wolves. Charlotte and Annie meandered out of the shop, trying to appear relaxed. When they were safely out of view, Charlotte pulled Annie into a small alley just around the corner. "It's there. It's hidden inside the plaster King Tut statue."

"The Cerulean Queen?" Annie looked like she was about to jump up and down and start yelling.

"Shhh. Yes."

"What do we do next? Call the police?"

"I don't know how sympathetic an Egyptian policeman will be if they don't understand the value of Egyptian antiquities. Heba might have local connections as well."

"Do we call Omar?"

"Yes. I think that's best." Charlotte imagined Heba back in the shop, taking the statue out of the box, preparing to move it to a different location. Hopefully the tourists would keep her busy until Charlotte spoke to Omar.

Heba's reaction was strange, though. She hadn't seemed overly angry or overly protective, more annoyed that Charlotte had trespassed beyond the shop floor.

It was almost as if she didn't know the value of what was in her back room. "Let's go find a phone," Charlotte said.

"I can wait here, in case she tries to leave," Annie offered.

"No, we have to stick together. I don't want to put you in danger."

Charlotte had barely finished the sentence when a hand grabbed her roughly by the back of her neck, and then she was flying through the air, landing on some boxes deep in the alley. She hardly had time to register what was going on before Annie was tossed on top of her, knocking the breath out of her lungs, the two of them flailing to get their bearings like a couple of beetles that had been turned onto their backs.

The air smelled of urine and rotting vegetables; the ground was slick with something wet and slimy. Charlotte's heart jolted in her chest as she caught sight of a pair of khaki-covered legs heading their way. Annie rolled off her and Charlotte tried to stand, but before she could get her feet under her, a hand smacked her hard across the face, sending her flying back to the ground, the skin on her cheek burning. She wanted to curl into a ball, protect herself, but she couldn't leave Annie exposed. They were trapped in an alley with a madman who clearly wanted to teach them a lesson, if not kill them. She threw her arms wide, trying to keep Annie safe beneath her.

The next time the man charged, Charlotte retracted one leg and kicked him hard. He cried out in pain and bent over, cupping his crotch. Charlotte again tried to scramble to her feet and lift Annie with her—they didn't have much time. When their attacker looked up, his face was filled with fury.

He had dark hair and dark eyes, and around his neck hung a silver ankh pendant.

"It's him," croaked Annie.

There was no way out, nowhere to run. The man stood tall and cracked his knuckles, taking his time, knowing they were trapped. As he cocked his arm back, Charlotte shielded Annie with her own body as best she could and braced herself for the blow, closing her eyes and praying that Mark wouldn't have to identify her bruised corpse.

But instead of feeling another sharp crack of pain, she heard a low "oomph."

Another man had his arm around the neck of their attacker, whose eyes now bulged in shock as he struggled to get free. They bounced off the alley walls like they were in a pinball machine before their attacker finally closed his eyes and slumped over. The other man laid him on the ground and checked for a pulse. "He's alive," he said.

Charlotte looking into their rescuer's eyes and realized she'd seen him before.

It was Jabari. The grandson of Mehedi, the Bedouin who'd been bitten by a cobra all those years ago and had promised to always keep Charlotte safe.

He'd kept his word.

CHAPTER TWENTY-SEVEN

Annie

The police came quickly, having already been alerted by some tourists who'd witnessed the attack as they passed by the alley. Charlotte yelled something about the woman inside the shop, and then Jabari yelled to the cops in Arabic, which sent two of the policemen racing to the store's front door.

Annie and Charlotte eased up to standing. Annie's entire right side pulsed with pain, but it was achy, not sharp. As far as she could tell, her bones were intact.

Charlotte put one hand gently under Annie's chin, scrutinizing her face. "Are you hurt?"

"Just a little sore. I think you took the worst of it," said Annie. Charlotte's cheek was bright red. "Thank you for protecting me."

Charlotte focused on brushing the dirt off Annie's backside. "Of course."

Annie tried to imagine Joyce in a similar situation. She doubted her mother would've risked damaging her face to protect her.

Annie shivered at the thought of what would have happened if

Jabari hadn't appeared. Charlotte wouldn't have been able to hold the man off for very long, and they would've both been knocked unconscious. Or worse. He was clearly out to do damage.

"I think he was surprised that you fought back the way you did," said Annie. "Do you want to get some ice on your cheek?"

"I'm fine for now," said Charlotte. "Let's go inside and I'll call Omar."

In the back room of the Farid Gallery, Heba stood against one wall, arguing in Arabic with two policemen. Jabari was explaining something loudly to what looked like the head cop, everyone speaking over each other. Charlotte phoned the museum and the chaos finally came to a halt when Omar burst through the front door, followed by another man, a conservator, who pulled on a pair of gloves and carefully lifted the King Tut mask statue that Charlotte pointed to out of the box. As he placed it on top of a small table and began unwrapping it, Heba asked a question. Although Annie couldn't understand the words, her tone was one of confusion.

"Take her out of here," instructed Omar.

Once Heba had been escorted away, the conservator examined the statue. Charlotte showed him where she'd chipped away at the underside, and he took out some tools from a bag and began gently scraping off the plaster. A large chunk dropped onto the table, and Annie spied a section of shiny blue stone. As another came loose, the curved lips of the queen emerged.

The technician murmured something to Omar, who turned to Charlotte and Annie.

"He's certain it's the Cerulean Queen. You've found it."

Annie let out a loud whoop, which made the policemen laugh. "We did it!" she said to Charlotte.

"We certainly did," answered Charlotte before turning to Omar. "Where does it go from here?"

"For now, they'll transport it to the Egyptian Antiquities Organization, where our conservator will resume freeing it without damage."

"Just think, you've discovered two queens," said Annie to Charlotte. "Not bad for your first time back to Egypt since the dark ages."

Charlotte smiled, but it didn't reach her eyes. "I suppose so." She turned to Omar. "What about Heba?"

"She'll no doubt be charged with smuggling and theft of a major artwork. If Ma'at is behind this, it means we have a big lead."

Annie pictured Heba in jail, her manicured nails chipping and her hair undone. Her face, as she'd been led out of the shop, was filled with anguish. Not exactly what Annie would've expected for a hardened Ma'at disciple.

"Thank you for everything you've done," said Omar to Charlotte. "The moment we identified Hathorkare will no doubt remain the highlight of my career. Second only to this."

"And mine as well," said Charlotte.

They'd done it. They'd located the Cerulean Queen. Even though there were moments when Annie had been confused or even terrified, it had been wonderful having a purpose in the world. She envied Charlotte's life. Not that Annie wanted to unearth any more mummies anytime soon, but to have a job that made you want to go to the ends of the earth to figure out the truth, or pursue something beautiful? That sounded like a pretty good way to spend one's days and, sadly enough, reminded her of her time with Mrs. Vreeland.

Charlotte lingered, speaking with the conservator, and a wave of fatigue settled over Annie. They'd been going nonstop since they'd arrived in Egypt, and now that her adrenaline had subsided, she was beginning to feel the physical effects of being tossed around like a rag doll. Her right side, especially, ached from the brawl.

Annie took a seat at Heba's desk, happy to be off her feet. A bunch of manila files were stacked in a pile, and she glanced through them, imagining the elation in Charlotte's eyes as she held the missing research file aloft. But that would be too much to ask for. They were just sales receipts or boring forms in Arabic.

A policeman came over and asked Annie in English to not touch anything.

"*Ana asfa*," she answered, pleased with herself for remembering the phrase for "I'm sorry" from her guidebook.

As she rose out of the chair, she accidentally bumped into the desk—her klutziness getting the better of her again—and a framed photograph that was sitting on the other side of the stack of files fell over. Annie reached over to right it, apologizing again to the policeman, but froze when she understood what she was looking at.

She blinked twice. It couldn't be. But somehow, it all made sense.

The mastermind behind the theft of the Cerulean Queen was staring right back at her.

CHAPTER TWENTY-EIGHT

Charlotte

The plane carrying Charlotte and Annie chased the sunrise back to New York, landing in a wash of yellows and oranges. Charlotte was distraught she'd had to leave Cairo so quickly; the timing couldn't have been worse. There were still so many unanswered questions about Henry and Layla—his whereabouts, what had happened the night of the sinking and in the intervening years, where on earth Layla was—but at the moment, capturing the thief of the Cerulean Queen had to come first. They would only have one chance, and retaining the element of surprise was of the utmost importance.

Back in Egypt, after Annie had shown Charlotte the photograph at the Farid Gallery, Charlotte had looked at her in confusion. But when Annie explained—and once again Charlotte thanked her lucky stars that the girl had invited herself on this trip—it all began to fall into place. Charlotte had spun into action, talking rapidly to the police and Omar in Arabic, making several calls to New York, and then sprinting to their hotel to collect their things before taking the next direct flight out.

After passing through customs, they caught a cab and proceeded to the Met. At the information desk, Charlotte wrote a quick note, and then she and Annie walked to the Met's auditorium. Inside, the curator of the Arms and Armor department stood behind a dais on the stage, describing an Italian suit of armor from the fourteenth century to a room that was only about a quarter filled, mainly with women. Charlotte handed the note to an usher standing at the back of the room, and Annie pointed out to whom it should be delivered. As the intern strode down the aisle, Charlotte and Annie slipped out of the auditorium and proceeded to the Temple of Dendur gallery. They weaved around the rope and stanchions that blocked the entrance with a "Closed to the Public" sign attached and waited, tucked behind the huge stone gate that stood directly in front of the temple. The once brilliantly painted walls and columns had long ago faded, leaving only the outlines of bygone pharaohs and gods carved in sandstone.

Less than two minutes later, a woman walked into the gallery.

"Hello?" she called out. "Is anyone here? I was told to report to the Temple of Dendur?"

Charlotte stepped from behind the gate, followed by Annie. They waited in the temple's courtyard as the woman approached, looking confused.

She was the same docent trainee who had helped her friend through a disastrous presentation about the Cerulean Queen two weeks prior, the one who had mouthed answers from the back of the room.

The one named Mona.

"What's going on?" Mona stood perfectly straight in her Chanel tweed suit, her words echoing in the spacious gallery.

Back in Cairo, once Annie had explained to Charlotte that the woman standing next to Heba in the photograph was one of the Met's docent trainees, Charlotte realized that she *had* seen her, albeit briefly, standing near her and Frederick during an error-filled history of the Cerulean Queen in the Egyptian Art collection, the same statue this woman later arranged to have stolen during the Met Gala. And now they were face-to-face. Everything depended on this single conversation.

"Mona. I'm Charlotte Cross, as you know."

"I'm sorry, how would I know you?" Mona's expression was one of polite interest.

"You arranged to steal my research folder." Mona opened her mouth to deny it, but Charlotte cut her off. "I don't know why. I don't care. I just want it back."

"I assure you I have no idea what you're talking about. If you don't mind, I'll head back to my lecture now." She turned to go.

"I'd stick around if I were you. We know you were behind the theft of the Cerulean Queen."

Mona turned back. A small muscle twitched at the corner of her mouth. "I heard about the theft. A terrible loss," she said.

"We're aware that you're involved with Ma'at, along with Leon Pitcairn."

At the mention of Leon's name, Mona stiffened. She glanced back and forth between Annie and Charlotte, her composure rattled. "How do you know Leon?"

"That doesn't matter right now," said Charlotte. "I care about my file, nothing else."

"Your file. Even if I did have it, why would I give it back to you?"

"Because otherwise I will tell Mr. Lavigne that you were behind the theft of the Cerulean Queen. Look, as far as I'm concerned, it should be on Egyptian soil, I don't care if the Met never gets it back," she lied. "What I *do* care about is my career, and that file, as you know, is vitally important."

Mona looked around the courtyard, as if assessing whether it was safe to speak. "It looks like we each have something to hold over the other. How do I know if I give you back the file that you'll keep your mouth shut?"

"You don't. You'll have to trust me." Charlotte looked at Annie. "Trust us."

Mona looked Annie up and down. "I thought you were banned from this place."

"I've been assisting Charlotte."

Mona let out a breezy laugh. "Good luck with that. Mrs. Vreeland is ruing the day she ever hired you."

The direct approach wasn't working, so Charlotte would try a different tack. "In any event, Ma'at appears to be shaking up the stodgy art world. I'm curious, what exactly is Ma'at up to? It's not as if they can place a stolen work in an Egyptian museum without international outcry. Why bother?"

"Why bother? How would you feel if your beloved Constitution was on display in the Soviet Union? You'd want it back, right?"

She had a point. "I suppose so."

Charlotte's concession appeared to embolden Mona. "Ma'at is named for the Egyptian goddess of truth and justice. Our country has either given away or sold off some of its most important treasures, and Ma'at is fighting for the repatriation of Egyptian art and antiquities from those who plundered our past." The more she spoke, the more animated she became, clearly thrilled to toss off the docent-trainee guise. "We see no difference between objects that were smuggled out and those that were looted with the full approval of the government. They all belong to the people. They should be in the

Egyptian homeland, not flaunted in the trophy cases of museums like the Met."

If Mona had her way, the only way to view the Benin bronzes or an Egyptian stela would be to go to the countries themselves. What a shame that would be for scholars and educators, or for children who would lose the chance to see actual antiquities from around the world up close. For Mona, there were no shades of gray whatsoever. Yet after Charlotte's conversations on the subject with Annie while they were in Egypt, she'd come to understand that there were no easy answers to the question of repatriation.

Annie spoke up. "Are you the one who called the Museum of Natural History and told them to switch the butterflies for moths?"

This seemed like the least pressing of questions, but Charlotte kept quiet.

Mona laughed. "When Priscilla told me about your little project, I figured it would make the perfect distraction. And you pulled it off brilliantly. What an absolute travesty."

"I'm guessing that you and your husband are the donors behind the loan of the broad collar," said Charlotte. "Weren't you worried that would attract undue attention, considering you were planning a major heist?"

Mona was obviously proud of what they'd done and eager to show off. "In order to steal the statue, I needed to gain inside access to the museum, and the best way to do so was by securing a place in the docent-training course—that way I could roam freely. The waiting list at the Met was ridiculously long, so the one-year loan was a way to fast-track my application, bump me to the head of the line. Then it was just a matter of figuring out when to pull our plan off. Unfortunately, you started asking questions, which made me think you needed to be put in your place."

"So you stole my research file."

Mona gave a catlike smile.

"How did you get into the administrative offices? And how did you even know about it in the first place?"

"Mr. Lavigne complained about your research when we had coffee one day. Before the Met Gala, when the Egyptian wing had cleared out, I persuaded one of the Lebanese janitors to let me in. It was easy enough to convince him that I was a curator and had forgotten my key with a little Arabic sweet talk. I figured I'd steal something valuable of yours so you could see what that feels like."

Touché, thought Charlotte. "Where did you get the broad collar?"

"What do you care about that?"

"It's a beautiful piece. I'm curious."

Mona puffed with pride. "After my parents separated when I was a baby, my mother ran the Farid Gallery in Cairo and my father took over the branch in Geneva," said Mona. "I'd visit him during the summer, but I rarely went outside—the other children were cruel to me. Instead, I entertained myself with what I found around the house. One day, I pulled out a drawer in his study and found it tucked way in the back. I put the collar around my neck, pretended at playing princess. When he caught me, I'd never seen him so angry. I thought he was going to murder me.

"As I grew older, I realized his hypocrisy. This respected antiquities dealer who spoke out against the black market had a hidden treasure. A few years ago, I went to visit and took it with me when I left. He arrived in Egypt not long after, searching for me. He was furious, not only because of what I'd done, but because he suspected I'd gotten involved in Ma'at and didn't approve. When he finally tracked me down in Luxor, he demanded it back, but I laughed in his face, told him he should go to the police if he wanted it so badly."

"How did your father acquire the broad collar in the first place?" Charlotte's heart raced as she tried to process what Mona was saying.

Mona shrugged. "No idea. Never bothered to ask. It was a means to an end. We dangled it in front of Mr. Lavigne at the Met, had a forger produce some foolproof fake documentation, and soon enough, the Met agreed to the loan."

"Why did the other children tease you?" asked Annie.

Another waste of a question, but Mona's expression turned ugly. Annie had hit a nerve. "When they heard me speaking with my father, they said I must be adopted."

"Why?" Charlotte straightened.

"Our accents are different. I was raised in Egypt speaking Arabic, but my father wasn't. They laughed when I spoke with my strange accent."

"Where was your father raised?" Charlotte tried to sound cavalier, not desperate.

"He was born in England."

With shaking fingers, Charlotte reached into her handbag and pulled out the ripped photo of Henry. The same one that had sent Heba running into the back of the store to find a pair of glasses she didn't need.

"Is this your father?" Charlotte asked.

Mona stared at the photograph, taking it from Charlotte's hand to study it closer. "Yes, when he was younger, though. Where did you get this?"

"He was my husband," Charlotte said simply. "Henry Smith."

Mona shook her head. "My father's name is Darius Farid."

Charlotte stared at Mona, momentarily at a loss for words. Three years ago, Henry had argued with Leon about his daughter, and also had a confrontation with Mona.

Mona, his daughter.

Charlotte guessed that Mona was probably around the same age as Layla would be. Yet as much as she tried, she didn't feel any kind of connection with the rigid woman standing opposite her. Wouldn't a mother recognize her daughter, even after so many years? Wouldn't there be some kind of pheromone or something that drew them together? Charlotte studied Mona's features, trying to see if there was any resemblance at all. She had her father's ears, visible when she tucked her hair back. But what of Charlotte?

"Darius Farid *is* Henry Smith," Annie said.

Charlotte gathered herself. "This is uncomfortable to bring up; I'm not sure how to say it. Henry—Darius—and I had a child together. A child I never saw again, a child who was only three months old when she and Henry disappeared. I've been looking for her. She would be around your age, I'm guessing."

The color drained from Mona's face. Charlotte imagined the thoughts that were swirling through Mona's head: What if she was the daughter of Henry and Charlotte? What if her strident patriotism for Egypt was all wrong and, in fact, she had no Egyptian blood in her at all?

What an awful reunion, if that was true. A mother and daughter staring at each other, an intractable void between them. A far cry from the tear-filled hugs that Charlotte had envisioned the few times she'd allowed herself to imagine such a thing.

If it was true, then Charlotte wished she'd never known.

CHAPTER TWENTY-NINE

Annie

Annie watched as Charlotte and Mona reassessed each other in front of the Temple of Dendur. They both had dark hair and eyes, but that was about it. Mona's face was a different shape from Charlotte's; their profiles were different as well. But then again, Annie hardly resembled her mother at all. That kind of thing happened all the time.

If Mona was indeed Layla, how awful for Charlotte. She would have found her daughter, but one who had done a terrible thing by stealing the Cerulean Queen. A daughter who fought against everything Charlotte believed in.

"When were you born?" asked Charlotte after an interminable silence.

"The tenth of February 1939."

"My daughter was born in August of 1937."

Close, but not that close. Even Annie, who'd had little interaction with young children, knew it would've been hard to pass a five-year-old off as a three-year-old.

Of course, if Henry had changed his name, he could have easily changed Layla's and falsified the birth record.

Mona looked Charlotte up and down. "Rest assured, I am *not* your daughter, if that's what you're thinking."

Charlotte didn't seem so convinced. "Did your father ever mention me?"

"Did he ever tell me that he'd been married before? No, of course not."

"What about your mother?"

"What about her?"

"She obviously recognized him in the photograph I showed her, even if I called him Henry Smith."

Mona's mouth shot up in a snarl. "What are you talking about? When did you see my mother?"

Charlotte, caught up in the moment, had given away too much. She looked over at Annie, as if she was unsure how to respond, so Annie stepped in. "We just got back from Egypt. We tracked down Leon Pitcairn in Luxor last week, and ran into your mother when we stopped by the Farid Gallery," she said.

"You were in Luxor and Cairo? Why were you at the gallery?" Mona's accent had become more pronounced, and now that Annie had spent time in Egypt, she recognized it as Arabic, a fact she never would have picked up before. She recalled their conversation before the Met Gala, as the bartenders were setting up, when Mona had complained about the many traffic lights in New York. Now it made sense: She had been comparing it to the free-flowing mayhem of Cairo.

It had been Mona all along.

Charlotte was pale, probably still in shock from the revelation about Mona's father being Henry, so Annie took over. "The Farid

Gallery is where we first saw the King Tut plaster statue, the one that had the Cerulean Queen hidden inside it."

Mona took a couple of steps back. "Wait, how do you know that?"

Before they'd left Egypt, Omar had told Annie and Charlotte what the police learned from Heba's assistant, Nephi Nasr—the man Heba had called out for the first time they'd visited the shop and the same one who'd attacked her and Charlotte both at the Met and in Cairo.

Annie took a deep breath. "We know you were working with Leon, Ma'at's logistics coordinator, who handled the customs arrangements for the King Tut plaster to get from New York to Cairo. After Nasr stole it from the Met, he sent it back to Egypt in a box filled with cheap souvenirs bound for the Farid Gallery. From there, it was supposed to be handed off to another operative by Nasr, but we intercepted it before that could happen."

Annie didn't reveal the rest of the story: that once in custody, Nasr admitted that he'd recognized Annie from the Met heist when she and Charlotte first wandered into the Farid Gallery. He'd retreated to the back room, listened in on their conversation, and decided to trail them, make sure they didn't get too close. Luckily, Jabari's grandfather had insisted Jabari keep an eye on Charlotte and Annie until they were safely out of the country, which meant their stalker had a stalker of his own.

It was Mona's turn to be speechless. "How do you know all this?" she finally sputtered.

"I saw a photo of you and your mother on her desk." In the photo, Mona's arm was draped over Heba's shoulders during a trip to the seashore. They were laughing, obviously comfortable in each other's company, obviously close. Mona's mother was her weak point, her Achilles' heel.

It was time to go in for the kill, and Charlotte took over.

"The police raided the shop," said Charlotte. "Nasr led the Egyptian police to a storage unit where they recovered the other antiquities, similarly hidden inside King Tut plaster statues. Nasr, Leon Pitcairn, and your mother have all been arrested, and we're told there will be more Egyptian arrests announced soon."

Mona's scornful pride crumbled. "They arrested my mother? She had nothing to do with it, nothing at all. We kept her out of it, to protect her."

"You used your mother's shop assistant to funnel stolen items into the country," said Charlotte. "How are you surprised she got caught up in the police raid?"

The confusion and fear on Heba's face finally made sense. She might have wondered what Charlotte and Annie were up to after they showed her the photo of the man she knew as Darius, and lied because she didn't trust them. But she had no idea that her daughter was part of Ma'at.

"I have to go. Consider your file destroyed." Mona spun on her heel but came to a sharp halt as Mr. Fantoni and his security team, along with Frederick and Mr. Lavigne, streamed out of the Temple of Dendur. At the same time, uniformed police officers stepped out from where they'd been posted at each gallery exit.

One policeman handcuffed Mona as another read her her rights. "The police are currently searching the Upper East Side apartment you share with your husband, the importer/exporter named Karim Salah," said Mr. Fantoni. "Karim is in the process of being arrested in Munich, where we believe he's been surveying another museum for a possible hit."

"My mother?" Mona cried. "How is she? Where is she?"

The transformation of Mona from a haughty, overconfident Upper East Side matron into a panicked, frightened daughter was sudden and shocking. While she might love her mother, her single-minded zeal had brought them both down.

Mona swiveled her head around as the police began to lead her away. "Wait a minute. You want to find your daughter? I know where she is."

"You do?" Charlotte stepped toward her. "Where?"

Mona gave her a dark look and spit on the floor. "I'll never tell. You go after my mother? This is what you get in return. And to think she was right under your nose."

"Please. What are you saying?"

She smirked, as if enjoying a private joke. "It will be a cold day in hell when I tell you. Very, very cold."

Mona's laugh echoed off the walls as she was led away.

After the arrest, Mr. Lavigne, Frederick, and Mr. Fantoni congratu-lated Charlotte for a job well done and she insisted they extend the same courtesy to Annie. "I couldn't have accomplished any of this without Annie Jenkins," she said, and they made a point of shaking Annie's hand as well. On their way out, at the information desk in the Great Hall, Charlotte asked for an interoffice memo and placed the slides of the faded hieroglyphs from Hathorkare's tomb inside, along with a note to her conservator friend Helen. "It's worth a try," she said to Annie with a shrug.

Outside the Met, the air smelled like snow and Annie shivered in her windbreaker, already missing the desert warmth of Egypt. Nei-ther she nor Charlotte had been home yet—not that Annie had a home—and it felt odd to be parting after the roller coaster of the past few days. She didn't want to have to say goodbye just yet.

"Do you think Mona really knows where Layla is? Or that she *is* Layla? She said, 'Right under your nose.' Does that mean herself?"

Charlotte hugged her arms to her chest. "I have no idea anymore. I wouldn't put it past her to lie in order to torture me. In the end, only Henry can tell me the truth. If she *is* Mona, I'll be relieved that she's alive, but bereft at who she turned out to be."

"So you're going to try to find Henry?"

"Yes. I have to find out what happened, hear his side of the story. I'll head to Switzerland as soon as I've had time to go home and repack."

Her voice trailed off and her eyes grew watery.

Annie had gotten what she was after by going to Egypt, and she should be bursting with excitement that she'd helped track down the Cerulean Queen and bring the thief to justice. But she wasn't, because Charlotte had come away empty-handed, with even more questions than she had when she'd started.

"I'm happy to come to Switzerland with you," offered Annie. "We make a good team, and you might need someone around to divert bad guys with broken perfume bottles."

Charlotte pulled Annie into a deep hug. "I have to do this on my own," she whispered into her ear. "You understand, don't you?"

Now they were both crying. "Of course I do."

CHAPTER THIRTY

Charlotte

At home, Mark was careful with Charlotte at first, holding her like she might break, but then they got coffee and sat in the living room and she told him everything she'd learned, everything she and Annie had done, and by the end of her story he kissed her hand and told Charlotte how proud he was of her. When she added that she now had to go to Switzerland to find Henry, he insisted on coming along.

She changed the subject. "How is Lori?"

"Well, she didn't get the soap opera," said Mark. "But she did land a national commercial for toothpaste, which apparently, after it airs, will bring in some 'serious dough,' as she called it."

"That's great news."

"Yes. So you can have your office back, finally."

"That's all right. Lori can stay there."

Mark shook his head. "No, you've put up with enough."

"What I mean is, I'm going away, and I may not be back for a while."

"I thought *we* were going away. Didn't I just say that?" he asked testily.

She'd mulled over this conversation during the plane ride home, when she'd realized she wasn't looking forward to returning to the apartment. It wasn't her home, never had been. In fact, as she looked around the room, she didn't recognize anything as hers, not the books in the bookshelf, nor the armchair by the fireplace, nor the silk curtains on the windows. Her imprint was difficult to find because the apartment had first belonged to Mark's mother, followed by his wife. For whatever reason—Charlotte was always too busy with work; interior decorating didn't appeal—she'd never claimed any spot other than her office as her own. It was as if she'd known deep down she wasn't going to be here forever. "I don't want you to come with me," she said finally. "I need to take some time. Alone."

"For how long, exactly?"

"I don't know."

He sat back on the couch and placed his hands on his legs. "Huh. What about your job? King Tut opens in two weeks."

"Please don't talk to me like I'm a child."

He took a breath. "You're right, I'm sorry. What is it you're trying to say?"

"I'm sorry, but I'm leaving for good, Mark. I love what we had, but it's time for me to move on. This isn't working, and I feel like I'm in the way." She shook her head. "No, that's not it, or at least not all of it. We want different things for our lives. You want a wife, and I need to be free."

To her surprise, he didn't seem hurt or shocked. Maybe he was thinking of Lori and how, without Charlotte present, they would be able to reconnect in a way that was impossible right now. Or maybe he was putting up a brave front to save face.

"I'm sorry to hear it, Charlotte," he said. "To be honest, I've been thinking about our relationship ever since our discussion on the steps of the Met. The fact that you only recently told me about a momentous event in your life indicates that yes, maybe you're looking for something different. That I'm not the right man for you."

But I'm not looking for a man, Charlotte thought. The narrow way he framed the issue only served to confirm that she was making the right decision, as difficult as it was. "You deserve someone who is as committed as you are, and I can never be." She paused. "I'm sorry if I misled you."

He laughed softly. "You never misled me. I just refused to see it, until now. I guess I hoped eventually you'd be all mine."

An impossible ask.

Because only Layla could claim that mantle.

The next available flight to Switzerland didn't leave for two days, so Charlotte enjoyed a leisurely breakfast with Mark and Lori the next morning before heading to work. Mark had told Charlotte the prior evening to take all the time she needed, that there was no need for her to rush to pack her things or find a new place to live, and now that the air between them was finally cleared, she was able to see him in a new light. The gentle kindness with which he treated his daughter, and way the two teased each other and laughed, brought tears to Charlotte's eyes. She was lucky to know them both, and hoped she could remain in their lives in some way.

At the Met, Frederick sidled over to Charlotte as soon as she sat down at her desk.

"Welcome back, conquering hero," he said, giving a slight shake of his head. "How was Egypt, then?"

"It was beautiful," answered Charlotte.

"Quite the detective you were, tracking down the Cerulean

Queen. Of course, now we have to give the broad collar back to the Egyptian authorities, which is a shame as our one-year loan only lasted two weeks, but so be it."

Of course he focused on the negative. "It had been stolen, of course it has to go back."

"We don't even have our Queen, or at least, not for a while. The Egyptian Museum has asked for some sort of time-sharing arrangement: They get it for a year, then we do. The director is actually considering it."

"As long as they keep it safe and sound, I don't see why not. It was theirs to begin with."

He pulled his chin into his neck like a chicken whose egg had just been stolen. "That's not the Charlotte Cross I know. What happened to you over there?" He didn't wait for an answer. "Anyway, I've been giving interviews to newspapers nonstop. I'm exhausted, but thanks to you we have a happy ending."

"You're welcome."

He lowered his voice. "What about your other project?"

"Hathorkare?"

"Yes. Anything?"

"We identified her mummy, but that news will be broken by Omar Abdullah at the Egyptian Museum."

"I see. Were you able to uncover any evidence disputing the fact that Saukemet II destroyed her images in revenge?"

She thought of the faded hieroglyphics. There had been no return message from Helen this morning, unfortunately. And Hathorkare's tomb was irreparably damaged. "I'm afraid not."

Frederick looked like he was about to rise into the air, his relief was so palpable. "That's too bad. But at least it means we don't have to change her entry in the department catalog."

It also meant Frederick's standing was secure.

She was gathering the courage to tell him that she was leaving again, this time for Europe, when her phone rang.

She picked up the receiver. "This is Charlotte Cross."

A familiar voice answered. "Charlotte, it's Helen. Come downstairs. I have something you might want to see."

"Annie!"

Charlotte called out to Annie in the basement of the Met, thrilled to see her.

"You haven't left for Switzerland yet?" asked Annie, giving Charlotte a generous hug. She wore platform heels, striped pants, and a man's vest over a white blouse, and walked with a newfound confidence.

"Not yet. In fact, you have to come with me."

Annie checked her watch. "I've been summoned to see Mrs. Vreeland, but I'm early. Where are we going?"

"To visit my friend Helen." Charlotte explained about the phone call. "I don't know if it's good news or bad, but either way, it would be nice to have you there."

"Of course."

Charlotte led the way into the Met's conservation workshop, where several oversized paintings in various stages of restoration perched on paint-splattered easels. On the other side of the room were large worktables used for panel work and varnishing. Helen's altarpiece panels were near completion, with only a few sections of gilding left on the final panel. The other two looked much like they would have when they were finished in the 1400s, a substantial achievement.

However, Helen's chair was empty.

"Over here!"

She waved to them from a door near the back of the room. Inside was a projector and a large screen. "Come in, sit. How was your trip?"

Charlotte introduced Annie and gave Helen a quick summary. "You're really sweet to put your work aside to play with my slides. I know they're not very good."

"You're telling me. You didn't give me much to work with."

Charlotte's heart sank. She hadn't realized how much she was hoping for a miracle. "What a waste of time. Thanks for trying."

"Oh, I did more than try. I've been here all night."

"All night? You didn't have to do that."

"Your note said it was urgent, and I have to say I was intrigued."

Helen turned off the lights and turned on the projector. The faint images that appeared looked even worse on the bright white screen than Charlotte remembered, only pitiful wisps of random color and lines.

"Ugh," said Charlotte. "I can't make out a single symbol."

"That's true," said Helen. "But instead of projecting the slides onto a screen the way I'm doing now, I used a large piece of drawing paper and painstakingly filled in whatever I could discern. I have a few more slides left to do, but I wanted you to see the initial results." She turned off the projector, turned on the lights, and retracted the screen. Behind it hung the result of her efforts: marvelous, fully colorized hieroglyphics and paintings from the walls of Hathorkare's tomb as they must have looked right before it was sealed.

Annie squealed with delight.

Charlotte drew close and pointed to the symbols. "These are incredible. Over here, she's shown as a masculine ruler, from the reddish skin and the way her left foot is extended forward, but the text retains her feminine name. This depicts her divine birth and coronation. And over here she's making an offering to her husband, Sauke-met I. This last one includes the cartouche of a scribe who worked first for Hathorkare, and later for Saukemet II, Ankhsheshonq."

A vague memory rose in Charlotte's jet-lagged brain of Henry making fun of the name after she mentioned she'd translated an os-tracon between the scribe and a master craftsman. *Sounds like a cam-el's sneeze*, he'd said.

Ankhsheshonq.

She closed her eyes, remembering the Egyptian heat, the feel of limestone under her fingertips. "Huh."

"What?" asked Helen. She and Annie gathered on either side of Charlotte.

"Ankhsheshonq," she repeated. "When I was first in Egypt, one of my jobs was translating contracts, wills—even shopping lists—found in a small village near the Valley of the Kings, all the day-to-day evidence of what life was like in ancient Egypt. One of the pieces was a contract between the scribe Ankhsheshonq, acting on behalf of Saukemet II, and a master craftsman. What stood out at the time—and I'd forgotten this completely until now, as I had no context—was that instead of being asked to decorate a temple wall, he was being asked to alter an existing relief, by carving it out and changing the cartouche from the former queen to that of the future king. Hathorkare to Saukemet III."

"So Ankhsheshonq was involved in the campaign to erase Ha-thorkare?" said Annie.

"Yes, but I can't remember the wording of the contract exactly."

"Where did the ostracon end up?" asked Helen.

"I have no idea. Possibly here at the Met, if we're lucky."

The three headed to the Met's library, where the librarian handed over a copy of the *Egyptian Arts Collection Catalog, Volume I.* Charlotte turned to the index and ran her finger down a column. She found the corresponding page and gave out a yelp. "Yes! That's it. It's here in the building."

They flew off to the storage area listed in the entry.

Charlotte had a new appreciation for the catalog, even if it included sexist views of Hathorkare and was a beast to update. Its format also made locating anything in the collection easy, and in no time they were standing in front of a large cabinet in one of the smaller basement storage rooms. Charlotte gently pulled out the third drawer from the bottom.

Inside, several large pieces of limestone filled with hieratic writing lay in shallow, custom-made foam dishes. "This is it," said Charlotte. "Oh my God."

"What?" said Annie and Helen in unison.

She pointed to one of the shards with her pen without touching it. "Here Ankhsheshonq writes that Saukemet II only wants the images of Hathorkare as a king to be erased. He requests that, when possible, her likeness be replaced with that of his son, who is to be referred to as 'Egypt's next divine king.' Here it has the date." Excitement rippled through her. "Do you know what that means?"

"You have proof that the erasures were ordered long after Hathorkare's death, as well as the reason why," Annie proclaimed.

"Exactly. Saukemet II was worried about his son being trounced by a female rival, not angry at his long-dead stepmother. And to think it was right under my nose all along, locked away in storage, long forgotten. When I first translated the contract, I didn't understand its importance. Hathorkare was a minor pharaoh, so no one really cared. But now we have solid evidence of the reason why the erasures occurred, as well as the date. We did it!"

"*You* did it," said Helen.

"Group effort, shall we say?" said Charlotte, putting her arms around her friends.

"Frederick is going to have a fit," said Helen.

Charlotte thanked Helen profusely, promising to fill her in on the rest of the details from the trip as soon as she had a spare minute, then gave Annie a hug and wished her good luck in her meeting with Diana Vreeland.

Poor Frederick. He'd challenged Charlotte to find proof, and she had, but the joy derived from the validation of her theory was tempered by the impact it would have on her boss. He wasn't an easy man to work with, but she wished him the best. Hopefully the financial success of the King Tut exhibit would lessen the blow of a junior colleague undermining his area of expertise.

Just as Charlotte had been reluctant to return to the apartment she shared with Mark after her adventures in Egypt, it suddenly occurred to her that she didn't want to have to spend another day in her cubby at the Egyptian Art department, either. Her time in Egypt had been painful and wondrous, but she wasn't ready to leave it behind. Not just yet.

Furthermore, she'd saved a good deal of her salary, and had nothing left in New York to tie her down. Which meant she had the freedom to choose what she wanted to do with the rest of her life, and where she wanted to do it. With growing excitement, she considered going to Switzerland to track down Henry and then heading straight to Egypt.

Mark, no doubt, would say she was being rash. She had a position most would envy, and she'd miss her fellow employees at the Met, from the security guards who greeted her each morning to the technicians and handlers who loved the objects they encountered every day as much as she did.

But it was time to move on.

She went straight to Frederick's office and told him about the evidence she'd uncovered. He looked at her in disbelief and rose out of his chair. "I need to see this for myself."

Charlotte stopped him. "There's something else."

He sat back down with a frown. "Yes?"

"I have some family business I need to attend to, in Europe. I'll be leaving tomorrow."

"You can't. King Tut—"

She cut him off. "I'll be heading to Egypt after that. That's where I belong, and there's so much lost time to make up for."

He cocked his head, as if she had to be joking. "You're saying you're leaving the Met?"

"I suppose I am."

"May I remind you that you're sixty, Charlotte?"

She remembered Annie's advice. "So what? In three years I'll be sixty-three and wishing I'd done so when I was sixty. It's just a number."

"You can't go. What about me and the exhibition?" he pleaded. "You're too old to be making drastic life changes, stop and think for a minute."

How lovely of him to make it so easy, thought Charlotte. "Thank you for all the responsibility you've given me, Frederick, and I'm sorry to miss the King Tut exhibition. But this is what I have to do."

CHAPTER THIRTY-ONE

Annie

Annie's homecoming hadn't been as terrible as she predicted it would be. Sure, she still didn't have a place to live or a job, but after the trip with Charlotte, her world had opened up, and now she understood that clinging to her old life wasn't worth it.

Yesterday, after the successful arrest of Mona, Joyce's boyfriend had let Annie into the basement apartment with a look of confusion on his face. Brad—a mild-mannered guy with no chin or shoulders to speak of, which gave the unfortunate impression he was slowly melting into the ground—seemed uncertain as to who exactly Annie was.

Joyce had never even mentioned Annie's existence.

So while Joyce got herself out of the bath and dressed at warp speed after Brad announced Annie was here, Annie genially introduced herself as Joyce's daughter. The irony that Charlotte was desperate to find her missing child while Joyce was doing everything she could to erase Annie from her life was not lost on Annie. But it also didn't crush her the way it might have two weeks earlier.

Annie was no longer angry at Joyce for her terrible decisions.

Those were her mother's choices, and Annie didn't need to fix them or change them. Whether Joyce's marriage to Brad worked out or not was not Annie's problem. She hoped it would work out, but if it failed, she would be there for Joyce in a new way, as a sympathetic observer, not as a fixer.

Joyce had emerged from the bedroom, her hair up in a towel, and sheepishly introduced them. By then, they'd had a pleasant enough discussion about the best place to get a burger in the neighborhood as well as the various eccentricities of Mrs. Hollingsworth upstairs. Joyce went on and on about their plans for the future while not asking a thing about Annie's trip nor her plans, and so after ten minutes Annie excused herself and left.

Upstairs with Mrs. H, Annie explained that she'd need a place to stay for a few weeks until she got settled, and thanked her for having the foresight to withhold some of Annie's pay each week, that the trip she'd taken to Egypt had turned her life around in a good way. Mrs. H smiled and put her bony hand over Annie's. "That's my girl," she said. "By the way, Mrs. Vreeland called me a little while ago. She's trying to track you down. Looks like you have a second chance."

Then, this morning, Annie had got caught up in the whirlwind of seeing Charlotte and the revelation of Helen's drawings made from the Kodachrome slides, not to mention the rediscovery of the ancient contract, which left Annie no time to get nervous for her meeting with Mrs. Vreeland.

The Costume Institute workroom was empty now that the exhibition was up and running, and Mrs. Vreeland warmly welcomed Annie into her office, lit a cigarette, and asked all about the trip, more than making up for Joyce's indifference. Rather than making the standard inquiries—did she see the pyramids (unfortunately, no) and did she ride a camel (again, no)—Mrs. Vreeland asked what the Egyptian women were wearing and raved about the softness of the

Egyptian cotton button-down shirts she'd bought her last time in the country.

"Were any of the clothes from the exhibition damaged?" Annie asked. That was her one worry, that the moths had gotten to the delicate silks and embroidery on display.

"They fumigated that evening, so not a flying insect was left. All is in order." She drew on her cigarette. "What now, for you?"

"I'm not exactly sure."

"I'd like you to come back and work for me, if you're willing. I thought we did well together, until I overreacted and sent you packing. Your involvement in the recovery of the Cerulean Queen has this place in an uproar, and I have to admit I'm mightily impressed with your gumption."

"I'm not sure I'm up to your standards, Mrs. Vreeland," Annie admitted honestly.

"Don't sell yourself short, girl. I believe in the rare, the extravagant, the utmost of everything. I don't believe in the middle of the road because I don't think it's good company. But ultimately, it is for you to discover for yourself, within yourself." Mrs. Vreeland looked off into the distance, lost in her own verbiage. "Within the silent green-cool groves of an inner world where, alone and free, you may dream the *possible* dream: that the wondrous is real, because that is how you feel it to be, that is how you wish it to be. And how you wish it into being."

Annie was flummoxed by what exactly Mrs. Vreeland had just said. "English, please."

Mrs. Vreeland let out a girlish laugh. "*That's* what I like about you. You don't put up with my nonsense. Please, give me a second chance. I'm already dreaming up themes for next year's exhibition." She held both hands up in the air, palms out, fingers spread. "*Fashions of the Hapsburg Era: Austria-Hungary.* Can't you just see it?"

"Not exactly, but it sounds intriguing."

"I'm off to Vienna and Budapest next week. Care to join me?"

No matter Mrs. Vreeland's quirks, she had a lot to teach Annie. The offer was too good to pass up, and Annie accepted the job without any reservations. She'd grown so much since the first time she'd walked into the Costume Institute carrying Mrs. H's feather boa in a paper bag. She had a newfound faith in herself and her capabilities, one she was eager to apply to her role as Mrs. Vreeland's assistant.

As Annie passed through the basement gallery of the Western European Arts collection on her way upstairs, she heard her name called out.

Billy strode over and gave her hand a hearty shake. "Annie Jenkins! You're the hero of the Met. We heard all about how you found the Cerulean Queen and took out the thief in the process. Just amazing." His grip was strong and warm, and his eyes shone.

"Well, it wasn't quite like that."

"Can I buy you a coffee to celebrate? And as thanks? I learned yesterday that I can still stay on at the job, thank goodness."

Seeing Billy so happy and enthusiastic was a relief. She would've hated to think their friendship had cost him his job.

In the staff caf, she answered his questions about her trip (pyramids, no; camel ride, no; mummies, yes) and then they settled into an easy conversation about his application to New York University, which he'd just submitted. "Fingers crossed I get good news in April," he said. "And what about you? Are you coming back to the Met?"

"Actually, I accepted, for the second time in a month, the job of assistant to Mrs. Vreeland," said Annie.

"That's great! She's lucky to have you."

"I realized I'm no longer intimidated by her. Well, not as much as I was before. Being in Egypt—it's hard to explain—but it changed everything. After almost being killed during a tomb cave-in, asking Mrs. Vreeland what on earth she means is no big deal."

"You seem different. Not that you weren't extremely compelling before." Billy looked straight at her with his big brown eyes.

Annie took a sip of her coffee to hide the blush that she was certain was crawling across her cheeks.

"Well, now that you're back at the Met," he said, "I hope I can take you out on a real date. Would that be all right?"

"I couldn't think of anything better."

Annie was still beaming from her conversation with Billy as she crossed the Great Hall on her way out. At the information desk, she overheard a man ask for Charlotte Cross. She turned to see who it was, but he had his back to her. The clerk informed the man that Charlotte wasn't at the museum, and she was unsure of her exact return date.

"Blast it!" said the man.

In an English accent.

He was tall, wearing a tan overcoat, with curly gray hair cut short. Short enough that Annie could see a large pair of ears sticking out from either side of his head.

It was Henry.

Charlotte's Henry was here.

CHAPTER THIRTY-TWO

Charlotte

As Charlotte was cleaning out her desk, the phone rang, a jarring sound in the tiny cubby.

She picked up the receiver. "Hello?"

"Charlotte, it's Annie." She was breathless, as if she'd run a marathon. "He's here at the information desk. You've got to come at once. He's here, asking for you."

All sorts of terrible images flew through Charlotte's mind at the panic in Annie's voice: that Leon had escaped from the Egyptian authorities and was after them, or another Ma'at goon was out for revenge. "Calm down. Who? Who is asking for me?"

She heard Annie take a deep breath.

"Henry," she said finally. "Henry's here. He's waiting for you."

Charlotte registered nothing but the path directly in front of her as she made her way to the Great Hall. She still couldn't believe Henry was at the Met.

After decades apart, she wasn't sure how she was supposed to behave. Pummel his chest with her fists? Offer to shake hands? The last time they'd seen each other had been the most traumatic experience of her life, and now he'd shown up out of the blue. She resented that he had the element of surprise. That was what she'd been counting on by going to Geneva—having the upper hand—but at the very least, Henry was on her home turf. The Met was her domain, not his.

She stepped clear of the tourists and spotted Annie and, standing next to her, Henry. He carried himself much the same, the only difference a slight stoop to his shoulders and a heaviness about his eyes. This was the man who she'd once shared all her secrets, hopes, and dreams with. They'd created another human being together and marveled over their baby's ears and toes. He was obviously older, his hair gray instead of brown, but in looking at him, she saw the ghost of his younger self, which shimmered past the age spots on his temples and the folds around his eyes.

At first, Henry appeared stuck, like the marble floors had turned to quicksand, but then he took a step forward. "Charlotte. My God. It's you."

They stood a yard apart, surveying each other, Henry shifting uncomfortably from foot to foot, as if he wanted to take her into his arms. Charlotte remained where she was, stiff, her body turned to ice. If he dared to approach her, she was sure she'd crack into pieces. This was the man she'd married, the man she'd carried a child for, the man who had run away and disappeared into the ether. Until now.

"Follow me," Charlotte said to Henry. She turned to Annie. "Thanks for the call. I've got it from here."

Annie nodded and stepped back, her eyes worried.

Charlotte took Henry to the most private place in the museum, the rooftop, where visitors weren't allowed.

"You planning on pushing me off?" Henry quipped as they stepped out onto a large, unoccupied balcony. Charlotte hadn't seen him for just over four decades, but she knew from his tone that he was only half joking. Good. Let him wonder whether or not she was unhinged. She wasn't sure herself, at this very moment.

"Figure I'd give myself the option," she answered back.

Neither of them smiled.

In the watery winter light, their days in the desert seemed like another lifetime. Charlotte's stomach felt like it was full of rocks, her head reeled. She noticed Annie emerging from the shadows of the doorway but didn't mind the intrusion. The girl held back, giving them some privacy while keeping a wary eye on Charlotte, her presence a comfort to what was sure to be a difficult conversation.

"What are you doing here?" Charlotte asked Henry. "After forty-one years. *Forty-one years.* Now you show up?"

"Friends in Cairo phoned me to say there had been some kind of a raid, that the gallery was shut. I tried to reach Heba with no luck, and then I learned that Mona had been arrested here in New York. I was sick with worry and flew out immediately. She wouldn't tell me what was going on, other than to say that the person responsible for her arrest was Charlotte Cross, from the Met. She added that she was fairly certain I'd know who that was."

The way the names of Henry's new family so easily tripped off his tongue made Charlotte sick with jealousy and resentment. *She* had been there first. Hers and Layla's should be the names on his lips, not those of these two strangers. He'd created a whole other life after ruining hers, and now he thought he could share his concern for their well-being with her as if she were some random bystander?

He must've read the fury in her face. He reached out helplessly with his hands. "I didn't know you were alive. You have to believe me, Charlotte. I thought you'd died in the shipwreck."

"Did you bother to look for me, even?"

"Of course. It was chaos, no one knew what was going on. What happened?"

She shook her head, remembering. "It was terrible."

"Tell me."

The words came out slowly. "They brought me to a hospital at first, but I was out of my mind with worry, and I was screaming, I couldn't stop screaming. They gave me some kind of sedative, and the next thing I knew, I woke up in a psychiatric hospital. I was in and out for days, weeks, maybe, before I was able to pull myself together and face what happened. They said you were never found." She couldn't say Layla's name out loud. She wouldn't say it. He didn't deserve to hear it.

"Please believe me, I tried," implored Henry.

She cut him off, hating the distraught look in his eyes. "But there were extenuating circumstances, weren't there? You and Leon had to flee the country, that's why we left in such a rush, right?" She waited, but Henry didn't deny it. "Maybe, if you weren't on the run, you would have found me eventually. Leon said it was your idea to smuggle antiquities out of the country in the first place."

"No, that's not true. Leon had been doing it long before he convinced me to join in, during that summer we worked at the Egyptian Museum. He said it would be better to get the antiquities into the hands of a buyer who would take care of them, not the Egyptian Museum, where they'd be stuck in crates in the basement and never seen again. But that's all nonsense, I realize now." He thrust his hands into his pockets. "To be honest, I was desperate to make something of myself, prove to you and your parents that I was worthy of you. My salary was a pittance, and on top of that we were starting a family. Meanwhile, I was struggling to pay the rent on the apartment in Cairo. I kept wondering how on earth I could afford to take care of a wife and daughter."

"Why didn't you tell me this?"

"I couldn't bear to see the disappointment in your eyes. I figured the money would give us a head start and your parents would see that I was a good husband, a good provider.

"The night of the shipwreck and for the next two days I scoured the hospitals until one of the doctors told me to stop pestering them, that you were most likely dead. I was in shock. I went to the airport and took the next plane out using the forged documents Leon had given me. I'm so, so sorry." He was pleading now. "I wrote your parents a letter a few months after the accident, telling them how much I loved you and how sorry I was for their loss. I wanted them to know that I thought of you every day."

Charlotte's head spun as she tried to digest this new information. "You wrote to my parents?"

"Yes. Your father wrote back, saying that they were in mourning and requesting that I never contact them again. I'm sure they wanted nothing to do with me, which I understood, of course."

That couldn't be right. "In mourning?"

"Yes. In mourning. So you can imagine my shock hearing your name from Mona."

It was no surprise that Charlotte's parents would want to keep Henry as far away from her as possible. After all, he was the man who'd ruined their daughter. And it wasn't the only instance that important information had been kept from Charlotte. Her mother had burned the letter from Mr. Zimmerman offering her a job, and the only reason she'd known was that she'd overheard their exchange. Otherwise, her life might have taken an entirely different trajectory, as it also would have if they'd informed her of Henry's correspondence.

Henry *had* tried to contact her. She remembered her mother's words on her deathbed. She'd said a man had been looking for Charlotte; she'd apologized for having interfered. It was Henry, all that time. "They lied to you. I was alive."

"As was I." Henry inhaled hard. "My God. Charlotte. All these years, lost."

Charlotte collected herself as best she could, unable to process the latest revelation. There were still more questions to be asked.

"So you stayed in Geneva?"

"I started a small gallery. Although I financed it by selling some of the smuggled goods, I vowed from then on I would be aboveboard in my dealings."

"How honorable of you," she said dryly. "Was it in Geneva that you acquired your new family?"

He flinched. "Heba, who was living in Geneva at the time, came on as my business partner, and we fell in love and then she became pregnant."

Which meant Mona was Heba's daughter, She wasn't Layla.

Charlotte had the sensation of falling off a cliff, only to find herself suspended in midair. "Mona is not our daughter?"

Henry blinked. "No. Of course not. To be honest, it made me sick, the idea of having another child. It brought up so many memories, and eventually I told Heba that I'd been married before. That I'd had a daughter before. She was furious, and moved back to Cairo to open a shop while I stayed in Geneva."

Which explained why Heba didn't admit to knowing Henry/Darius after being shown the photograph in the Farid Gallery. No doubt Charlotte's presence had dredged up all kinds of resentment and hurt.

"Although the galleries shared the same name," continued Henry, "we ran them as separate entities—Heba insisted on that. Mona visited me during the summers and I tried to be a good father, but it was hard from that distance. Then, after she married Karim, she became more strident about her Egyptian heritage, about the corruption in the antiquities trade. She became even angrier at me."

"How did she know Leon?"

Henry grimaced, as if the memory hurt physically. "Several years ago, I went to Cairo and took her out to dinner. We ran into Leon, who, unbeknownst to me, was working with Ma'at by then." There was a short pause. "To think the same man who'd served prison time for smuggling antiquities *out* of Egypt was now involved with an illegal organization trying to smuggle them back *in*. In any event, it kills me that I was the reason for their connection."

"And at one point, you went to Luxor to confront him."

"Yes. I knew Mona was putting herself in danger and I tried to warn her, which resulted in a blowup in the lobby of the Winter Palace Hotel. I confronted Leon at his apartment and told him to keep away from Mona, which didn't do much good at all. Now Mona's gone and taken Heba down with her. It should be me in that Egyptian jail cell."

Henry's bad decision all those years ago had wreaked disaster after disaster. At the same time, Charlotte's own parents had lied to her, taking away her chance of closure, although any rage directed their way was wasted. They were long gone, having taken the secret to their graves.

As for Henry, he would remain tortured the rest of his life. There would be no peace for Henry.

But maybe there would be for Charlotte. It was time.

"What about Layla?"

"What about her?" Henry genuinely looked confused.

"What happened after you went up to the top deck of the ship?"

"You don't know? Of course you don't. I explained it in my letter." He walked to the edge of the rooftop and then back to Charlotte, his fists clenched. "The letter that your parents never showed you. What a heartless thing to do."

"Please. Tell me now."

CHAPTER THIRTY-THREE

Annie

Annie watched the scene between Charlotte and Henry with a heavy heart. Around them, the city fanned out in every direction, but for some reason the sounds of traffic and car horns didn't reach the roof of the Met; all was silent other than the hiss of the wind and the words of Charlotte and the man she'd once loved. Annie knew it was wrong to follow them, but she didn't trust Henry and wanted to be there for Charlotte in case she needed her.

Henry took a deep breath, his face stricken. "I'm so sorry, Charlotte. They told me Layla died."

Charlotte held very still but otherwise betrayed no emotion. "Did they find her body?"

"No. There was no body."

"Then how do they know for sure she's gone?"

"How could she have survived? Once I got to the top deck, the few lifeboats that worked had been released. The ship went down quickly, and we went down with it. I held on to her for as long as I could, but she was sucked out of my arms by the current. I promise you, I tried." Henry had tears in his eyes. "I didn't care what happened after that, I gave up, but someone grabbed me and pulled me onto a lifeboat and I passed out. The next thing I knew, I was on land, coughing up water. I crawled to the riverbank, determined to sink back into the Nile where Layla and you were, but they stopped me and took me away."

A sob burst from Charlotte's mouth and Henry's expression crumpled, but neither moved to comfort the other; they stood in place, individual statues of a shared agony.

"I wonder about her every day," said Henry. "If she would have had my ears. Or your hair, that silver streak passed down from mother to child."

For the first time, Annie really noticed the stripe of gray that ran from Charlotte's right temple, a sharp contrast to the dark brown around it. Before, her short haircut had made it almost imperceptible, but it had grown out since they'd first met.

Charlotte spoke. "Mona, before she was taken away, said that Layla was alive, that she knew where she was but would never reveal it."

"You think she was telling the truth?" asked Henry. He looked unconvinced.

"I don't know. At first I thought Mona *was* Layla, and for a moment, I think, so did she. But she didn't appear to consider that theory very long. As if she knew otherwise."

"What did she say?"

"She said that Layla was right under my nose, and that it would be a cold day in hell before she told me."

"Very, very cold."

Annie didn't realize she'd voiced her thoughts out loud until she looked up to see Charlotte and Henry staring at her.

"I didn't realize we had company," said Henry. "I'm sorry, what did you say?"

"Mona said it would be a 'very, very cold day in hell,'" repeated Annie.

"What does that mean?" said Henry.

A swirl of images ran through Annie's head. The way Mona had looked as she spoke to them, as if venom dripped off her lips, the sheer joy of torturing someone else too good to pass up. Mona was telling the truth.

Somewhere, Mona had met Layla.

But where? Cairo? New York?

Right under your nose.

She closed her eyes and remembered the soothing light of chandeliers, the feel of a thick carpet underfoot, and, in a rush, the cold, stale air of New York was replaced by the scent of vanilla, the murmuring of soft voices, and the ding of a bell.

She knew exactly where to find Layla.

CHAPTER THIRTY-FOUR

Charlotte

EGYPT, 1979

Death, to the ancient Egyptians, was not an end; it was a continuation of the life already lived. In the underworld, the spirit ultimately faced judgment by Osiris, its leader. After offering up a list of denials of wrongdoing, the truth of the matter was tested: The spirit's heart was placed on one side of a scale, and a feather—the symbol of truth and justice—was placed on the other. If the scales were balanced, the eternal life of the person's spirit would be much like that of an abundant earthly life, surrounded by riches, servants, and plenty of food and drink. Those who failed the test had their hearts fed to Ammut, "the Devourer"—a beast that was part crocodile, part lion, and part hippo—and their souls cast into darkness.

For the past forty-one years, Charlotte had believed her daughter was no longer on this earth. If the ancient Egyptians were right about the afterlife, it meant that Layla's innocent heart weighed the same as a feather, and that her spirit would enjoy the same pleasures she'd experienced during her time on earth—sitting in the garden behind the house in Luxor, laughing at the bees leaping from flower to flower, feeling loved and safe. The pain of her loss had been so visceral that sometimes it brought Charlotte to her knees, but it had helped to imagine Layla in the spirit world, dancing with Hathorkare.

Yet as Charlotte, Henry, and Annie walked along a dirt path on the edge of the Nile, the tiny spark of hope that Layla was alive had turned into a conflagration; it was as if Charlotte's heart itself was on fire, the anticipation almost too much to bear. She focused on putting one foot in front of the other. Just ahead, a square fisherman's hut covered in bougainvillea and surrounded by palms rose out of the sandy soil, exactly as it might have five thousand years earlier. A water buffalo standing in the grasses stared idly as they passed.

Two months after reconnecting with Henry, Charlotte was now based in Egypt full-time. Mr. Lavigne, loath to lose her, had offered Charlotte the position of curatorial consultant to the Met, acting as a liaison between the Met and the Egyptian Museum. When she wasn't in Cairo, she headed to the Valley of the Kings to assist with the newly formed Theban Mapping Project, led by an esteemed archaeologist who had begun surveying the historical sites on Luxor's West Bank. Meanwhile, Charlotte's missing folder on Hathorkare had been recovered intact in Mona's apartment, which meant that, in her spare time, she was writing her article on the reclamation of the female pharaoh, to be published in the fall, as well as cowriting an article with Omar regarding the discovery and identification of Hathorkare's mummy. The work Charlotte was doing was more fulfilling than she could have imagined, although she'd been pleased to hear that the King Tut exhibit at the Met had broken all previous records, the ticket line stretching twenty-three blocks down Fifth Avenue.

Annie had traveled to Egypt from Vienna, where she'd been conducting research with Diana Vreeland for the next Costume Institute exhibition. Charlotte was pleased at Annie's excitement over her work with Mrs. Vreeland; the girl was flourishing. Henry had flown to Luxor from his gallery in Geneva, landing that very morning.

Charlotte had found it in her heart to forgive Henry. After all, they most certainly would have found each other if it weren't for her parents' meddling, and now they both could move forward with their lives with clarity. The ship sinking hadn't been his fault, even if he was the reason they had climbed aboard in the first place.

Meanwhile, Mona and her husband were in jail in New York, awaiting trial, denied bail due to the fact that they were considered a flight risk. Ma'at had been effectively dismantled, its leadership locked away thanks to the address on the letter Annie had stolen from Leon. Heba had been released, although her store had been seized by the Egyptian government.

An old woman emerged from the fishing hut and invited them to sit at a table and chairs under a torn red canopy. In broken English, she spoke of a night many years ago during a frightening storm, when a steamer and a felucca had collided in the middle of the river, the captains blinded by the pouring rain. Her son had gone out in a boat to help with the rescue and plucked a baby girl from the water just after the man holding her was swallowed up by the river. Her son had brought the baby home, and her son's wife, who had recently given birth to a stillborn child, insisted they keep the girl for a few days. He had agreed, eager to comfort his distraught wife, to ease her pain. A few days turned into months, and then years.

As she spoke, a woman in her forties appeared on the footpath and joined them.

"Fatima, there you are," said the older woman.

"I'm so sorry, I got held up at work." She stood near her grandmother, one hand on the woman's shoulder. They both wore headscarves, and the younger of the two stood with a straight back, as if she were bracing herself for a blow.

Charlotte remained seated, unsure of what to do next, what to say, even though the electricity between them was palpable. It took all her strength not to run to the woman and pull her close. Not yet. She didn't want to spook her. Charlotte scrutinized her face, just as she had Mona's a couple of months earlier. The woman had Charlotte's small ears, thank goodness, and Henry's nose, and Charlotte recognized her mother's high cheekbones. She was taller than Charlotte—about Annie's height—with narrow shoulders. Her eyes were a golden brown. She was beautiful.

It was Layla.

Fatima, the clerk from the Winter Palace Hotel, was Layla.

That day, on the rooftop of the Met, when Annie had figured out the puzzle to Mona's vague declarations, Charlotte's first impulse had been to head to the airport and take the next flight to Egypt. But Henry had advised taking a more measured approach, instead sending a letter to Fatima, care of the Winter Palace Hotel, which would allow her time to process what they were asserting.

They'd received a reply a month later—it felt like centuries to Charlotte, who luckily had been kept busy with the relocation from New York to Cairo. The letter had been sent to Henry in Geneva, as he had a fixed address, and he'd called Charlotte immediately with the news: Fatima wanted to meet them in Luxor.

And now here they were. "I hope our letter wasn't too overwhelming," said Charlotte.

"No." Fatima looked back and forth between Charlotte and Henry. "I knew who you were. Even before you found me."

Charlotte had imagined all kinds of reactions that Fatima could have had upon receiving their letter: disbelief, anger, resentment at having her world turned upside down. The last thing Charlotte expected to hear was that she already knew.

"I'm sorry," sputtered Henry. "What? When did you find out?"

"When I was a teenager, I needed a birth certificate for something, and when my parents couldn't provide one, they eventually admitted that I was a foundling. They mentioned something about a shipwreck and how I was miraculously rescued, and so I went to the library and scoured old newspapers, found articles written about the collision. Your photos and names were included—as victims of the sinking—along with the name of a baby girl, the only infant on board, Layla Smith. I knew that had to be me. The article said you'd come to Luxor to work for the Metropolitan Museum."

"Did you tell your parents what you discovered?" asked Henry.

She shook her head. "It would've hurt them."

"They passed away last year," said the grandmother. "Within a month of each other."

"I'm sorry to hear that," said Charlotte.

Fatima's chin quivered. "They were good parents, raised me well. They insisted I learn English, and because of that, I got a job at the hotel, starting as a maid and working my way up to the position of desk clerk. I was pleased to land a position at the hotel popular with the foreign archaeologists because I liked the idea that maybe my birth parents once walked down the same halls."

Her grandmother nodded from her chair. "She is a good girl, she takes care of me. I told her to marry, but she said she wanted to stay here with me. A good girl," she repeated.

"Of course, gídda," said Fatima. "It's true. I never married or had children. I preferred to work, to support myself and my grandmother instead of relying on someone else." She glanced up shyly at Henry. "A few years ago, a man rushed up to the check-in desk at the hotel and asked if Henry Smith was available, but then quickly shook his head and said, 'No, sorry, Darius Farid is his name.' The guest was out, but when he arrived to collect his messages, I recognized him from the newspaper photo I carried with me. Your faces and names had been etched in my brain ever since I first saw them, and I knew he was the same man. I knew *you* were the same man."

"I remember that day," said Henry.

"I couldn't believe you were alive, after all this time. But you were distracted, and there was a woman with you, she called you Father. I watched as you argued in the lobby. I could tell there was something terribly wrong."

"That was Mona, my other daughter. Your half sister."

"I didn't think it was right for me to approach at that time. When your daughter came to the desk to check out a couple of hours later, I pulled her aside and said that I believed I was also the daughter of her father. I tried to explain about the shipwreck, but I was flustered and it must have sounded crazy. She laughed at me, said if I didn't leave her alone she'd complain to the manager that I was harassing her and her family. I probably went about it all wrong, I see that now." Fatima's forehead wrinkled at the recollection. "She stormed off."

"Sounds like Mona," said Henry, a pained look on his face.

"My parents were still alive then, and I decided to forget about it, so as not to cause them any hurt or get myself into trouble." She glanced over at Charlotte. "And then, a few years later, you showed up."

"Did you recognize me as well?" asked Charlotte.

"Yes. Right away. After the shipwreck, the newspapers identified you as Charlotte Smith née Cross. After you told me your name and that you worked at the Met Museum, I knew it was you."

"That's why you asked us so many questions when we first arrived," said Charlotte. "I remember thinking it was like going through customs all over again. Why didn't you say something, if not that day, then before we left?"

"She tried to," answered Annie. She turned to Fatima. "You took me outside to show me the way to the camera store and seemed eager to talk. I remember you mistook me for Charlotte's daughter."

"I thought you were her daughter, or granddaughter, perhaps."

"I didn't correct you because I rather liked the idea. I'm sorry if I gave you the wrong impression, or somehow discouraged you."

"It wasn't just that. Miss Cross seemed very preoccupied, very upset, and after seeing how the other daughter reacted, I decided it was better not to be rejected again. I'd rather not know the truth."

This was all so formal, so stilted. Charlotte wanted to scream, to jump up and yell to the hills that she'd found her baby girl. They'd lived very different lives yet were connected at the most primal level.

"That's how I knew who you were, but how did you find me?" Fatima asked.

"Annie here figured it out," said Henry.

Annie shrugged. "Mona said that you had been 'right under our nose,' and that it would be a 'very, very cold day in hell' when she told us where you were. She knew we'd been in Luxor and that you worked at the Winter Palace Hotel, where archaeologists were known to stay. It was a play on the hotel's name. Mona guessed correctly that we had probably crossed paths."

"But how did you know it was me and not some other employee?"

"Your hair."

Fatima touched her headscarf, confused.

"When we were on the steps of the hotel that day, your headscarf came loose in the wind and I noticed the gray," said Annie. "But it wasn't until later, when Henry mentioned that Charlotte's silver streak was hereditary—her mother had one as well—that I put two and two together."

Slowly, Fatima unwrapped her headscarf and pulled it off. The gesture was childlike, trusting. Her hair was thick and shiny, falling halfway down her back in a rich brown hue, the same color as Charlotte's.

And, just like Charlotte, a streak of gray ran from her right temple, like a silver waterfall.

Charlotte rose and crossed the space between them, softly touching Fatima's hair. "I'm sorry we lost you for so long. I've missed you terribly."

Fatima's eyes filled with tears. Charlotte enveloped her daughter in a hug as they wept into each other's shoulders, Fatima catching her breath only to cry some more. They cried for all the years Charlotte was unable to soothe Fatima when she was hurt, or share in her triumphs. For all the birthdays spent wondering about the missing, and the choices they'd made to avoid further pain.

Lost year after lost year.

Henry stood and joined them, placing his arms around them both.

For most of her life, Charlotte had prevented others from getting close in order to avoid another loss. Only recently had she come to understand that doing so actually increased the anguish, and that interacting with others, letting her real self be known, served as a gentle buffer to what had come before, stopping the pain from becoming overwhelming. It was the only way to repair the agony of the past without obliterating it.

But the dark clouds of her past had lifted. Her daughter was alive. Although nothing could make up for the decades lost, there would be many years ahead for them to get to know and understand each other.

Annie walked over, holding two sprigs of jasmine, and offered one to Charlotte and the other to Fatima. "I'm glad you found each other."

Charlotte placed her sprig behind Annie's ear. "I'm glad I found *you* as well."

For so long, Charlotte had felt incomplete and unknowable, misunderstood and damaged, much like the Cerulean Queen and Hathorkare. Many questions had gone unanswered. Now Hathorkare was about to take her rightful place in history as a strong, admired woman of power, and the rediscovered Cerulean Queen was attracting hordes to the Egyptian Museum, not to mention substantially increasing the museum's coffers.

And Charlotte was finally whole. She knew the truth, and silently vowed to honor the memory of Hathorkare, to celebrate the rediscovery of her daughter, and to spend the rest of her days in Egypt among the whispers of ancient pharaohs and the joyful laughter of those she loved.

AUTHOR'S NOTE

Fans of ancient Egyptian history will easily recognize the pharaoh Hatshepsut as the inspiration behind Hathorkare in *The Stolen Queen*. Due to storyline constraints, I had to alter dates and locations, and so instead created a fictional version of the female pharaoh who ruled Egypt during the Eighteenth Dynasty. In the same vein, Saukemet I and II are fictionalized versions of Thutmose II and III.

Here are the facts of Hatshepsut's story: In 1903, British archaeologist Howard Carter came upon two mummies in tomb KV60 in the Valley of the Kings, one of which had a bent left arm, a mark of royalty. Egyptologist Elizabeth Thomas was one of the first to suggest it might be Hatshepsut, in the 1960s.

Early editions of the Met Museum catalog did indeed describe Hatshepsut as a "vain, ambitious, and unscrupulous woman," based on the erasures of her image by her successor. However, in 1966, Charles F. Nims published an article in *The Journal of Egyptian Language and Archaeology* that questioned the timing of the destruction and erasures, and posited some of the reasons mentioned in the novel as to why they might have been carried out.

In 2007, Egyptian archaeologist Zahi Hawass placed the mummies from KV60 and a canopic box marked with Hatshepsut's cartouche—containing her internal organs as well as a molar tooth lacking one root—through a CT scanner and declared the mummy with the bent arm to be that of Hatshepsut, who is now exhibited at the National Museum of Egyptian Civilization in Cairo.

For more information on Hatshepsut, I recommend reading the Met's exhibition catalog for *Hatshepsut: From Queen to Pharaoh*, edited by Catharine H. Roehrig, with Renée Dreyfus and Cathleen A. Keller.

Much of Charlotte's early experiences in Egypt are inspired by the famed female French archaeologist Christiane Desroches-Noblecourt, who is the subject of a terrific biography by Lynne Olson, *Empress of the Nile: The Daredevil Archaeologist Who Saved Egypt's Ancient Temples from Destruction*. It's a fantastic read.

The Cerulean Queen statue is based on a Met antiquity called Fragment of a Queen's Face, which was possibly modeled after Nefertiti, Kiya, or Meritaten. Sculpted out of yellow jasper, the piece is hauntingly beautiful and has never been stolen, nor has its provenance been questioned. The theft in the book is inspired by one that occurred at the Met in 1979, when a thief plucked a 2,500-year-old marble head from a pedestal in the Greek and Roman galleries. Luckily, the head was recovered from a locker at Grand Central Terminal less than a week later.

The Ma'at organization mentioned in the novel is completely fictional. The Theban Mapping Project, on the other hand, is very real and, since its founding in 1978 by Dr. Kent Weeks, has become an important resource for scholars, tourists, and educators in its mission to protect and survey the hallowed grounds of the ancient pharaohs while also keeping them accessible to the public.

The staff of the Met Museum were incredibly generous with their

AUTHOR'S NOTE

time and expertise as I researched this book. While the plot and characters are completely fictional, I hope readers will seek out Hatshepsut's likenesses, linger in front of the Fragment of a Queen's Face statue, and wander the many galleries of this iconic New York City institution in order to appreciate the inspiration behind *The Stolen Queen*. You never know what you might find . . .

Finally, the Met Gala did not have a red carpet for its guests in 1978, but the image is so iconic, I simply couldn't resist including one in the novel.

Further Reading

All the Beauty in the World: The Metropolitan Museum of Art and Me, by Patrick Bringley

Diana Vreeland: Bon Mots: Words of Wisdom from the Empress of Fashion, edited by Alexander Vreeland, illustrated by Luke Edward Hall

D.V., by Diana Vreeland

Egypt's Golden Couple: When Akhenaten and Nefertiti Were Gods on Earth, by John Darnell and Colleen Darnell

Empress of Fashion: A Life of Diana Vreeland, by Amanda Mackenzie Stuart

Empress of the Nile: The Daredevil Archaeologist Who Saved Egypt's Ancient Temples from Destruction, by Lynne Olson

Hatshepsut: From Queen to Pharaoh, edited by Catharine H. Roehrig with Renée Dreyfus and Cathleen A. Keller

Making the Mummies Dance: Inside the Metropolitan Museum of Art, by Thomas Hoving

Metropolitan Stories: A Novel, by Christine Coulson

Rogues' Gallery: The Secret History of the Moguls and the Money That Made the Metropolitan Museum, by Michael Gross

Stealing the Show: A History of Art and Crime in Six Thefts, by John Barelli with Zachary Schisgal

ACKNOWLEDGMENTS

As I researched and wrote *The Stolen Queen*, I was incredibly lucky to meet several wonderful people associated with the Met Museum who lent their time and expertise to this story, including Ken Weine, Patrick Bringley, Adela Oppenheim, Alexandra Fizer, Seth Zimiles, Anna Serotta, Annie Bailis, Nancy Chilton, Dina Sheridan Grant, Jeff L. Rosenheim, Elizabeth L. Block, and Christine Coulson.

Others who were instrumental in the writing of this book include Lynne Olson, Kent R. Weeks, Colleen Darnell, Sree Sreenivasan, Anne Seelbach, Heather Hornbeck, Jenny Bruce, Jennifer Quinlan, Lynda Cohen Loigman, Andrew Alpern, Nikki Slota-Terry, Michael Rubenstein, Robert Clauser, and Sherif Samy. Any errors are my own.

I'm lucky to have the power trio of Stefanie Lieberman, Molly Steinblatt, and Adam Hobbins behind me, and I'm indebted to the entire team at Dutton: my brilliant editor, Lindsey Rose, Christine Ball, John Parsley, Ivan Held, Allison Dobson, Amanda Walker, Stephanie Cooper, Alice Dalrymple, Sarah Thegeby, Nicole Jarvis, Diamond Bridges, Caroline Payne, Charlotte Peters, Christopher Lin, Olga Grlic, Sarah Oberrender, and Kelly Gildea.

ACKNOWLEDGMENTS

Thanks also to Olivia Fanaro and Orly Greenberg at UTA, Kathleen Carter of Kathleen Carter Communications, and Authors Unbound. And, of course, a huge shout-out to all the book influencers, readers, bloggers, reviewers, and bookstore owners and staffers who make this such a warm and welcoming community.

To the readers who donated their names as characters in various charity auctions, I hope you enjoy your walk down the red carpet. Thank you for your generous support.

During the pandemic, a group of writers turned to each other for laughs, book talk, and wine over weekly Zoom happy hours. I consider myself lucky to be part of the Thursday Authors crew: authors Amy Poeppel, Lynda Cohen Loigman, Susie Orman Schnall, Nicola Harrison, and Jamie Brenner, as well as book maven Suzanne Leopold.

Thank you to my family: Dilys, Martin, Mace, Caitlin, Erin, Alex, and Lauren. Finally, I am lucky to share my life with Greg Wands: thank you for your boundless love and inspiration.

ABOUT THE AUTHOR

Fiona Davis is the *New York Times* bestselling author of several novels, including *The Spectacular, The Magnolia Palace,* and *The Lions of Fifth Avenue*, which was a *Good Morning America* Book Club pick. She's a graduate of the Columbia Journalism School and is based in New York City.